THE EU SONGBOOK

The EU Songbook

The EU Songbook
Copyright © The EU Songbook Association, Dansk Sang Publishing and Gads Forlag A/S
First printed in 2024

Cover design: Spine Studio
Graphic design and layout: The EU Songbook Association & the central editorial team
All illustrations (except song 28): David Drachmann Laureng

Printed by in Estonia by Print Best OÜ
ISBN: 978-87-12-07255-3

eu-songbook.org
dansksang.dk
gad.dk

This book is generously supported by The Augustinus Foundation

The publishers have made every effort to obtain permission to use the songs in this songbook. In the event that we have not succeeded in contacting the true copyright holders of the music or words to a song included in this book, thus infringing their copyright, this has not been intentional. Naturally, any claims made in the event of such infringement shall be met in accordance with the same guidelines as those applied to the other copyright holders.

The EU Songbook Web-App **(FREE)**

with all 164 song titles organized either

per member state or per song category,

164 introductions and YouTube-links,

– and a score compendium for the annual **EUROPE DAY**, May 9th:

https://www.webapp.eu-songbook.org

The EU Songbook YouTube-Channel

with videos of the all the 164 songs:

https://www.youtube.com/@eu.songbook

CONTENTS

8   In gratitude: funders & endorsers
10 In gratitude: 103 assisting music NGO's & institutions in the EU
13 List of 67 EU Songbook editors

16 Foreword – by the EU Songbook Association
20 Remarks on notation & translations
22 Chords & Signs

SIX SONG CATEGORIES (per song number):

Freedom & Peace: 1 - 28

Love songs: 29 - 55

Nature & Seasons: 56 - 82

Folksongs & Traditionals: 83 - 110

Faith & Spirituality: 111 - 137

Children's songs: 138 - 164

The European Anthem (Ode an die Freude / Ode to Joy): 28

PER MEMBER STATE (per song number):

Austria – 23, 48, 66, 104, 111, 147

Belgium – 25, 29, 80, 91, 129, 158

Bulgaria – 24, 49, 58, 96, 123, 140

Croatia – 21, 54, 78, 84, 114, 148

Cyprus – 5, 30, 60, 98, 115, 162

Czechia – 6, 38, 79, 88, 116, 146

Denmark – 9, 50, 77, 102, 117, 144

Estonia – 22, 31, 57, 90, 136, 159

Finland – 13, 37, 76, 109, 122, 143

France – 2, 51, 61, 95, 120, 138

Germany – 4, 39, 68, 101, 121, 141

Greece – 10, 34, 69, 94, 119, 149

Hungary – 1, 44, 62, 92, 113, 151

Ireland – 14, 36, 63, 89, 124, 163

Italy – 7, 52, 70, 103, 112, 152

Latvia – 15, 55, 75, 85, 126, 153

Lithuania – 19, 35, 67, 100, 127, 155

Luxembourg – 18, 46, 72, 106, 128, 157

Malta – 11, 40, 64, 105, 125, 156

Netherlands – 12, 47, 82, 108, 130, 154

Poland – 26, 32, 65, 87, 135, 139

Portugal – 3, 41, 56, 93, 118, 164

Romania – 17, 43, 73, 86, 133, 150

Slovakia – 8, 42, 74, 99, 134, 161

Slovenia – 16, 53, 71, 107, 132, 142

Spain – 27, 45, 59, 97, 137, 160

Sweden – 20, 33, 81, 83, 131, 145

* * *

The U.K. (Brexit) – 110

INDEX:

422 *Song categories*

424 *Member states*

428 *Song titles – in original language*

431 *Song titles – in European English*

434 *Composers*

436 *Lyricists*

438 Special mention & thank you list

439 Quotes about the EU Songbook

In gratitude: funders & endorsers

With gratitude for crucial economic support for making singable translations:

Aage og Johanne Louis-Hansens Fond, Denmark

William Demant Fonden, Denmark

Wistifonden, Denmark

The Czech Music Fund Foundation (Nadace Český hudební fond, NČHF)

Minister of Arts, Culture, Civil Service & Sport, State Secretary Andrea Mayer, Austria (2020)

Minister of Science and Culture, Annika Saarikko, Finland (2020)

Minister of Education, Culture and Science, Ingrid van Engelshoven, The Netherlands (2020)

Minister of Art, Ministry of Culture, Tõnis Lukas, Estonia (2020)

Minister of Culture, Sam Tanson, Luxembourg (2020)

Minister president of Flanders, Jan Jambon, Belgium (2020)

Minister for Culture and National Heritage, Piotr Gliński, Poland (2021)

Minister of Culture and Media, Nina Obuljen Koržinek, Croatia (2021)

Minister of Culture, dr. Vasko Simoniti, Slovenia (2020)

Secretary of State, Péter Fekete, Hungary (2021)

Minister for National Heritage, Arts & Local Government, Dr. Owen Bonnici, Malta (2022)

Minister of Education, Culture, Sport and Youth, Prodromos Prodromou, Cyprus (2020)

With gratitude for endorsements from:

The European Parliament (*The European Citizen's Prize 2023*)

Minister of Culture, Graça Fonseca, Portugal (2021)

Minister of Culture and Sport of the Hellenic Republic, Dr. Lina G. Mendoni, Greece (2020)

Minister of Culture, Boil Banov, Bulgaria (2021)

Minister of Culture, PhDr. Lubomir Zaorálek, Czech Republic (2020)

Minister of Foreign Affairs, Martin Lidegaard, Denmark (2015)

Minister of Culture, Marianne Jelved, Denmark (2015)

Minister of Education and Research, Sofie Carsten Nielsen (2015)

Minister of culture, Joy Mogensen, Denmark (2020)

Minister for Justice, Culture & European Affairs, Anke Spoorendonk, Schleswig-Holstein (2016)

Deputy State Secretary for Cultural Policy, Uldis Zariņš, Latvia (2020)

The European Movement, (former) chairwoman Stine Bosse, Denmark

In gratitude: 103 assisting music NGO's & institutions in the EU

With gratitude to all music NGO's or institutions (partners highlighted) who assisted with the 27 song nominations or/and song votes 2015-20:

1. **University of Music and Performing Arts Graz (KUG) – AUS**
2. **Steirisches-Volksliedwerk – AUS**
3. **Koor&Stem – BEL**
4. **À Cœur Joie, Fédération Chorale Wallonie-Bruxelles – BEL**
5. Conservatoire de Gand (KASK) – BEL
6. Kunstenpunt – BEL
7. **The Academy of Music, Dance and Fine Arts "Prof. Asen Diamandiev" – Plovdiv – BUL**
8. **University of Zagreb, Music Academy – CRO**
9. **Hrvatski sabor culture – HRSK (The Croatian Cultural Association) – CRO**
10. Hrvatsko društvo skladatelja (The Croatian Composers' Society) – CRO
11. The Josip Juraj Strossmayer University of Osijek, Department of Music – CRO
12. **Music Academy ARTE – CY**
13. University of Cyprus – CY
14. Cyprus Music Information Centre (CyMIC) – CY
15. **Academy of Performing Arts in Prague (HAMU) – CZ**
16. **The Czech Choral Union (Unie českých pěveckých sborů, UCPS) – CZ**
17. **Ochranný svaz autorský pro práva k dílům hudebním (OSA) – CZ**
18. **Rytmisk Musikkonservatorium / Rhythmic Music Conservatory (RMC) – DK**
19. Musiklærerforeningen / The Music Teachers Association in Denmark – DK
20. Sankt Annæ Gymnasium (SAG) / Sct. Ann Music High School – DK
21. The Royal Danish Music Academy / Det Kgl. Danske Musikkonservatorium (DKDM) – DK
22. **Estonian Choral Association (ECA) – EST**
23. **Estonian Society for Music Education – EST**
24. Eesti Muusika- ja Teatriakadeemia – EST
25. **Sulasol – The Finnish Amateur Musicians' Association – FIN**
26. **Sibelius Academy – University of the Arts, Helsinki – FIN**
27. **Music Archive Finland – FIN**
28. Music Finland – FIN
29. Musiikkimuseo Fame (Fame Music Museum) – FIN
30. **Training Center for Teachers of Music (CEFEDEM) – FRA**
31. **Lyon Conservatoire National Supérieur Musique et Danse – FRA**
32. **Association of German Concert Choirs (VDKC) – GER**
33. **Hochschule für Musik "Carl Maria von Weber" Dresden – GER**
34. Der Deutsche Chorverband (The German Choir Association) – GER
35. Deutsche Chorjugend (DCJ) – (The German Choir Youth) – GER

36 Deutscher Tonkünstlerverband e.V (DTKV) – GER
37 Die Hochschule für Musik Würzburg (University for Music Würzburg) – GER
38 **The Hellenic Choirs Association – GR**
39 Ionian University, Corfu / Music Department – GR
40 **KÓTA, Magyar Kórusok, Zenekarok és Népzenei Együttesek Szövetsége – HU**
41 Papageno – Élménykalauz – HU
42 Jeunesses Musicales Hungary (JM Hungary) – HU
43 Magyar Műfordítók Egyesülete (the Association of Hungarian Literary Translators) – HU
44 **CIT Cork School of Music – IRE**
45 **Sing Ireland – IRE**
46 **Istituto Superiore di Studi Musicali "Vincenzo Bellini", Catania – ITA**
47 **National Academy of Jazz, Siena – ITA**
48 Conservatorio di musica "Giuseppe Verdi" (Milano) – ITA
49 Conservatorio Statale di Musica "G. Frescobaldi" (Ferrara) – ITA
50 Coro Giovanile Diapason (Roma) – ITA
51 **Latvian Music Teachers' Association (LVIIMSA) – LAT**
52 Jāzepa Vītola Latvijas mūzikas akadēmija (Jāzeps Vītols Latvian Academy of Music) – LAT
53 **Lithuanian Choral Union – LIT**
54 Music Information Centre Lithuania (MICL) – LIT
55 Vytautas Magnus University (VMU), Musica Academy – LIT
56 Lithuanian National Culture Center, Music Division – LIT
57 Lithuanian Literature and Folklore Institute – LIT
58 **Union Grand-Duc Adolphe (UGDA) – LUX**
59 **Institut Européen de Chant Choral Luxembourg (INECC) – LUX**
60 **Conservatoire de la Ville de Luxembourg – LUX**
61 **School of Performing Arts, University of Malta – MAL**
62 Malta School of Music – MAL
63 **Prins Claus Conservatorium, Groningen – HOL**
64 **Hogeschool voor de Kunsten Utrecht (HKU) – HOL**
65 **Academy of Music, Stanisław Moniuszko in Gdańsk – POL**
66 Academy of Music. I.J. Paderewski, in Poznan – POL
67 Bydgoszcz Music Academy – "Feliks Nowowiejski" – POL
68 Association of Polish Choirs and Orchestras / PZChiO – POL
69 The Association of Philharmonic Orchestras in Poland – POL
70 National Institute of Music and Dance – POL
71 **Portuguese Association for Music Education (APEM) – POR**
72 **Association for Choirs in Lisbon (AMLC) – POR**
73 Institute of Ethnomusicology, Center for Studies in Music and Dance – POR
74 Academia de Música de Lagos (Academy of Music – Lagos) – POR
75 Grupo Coral Stravaganzza – POR
76 **Romanian National Association of Choral Music (ANCR) – RO**

77 **National University of Music, Bucharest (UNMB) – RO**
78 **Faculty of Music, Transilvania University of Brașov – RO**
79 Academia de Muzica, Gheorghe Dima' din Cluj-Napoca – RO
80 **Slovak Music Teacher Association (AUHS) – SLOVA**
81 **Academy of Music Bratislava (VŠMU) – SLOVA**
82 Bratislava Music Agency (Viva Music Agency) – SLOVA
83 Hudobné Centrum (Music Centre) – SLOVA
84 **University of Ljubljana, Academy of Music – SLOVE**
85 **Slovene Society of Composers (DSS) – SLOVE**
86 Republic of Slovenia Public Fund for Cultural Activities (JSKD) – SLOVE
87 Zbor sv. Nikolaja Litija – SLOVE
88 **Escuela Superior de Canto de Madrid (ESCM) – SPA**
89 Real Conservatorio Superior de Música de Madrid (RCSMM) – SPA
90 Departamento de Didáctica de la Expresión Musical, Universidad de Granada – SPA
91 Escuela Superior de Música Reina Sofía – SPA
92 Universitat Autònoma de Barcelona, Departament d'Art i de Musicologia – SPA
93 European Association of Music in Schools, Spain (EAS) – SPA
94 **Royal College of Music in Stockholm (KMH) – SWE**
95 **Musikwerket – SWE**
96 Musikhögskolan i Malmö – SWE
97 Svensk Visarkiv – SWE
98 Skap – Composers Union of Sweden – SWE
99 **Royal Birmingham Conservatoire – UK**
100 Royal Academy of Music, Open Academy – UK
101 Royal College of Music – UK
102 Association of British Choral Directors – UK
103 British Music Teachers – UK

Illustration (orginally in color): David Drachmann Laureng

List of 67 EU Songbook editors

Central editors:

(The EU Songbook Association)

Jeppe Marsling (DK), main editor
Lars Kynde (DK), music editor
Anders Monrad (DK), music editor
Connor McLean (CAN), music editor
Liesbeth Segers (BEL), music editor
David Drachmann Laureng (DK), translations

61 national editors from 27 member states:

AUSTRIA
Dr. *Sarah Weiss*, Kunst Universität Graz, KUG
Dr. *Eva Maria Hois*, Steirisches Volksliedwerk
Dr. *Helmut Brenner (R.I.P.)*, Kunst Universität Graz, KUG

BELGIUM
Liesbeth Segers, Koor & Stem
Erik Demarbaix, Koor & Stem
Noël Minet, chairman, À Cœur Joie, Fédération Chorale Wallonie-Bruxelles
Reynald Sac, À Cœur Joie, Fédération Chorale Wallonie-Bruxelles

BULGARIA
Toni Shekerdzhieva-Nowak, Academy of Music, Dance and Fine Arts – Plovdiv
Jean Pehlivanov, Academy of Music, Dance and Fine Arts – Plovdiv

CROATIA
Jasenka Ostojić, head of Dep. for Conducting, University of Zagreb, Music Academy
Valentina Badanjak Pintarić, The Croatian Cultural Association (HRSK)

CYPRUS
Egli Spyridaki, Music Academy ARTE
Ayis Ioannides, Music Academy ARTE

CZECHIA
Hanuš Bartoň (R.I.P.), head of Dep. of Composition, Academy of Performing Arts in Prague (HAMU)
Lukáš Prchal, Czech Choral Union (UČPS)
Adam Klemens, Copyright Protection Association for Musical Works (OSA)

DENMARK
Henrik Marstal, associate professor at Rhythmic Music Conservatory (RMC)
Jesper Moesbøl, contributing editor (introductions)

ESTONIA
Kaie Tanner, Sec. General, Estonian Choral Association (ECA)
Siim Aimla, Estonian Choral Association (ECA)
Kadi Härma, Estonian Society for Music Education

FINLAND
Reijo Kekkonen, publishing director, The Finnish Amateur Musicians' Association (SULASOL)
Dr. *Vesa Kurkela*, Sibelius Academy, University of the Arts Helsinki
Juha Henriksson, director, Music Archive Finland

FRANCE
Jacques Moreau, dir., CEFEDEM, Training Center for Teachers of Music, Auvergne Rhône-Alpes
Jean Blanchard, CEFEDEM, Training Center for Teachers of Music, Auvergne Rhône-Alpes

GERMANY
Ekkehard Klemm, president, The Association of German Concert Choirs (VDKC) / Prof. of conducting, Hochschule für Musik *Carl Maria von Weber* Dresden

GREECE
Thomas Louziotis, president, The Hellenic Choirs Association

HUNGARY
Zsuzsanna Mindszenty, president, KÓTA, Association of Hungarian Choirs, Orchestras & Folk Ensembles
Ágnes C. Szalai, contributing editor, called by KÓTA
David Zsoldos, president, The Hungarian Music Council / Jeunesses Musicales Hungary

IRELAND
Mark Armstrong, SING IRELAND
Dermot O'Callaghan, Chief Executive, SING IRELAND
Maria Judge, head of Musicianship and Academic Studies, Cork School of Music (MTU)

ITALY
Alfonso Santimone, National Academy of Jazz, Siena
Stefano Sanfilippo, Istituto Musicale "Vincenzo Bellini" Catania

LATVIA
Rūta Kanteruka, president, Latvian Music Teachers' Association (LVIIMSA)

LITHUANIA
Dr. *Arvydas Girdzijauskas*, Lithuanian Choral Union

LUXEMBOURG
Robert Köller, Union Grand-Duc Adolphe (UGDA)
Raoul Wilhelm, Union Grand-Duc Adolphe (UGDA)
Arend Herold, director, Institut Européen de Chant Choral Luxembourg (INECC)

MALTA
Dr. *Albert Pace*, School of Performing Arts, University of Malta
Dr. *John Galea*, School of Performing Arts, University of Malta

THE NETHERLANDS
Christiane Nieuwmeijer, Leiden University of Applied Sciences (since 2020) / Hogeschool voor de Kunsten Utrecht, HKU (2017-20)
Lieuwe Noordam, Prins Claus Conservatorium, Groningen

POLAND
Dr. *Marcin Tomczak*, head of Faculty of Choral Conducting, Academy of Music, Stanisław Moniuszko in Gdańsk
Dorota Stefaniak, librarian, Academy of Music, Stanisław Moniuszko in Gdańsk

PORTUGAL
Manuela Encarnação, president, Portuguese Music Education Association (APEM)
Nuno Bettencourt Mendes, board member (APEM)
Lina Trindade Santos, board member (APEM)
Jorge Alves, Artistic Director, Association for Choirs in Lisbon (AMLC)

ROMANIA
Dr. *Grigore Cudalbu*, Romanian National Association of Choral Music (ANCR) / National University of Music, Bucharest (UNMB)
Alexandra Belibou, assoc. Prof. PhD Lecturer, Faculty of Music, Transilvania University of Brașov

SLOVAKIA
Eva Čunderlíková, Slovak Music Teacher Association (AUHS) / Academy of Music Bratislava (VŠMU)

SLOVENIA
Dušan Bavdek, vice dean for Int. Affairs and Quality, University of Ljubljana, Academy of Music / Slovene Society of Composers (DSS)
Dr. *Leon Stefanija*, University of Ljubljana, Faculty of Arts

SPAIN
Julio Muñoz, directior, Escuela Superior de Canto de Madrid (ESCM)
Maria del Carmen García Jiménez, head of studies, Escuela Superior de Canto de Madrid

SWEDEN
Susanne Rosenberg, head of Choir Depart. Royal College of Music in Stockholm (KMH)
Kerstin Carpvik, head of library, Musikverket

***

THE UNITED KINGDOM
(Should Old Acquaintance Be Forgot)
David Saint, former principal of Birmingham Conservatoire

Foreword – by the EU Songbook Association

Opening statement

With the completion of the EU Songbook, a European dream has come true for all of us wishing to exchange national differences and share common ground, at home and abroad, via songs. And to all you 87,000+ citizens, music teachers, music students and choir singers who nominated and/or voted for the 164 songs in the 27 member states and have waited a decade for this pioneering publication: *Thank you for your patience and engagement!* We 67 editors and 39 translators, as well as our publishers clearing the copyrights, had to work in 25 languages — and three alphabets — which is why we had to submit to the motto: *Great things take time*. We were both prompted by Brexit, the Covid-19 pandemic, and the terrible war in Ukraine and inspired by learning from the many wonderful songs along the way, both through the emerging translations and the daily conversations about these songs with EU citizens everywhere. Like dreams, songs are shortcuts to the depths of our souls and our common history, both individually and collectively: a magic wand to inspire confidentiality. We learned, firsthand, that through the exchange of our separate national cultures we can experience being Europeans together: in the feeling of common ground, in understanding our differences, across the categories of both life and of songs in this publication: love, freedom, peace, nature, seasons, folksiness, spirituality, childhood. Now it is up to you all to hopefully embrace and use the EU Songbook in your social life, at work, at home and abroad. The EU Songbook WebApp is meant as a tool to enable cultural exchange when you do not have the songbook with you: here you can easily find the six song titles from each member state and hear all the songs on YouTube.

Why and how we made the 1st EU Songbook

'The EU' is — like 'the U.S.A' — not a protected title; it is accessible to everyone who wishes to be a part of it and 'own it'. The EU Songbook project did not originate from the EU establishment, but is a grassroots publication, assembled democratically by a non-profit NGO — the EU Songbook Association — in collaboration with the civil societies in all 27 member states; it is a book 'of, by and for the people'.

Our mission was — and is — for the EU populations to live less parallel lives, culturally speaking. With the EU Songbook, our association hopes to provide a tool for people to embody their union with their many diverse voices, and, via translations of a part of their song treasures into the currently most spoken EU language, we wished for them to better get to know each other. And we wanted to dig deeper culturally, since the self-Americanised mainstream culture often becomes a safe zone where Europeans rarely dare to present their lesser-known original differences: while most know a song from France, Germany, or Italy, how many know one from Poland, Hungary, or Romania? This is problematic, as the less economically developed East is not less valuable culturally than the West.

Our union is almost 70 years old. The main reason why a union songbook has not been made until now is obviously the language diversity- and barrier. We believe there can be no valid *cultural* argument behind choosing a language for our singable translations, solely a *practical* argument: the most commenly spoken tongue in the EU. Therefore, all 164 songs in the EU Songbook are printed, side by side, in both 24 original EU languages (+ Luxembourgish), spanning three alphabets and in singable/cantabile 'European English'. By using the term 'European English' we wish to underline that English, both for most of our translators and songbook users, is not a mother tongue, but a second language, a so-called 'vehicle language' formed and coloured by all those who speak it.

A key question for us has been that of 'representation': how to truly make the EU Songbook a democratic symbol that people would feel represented by and wish to embrace? The easiest way would have been to organise an 'expert seminar' (wine and a city tour) and invite 27 music experts or 27 of the most popular songwriters to each select their population's six songs. However, the ideal — and hardest way — is always direct democracy. Both founding our non-profit NGO and discovering 'SurveyMonkey' — a digital survey to collect 'unlimited' responses — enabled us to communicate in 24 languages and involve other NGOs and public institutions, as well as the wider public via media. It took eight years to complete, since our union is vast and our diversity complex.

The 164 songs were identified in three democratic phases lasting over six years from 2015-20: Firstly, six song categories were decided as a compromise between suggestions from 17 music academies in 14 member states: 1) *Love Songs* 2) *Nature & Seasons* 3) *Freedom & Peace* 4) *Folksongs & Traditionals* 5) *Faith & Spirituality* (beliefs in general) and 6) *Children's Songs*. These pan-European (and universal) categories provided a frame, a unity, for the comparison of all the populations' diversity.

Secondly, songs somehow originating from EU were nominated by more than 2,100 music teachers, music students, choir singers and composers. The nomination criteria: a minimum of affiliation (either the composer or the lyricist had to originate from the member state, or the song had to be written in that member state by non-nationals). This ensured that we did not end up with dominantly common denominator 'safe zone' songs from the UK and US, which everyone already knows so well. Twenty-seven voting lists containing the six to ten most nominated songs in each category were formed by our engaged national EU Songbook editors, who were permitted to nominate a song title in each category themselves.

Thirdly and finally, the selection process was concluded in 27 consecutive public song votes, one in each member state, and conducted in the national languages (for Belgium, the two largest language groups — Dutch and French — were invited to each choose half of their six songs). Facilitated by a total of 103 music organisations and institutions, and publicised by more than 400 media outlets, the song votes reached more than 87,000 people. Our association's lower bar was set at a minimum of 1,000 voters per population, a statistical criterium. Finally, we were able to narrow down the number of songs to 164 of the most preferred 'classics' originating from the European Union.

So, how do 'the lives of the others' sound? With this final selection, users are invited into seven centuries of European cultural history, encompassing various musical genres from folksong, chant and waltz to tango, jazz, rock and pop. Overall, the EU Songbook is a mixed soundscape of both the provincial, regional and continental, with rhythmic influences from the US and South America—continents that have inspired Europe's songwriters of the 20th and 21st century. While some songs are "signature songs" or "identity card songs", resonating a specific population's majority culture, others are universal songs. Some have been international classics for decades, even centuries, but most of them are still unknown to many.

Just like when we were in school and received a class photo to first identify our own faces in the crowd ('How do I look?!'), we expect everyone to first examine their own population's songs ('How do we sound?'): however, accordingly, we invite everyone to wander and discover the cultures of the others'. Sixty-one engaged national songbook editors have generously provided authentic, 'most commonly used' scores and written fascinating introductions to offer a view into the European narrative and identity—not as elusive theory, but as a complex mosaic, a choir of voices singing out our union's motto: *Unity in diversity*.

It is a great challenge to translate/adapt a song! Some of the local fragrance is destined to be "lost in translation", but conversely, some fragrance is 'found in translation', which is why we sincerely hope for the understanding of our songbook users. May the citizens' heartfelt wish to communicate and to express themselves bridge the language gap. Since what matters above correctness are the voice-to-voice and heart-to-heart meetings between Easterners, Westerners, Northerners and Southerners. There are so many people to meet and so much to learn in the EU: we believe talking about the classic songs in the EU Songbook will turn many strangers into friends.

Making the first EU Songbook has been a mountain to climb, and the publication will remain in this version for many years to come. However, just like the British left with their chapter (except for a single song, 'Should Old Acquaintance Be Forgot'), upcoming chapters of any 'EU candidate countries' — like Albania, Moldova, the Republic of North Macedonia, Montenegro, Serbia, Turkey and Ukraine — will be added to the songbook. Potentially, a seventh song category could be added.

With the first EU Songbook, our association hopes to contribute to more open windows between the EU populations, and bring the lesser-known songs into the Western mainstream; to reach out to those dreaming the European Dream in upcoming member states; to contribute to making the cultural bridge to the USA a fairer two-way street; to contribute to music life across society, in education and exploration, in debate and commemoration; for choir life, for friends and families, festivals, Interrail, on squares and in parks.

The European Anthem

Allow us to reflect for a moment. What is the opposite of "164 songs in 25 languages"? Is it a single song in 25 languages? Or perhaps a song without words, or: the sound of silence? The European Anthem, adopted in 1985, consists solely of a melody and is not a song in the traditional sense. Yet an EU Songbook without the European anthem would feel incomplete! This music draws nourishment from one of the most fertile layers of European history — the age of idealism, Enlightenment and revolution that laid the foundation for our democracies. The vision of universal rights and brotherhood was captured in words when 26-year-old Schiller (1759-1805) wrote his inspired poem 'An die Freude' (To Joy) in Germany in 1785. By 1822-24, at the end of his life, Beethoven—now old and deaf—knew that singing joyously together about joy could bring about peace and brotherhood to any community. The music, having 200th anniversary this year, is deserving of special honour, especially on *Europe Day, May 9th*—our European *'Dependence Day'*. But how should we celebrate it?

From our friend at the Citizens' Library Unit at the European Parliament, Étienne Deschamps, we learned that the bureau of the European Parliament attempted to launch a competition in 1986 to add lyrics to the anthem, but failed. This attempt was repeated during the negotiations for the *Lisbon Treaty* in 2004, also without success. Historian Timothy Garton Ash noted that even Czech writer-president Václav Havel (1936-2011) had tried too. Therefore, when the EU Songbook Association received the European Parliament's *European Citizen's Prize* in 2023, we dared "to ask the EU" whether we, the civil society, could launch a competition to create lyrics for the European Anthem in 24 languages. To our surprise, the Vice-President of the European Commission, Greek Margaritis Schinas, invited us to Brussels in 2024, where he endorsed the idea. This initiative soon garnered support from *The International Association of Music Centres (IAMIC), the European Association of Conservatoires (EAC)* and *the European Union of Music Competitions for Youth (EMCY)*, and 17 national choir unions and conservatories. The coming year will reveal whether we can secure the funding and, more importantly, gain the necessary backing from the Parliament and the Council, to produce official lyrics for the European Anthem, so that we citizens can celebrate *Europe Day* with it.

In this first edition of the EU Songbook, and out of respect for the official stance, we have printed the anthem's notes without Schiller's lyrics beneath them. However, since Beethoven's inspired music is inseparable from Schiller's poem, we have included both the three verses which Beethoven used in the choral part of the 9th Symphony, both in original German and in a fine literal (non-singable) English translation, as well as the remaining six verses of the poem.

Finally, a little-known anecdote about the EU and song: at the funeral march of Jean Monnet, the "Father of Europe", held in a small French village church in 1979, the many heads of state in attendance were in for a surprise. Monnet had arranged for six songs to be performed—one for each of the founding member states! Then, to everyone's confusion, a seventh song was played. According to his wife, it was one of Monnet's favourites: the American civil war song, "Battle Hymn of the Republic, *Glory, Glory, Hallelujah*", written by abolitionist writer Julia Ward Howe in 1861.

Culture, it seems, had the last word over economy. And the EU and US briefly embraced, unified in diversity. To us, Monnet's posthumous 'happening' formed the first little EU Songbook. If only he'd had a mailbox in Elysium, so we could mail him a copy...

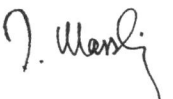 *By Jeppe Marsling, co-founder / Copenhagen 15.08.24*

Remarks on notation and translations

On scores and singable translations

The scores for this songbook were collected by our 57 national EU Songbook editors from music communities, or sent directly to us by the copyright holders, including record companies or foundations managing the legacy of the original composers. Once we received the authentic 'commonly used' or authorised versions, provided by our national editors, we, the central editors, initiated a dialogue concerning transcriptions and user-friendliness. In most cases, the typing and layout were done centrally to create a uniform collection, while adhering to the preferences of the national editors as a rule. This approach, which respected differences in methodology and prioritised authenticity, resulted in varying standards across different member states.

The scores were tested on piano and voice, with each compared to available audio versions on YouTube. Where necessary, missing tempi or chords were added, and various songs were transposed into more user-friendly keys. For the intro, pre-chorus or bridge sections of certain scores, cue notes (in smaller sizes) were added to enhance the character of the song. In other cases, similar notes were excluded to maintain space or uniformity.

The lyrics often existed in various versions, with differences in punctuation, spelling, or even wording. In some instances, entire verses were exchanged or replaced by newer ones. Where discrepancies were found, the national editors were consulted to decide which version should be printed. The lyrics appearing below the notes and those in the verse section have been harmonised, though in some cases differences may be noticeable where older forms have been updated. In such cases, the older version is found below the notes, while the newer form is in the verse section. Proofreading across 25 languages, many of which were unfamiliar to the central editors, required significant focus. Thankfully, the 61 national EU Songbook editors were vigilant, with additional support from lyrics translators and copyright holders, who worked closely with the 'approved' scores.

Lost 'n found—in translation

Most of the singable translations in the EU Songbook are newly created. However, some pre-existing translations were retained, either due to copyright holder requirements or because they were found to be excellent versions, used for decades, and unnecessary to replace (as often recommended by our recruited translators). The goal for the translators was to strike a balance between remaining loyal to the original and creating a singable English version that could stand on its own. How meaning, rhyme, poetry, and singability were balanced in an English translation depended on the character of the song, including its melody and cultural significance to the population that chose it. For songs that hold deep symbolic meaning to a member state's population, translators — often individuals with origins in or strong affiliations with those populations — understandably prioritised conveying the meaning over rhyme or singability. Some of these nationally famous songs had never been translated in a singable version before, perhaps because no one was prepared to take on the challenge. What is most important is to remain open to what is being shared and to learn from it.

Some songs have a cabaret-like style where the rhythm is more spoken (recitative) and the lyrics are freer in the original language. For these songs, translators had more room to improvise rhythmically. Where these rhythmical differences were minor, we added supporting notes in brackets. However, where the differences were significant, we left it up to the reader to freely interpret the rhythm by adding pressure, anticipations, and upbeats.

Finally, there are fundamental differences between melodies that were composed as notated music and those transcribed from a singing voice, as well as between songs composed for community singing and those composed for a skilled soloist. Lyrics translators always prefer the former category over the more challenging latter. Each of the 25 EU languages also has its own rhythms and melodies, which can pose challenges in creating a singable translation. This is reminiscent of the differences between opera in Italian versus in English, Rossini versus Britten, or jazz standards translated from English into singable German or Danish.

All in all, we are grateful to have found so many brave songwriters, singers or literary translators who dared to — sometimes in pairs — adapt these national classics, allowing us to present and exchange them in the EU Songbook! All of them are pioneers, and we encourage anyone who feels that something vital was 'lost in translation' from their own language to instead seek out what could be 'found in translation' from other populations' languages. Those unfamiliar with Greek or Cyrillic could start there.

The central editors

Chords & Signs

In the EU Songbook we use the standard notation signs:

𝄋 = **Segno** ("sign") 𝄌 = **Coda** ("tail") and **Fine** (the end)

D.S. al Coda (Dal Segno al Coda, "from sign to tail")
Jump to 𝄋 and play until you reach **to Coda** and then jump to 𝄌

D.S. al Fine (Dal Segno al Fine, "from sign to the end")
Jump to 𝄋 and continue until you reach **Fine**.

D.C. (Da Capo, "from the head") – start all over

Rep. ad. lib. ("repetition ad libitum")
Repeat as much as you like (and finish at **Fine**, if there is one)

Chapter I

Freedom & Peace

FREEDOM & PEACE   HUNGARY

1
Ha én rózsa volnék
If I Was a Rose

The folk melody is from Csongrád county, and around 1969, it took a new lease of life, becoming the hymn of the Hungarian resistance against communist oppression of millions. The song was released on Hungarian singer Zsuzsa Koncz' solo-album "Jelbeszéd" – Sign Language – which shortly after was banned by the censor (only to be re-released ten years later). The forceful lyrics are by singer-songwriter, rock musician János Bródy (1946-): "If I was a banner, rarely would I wave, / no wind would dare tell me how I should behave, / I would be most joyful, if they stretched me thin, / never be a plaything of any blasting wind.."

By Ágnes C. Szalai, called by the National Association of Hungarian Choirs and Orchestras, KÓTA

Lyrics: János Bródy (1946-)   Music: folk song

1. Ha én rózsa volnék, nem csak egyszer nyílnék,
   Minden évben négyszer virágba borulnék,
   Nyílnék a fiúnak, nyílnék én a lánynak,
   Az igaz szerelemnek, és az elmúlásnak.

   1. If I was a rose, to hide I'd have no reason,
   I would bare my flowers each and every season,
   I'd blossom for the boy, I'd blossom for the girl,
   I'd blossom for true love, and for the passing world.

1. Ha én rózsa volnék,
   nem csak egyszer nyílnék,
   Minden évben négyszer
   virágba borulnék,
   Nyílnék a fiúnak
   nyílnék én a lánynak
   Az igaz szerelemnek
   és az elmúlásnak.

2. Ha én kapu volnék,
   mindig nyitva állnék,
   Akárhonnan jönne,
   bárkit beengednék,
   Nem kérdezném tőle,
   hát téged ki küldött,
   Akkor lennék boldog,
   ha mindenki eljött.

3. Ha én ablak volnék,
   akkora nagy lennék,
   Hogy az egész világ
   láthatóvá váljék,
   Megértő szemekkel
   átnéznének rajtam,
   Akkor lennék boldog,
   ha mindent megmutattam.

4. Ha én utca volnék,
   mindig tiszta lennék,
   Minden áldott este
   fényben megfürödnék,
   És ha egyszer rajtam
   lánckerék taposna,
   Alattam a föld is
   sírva beomolna.

5. Ha én zászló volnék,
   sohasem lobognék,
   Mindenféle szélnek
   haragosa lennék,
   Akkor lennék boldog,
   ha kifeszítenének,
   S nem lennék játéka
   mindenféle szélnek.

1. If I was a rose,
   to hide I'd have no reason,
   I would bare my flowers
   each and every season,
   I'd blossom for the boy,
   I'd blossom for the girl,
   I'd blossom for true love,
   and for the passing world.

2. If I was a portal,
   I would always welcome
   every traveler, no matter
   where they came from,
   I would never ask them,
   "hey, who sent you here,"
   I would be delighted,
   if everyone were near.

3. If I was a window,
   wide open and grand,
   you could gaze right through me,
   all across the land,
   I'd reveal the world to
   understanding eyes,
   show you every wonder
   'neath our starry skies.

4. If I was a street,
   I'd always be gleaming,
   I would bathe in brightness
   every blessed evening,
   and if heavy armor
   tread upon my skin,
   the very ground below
   would weep and then cave in.

5. If I was a banner,
   rarely would I wave,
   no wind would dare tell me
   how I should behave,
   I would be most joyful,
   if they stretched me thin,
   never be a plaything
   of any blasting wind.

Translation by József Váradi (2021)

FREEDOM & PEACE　　　　　　　　　　　　　　　　　　　　　　　　　FRANCE

2
Le chant des partisans
Song of the Partisans

This song is an integral part of the French history of the Second World War. The melody is influenced by Anna Marly's Russian origins. The song, broadcast on Radio London during the conflict, is a call to resistance and insurgency against the occupier. Its lyrics, written in 1943 by Kessel and Druon, testify to the violence of that time. The song is performed by children's choirs in French schools during ceremonies to celebrate the end of the Second World War, limited, however, to verses 1 and 4.

By Jean Blanchard, Training Center for Teachers of Music, Auvergne Rhône-Alpes, CEFEDEM

Lyrics: Joseph Kessel (1898-1979) & Maurice Druon (1918-2009)

Music: Anna Marly (1917-2006)

1. A - mi, en - tends - tu le vol noir des cor-beaux sur nos plai - nes?
1. My friend hear the sound of the crows swoop-ing o - ver the plains?

A - mi, en - tends - tu les cris sourds du pa - ys qu'on en - chaî - ne?
My friend hear the cries, it's the plight of our na - tion in chains?

O - hé! par - ti - sans, ou - vri - ers et pa - y - sans, c'est l'a - la - rme! Ce soir l'en-ne - mi con-naî-tra le prix du sang et des lar - mes!
Make haste par - ti - sans and all wor - kers of the land, time is near! For soon we will show our foe the cost of blood, grief and tears!

1. Ami, entends-tu
   le vol noir des corbeaux
   sur nos plaines?
   Ami, entends-tu
   les cris sourds du pays
   qu'on enchaîne?
   Ohé! partisans,
   ouvriers et paysans,
   c'est l'alarme!
   Ce soir l'ennemi
   connaîtra le prix du sang
   et des larmes!

2. Montez de la mine,
   descendez des collines,
   camarades!
   Sortez de la paille
   les fusils, la mitraille,
   les grenades...
   Ohé! les tueurs,
   à la balle et au couteau,
   tuez vite!
   Ohé! saboteur,
   attention à ton fardeau:
   dynamite!

3. C'est nous qui brisons
   les barreaux des prisons
   pour nos frères,
   la haine à nos trousses
   et la faim qui nous pousse,
   la misère...
   Il y a des pays
   où les gens au creux de lits
   font des rêves;
   ici, nous, vois-tu,
   nous on marche et nous on tue,
   nous on crève.

4. Ici chacun sait
   ce qu'il veut, ce qu'il fait
   quand il passe...
   Ami, si tu tombes
   un ami sort de l'ombre
   à ta place.
   Demain du sang noir
   séchera au grand soleil
   sur les routes.
   Chantez, compagnons,
   dans la nuit la Liberté
   nous écoute...

---

1. My friend hear the sound
   of the crows swooping
   over the plains?
   My friend hear the cries,
   it's the plight of our nation
   in chains?
   Make haste partisans
   and all workers of the land,
   time is near!
   For soon we will show
   our foe the cost of blood,
   grief and tears!

2. And come up from the mines
   come down from the pines,
   fellow comrades!
   Kept stowed in the bails,
   fetch the guns and the shells,
   the grenades...
   To you who shall kill
   with a bullet or a blade,
   do it swiftly!
   And you, saboteur,
   mind the dynamite, the burden
   you carry!

3. No brother in arms
   shall be kept behind bars,
   we are coming,
   With hate at our heels,
   we are chased, we are killed,
   we are starving...
   There are other places
   where children, lying careless,
   are dreaming:
   But we kill and run,
   with our bullets and our guns,
   undefeated.

4. For each of us know
   what will come with a blow,
   with a whisper...
   My friend if you fall,
   you can count on us all,
   brother, sister.
   Tomorrow the sunlight
   will dry the blood they shed
   on the trails.
   Let's sing to the nighttime,
   for in the darkness
   freedom prevails...

Translation by Claire Moreau & Lara Taska (2023)

Copyright © Editions Raoul Breton. International Copyright Secured. All Rights Reserved.
Reprinted by permission of Gazell Music, Sweden

FREEDOM & PEACE   PORTUGAL

3
Grândola Vila Morena
Grândola, Swarthy Town

Given their political content, often indirectly protesting about social injustice, misery and extreme poverty, many of Zeca Afonso's songs were censored under the far-right Dictatorship which lasted in Portugal for 48 years (1926-74). However, during a concert in March 1974, the audience joyfully dared to defy censorship and sing a song describing the brotherhood of men amongst the villagers around Grândola, a small town in Alentejo. One month later, this song was broadcasted by Radio Renascença as a signal for the rebellious armed forces to begin the Carnation Revolution which would finally lead to democracy. On the 25th day of April every year, "Grândola..." is sung across the country, working like an anthem with a very basic major harmonic progression, to celebrate freedom, democracy and the peaceful Revolution of '74.

By Manuela Encarnação & Nuno B. Mendes, Portuguese Music Teacher Association, APEM
& Jorge Alves, Association for Choirs in Lisbon, AMLC

Lyrics: Zeca Afonso (1929-87)   Music: Zeca Afonso (1929-87)

♩ = 100   No Chords - To be sung a cappella

1. Grân-do-la, vi-la mo-re - na,   ter - ra da____
1. Grân-do-la, swarth-y town,____   is   to us____

____fra-ter-ni-da - de,   o po-vo é quem mais or-
____land of fra-ter - ni - ty,   peo-ple are here to com-

de - na   den-tro de ti, ó ci-da - de.
mand____   with-in you, our dear ci - ty.

Den-tro de ti, ó ci-da - de   o po-vo é____
With-in you, our dear ci - ty,   peo-ple are____

1. Grândola, vila morena,
   terra da fraternidade,
   o povo é quem mais ordena
   dentro de ti, ó cidade.

   Dentro de ti, ó cidade
   o povo é quem mais ordena.
   Terra da fraternidade,
   Grândola, vila morena.

2. Em cada esquina um amigo,
   em cada rosto igualdade,
   Grândola, vila morena
   Terra da fraternidade!

   Terra da fraternidade!
   Grândola, vila morena
   Em cada rosto igualdade
   O povo é quem mais ordena!

3. À sombra de uma azinehira
   Que já não sabia a idade
   Jurei ter por companheira
   Grândola a tua vontade!

   Grândola a tua vontade
   Jurei ter por companheira
   À sombra duma azinheira
   Que já não sabia a idade!

1. Grândola, swarthy town,
   is to us land of fraternity,
   people are here to command
   within you, our dear city.

   Within you, our dear city,
   people are here to command.
   Land of fraternity,
   Grândola, swarthy town.

2. In each corner there's a friend,
   in each face equality,
   Grândola, swarthy town,
   is to us land of fraternity!

   Is to us land of fraternity!
   Grândola, swarthy town,
   in each face equality.
   People are here to command!

3. Right under the holm oak tree
   that forgot how old it is,
   I swore to have by my side
   Grândola, you and your will!

   Grândola, you and your will
   I swore to have by my side.
   Right under the holm oak tree
   that forgot how old it is!

Translation by Luísa Sobral (2022)

Copyright © Vydia Music Publishing/Strengholt Music. Reprinted by permission of CTM Outlander Music LP

FREEDOM & PEACE   GERMANY

4
Die Gedanken sind frei
All My Thoughts Are Truly Free

Originating from Switzerland in the decade of the French revolution this freedom song takes up the ancient idea of the freedom of thought, which already in the 12th century occupied the "Urvater" of the German song, Walther von der Vogelweide (c. 1170– c. 1230). The merry melody and serious lyrics were given their common form from various versions by Hoffmann von Fallersleben (1798 – 1874). Since its publication in 1842 this symbol of freedom of thought – and speech! – and struggle against oppression, was actualized in many conflict situations in German history. It was forbidden both during German Revolution (1848) and Nazism. Anti-Nazi political activist Sophie Scholl (1921-43) played it on flute by the prison wall for her imprisoned father, who had been critical of Hitler.

By Ekkehard Klemm, president, Association of German Concert Choirs (VDKC)/
Hochschule für Musik "Carl Maria von Weber" Dresden

Lyrics: possibly Ferdinand Freiligrath (1810-76)   Music: folksong

1. Die Ge-dan-ken sind frei, wer kann sie er-ra-ten, sie flie-hen vor-bei wie nächt-li-che Schat-ten. Kein Mensch kann sie wis-sen, kein Jä-ger er-schie-ßen, es blei-bet da-bei: die Ge-dan-ken sind frei.

1. *All my thoughts are tru-ly free, no-bo-dy can know them, like sha-dows in the night I don't have to show them. No hunt-er can kill them, no care-less bloke spill them, it's ea-sy to see: All my thoughts are tru-ly free.*

1. Die Gedanken sind frei,
   wer kann sie erraten,
   sie fliehen vorbei
   wie nächtliche Schatten.
   Kein Mensch kann sie wissen,
   kein Jäger erschießen,
   es bleibet dabei:
   die Gedanken sind frei.

2. Ich denke, was ich will,
   und was mich beglücket,
   doch alles in der Still,
   und wie es sich schicket.
   Mein Wunsch und Begehren
   kann niemand verwehren,
   es bleibet dabei:
   die Gedanken sind frei.

3. Ich liebe den Wein,
   mein Mädchen vor allen,
   sie tut mir allein
   am besten gefallen.
   Ich bin nicht alleine
   bei meinem Glas Weine,
   mein Mädchen dabei:
   die Gedanken sind frei.

4. Und sperrt man mich ein
   im finsteren Kerker,
   das alles sind rein
   vergebliche Werke;
   denn meine Gedanken
   zerreißen die Schranken
   und Mauern entzwei:
   die Gedanken sind frei.

5. Drum will ich auf immer
   den Sorgen entsagen
   und will mich auch nimmer
   mit Grillen mehr plagen.
   Man kann ja im Herzen
   stets lachen und scherzen
   und denken dabei:
   die Gedanken sind frei.

1. All my thoughts are truly free,
   nobody can know them,
   like shadows in the night
   I don't have to show them.
   No hunter can kill them,
   no careless bloke spill them,
   it's easy to see:
   All my thoughts are truly free.

2. What I think is up to me,
   I follow my calling.
   But I do it silently
   and never appalling.
   To what I aspire
   remains my desire,
   it's easy to see:
   All my thoughts are truly free.

3. Let's have some more wine,
   my girl is a treasure,
   so fair and so fine,
   she gives me such pleasure.
   Let's drink to life's chances,
   to love and romances,
   so lovely is she -
   all my thoughts are truly free.

4. If they give me ball and chain
   for long or forever -
   their hate is in vain,
   they'll change my mind never.
   My thoughts have the power
   to crush any tower
   and all misery -
   all my thoughts are truly free.

5. So that's what I plea:
   No pain and no sorrow.
   There always will be
   a joyful tomorrow.
   Sometimes saint, sometimes sinner,
   but my heart is a winner
   and always will be:
   All my thoughts are truly free.

Translation by Heinz Rudolf Kunze (2022)

English translation: Copyright © 2022 Weltverbesserer Musikverlag.

FREEDOM & PEACE   CYPRUS

5
Η δική μου η πατρίδα
My Own Fatherland

This song from 1998 refers to the divided Cyprus. It is written by a male Greek Cypriot composer and a female Turkish Cypriot poet. The song poses the question that is in the hearts of the Cypriots: Which part of my divided country should I love?

By Egli Spyridaki, Music Academy ARTE

Lyrics: Neşe Yaşin (1959-)
Greek translation: Elli Peonidou (1940-)

Music: Marios Tokas (1954-2008)

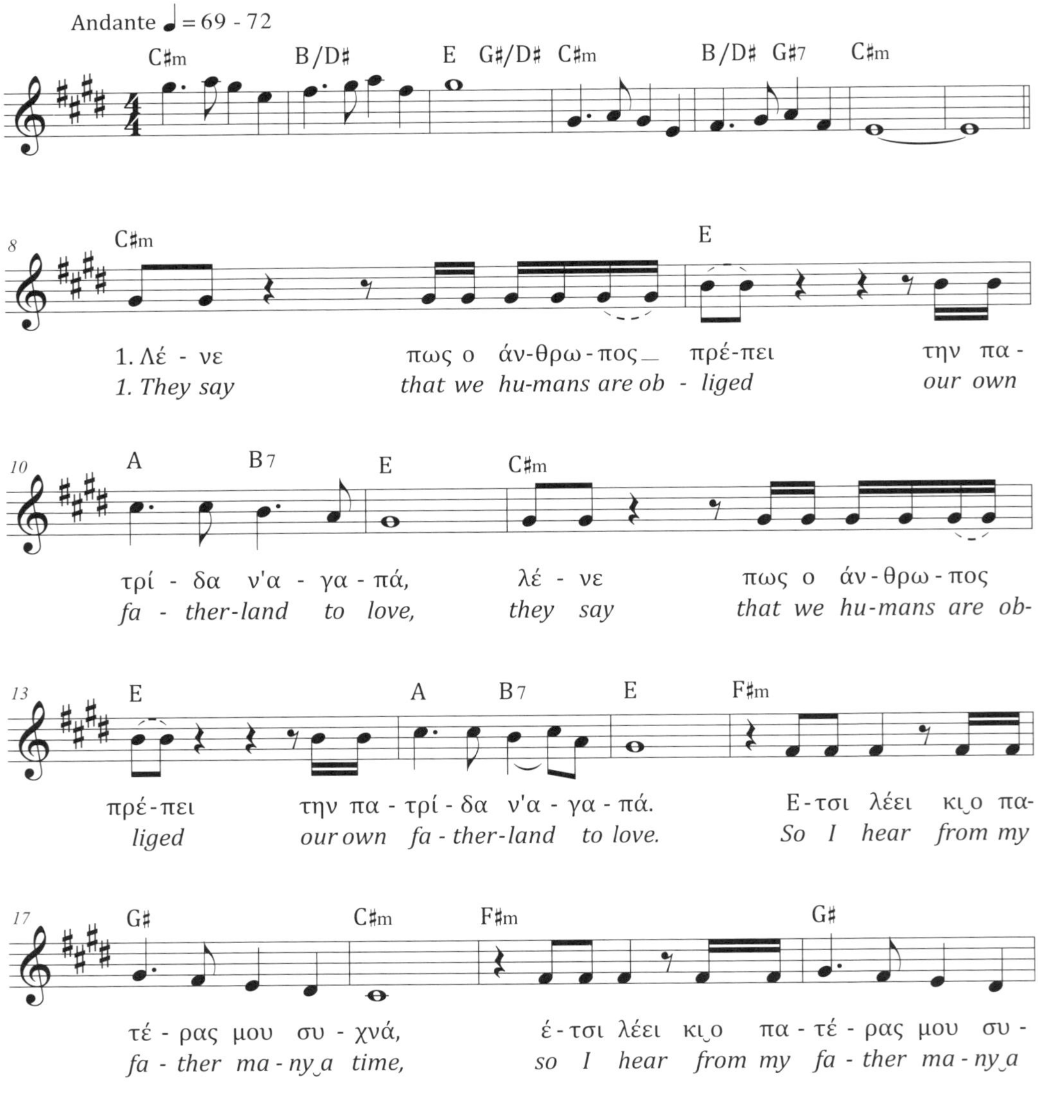

Andante ♩ = 69 - 72

1. Λέ - νε πως ο άν-θρω-πος πρέ-πει την πα-τρί - δα ν'α - γα - πά, λέ - νε πως ο άν-θρω-πος πρέ-πει την πα-τρί - δα ν'α - γα - πά. Ε-τσι λέει κι ο πα-τέ - ρας μου συ - χνά, έ-τσι λέει κι ο πα-τέ - ρας μου συ -

1. They say that we hu-mans are ob - liged our own fa - ther-land to love, they say that we hu-mans are ob - liged our own fa - ther-land to love. So I hear from my fa-ther ma-ny a time, so I hear from my fa-ther ma-ny a

Λένε πως ο άνθρωπος πρέπει
την πατρίδα ν' αγαπά,
λένε πως ο άνθρωπος πρέπει
την πατρίδα ν' αγαπά.
Ετσι λέει κι ο πατέρας μου συχνά,
έτσι λέει κι ο πατέρας μου συχνά.

Η δική μου η πατρίδα
έχει μοιραστεί στα δυο,
η δική μου η πατρίδα
έχει μοιραστεί στα δυο.
Ποιό από τα δυο κομμάτια
πρέπει ν' αγαπώ;
Ποιό από τα δυο κομμάτια
πρέπει ν' αγαπώ;

They say that we humans are obliged
our own fatherland to love,
they say that we humans are obliged
our own fatherland to love.
So I hear from my father many a time,
so I hear from my father many a time.

But my own, my dearest native fatherland
is divided in two,
but my own, my dearest native fatherland
is divided in two.
Which of the two parts
should I then love?
Which of the two parts
should I then love?

Translated by Ayis Ioannides (2021)

FREEDOM & PEACE   CZECHIA

6
Modlitba pro Martu
Prayer for Marta

When the Warsaw Pact troops invaded Communist Czechoslovakia on August 21, 1968, the hopes of the Prague Spring were definitively crushed. In that same moment the song "Prayer for Marta" was created, for the TV series "Song for Rudolf III". It immediately became a symbol of protests against the occupation, mainly due to the fact that only a few days after the invasion it was recorded by Marta Kubišová (b. 1942) and successfully passed to the radio, which protested against the occupiers. The song was subsequently banned during the normalization period and was not allowed to be broadcast on radio or television. Finally, during the Velvet Revolution in November 1989, "Prayer for Marta" resounded throughout Wenceslas Square in Prague.

By Czech Copyright Protection Association for Musical Works, OSA

Lyrics: Petr Rada (1932-2007)   Music: Jindřich Brabec (1933-2001)

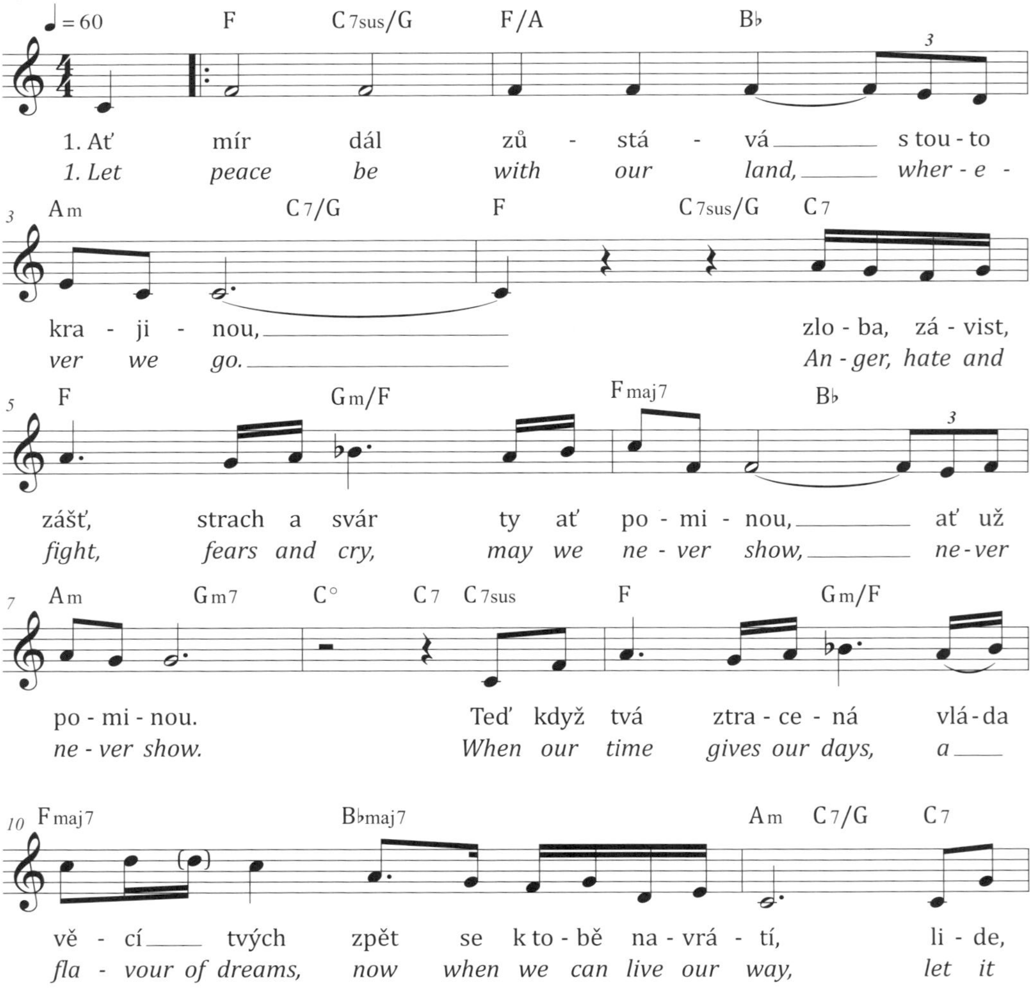

1. Ať mír dál zůstává s touto krajinou, zloba, závist, zášť, strach a svár ty ať pominou, ať už pominou. Teď když tvá ztracená vláda věcí tvých zpět se k tobě navrátí, lide,

1. Let peace be with our land, wherever we go. Anger, hate and fight, fears and cry, may we never show, never never show. When our time gives our days, a flavour of dreams, now when we can live our way, let it

1. Ať mír dál zůstává s touto krajinou,
   zloba, závist, zášť, strach a svár
   ty ať pominou, ať už pominou.
   Teď když tvá ztracená vláda věcí tvých
   zpět se k tobě navrátí, lide, navrátí.

Chorus:
   Z oblohy mrak zvolna odplouvá,
   a každý sklízí setbu svou.
   Modlitba má, ta ať promlouvá
   K srdcím, která zloby čas nespálil
   Jak květy mráz, jak mráz.

2. Ať mír dál zůstává s touto krajinou,
   zloba, závist, zášť, strach a svár
   ty ať pominou, ať už pominou.
   Teď když tvá ztracená vláda věcí tvých
   zpět se k tobě navrátí, lide, navrátí.

1. Let peace be with our land, wherever we go,
   anger, hate and fight, fears and cry
   may we never show, never-never show,
   when our time gives our days, a flavour of dreams
   now when we can live our way, let it be this way.

Chorus:
   Clouds on the sky slowly go away,
   now we must reap all that we've sown.
   This prayer of mine calls for better days,
   there's a chance, a brand new start,
   I can feel it in my heart, my heart.

2. Let peace be with our land, wherever we go,
   anger, hate and fight, fears and cry
   may we never show, never-never show.
   When our time gives our days, a flavour of dreams,
   now when we can live our way, let it be this way.

Translation by Michal Bukovič (1990)

FREEDOM & PEACE ITALY

7
Bella Ciao

After WW2, this song became the symbol of the resistance (Resistenza) against fascism and is for the Italian people a hymn to freedom and liberation from tyranny. Today it's a song of freedom very much felt in the emotional sense by all those citizens protesting against the continuous attempts of the authoritarian and populist right wing and is sung often and spontaneously by the multitudes in street demonstrations and on April 25th (the end of WW2 in Italy) or May 1st (Labour Day). The melody of "Bella Ciao" is so well known that it is often used in the most different contexts also with other lyrics, for example in the anthems of soccer fans. However, it is always important to remember the authentic origins of this song that still reflects the political struggle between opposing factions.

By Alfonso Santimone, National Academy of Jazz, Siena

Lyrics: Anonymous, (based on workers song, Po Valley)   Music: Folksong, 19th century

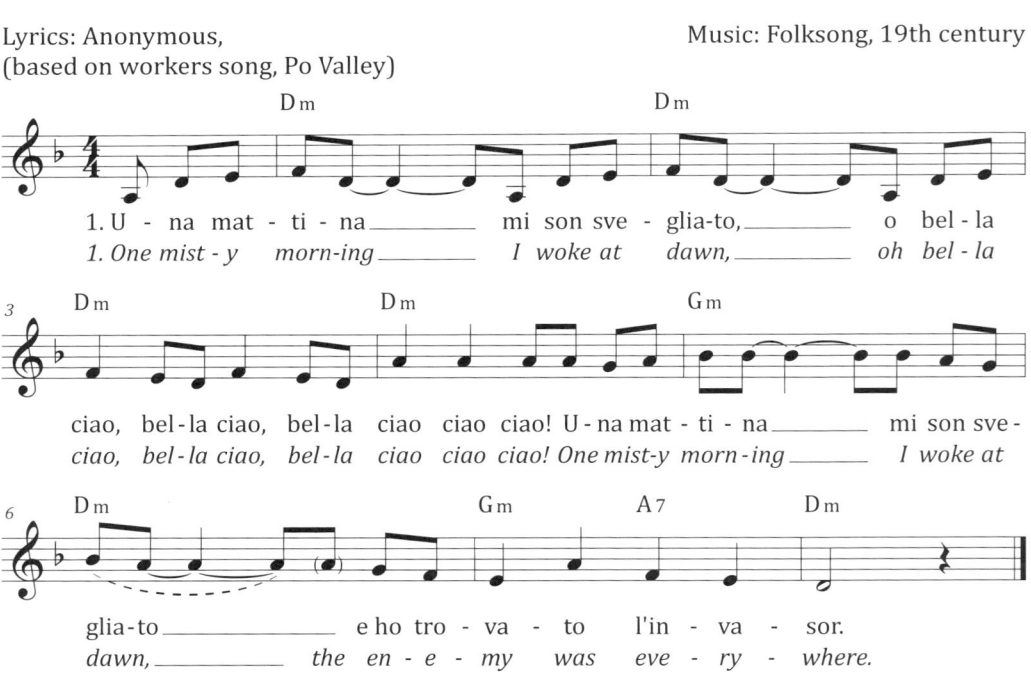

1. Una mattina mi son svegliato,
   o bella ciao, bella ciao, bella ciao ciao ciao!
   Una mattina mi son svegliato
   e ho trovato l'invasor.

2. O partigiano portami via,
   o bella ciao, bella ciao, bella ciao ciao ciao
   o partigiano portami via
   che mi sento di morir.

1. *One misty morning I woke at dawn,*
   oh bella ciao, bella ciao, bella ciao ciao ciao!
   One misty morning I woke at dawn
   the enemy was everywhere.

2. *Oh partisan, take me away!*
   oh bella ciao, bella ciao, bella ciao ciao ciao!
   oh partisan, take me away!
   for I am very close to die.

3. E se io muoio da partigiano,
   o bella ciao, bella ciao, bella ciao ciao ciao,
   e se io muoio da partigiano
   tu mi devi seppellir.

4. Seppellire lassù in montagna,
   o bella ciao, bella ciao, bella ciao ciao ciao,
   seppellire lassù in montagna
   sotto l'ombra di un bel fior.

5. E le genti che passeranno,
   o bella ciao, bella ciao, bella ciao ciao ciao,
   e le genti che passeranno
   mi diranno «che bel fior.»

6. Questo è il fiore del partigiano,
   o bella ciao, bella ciao, bella ciao ciao ciao,
   questo è il fiore del partigiano
   morto per la libertà.

3. And if I die as partisan,
   oh bella ciao, bella ciao, bella ciao ciao ciao!
   and if I die as partisan
   you will have to bury me.

4. You'll bury me, up in the mountains,
   oh bella ciao, bella ciao, bella ciao ciao ciao!
   you'll bury me, up in the mountains,
   under the shade of a wild rose.

5. And all the people who'll pass by me,
   oh bella ciao, bella ciao, bella ciao ciao ciao!
   and all the people who'll pass by me,
   they'll whisper «What a rose!»

6. This partisan became a wild rose,
   oh bella ciao, bella ciao, bella ciao ciao ciao!
   this partisan became a wild rose
   who died to set the peoples free.

Translation by Massimo Bubola (2023)

FREEDOM & PEACE   SLOVAKIA

8
Na Kráľovej holi
On the King's Highland

This is a Slovak folksong from the area of Horehronie (upper part of the river Hron). According to legend, the lyrics were written during World War II on the Russian front by a wounded Czechoslovakian soldier who thought he would probably never return home. An alternative interpretation is that the song is about a convicted man just before his execution by hanging. Even though nowadays there is no tree at the top of the "King's Hill" to resemble a gallows, this place is one of the most attractive tourist routes due to its beautiful nature. "Na Kráľovej holi" is also considered part of the Slovak history as significant figures had visited it (e.g. Bulgarian king Ferdinand, king Matthias Corvinus, and others). In 2019 a version of the song became the anthem and battle hymn of the football club "Slovan Bratislava".

*By Dr. Eva Čunderlíková, Slovak Music Teacher Association, AUHS/
Academy of Music Bratislava, VŠMU*

Lyrics: folk poem   Music: folksong

1. Na Krá - ľo - vej ho - li sto - jí strom ze - le - ný.
1. On the King's High-land, see, there stands a tall green tree.

Na Krá - ľo - vej ho - li sto - jí strom ze - le - ný.
On the King's High-land, see, there stands a tall green tree.

Vrch má na - klo - ne - ný, vrch má na - klo - ne - ný, vrch má na -
Bend-ing, its leaf-y crown, bend-ing, its leaf-y crown, bend-ing, its

klo - ne - ný do slo - ven - skej ze - mi.
leaf - y crown to Slo - vak earth bows down.

1. ||:Na Kráľovej holi
   stojí strom zelený. :||
   ||:Vrch má naklonený,
   vrch má naklonený,
   vrch má naklonený
   do slovenskej zemi. :||

2. ||: Odkážte, odpíšte
   tej mojej materi, :||
   ||: že mi svadba stojí,
   že mi svadba stojí,
   že mi svadba stojí
   na Kráľovej holi. :||

3. ||: Na nebi hviezdičky
   sú moje sestričky :||
   ||: a guľa z kanóna
   a guľa z kanóna
   a guľa z kanóna,
   to je moja žena. :||

4. ||: Odkážte, odpíšte
   mojím kamarátom, :||
   ||: že už viac nepôjdem,
   že už viac nepôjdem,
   že už viac nepôjdem
   na fraj za dievčaťom. :||

5. ||: Nezomrem na zemi,
   zomrem na koňovi, :||
   ||: a keď s koňa spadnem,
   a keď s koňa spadnem,
   a keď s koňa spadnem,
   šabľa mi zazvoní. :||

6. ||:Šabľa mi zazvoní,
   karabín zabrinká, :||
   ||:ozdaj me počuje,
   ozdaj me počuje,
   ozdaj me počuje
   tá moja frajerka. :||

---

1. ||: On the King's Highland, see,
   there stands a tall green tree. :||
   ||: Bending, its leafy crown,
   bending, its leafy crown,
   bending, its leafy crown
   to Slovak earth bows down. :||

2. ||: Let your report be clear,
   telling my mother dear:
   ||: now I've my wedding planned,
   now I've my wedding planned,
   now I've my wedding planned,
   here on the King's High Land. :||

3. ||: Stars that so brightly shine,
   sisters they shall be mine. :||
   ||: A cannonball in flight,
   a cannonball in flight,
   a cannonball in flight,
   shall be my wife tonight. :||

4. ||: Let your report be clear,
   telling my comrades dear: :||
   ||: I shall no longer come,
   I shall no longer come,
   I shall no longer come,
   to court the girls at home. :||

5. ||: On foot I shall not die,
   but on my saddle high. :||
   ||: When horse and I shall yield,
   when horse and I shall yield,
   when horse and I shall yield,
   like bells my sword will peal. :||

6. ||: My sword peal like a bell,
   my carbine call as well, :||
   ||: and maybe she will hear,
   and maybe she will hear,
   and maybe she will hear,
   that girl I love so dear. :||

Translation by John Minahane (2023)

FREEDOM & PEACE — DENMARK

9
Man binder os på mund og hånd
They Try to Tie Us, Lips and Hand

The song originates from a cabaret, written shortly after the German occupation in 1940. Apparently the lyrics – written by one of Denmark's most progressive poets and intellectuals – are solely about free love and the occupying force of marriage, but between the lines it was also directed toward the military occupation. The melancholic tango outsmarted censorship and became an all-time national unifier.

By Jesper Moesbøl, editor of "Sanghåndbogen"/The Song Handbook

Lyrics: Poul Henningsen (1894-1967)   Music: Kai Normann Andersen (1900-67)

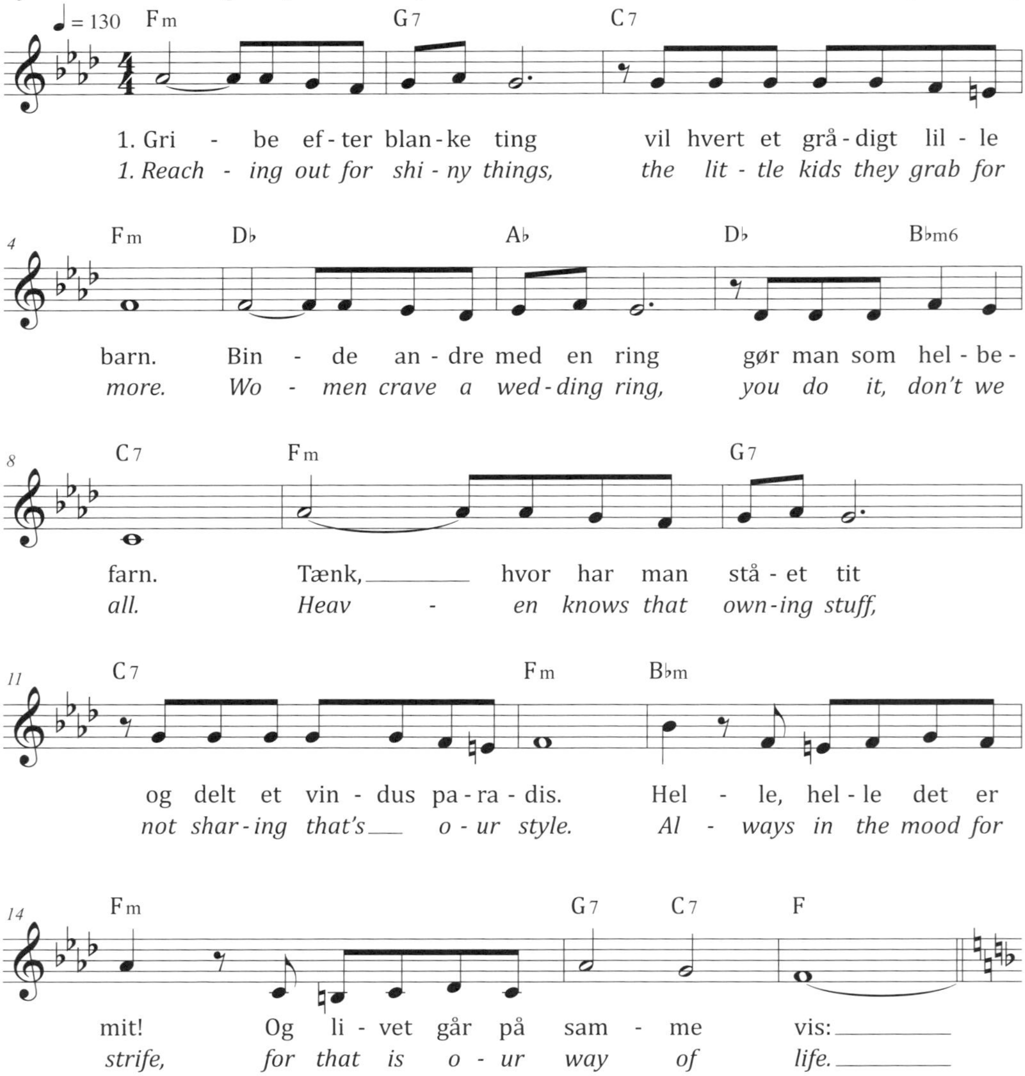

1. Gri - be ef - ter blan - ke ting vil hvert et grå - digt lil - le
1. Reach - ing out for shi - ny things, the lit - tle kids they grab for

barn. Bin - de an - dre med en ring gør man som hel - be -
more. Wo - men crave a wed - ding ring, you do it, don't we

farn. Tænk, hvor har man stå - et tit
all.   Heav - en knows that own - ing stuff,

og delt et vin - dus pa - ra - dis. Hel - le, hel - le det er
not shar - ing that's o - ur style. Al - ways in the mood for

mit! Og li - vet går på sam - me vis:
strife, for that is o - ur way of life.

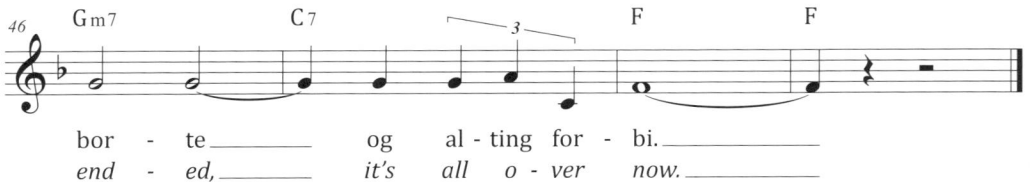

bor - te___ og al - ting for - bi.___
end - ed,___ it's all o - ver now.___

1. Gribe efter blanke ting
   vil hvert et grådigt lille barn.
   Binde andre med en ring
   gør man som helbefarn.
   Tænk, hvor har man stået tit
   og delt et vindus paradis.
   Helle, helle det er mit!
   Og livet går på samme vis:

1st chorus:
   Man binder os på mund og hånd,
   med vanens tusen stramme bånd,
   og det er besværligt
   at flagre sig fri.
   Vi leger skjul hos en, som ved
   at skærme os mod ensomhed
   med søde kontrakter
   vi luller os i.

   Kunne vi forbyde de tre ord:
   jeg lover dig,
   var vi vist i kærlighed
   på mere ærlig vej.

   De ord, vi svor med hånd og mund,
   de gælder kun den korte stund,
   til glæden er borte
   og alting forbi.

2. Kærlighed og ægteskab,
   hvad kommer de hinanden ved?
   Kedsomhedens tomme gab,
   til kæben går af led.
   Elskov er den vilde blomst:
   I gartnerhænder går den ud.
   Skærmet får den sin bekomst,
   men blomstrer hedt i storm og slud.

1. Reaching out for shiny things,
   the little kids they grab for more.
   Women crave a wedding ring,
   you do it, don't we all.
   Heaven knows that owning stuff
   - not sharing - that's our style.
   Always in the mood for strife
   for that is our way of life.

1st chorus:
   They try to tie us, lips and hand,
   the spirit of a wicked land,
   so hard to be free,
   I wish it was me.
   The game we play is hide and seek,
   with those who promise they won't cheat.
   Don't want to be lonely,
   be my guarantee.

   Let's stop signing contracts
   just like lawyers always do.
   Truer to ourselves we'd be,
   if I let go of you.

   The promises we'd want to keep,
   won't even last another week.
   Our love joy has ended,
   it's all over now.

2. Love & marriage hand in hand –
   invite a tiger in for tea.
   Loneliness and boredom will
   surely be maddening me.
   Flower power, making love -
   repression comes for sure.
   Love must flourish as a song
   just like the stormy weather's cure.

2nd chorus:
  Man binder os på mund og hånd,
  med vanens tusen stramme bånd,
  men ingen kan ejes.
  Vi flagrer os fri.
  I alle kærtegn er en flugt
  de røde sansers vilde flugt
  fra pligternes tvungne fortrampede sti.

  Du må ikke eje mig.
  Jeg ejer ikke dig.
  Alle mine kys er
  ikke ja og ikke nej.

  De ord vi svor med hånd og mund
  de gælder kun den svimle stund,
  det netop er kysset
  fra dig jeg ka li.

3. Møde hvad der venter os,
  og ingen ve hvordan det går.
  Bære skæbnen uden trods,
  hva der så forestår.
  Glad ved hver en venlighed,
  men uden tro, at det blir ved.
  Søge fred, idet vi ved
  at vi har ingen krav på fred.

3rd chorus:
  Man binder os på mund og hånd,
  men man kan ikke binde ånd,
  og ingen er fangne,
  når tanken er fri.
  Vi har en indre fæstning her,
  som styrkes i sit eget værd,
  når bare vi kæmper
  for det, vi ka li.

  Den, som holder sjælen rank,
  ka aldrig blie træl.
  Ingen ka regere det,
  som vi bestemmer sel.

  Det lover vi med hånd og mund,
  i mørket før en morgenstund,
  at drømmen om frihed
  blir aldrig forbi.

2nd chorus:
  They try to tie us, lips and hand,
  the spirit of an evil land,
  I'll fight to get free,
  I want to be me.
  Caresses in the flight we need,
  no fear of wilderness and weed,
  the duty of habit is not who we are.

  I will not possess you,
  if you just let me go.
  All my kisses matter,
  but hardly yes or no.

  The words we promised, lips and hand
  are true this moment in this land,
  cause I love to kiss you,
  it's you I adore.

3. Meet whatever comes our way,
  and not to know our fate.
  Patience, just to bear it all,
  why, life is always late.
  Kindness from a stranger is
  a blessing in disguise.
  Seeking for some peace of mind,
  it feels like bliss though you are blind.

3rd chorus:
  They try to tie us, lips and hand,
  the spirit - our beloved land
  where no one is threatened,
  when thinking is free.
  We have an inner certainty
  of strength and sought-for liberty
  of things that we like and
  of things that we love.

  Soul upright, and you will
  never ever be a slave.
  Self determination rules
  because that is our way.

  Our morning promise we declare
  deep from the darkness of despair:
  Keep dreaming of freedom
  forever a day.

  Translation by Suzanne Brøgger (2022)

Copyright © 1940 Edition Wilhelm Hansen AS, Copenhagen. International Copyright Secured. All Rights Reserved.
Reprinted by Permission of Hal Leonard Europe Ltd.

FREEDOM & PEACE   GREECE

10
Πότε θα κάνει ξαστεριά
When Will There Be a Clear Sky

This song originates from the island of Crete (probably early 19th century), during the time when Crete was under Ottoman rule. Rebellions occurred regularly and often the rebels had to seek refuge up in the mountains. They lived there and sang this song, waiting for the "clear skies", actually a "bright day" compared to the dark hours of their life, in order to get down from the mountains with their rifles, fight and become free again. Later, in the 20th century, this song became a "resistance song", particularly during the time when Greece was under dictatorship, between 1967-1974. Here the song is brought in a shortened version to accommodate younger generations.

By Thomas Louziotis, chairman, The Hellenic Choirs Association

Lyrics & Music: Traditional (Crete, probably early 19th century)

1. Πότε θα κά-, πότε θα κάμει ξαστεριά,
   ε πότε θα φλεβαρίσει,
   πότε θα φλεβαρίσει
   να πάρω το, να πάρω το ντουφέκι μου

2. Να πάρω το, να πάρω το ντουφέκι μου
   ε την έμορφη πατρόνα,
   την όμορφη πατρόνα
   να κατεβώ, να κατεβώ στον Ομαλό

3. Να κατεβώ, να κατεβώ στον Ομαλό,
   ε στη στράτα τω Μουσούρω,
   στη στράτα τω Μουσούρο
   να κάνω μα-, να κάνω μάνες δίχως γιους

1. When will there be, when will there be a clear sky,
   oh when will the spring arrive,
   when will the spring arrive
   to grab my ri-, to grab my rifle in my arms.

2. To grab my ri-, to grab my rifle in my arms,
   oh my chiseled cartridge belt,
   my chiseled cartridge belt,
   head down to O-, head down to Omalos.

3. Head down to O-, head down to Omalos,
   oh the street of the Mousouro's,
   the street of the Mousouro's
   to leave the mo-, to leave the mothers without sons.

Translation by Monika & Stavros Xenides (2023)

FREEDOM & PEACE   MALTA

11
Tema '79 (minn 'Ġensna')
Theme '79

This song was written for the 50 Ġensna ('Our People'), in remembrance of Freedom Day in 1979, when the last of the British soldiers left Malta after almost two centuries of colonisation. Particularly in "Theme '79", which was always the rock opera's most popular song, one can see the deep patriotic passion of the Maltese nation.

By Dr. Albert Pace, School of Performing Arts, University of Malta

Lyrics: Ray Mahoney (1949-)   Music: Paul Abela (1954-)

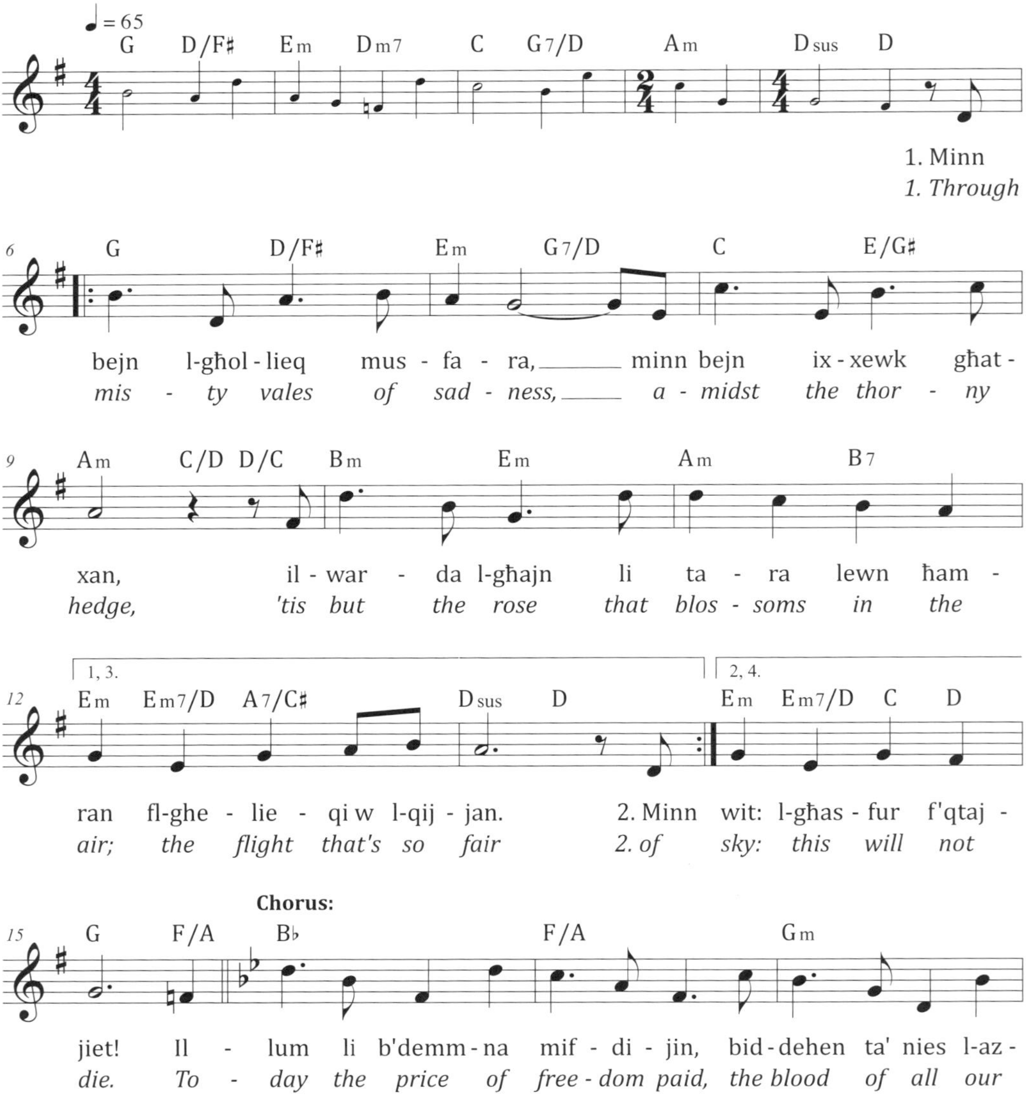

1. Minn bejn l-għol-lieq mus-fa-ra, minn bejn ix-xewk għat-xan, il-war-da l-għajn li ta-ra lewn ħam-ran fl-għe-lie-qi w l-qij-jan.
   Through misty vales of sadness, amidst the thorny hedge, 'tis but the rose that blossoms in the air; the flight that's so fair

2. Minn wit: l-għas-fur f'qtaj-jiet!
   of sky: this will not die.

Chorus:
Il - lum li b'demm-na mif-di-jin, bid-dehen ta' nies l-az-
Today the price of freedom paid, the blood of all our

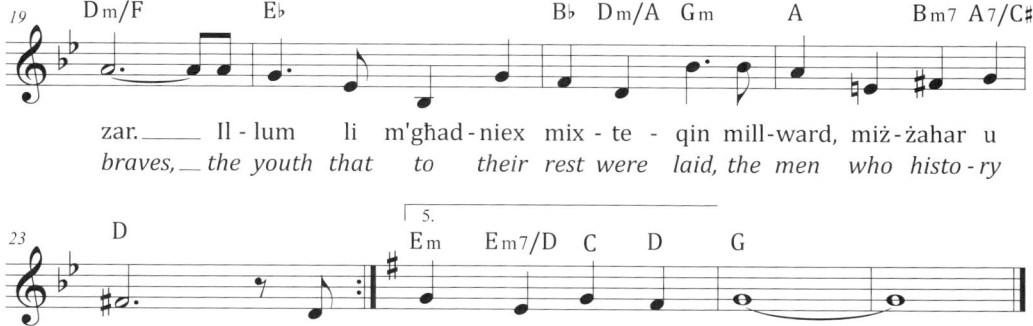

1. Minn bejn l-għollieq musfara,
   minn bejn ix-xewk għatxan,
   il-warda l-għajn li tara
   lewn ħamran fl-għelieqi w l-qijjan.

2. Minn bejn l-i-sħab imnikket,
   minn bejn iċ-ċparijiet,
   il-għanja ħadd ma jsikket
   mis-smewwit: l-għasfur f'qtajjiet!

Chorus:
   Illum li b'demm-na mif-dijin,
   bid-dehen ta' nies l-azzar.
   Illum li m'għadniex mixteqin
   mill-ward, miż-żahar u nwar.

3. Jifirħu ta' madwarna,
   il-ġnus u il-ġirien.
   Sa fl-aħħar ksibna darna,
   dan hu ż-żmien ta' ferħ kull ħolqien.

4. U l-ġwienaħ tal-meħlusa
   jittajru lejn ix-xemx,
   il-bajda w ħamra nbusha,
   bħala m'ħemmx, din ma tintemmx.

Chorus:
   Illum li b'demm-na mif-dijin...

5. O Alla, ħares fuqna.
   Dalġens qed jgħix mill-ġdid.
   Fil-hena saħħaħ ruħna,
   ħa nqimuk u infaħħruk.

1. Through misty vales of sadness,
   amidst the thorny hedge,
   'tis but the rose that blossoms
   in the air; the flight that's so fair...

2. ...of birds that found their freedom
   from captive cages, dark.
   'Tis theirs the song I hear now
   in the sky: this will not die.

Chorus:
   Today the price of freedom paid,-
   the blood of all our braves,
   the youth that to their rest were laid,
   the men who history made.

3. The neighbouring rejoicing,
   the bells that peal away,
   the marches play the glory
   of this day that homage we pay...

4. ...to those who fought with courage
   thar we may live in peace.
   Oh let me kiss the colours
   of my land, these will not end.

Chorus:
   Today the price of freedom paid,-...

5. Oh Lord look down upon us,
   we live each day anew.
   In this our height of glory
   give us strength for evermore.

Translation by Ray Mahoney (2022)

Copyright © the authors. International copyright secured. All rights reserved. Reprinted by permission

FREEDOM & PEACE   THE NETHERLANDS

12
Over de muur
Over the Wall

Written by Harrie Jekkers (born 1951) for one of the biggest Dutch peace demonstrations during the Cold War in the 1980s, "Over the Wall" tells its tale about the wall that separated not only Germany but all of Europe in two. Jekkers describes the situation without judgement; he sings about the good and bad from both sides. He got the idea that nature cannot be blocked by a wall when he witnessed a dog walking from one side to the other at Checkpoint Charlie. In the song this has been visualized with birds that "fly from East to West Berlin, because sometimes they want to be in the East, sometimes in the West."

By Christiane Nieuwmeijer, Leiden University of Applied Sciences
& Lieuwe Noordam, Prins Claus Conservatorium, Groningen

Lyrics: Harrie Jekkers (1951-)   Music: Léon Smit

1. Oost-Ber-lijn, Un-ter den Lin-den. Er wan-de-len men-sen langs vlag-gen en vaan-dels, waar Le-nin en Marx nog steeds op een voet-stuk staan. En ie-der-een werkt, ha-mers en sik-kels, ter-wijl in pa-ra-de-pas de wacht wordt ge-wis-seld. Veer-tig

1. East Ber-lin, Un-ter den Lin-den. Where peo-ple are stroll-ing past ban-ners and flags, and Le-nin and Marx are e-ven to-day raised high. And eve-ry-one works, ham-mers and sick-les, while sol-diers in goose step may be chang-ing the guard. De-cades

1. Oost-Berlijn, Unter den Linden.
   Er wandelen mensen
   langs vlaggen en vaandels,
   waar Lenin en Marx
   nog steeds op een voetstuk staan.
   En iedereen werkt,
   hamers en sikkels,
   terwijl in paradepas
   de wacht wordt gewisseld.
   Veertig jaar socialisme,
   er is in die tijd veel bereikt.
   Maar wat is nou die heilstaat
   als er muren omheen staan,
   als je bang en voorzichtig met
   je mening moet omgaan.

   (1. verse to be continued next page)

1. East Berlin, Unter den Linden.
   Where people are strolling
   past banners and flags,
   and Lenin and Marx
   are even today raised high.
   And everyone works,
   hammers and sickles,
   while soldiers in goose step
   may be changing the guard.
   Decades of socialism,
   an awful lot has been achieved.
   But what's great about this state
   when you're shut in by the wall,
   when you dare not even say
   what you are thinking at all?

   (1. verse to be continued on next page)

(1. verse continued)

Ach wat is nou die heilstaat,
zeg mij wat is hij waard,
wanneer iemand die afwijkt
voor gek wordt verklaard.

Chorus:
Alleen de vogels vliegen
van Oost- naar West-Berlijn,
worden niet teruggefloten,
ook niet neergeschoten.
Over de muur, over het IJzeren Gordijn,
omdat ze soms in het westen,
soms ook in het oosten willen zijn.
Omdat ze soms in het westen,
soms ook in het oosten willen zijn.

2. West-Berlijn, de Kurfürstendam
Er wandelen mensen
langs porno en peepshows,
waar Mercedes en Cola nog steeds
op een voetstuk staan.
En de neonreklames
die glitterend lokken:
Kom dansen, kom eten,
kom zuipen, kom gokken.
Dat is nou veertig jaar vrijheid,
er is in die tijd veel bereikt.
Maar wat is nou die vrijheid
zonder huis, zonder baan,
Zoveel Turken in Kreuzberg
die amper kunnen bestaan.
Goed, je mag demonstreren
maar met je rug tegen de muur.
En alleen als je geld hebt,
dan is de vrijheid niet duur.

Chorus:
En de vogels vliegen
van West- naar Oost-Berlijn,
worden niet teruggefloten,
ook niet neergeschoten.
Over de muur, over het IJzeren Gordijn,
omdat ze soms in het oosten,
soms ook in het westen willen zijn.
Omdat er brood ligt
soms bij de Gedächtniskirche,
soms op het Alexanderplein.

(1. verse continued)

Really, how well does it fare,
tell me who pays the bill,
when your critical mind
gets you stamped mentally ill?

Chorus:
Only the pigeons can fly
from East to West Berlin,
they are not stopped when trying,
nor shot once they're flying.
Over the wall, over the Iron Curtain,
because now it's in the west,
and then in the east they want to be.
Because now it's in the west,
and then in the east they want to be.

2. West Berlin, the Kurfürstendamm.
Where people are strolling
past porn shop and peepshow,
and Cola and Merc have been
and will be raised high.
And the neon adverts
that glitter and wink:
Come dine and come dance,
come gamble and with us come drink.
Decades of liberalism,
an awful lot has been achieved.
But what freedom is this then
for those with no house, no work,
with real poverty in Kreuzberg
for many a Turk.
You can take to the streets,
but with your back to the wall.
And unless you've got money,
there's no freedom at all.

Chorus:
Only the pigeons can fly
from West to East Berlin,
they are not stopped when trying,
nor shot once they're flying.
Over the wall, over the Iron Curtain,
because now it's in the east,
and then in the west they want to be.
Because there's bread crumbs
now at the Gedächtniskirche,
and then in Alexanderplatz.

Translation by Arnold Mühren (2021)

FREEDOM & PEACE   FINLAND

13
Finlandia-hymni
Finlandia Hymn

At the beginning of the 20th century, Jean Sibelius's orchestral piece "Finland awakens" – later known as Finlandia – became the central musical expression of Finland's struggle for independence from Russia, finally achieved in 1917. From the 1920s onwards, performing Finlandia was an integral part of all patriotic celebrations. As a song version, Finlandia was sung by American Finns as early as in the 1910s. In Finland, however, the hymn version did not become well known until the Second World War, when Veikko Antero Koskenniemi wrote new uplifting lyrics (1940): "Oi Suomi katso, sinun päiväs koittaa" (Finland, behold, thy daylight now is dawning). Finlandia has even been proposed as a new national anthem, emphasizing its central position at the heart of all patriotic songs in Finland.

By Dr. Vesa Kurkela, Sibelius Academy

Lyrics: Veikko Antero Koskenniemi (1885-1962)   Music: Jean Sibelius (1865-1957)

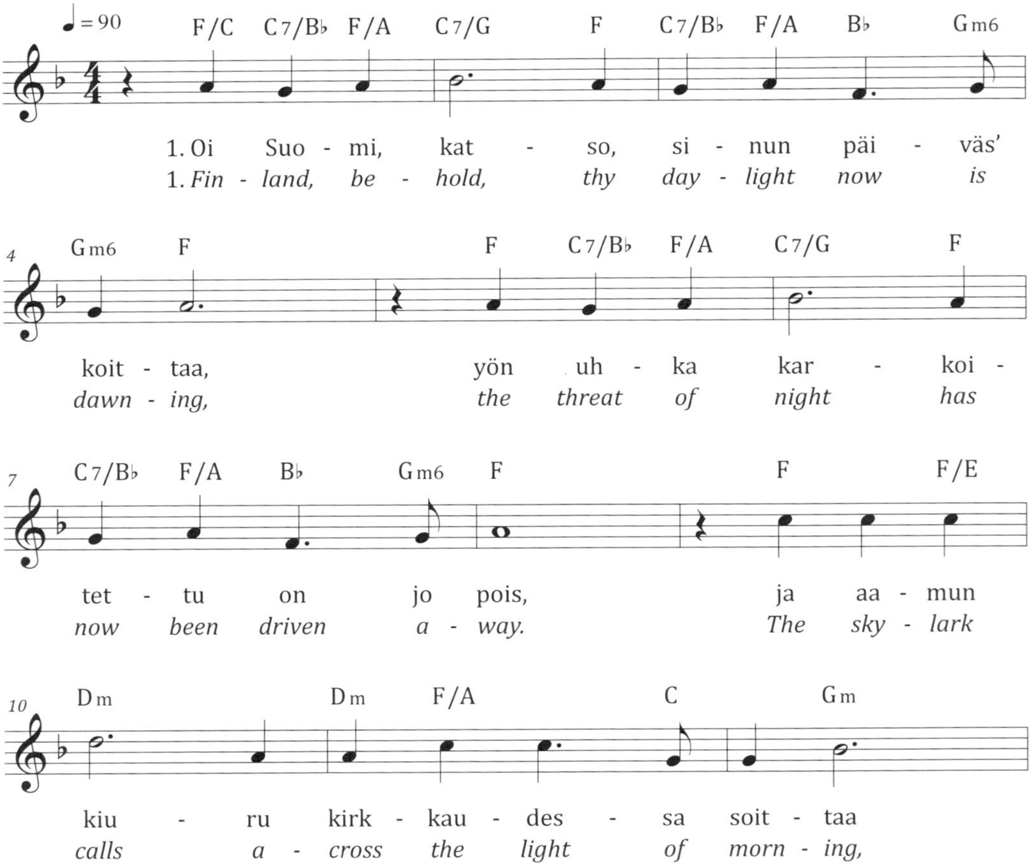

1. Oi Suomi, katso, sinun päiväs' koittaa, yön uhka karkoitettu on jo pois, ja aamun kiuru kirkkaudessa soittaa
1. Finland, behold, thy daylight now is dawning, the threat of night has now been driven away. The skylark calls across the light of morning,

1. Oi Suomi, katso, sinun päiväs' koittaa,
   yön uhka karkoitettu on jo pois,
   ja aamun kiuru kirkkaudessa soittaa
   kuin itse taivahan kansi sois.
   Yön vallat aamun valkeus jo voittaa,
   sun päiväs koittaa, oi synnyinmaa.

2. Oi nouse, Suomi, nosta korkealle
   pääs' seppelöimä suurten muistojen.
   Oi nouse, Suomi, näytit maailmalle
   sa että karkoitit orjuuden
   ja ettet taipunut sa sorron alle,
   on aamus' alkanut, synnyinmaa.

1. Finland, behold, thy daylight now is dawning,
   the threat of night has now been driven away.
   The skylark calls across the light of morning,
   the blue of heaven lets it have its way,
   and now the day the powers of night is scorning:
   thy daylight dawns, O Finland of ours!

2. Finland, arise, and raise towards the highest
   thy head now crowned with mighty memory.
   Finland, arise, for to the world thou criest
   that thou hast thrown off thy slavery,
   beneath oppression's yoke thou never liest.
   Thy morning's come, O Finland of ours!

Translation by Keith Bosley (1998)

Copyright © by Breitkopf & Härtel, Wiesbaden. Reprinted by permission

FREEDOM & PEACE   IRELAND

14
The Fields of Athenry

"The Fields of Athenry" was written in 1977 by Dublin-born singer songwriter Pete St. John. The song tells the story of a fictional man from Athenry, a town in County Galway in the west of Ireland who, having been caught stealing corn to feed his starving family during the Irish famine years (1840s), was deported to the penal colony at Botany Bay in Australia. The Fields of Athenry has become Ireland's unofficial sporting 'anthem' and may be heard from the terraces at many sporting events, in particular rugby and soccer, both at home games and on the international stage.

By Mark Armstrong, SING IRELAND

Lyrics: Pete St. John (1870 -1945)   Music: Pete St. John (1870 -1945)

1. By a lonely prison wall I heard a young girl calling: "Michael they have taken you away, for you stole Trevelyan's corn, so the young might see the morn, now a prison ship lies waiting in the bay."

Chorus:
Low lie the Fields of Athenry where

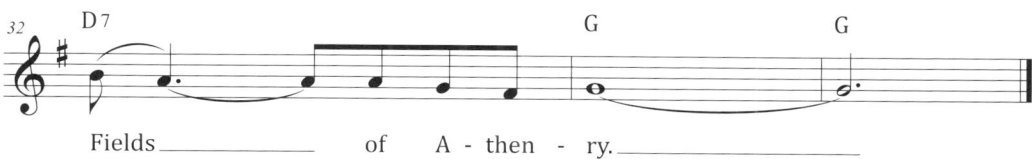

1. By a lonely prison wall,
   I heard a young girl calling.
   "Michael they have taken you away,
   for you stole Trevelyan's corn,
   so the young might see the morn,
   now a prison ship lies waiting in the bay".

   Chorus:
   Low lie, the Fields of Athenry
   where once we watched
   the small free birds fly.
   Our love was on the wing,
   we had dreams and songs to sing,
   it's so lonely round the Fields of Athenry.

2. By a lonely prison wall
   I heard a young man calling:
   "Nothing matters Mary, when you're free.
   'Gainst the famine and the crown,
   I rebelled, they cut me down.
   Now you must raise our child with dignity".

   Chorus:
   Low lie, The Fields of Athenry
   where once we watched
   the small free birds fly.
   Our love was on the wing,
   we had dreams and songs to sing,
   it's so lonely round the Fields of Athenry.

3. By a lonely harbour wall
   she watched the last star falling.
   As the prison ship sailed out against the sky.
   Sure she lived in hope and pray
   for her love in Bot'ny Bay.
   It's so lonely round the Fields of Athenry.

   Chorus:
   Low lie, The Fields of Athenry
   where once we watched
   the small free birds fly.
   Our love was on the wing,
   we had dreams and songs to sing,
   it's so lonely round the Fields of Athenry.

Copyright © Celtic Songs. Reprinted by permission of Edition Bjorlund AB

FREEDOM & PEACE   LATVIA

15
Saule, Pērkons, Daugava
Sun, Thunder, Daugava

When this song for choir appeared in 1988, three years prior to Latvian independence after 50 years of Soviet occupation, it was a call for a spiritual awakening. All those performing it – on stage, at choir festivals, on TV – defiantly voiced respect for the origin and strength of their occupied nation. The lyrics, written 100 years ago when Latvia was first declared independent, bring to life the voices of those who, between destiny and the elements, for centuries lived and guarded the banks of the Daugava River. For 30 years now, this song has been performed with both love and a sense of pride at cultural events. And when singers call out the forces of soul and nature, everyone rises: "Water of death, water of life: I feel both in the soul / The Sun is our mother / Daugav', nanny of pain / Thunder, who strikes devils / He is our father".

By Rūta Kanteruka, president, Latvian Music Teachers' Association, LVIIMSA

Lyrics: Jānis Krišjānis Pliekšāns "Rainis" (1865 -1929)   Music: Mārtiņš Brauns (1951-)

♩ = 60

1. Sau - le Lat - vi sē - di - nā - ja tur, kur ga - li sa - tie - kas, bal - ta jū - ra, za - ļa ze - me Lat - vei vār - tu at - slē - dzi - ņa 2. Lat - vei vār - tu at - slē - dzi - ņa, Dau - ga - vi - ņas sar - gā - tā - ja, sve - ši ļau - dis vār - tus lau - za, jū - rā kri - ta at - slē -

1. Moth - er Sun placed Lat-vi - a here, where the sea and fo - rest meet. White - foamed sea and ver-dant for - est, and a key to fas - ten the gate. 2. With the key they fas-tened the gate, guar - ded by the Dau-ga-va brave. Stran - gers came to break the gate down, and the key fell in - to

1. Saule Latvi sēdināja
   tur, kur gali satiekas,
   balta jūra, zaļa zeme
   Latvei vārtu atslēdziņa.

2. Latvei vārtu atslēdziņa,
   Daugaviņas sargātāja,
   sveši ļaudis vārtus lauza,
   jūrā krita atslēdziņa.

3. Zilzibeņu pērkons spēra,
   velniem ņēma atslēdziņu.
   Nāvi, dzīvi Latve slēdza,
   baltu jūru, zaļu zemi,
   nāvi, dzīvi Latve slēdza,
   baltu jūru, zaļu zemi.

4. Saule Latvi sēdināja
   baltas jūras maliņā,
   vēji smiltis putināja
   ko lai dzēra latvju bērni?

5. Dzīves ūdens, nāves ūdens
   Daugavā satecēja,
   es pamērcu pirkstu galu,
   abus jūtam dvēselē.
   Nāves ūdens, dzīves ūdens,
   abus jūtam dvēselē.

6. ||: Saule mūsu māte -
   Daugav' - sāpju aukle,
   Pērkons velnu spērējs,
   tas mūsu tēvs. :||

1. *Mother Sun placed Latvia here,*
   where the sea and forest meet.
   White-foamed sea and verdant forest,
   and a key to fasten the gate.

2. *With the key they fastened the gate,*
   guarded by the Daugava brave.
   Strangers came to break the gate down,
   and the key fell into the sea.

3. *Thunder rampaged blue in the sky,*
   down he came to rescue the key.
   Death and life were locked in one place,
   in this land where sand and sea meet.
   Death and life were locked in one place,
   in this land where sand and sea meet.

4. *Mother Sun placed Latvia here,*
   where the white-foamed water laps.
   Tempests churned the sandy beaches
   Oh, what will the children here drink?

5. *Living water, deadly water,*
   both flow through Daugava's stream.
   I bend down to touch the waters,
   I feel both within my soul.
   Deadly water, living water,
   I feel both within my soul.

6. ||: *Mother Sun, protect us*
   Daugava, caress us.
   Father Thunder, guard us,
   He fights for us. :||

Translation by Māra Walsh Sinka (2022)

FREEDOM & PEACE   SLOVENIA

16
Oj Triglav, moj dom
Oh, Triglav, My Home

Based on the lyrics by Matija Zemljič, the song was premiered in 1895 on the occasion of the opening of the famous Slovene alpine "tower", sponsored by and named after the composer himself, Jakob Aljaž, a priest and patriot. Aljaž bought the peak of Triglav, Slovenia's most celebrated and highest mountain – which rises imposingly to an altitude of 2864 meters – and sponsored the tower, now a cylindrical marker 2 meters high with space inside. This entire undertaking (buying the land; sponsoring, designing, transporting and building the tower) was a way to express the early idea of Slovene national sovereignty, an idea that patiently endured through three different political constellations until the country's independence in 1991. The simple 4-voice choral setting of the song, so specific for the Slovene music of the 19th century, is not only the hiking anthem of Slovenia, but it also symbolizes the important journey of Slovene cultural patriotism, from its early roots to today.

By Dr. Leon Stefanija, University of Ljubljana, Faculty of Arts

Lyrics: Matija Zemljič "Slavin" (1873-1934)   Music: Jakob Aljaž (1845-1927)

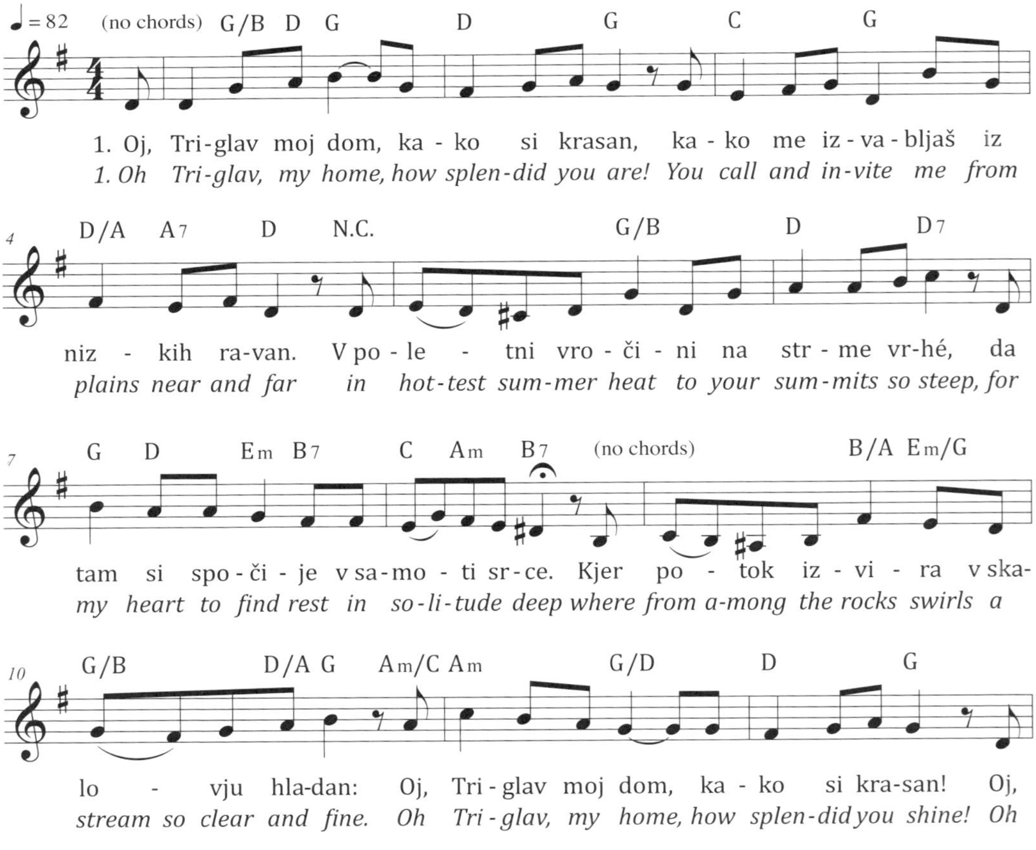

1. Oj, Tri-glav moj dom, ka-ko si krasan, ka-ko me iz-va-bljaš iz niz-kih ra-van. V po-le-tni vro-či-ni na str-me vr-hé, da tam si spo-či-je v sa-mo-ti sr-ce. Kjer po-tok iz-vi-ra v ska-lo-vju hla-dan: Oj, Tri-glav moj dom, ka-ko si kra-san! Oj,

1. Oh Tri-glav, my home, how splen-did you are! You call and in-vite me from plains near and far in hot-test sum-mer heat to your sum-mits so steep, for my heart to find rest in so-li-tude deep where from a-mong the rocks swirls a stream so clear and fine. Oh Tri-glav, my home, how splen-did you shine! Oh

1. Oj, Triglav, moj dom, kako si krasan,
   kako me izvabljaš iz nizkih ravan.
   V poletni vročini na strme vrhe,
   da tam si spočije v samoti srce.
   Kjer potok izvira v skalovju hladan:
   Oj Triglav, moj dom, kako si krasan!

Chorus:
   ||: Oj Triglav, moj dom,
   oj Triglav, moj dom!
   Oj Triglav, moj dom!
   Kako si krasan,
   kako si krasan! :||

2. Oj Triglav, moj dom, četudi je svet
   začaral s čudesi mi večkrat pogled,
   tujina smehljaje kazala mi kras,
   le nate sem mislil ljubeče ves čas,
   o tebi sem sanjal sred' svetlih dvoran:
   Oj Triglav, moj dom, kako si krasan!

Chorus:
   ||: Oj Triglav, moj dom... :||

3. Oj Triglav, v spominu mi je tvoj čar,
   zato pa te ljubim in bom te vsekdar,
   in zadnja ko ura odbila mi bo,
   pod tvojim obzorjem naj spava telo,
   kjer radostno ptički
                       naznanjajo dan:
   Oj Triglav, moj dom, kako si krasan!

Chorus:
   ||: Oj Triglav, moj dom... :||

1. Oh Triglav, my home, how splendid you are!
   You call and invite me from plains near and far
   in hottest summer heat to your summits so steep,
   for my heart to find rest in solitude deep
   where from among the rocks swirls a stream so clear 'n fine.
   Oh Triglav, my home, how splendid you shine!

Chorus:
   ||: Oh Triglav, my home,
   oh Triglav, my home,
   oh Triglav, my home,
   how splendid you are,
   how splendid you are! :||

2. Oh Triglav, my home, our world, has its might,
   its wondrous enchantments distracting my sight.
   Though lured on by the wonders of countries I've seen,
   still my love for you is the strongest it has been.
   Amidst the brightest halls I am dreaming from afar.
   Oh Triglav, my home, how splendid you are!

Chorus:
   ||: Oh Triglav, my home... :||

3. Oh Triglav, your charm remains such a thrill,
   and therefore I love you and I always will.
   So when the bells they chime and my last hour is 'nigh,
   'neath your wide horizon my body shall lie.
   There, joyfully the birds would declare the morning star:
   Oh Triglav, my home, how splendid you are!

Chorus:
   ||: Oh Triglav, my home... :||

Translation by Steve Klink & Boštjan Malus (2021)

FREEDOM & PEACE   ROMANIA

17
Acolo este țara mea
In My Beloved Land

The poem "In My Beloved Land" was written in the second half of the 19th century by poet Ioan Nenițescu (1854-1901), a Romanian playwright and prose writer, who enlisted in the Romanian Army and fought in the War of Independence (1877-78). It also inspired the music offered to us by Tudor Gheorghe, an actor by profession, and one of the most loved among living Romanian singers and composers. This song is truly patriotic music, expressing homesickness and grief, love for one's country and sung with fervour, elegiacally, with intensity, it also expresses the beauties of our country, from mountains, valleys and hills to plains, sea and delta, as well as famous legends known all around the world.

By Dr. Grigore Cudalbu, National University of Music, Bucharest, UNMB/
Romanian National Association of Choral Music, ANCR

Lyrics: Ioan Nenițescu (1854-1901)   Music: Tudor Gheorghe (1945-)

Free recitative - with guitar acc. with fast pace

1. A - co - lo un - des nalti ste - jari
1. Where trees are proud and oh so tall

Si cât ste - ja - rii, nalti îmi cresc
and oaks grow to the skies in grace

Flă - cãi cu piep - tu - ri - le tari
so are young men fear - less and strong

Ce moar - tean fa - ta o pri - vesc
and star - ing in - to death's pale face!

A - co - lo un - des stânci si munti,
Where cliffs and moun - tains stand in pride,

1. Acolo unde-s nalți stejari
   Și cât stejarii, nalți îmi cresc
   Flăcăi cu piepturile tari,
   Ce moartea-n față o privesc;

   Acolo unde-s stânci și munți,
   Și ca și munții nu clintesc
   Voinicii cei cu peri cărunți
   În dor de țară strămoșesc;

   Chorus:
   Acolo este țara mea,
   Și neamul meu cel românesc!
   Acolo eu să mor aș vrea,
   Acolo vreau eu să trăiesc!

2. Acolo unde-i cer senin
   Și ca seninul cer zâmbesc
   Femei, ce poartă l-al lor sân
   Copii ce pentru lupte cresc,

   Acolo unde întâlnești
   Cât ține țara-n lung și-n lat
   Bătrâne urme vitejești
   Și osul celor ce-au luptat;

   Chorus:
   Acolo este țara mea...

3. Și unde vezi mii de mormane,
   Sub care-adânc s-au îngropat
   Mulțime de oștiri dușmane,
   Ce cu robia ne-au cercat;

   Și unde dorul de moșie
   Întotdeauna drept a stat,
   Și bărbăteasca vitejie
   A-ncununat orice bărbat,

   Chorus:
   Acolo este țara mea...

1. Where trees are proud and oh so tall
   and oaks grow to the skies in grace,
   so are young men fearless and strong
   and staring into death's pale face!

   Where cliffs and mountains stand in pride,
   and as the mountains standing still,
   old warriors of quiet might,
   their love of country, greatest thrill!

   Chorus:
   For there in my beloved land
   I follow my Romanian ways!
   It's where I want my life to end
   and where I long to live my days!

2. There, skies are bright as they can be,
   and as these skies are filled with light
   so women raise their sons with pride
   for their homeland to stand and fight!

   And there, at every step you see
   throughout the country far and wide
   old marks that tell of victory
   and bones that died to win the fight!

   Chorus:
   For there, in my beloved land...

3. And there, you see thousands of heaps
   of bones of foes buried so deep,
   who died in shame, being defeated
   by those who fought freedom to keep!

   And to our Motherland beloved,
   we swore to never let her down
   and every father, son and brother
   from manhood forged a glorious crown!

   Chorus:
   For there, in my beloved land...

Translation by Beck Corlan & Alex Szollo (2022)

FREEDOM & PEACE　　　　　　　　　　　　　　　　　　　　　　　LUXEMBOURG

18
De Feierwon
The Fire-Wagon

Michel Lentz (1820-93) wrote what has become one of the two 'unofficial' national anthems of Luxembourg. The first railroads were built at a time when the country was suffering from a lack of transport infrastructure and industry, to the extent that 35% of the population had decided to leave for clearer skies. But within a few years it became possible to travel anywhere in the country in a matter of hours, where before the North had been cut off all winter for lack of a reliable bridge. Progress became obvious to everyone and people took pride in this, as is perfectly expressed by Lentz: 'Wherever you come from, we can now proudly show you the beauties of this small land'; but he added, in an age when others were seeking to take over control, 'We want to remain as we are, and happily so!'

By Robert Köller, Union Grand-Duc Adolphe, UGDA

Lyrics: Michel Lentz (1820-93)　　　　　　　　　Music: Jean Antoine Zinnen (1827-98)

March tempo ♩ = 110

1. De Fei - er - won, deen ass be - reet; Hie päift duerch d'Loft, a fort et geet am Dau - schen iw - wer d'Stroos vun Ei - sen, an hie geet stolz den No - per wei - sen, datt mir nun och de Wee hu fonnt zum éi - weg grous - se Vël - ker - bond.

1. When steam is up, the whis-tle blows a migh - ty blast, and off it goes, it clat - ters o - ver tracks of i - ron and shows the pro - gress we re - ly on which - ev - er na - tions lead the way, we're up there with them ev - ery day.

1. De Feierwon, deen ass bereet,
   Hie päift duerch d'Loft a fort et geet
   Am Dauschen iwwer d'Strooss vun Eisen,
   An hie geet stolz den Noper weisen,
   Datt mir nun och de Wee hu fonnt
   Zum éiweg grousse Vëlkerbond.

Chorus:
   Kommt hier aus Frankräich, Belgïe, Preisen,
   Mir wëllen iech ons Heemecht weisen:
   ||: Frot dir no alle Säiten hin:
   Mir wëlle bleiwe wat mir sinn! :||

2. Mir hale fest un onser Scholl.
   Vu Léift fir d'Land sinn d'Häerzer voll:
   Wa mir och keng Milliounen zielen.
   Dir gët ons uechter d'Welt ze wielen.
   Mir ruffen all aus engem Monn:
   Kee bessert Land beschéngt jo d'Sonn!

Kommt hier aus Frankräich...

*1. When steam is up, the whistle blows
   a mighty blast, and off it goes,
   it clatters over tracks of iron
   and shows the progress we rely on
   whichever nations lead the way,
   we're up there with them ev'ry day.*

Chorus:
   *So be you Belgian, French or Prussian,
   come see our homeland's pride and passion:
   ||: Ask any people, near or far:
   we want to stay the way we are! :||*

*2. We feel no pressing need to roam,
   because we're happiest at home.
   although it's true we are not many,
   you'd choose our country over any.
   You'll hear the cry from ev'ryone:
   No better land beneath the sun!*

So be you Belgian, French or Prussian...

3. D'Natur déi laacht ons iwwerall.
   Si rëscht de Biereg an den Dall:
   Mat Fielse wéi gewalteg Risen.
   Street Blummen iwwert Gaart a Wisen:
   Kee Këppchen Äerd, wou Halm a Räis
   Net riede vun deem eise Fläiss.

   Kommt hier aus Frankräich…

4. An d'Voll'k a mengem Heemechtsland
   Huet géint all Mënsch d'Häerz op der Hand;
   Seng Fräiheet deet ëm d'Aë blénken.
   An d'Trei déi deet seng Wierder klénken:
   Seng Sprooch matt hire friemen Téin,
   D'Gemittlechkeet, déi mëcht se schéin.

   Kommt hier aus Frankräich…

5. Mir hu keng schwéier Laascht ze dron
   Fir eise Staatswoon dunn ze goen:
   Keng Steiere kommen eis erdrécken.
   Keen Zwang de fräie Geescht erstécken:
   Mir maachen spuersam eise Stot.
   Kee Bierger a kee Bauer klot.

   Kommt hier aus Frankräich…

6. An huet dir dann de Wäert erkannt
   Vum klenge Lëtzebuerger Land,
   An dir musst fort 'rëm vun äis goen,
   Da kënnt dir an der Heemecht soen:
   'T´ass d'Gréisst net grad, déi d'Gléck bedeit.
   Well an deem Land si glécklech Leit!

   Kommt hier aus Frankräich…

3. *For Mother Nature's all around,*
   upon the hills and higher ground
   it's scattered many giant boulders,
   inspiring awe in all beholders,
   while in the countryside below
   the fruits of farmers' labour grow.

   So be you Belgian, French or Prussian…

4. *The people in my native land*
   are open-hearted, never grand,
   their freedom dazzles in its glory,
   their loyalty's a famous story.
   Their language with its singing tone
   reflects the cheerfulness they own.

   So be you Belgian, French or Prussian…

5. *We have no heavy burdens here*
   to make our wagon hard to steer,
   no taxes squeeze us to the limit,
   no force extinguishes our spirit:
   We keep a tight and frugal house;
   no citizen has cause to grouse.

   So be you Belgian, French or Prussian…

6. *So if you really must depart,*
   but Luxembourg has won your heart,
   when people ask where you were staying,
   just tell the honest truth, by saying,
   'size doesn't matter where I went:
   In that small country they're content.'

   So be you Belgian, French or Prussian…

   Translation by Edward Seymour (2021)

FREEDOM & PEACE   LITHUANIA

19
Laisvė
Freedom

The song "Laisvė" – Freedom – by Eurika Masytė was created in 1989 during the period of liberation from Soviet occupation, inspired by ideas of our country's independence and freedom. The author was not a professional musician, although the song "Laisvė" became extremely popular, gaining the status of a folk song. It has become a strong symbol of Lithuanian independence and freedom and is very dear to Lithuanians. The lyrics are based on a poem by legendary Lithuanian poet Justinas Marcinkevičius (1930-2011).

By Dr. Arvydas Girdzijauskas, Lithuanian Choral Union, LCHS

Lyrics: Justinas Marcinkevičius (1930-2011)   Music: Eurika Masytė (1967-)

1. Aš jau ne-pa-ke-liu min-čių a-pie ta-ve,
1. No more can I en-dure the weight of thoughts of you,

kaip o-be-lis, ap-sun-ku-si nuo vai-sių,
an ap-ple tree can't bear the weight of har-vest.

už-lau-žiu tra-giš-kai nu-svi-ru-sias ran-kas,
I can-not hold de-spair with tra-gic lif-ted hands,

o tu sa-kai: „Sto-vėk kaip sto-vi lais-vė",
and you tell me: "Stay strong as up-right free-dom",

o tu sa-kai: „Sto-vėk kaip sto-vi lais-vė".
and you tell me: "Stay strong as up-right free-dom".

1. Aš jau nepakeliu minčių apie tave,
   kaip obelis, apsunkusi nuo vaisių,
   užlaužiu tragiškai nusvirusias rankas,
   o tu sakai: „Stovėk kaip stovi laisvė",
   o tu sakai: „Stovėk kaip stovi laisvė".

Chorus:
   ||: Tai uždaryk mane, Tėvyne, savyje,
   kaip giesmę gerklėje mirtis uždaro,
   taip kaip uždaro vakarą naktis,
   o tu man atsakai: „Aš tavo laisvė". :||

2. O nesibaigianti kelionė į tave,
   jau kaip akmuo šalikelėj sukniubęs,
   aš pilku vakaru lyg samanom dengiuos,
   o tu sakai: „Eik taip kaip eina laisvė".
   o tu sakai: „Eik taip kaip eina laisvė".

Chorus:
   ||: Tai uždaryk mane,
       Tėvyne, savyje... :||

*1. No more can I endure the weight of thoughts of you,
   an apple tree can't bear the weight of harvest.
   I cannot hold despair with tragic lifted hands,
   and you tell me: "Stay strong as upright freedom".
   and you tell me: "Stay strong as upright freedom".*

Chorus:
   *||: So you, my fatherland, imprison me in you,
   as death imprisons songs within my throat,
   like evening is imprisoned by the night,
   and your response to me: "I am your freedom". :||*

*2. A never ending journey on the way to you,
   already like a stone, I've fallen on the road.
   I wrap myself in dusk as if I were in moss,
   and you tell me: "Walk on and on in freedom",
   and you tell me: "Walk on and on in freedom".*

Chorus:
   *||: So you, my fatherland,
       imprison me in you.... :||*

*Translation by Kerry Shawn Keys
& Sonata Paliulytė (2021)*

FREEDOM & PEACE   SWEDEN

20
Änglamark
Where Angels Tread

This song was written for "Äppelkriget" (The Apple War, 1971), a film by Hasse Alfredsson (1931-2017) and Tage Danielsson (1928-85), featuring Evert Taube (1890-1976) and his wife Astri (1898-1980). The idea that nature is a divine gift for humanity to take care of has always run through Taube's poetry, long before the advent of environmental activism. The song has a beautiful, lyrical style, and the opening words "call it the Angel Fields, or Heavenly Earth if you will, the earth we inherited and the green groves" can be seen as both a kind of testament and as Taube's epilogue after fifty years of developing his very own part of the Swedish canon of songs. The song is still one of the most popular sing-along songs.

By Kerstin Carpvik, head of library, Musikverket

Lyrics: Evert Taube (1890-1976)   Music: Evert Taube (1890-1976)

1. Kal - la den äng - la - mar - ken el - ler him - la - jor - den om du
1. Where an - gels tread are ver - y par - a - dis - al, E - den if you

vill, jor - den vi ärv - de och lun - den den grö - na.
will this earth we're giv - en, its wood - lands and mead - ows.

Vild - ro - sor och blå - klo - ckor och lind - blom - mor och ka - mo -
Butter - cups and blue - bells and dai - sies grow - ing on the

mill låt dem få le - va, de är ju så skö - na.
hill, leave them to grow there, they are so love - ly.

2. Låt bar - nen dan - sa som äng - lar kring lönn och alm,
2. Child - ren shall dance here as an - gels up - on the green,

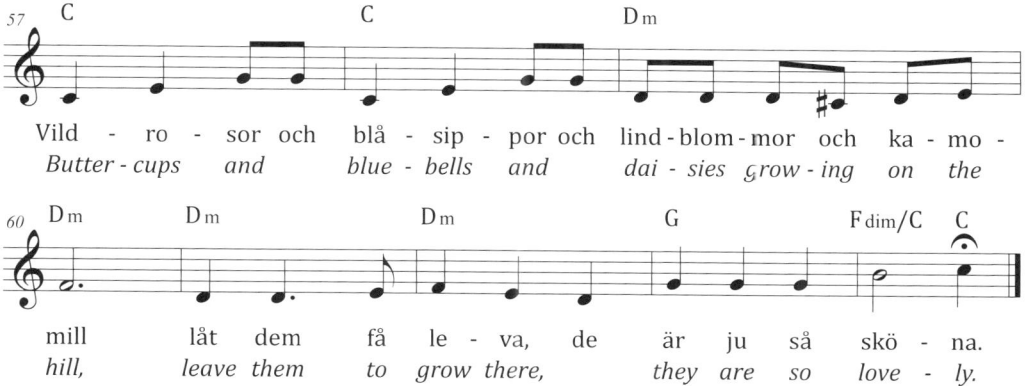

1.
Kalla den änglamarken
eller himlajorden om du vill,
jorden vi ärvde
och lunden den gröna.
Vildrosor och blåklockor
och lindblommor och kamomill
låt dem få leva, de är ju så sköna.

2.
Låt barnen dansa
som änglar kring lönn och alm,
leka tittut mellan blommande grenar.
Låt fåglar flyga och
sjunga för oss sin psalm,
låt fiskar simma bland bryggor
               och stenar.

3.
Sluta att utrota
skogarnas alla djur!
Låt örnen flyga, låt rådjuren löpa!
Låt sista älven som
brusar i vår natur
brusa alltjämt mellan fjällar
               och gran och fur!

4.
Kalla den änglamarken
eller himlajorden om du vill,
jorden vi ärvde
och lunden den gröna.
Vildrosor och blåsippor
och lindblommor och kamomill
låt dem få leva, de är ju så sköna.

1.
Where angels tread are very paradisal,
Eden if you will
this earth we're given,
its woodlands and meadows.
Buttercups and bluebells
and daisies growing on the hill,
leave them to grow there, they are so lovely.

2.
Children shall dance here
as angels upon the green,
play hide and seek mid the apple trees blossom,
birds sing their anthem
of praises in the ravine,
let all the fishes swim deep in our rivers.

3.
Cease all this slaughter
of wild creatures in the woods!
Eagles shall fly over mountains in freedom,
and the last river that roars
forming through the dale,
let it forever flow peaceful in the vale!

4.
Where angels tread are very paradisal,
Eden if you will,
this earth we're given,
it's woodlands and meadows.
Buttercups and bluebells
and daisies growing on the hill,
leave them to grow there, they are so lovely.

Translation by Paul Britten Austin (1972)

Copyright © 1971 UNIVERSAL/REUTER-REUTER FORLAG. Copyright Renewed. All Rights in the United States Administered by
UNIVERSAL - POLYGRAM INTERNATIONAL PUBLISHING, INC. International Copyright Secured. All Rights Reserved.
Reprinted by Permission of Hal Leonard Europe Ltd.

FREEDOM & PEACE   CROATIA

21
Moja domovina
My Croatia, My Home

The song "Moja domovina" (My Homeland) by songwriters Zrinko Tutić and Rajko Dujmić was created at the beginning of "the Homeland War", Croatian War of Independence in 1991. It was performed by Croatian Band Aid, a musical ensemble that numbered over a hundred well-known and recognized Croatian musicians. In the difficult times of war, it awoke both comfort, hope, and pride in Croatians, and today it is an indispensable song in the programs of Croatian radio and television stations, especially in the days of remembrance of the victims of the war, as well as in the days of gratitude and celebration of homeland.

By Dr. Jasenka Ostojić, University of Zagreb, Music Academy

Music & lyrics: Rajko Dujmić (1954-2020) & Zrinko Tutić (1955-)

♩ = 78

1. Sva - kog da - na mi - slim na te - be,
1. Eve - ry - where I go you're in my mind,

slu - šam vije - sti, bro - jim ko - ra - ke.
an - y - where I stay you're in my heart.

Ne - mir je u sr - ci - ma, a lju - bav u na - ma
You to me are eve - ry - thing, the sweet - est song to sing.

i - ma sa - mo je - dna i - sti - na
You're my old star til the end of time.

2. Sva - ka zvije - zda si - ja za te - be,
2. E - ven if I'm half a world a - way,

1. Svakog dana mislim na tebe,
   slušam vijesti, brojim korake.
   Nemir je u srcima, a ljubav u nama
   ima samo jedna istina.

2. Svaka zvijezda sija za tebe,
   kamen puca, pjesma putuje
   tisuću generacija noćas ne spava,
   cijeli svijet je sada sa nama... Sa nama!

Chorus:
   Moja domovina, moja domovina,
   ima snagu zlatnog žita,
   oma oči boje mora,
   moja zemlja Hrvatska.

3. Vratit ću se moram doći, tu je moj dom,
   moje sunce, moje nebo.
   Novi dan se budi kao sreća osvaja
   ti si tu sa nama... Sa nama!

Chorus:
Moja domovina, moja domovina...

1. Everywhere I go you're in my mind,
   anywhere I stay you're in my heart.
   You to me are everything, the sweetest song to sing.
   You're my old star til the end of time.

2. Even if I'm half a world away,
   a part of me is with you as I pray.
   Stars are shining just for you, the sky is always blue,
   mother country let God be with you...Be with you!

Chorus:
   My Croatia, my home, my Croatia, my home,
   golden valleys, silent seas,
   silver islands, olive trees,
   my Croatia, my homeland.

3. As the child of generations this is my land
   where I was born, where I'll die.
   For the children of my children this is my land
   where I was born, where I will die... Where I'll die!

Chorus:
My Croatia, my home, my Croatia, my home...

Translation by Stevo Cvikić & Zrinka Moslavac (1991)

Copyright © Tutico d.o.o., Zagreb. International copyright secured. All rights reserved

FREEDOM & PEACE ESTONIA

22
Koit
Dawn

Koit – Dawn – was written in 1988 during Soviet occupation by Estonian singer-songwriter Tõnis Mägi. This freedom song quickly became one of the anthems of the Estonian Singing Revolution: Lasting over four years, this unique bloodless protest movement unfolded in all three Baltic States, where protesters gathered to sing in defiance. Mägi uses the hypnotic bolero rhythm, which grows and grows; at first lyrics are allusive, referring to a "new dawn" breaking, but in the final lines the cry is outspoken: "Land, land of my fathers, so sacred a land /(..)/ Our song, our song of freedom will sound". The song is well-known to every Estonian, and its choral arrangements have been sung in several Song Celebrations ever since.

By Kaie Tanner, Secretary General, Estonian Choral Association

Lyrics: Tõnis Mägi (1948-)   Music: Tõnis Mägi (1948-)

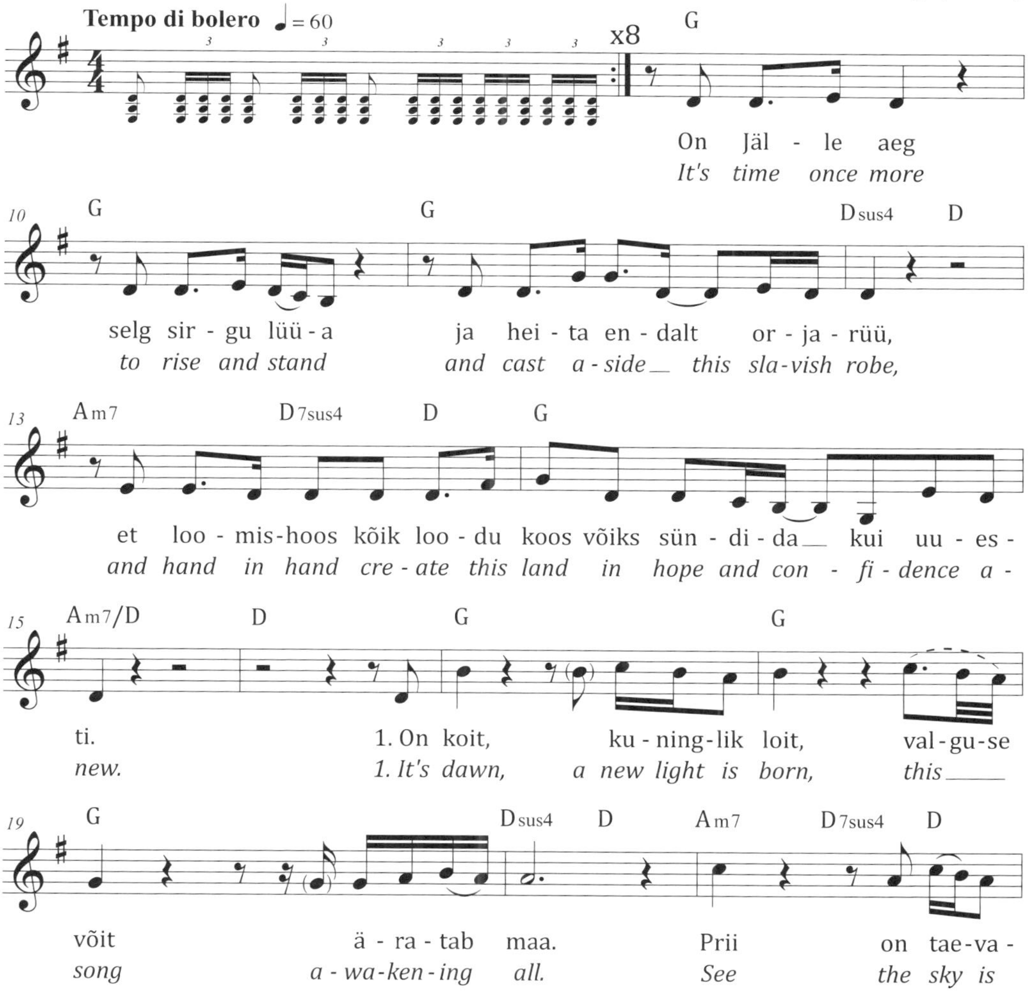

Tempo di bolero ♩ = 60

On Jäl- le aeg
It's time once more

selg sir- gu lüü- a ja hei- ta en- dalt or- ja- rüü,
to rise and stand and cast a-side this sla-vish robe,

et loo- mis- hoos kõik loo- du koos võiks sün- di- da kui uu- es-
and hand in hand cre-ate this land in hope and con- fi- dence a-

ti. 1. On koit, ku- ning- lik loit, val- gu- se
new. 1. It's dawn, a new light is born, this

võit ä- ra- tab maa. Prii on tae- va-
song a- wa- ken- ing all. See the sky is

On jälle aeg selg sirgu lüüa ja heita endalt orjarüü, et loomishoos kõik loodu koos võiks sündida kui uuesti.	*It's time once more to rise and stand and cast aside this slavish robe. and hand in hand create the land in hope and confidence anew.*

1. On koit, kuninglik loit,
   valguse võit äratab maa.
   Prii on taevapiir, esimene kiir
   langemas me maale.

   *1. It's dawn - a new light is born.
   this song awakening all.
   See - the sky is free, see the early glow
   greeting fields and forests.*

2. Hõik - murrame kõik,
   et vabana saaks hingata taas.
   Näe - on murdund jää
   ulatagem käed, ühendagem väed.

   *2. Voice - It's time to rejoice,
   breathing in the bright dawning hours.
   Ice broke in a trice,
   standing hand in hand, joining our powers.*

3. Nõul, ühisel nõul,
   ühisel jõul, me suudame kõik.
   Ees on ainus tee, vabaduse tee,
   teist ei olla saagi.

   *3. Rise - listen to the wise:
   we are the tribe. Sharing the vibe.
   Freedom is the way, our only way,
   freedom now and always.*

4. Võim, valguse võim,
   priiuse hõim, läheme koos.
   Huulil rõõmuhüüd -
   näe, on kaljust käe kätte saanud hiid.

   *4. Shine - this light is divine,
   glorious times together ahead
   singing out of joy:
   see, he's broken free - our epic hero!*

5. Usk edasi viib, taevane kiir
   saatmas on meid.
   Nii on võiduni jäänud veel üks samm,
   lühikene samm, samm.

   *5. Feel - deeply believe in heavenly lead -
   we are relieved.
   See the victory! Truth will be revealed:
   it's the freedom's seed, seed.*

6. Maa, isade maa, on püha see maa,
   mis vabaks nüüd saab.
   Laul, me võidulaul, kõlama see jääb,
   peagi vaba Eestit sa näed!

   *6. Land - ancestors' land, so sacred and dear,
   will now be unbounded.
   Our song of victory will now and always be:
   Estonia is Free! Is free!*

Translated by Doris Kareva (2021)

FREEDOM & PEACE　　　　　　　　　　　　　　　　　　　　AUSTRIA

23
Brenna tuat's guat
The Roof's on Fire

This protest song was composed and published in 2011 as commentary, in Austrian dialect, about world affairs at the time: the lingering world financial crisis; greed for capital; destruction of land and food production capability through climate change; and corruption in general. It was number 1 on the Austrian charts for 34 weeks and on the German top-100 charts for 40 weeks. About the song, Hubert von Goisern has said that he was stunned by the realization that people are actually aware that resources are mishandled and likewise the truth. We know that people are starving even as we turn food into fuel, and yet – we do nothing.

By Dr. Eva Maria Hois, Steirische Volksliedwerk & Dr. Sarah Weiss, Kunstuniversität Graz, KUG

Lyrics: Hubert von Goisern (1952-)　　　　　　　　Music: Hubert von Goisern (1952-)

Fast polka: ♩ = 135

1. Wo is der Platz, wo da Teifl seine Kinder kraigt,
1. Where's the place where the devil spawns a family,

wo is der Platz, wo oll's z'sam rennt. Wo is des
where's the place, where it all comes from? Where's the

Feuer, he, wo geht'n do da Blitz nieder, wo is 'n die
fire, hey, where did the lightning strike, where's the

1. Wo is der Platz,
   wo da Teifl seine Kinder kraigt,
   wo is der Platz,
   wo oll's z'sam rennt.
   Wo is des Feuer,
   he, wo geht 'n do da Blitz nieder,
   wo is 'n die Hittn,
   wo der Stodl, der brennt.

2. Hamma Pech oder an Lauf,
   fåll'n ma um oder auf,
   samma dünn oder dick,
   hab'n an Reim oder Glück,
   teil ma aus, schenk ma ein,
   toan ma uns obi oder g'frein,
   war'n ma Christ, hätt ma g'wisst,
   wo da Teifl baut an Mist.

Chorus:
   A jeder woaß,
   dass des Göld net auf da Wiesn wochst,
   und essen kau ma's a net,
   åber brenna tat's guat.
   Aber hoaz'n tuan ma Woazen
   und de Ruab'n und den Kukuruz,
   und wånn ma dann so weiter hoaz'n,
   brennt da Huat.

3. Wo is des Göld,
   des wås überall fehlt
   jo håt denn koana an Genierer,
   wieso kemman allweil de viara,
   de liag'n, de die Wåhrheit verbiag'n,
   und wånn's net kriag'n, wås wulln,
   dann wird's holt g'stohl'n,
   he de sull da Teifl huln.

4. Wo is da Plåtz,
   wo da Teifl seine Kinder kriagt,
   wo åll's zamm rennt.
   Wo is des Feier,
   wo geht'n grod a Blitz nieder,
   wo is'n die Hitt'n,
   wo der Stodl, der brennt.

Chorus:
   A jeder woaß, dass des Göld …

Jodlen:
   Heeeeee-a-he-o-hio-ho-ho-ho

Chorus a cappella

1. Where's the place
   where the devil spawns a family,
   where's the place,
   where it all comes from?
   Where's the fire, hey,
   where did the lightning strike,
   where's the hut,
   where the barn that's ablaze?

2. Bad break or on a roll,
   filthy rich or on the dole,
   fake smile, drowning shame,
   a simple life, chasing fame,
   playing smart, playing dumb,
   men in suits sucking their thumbs,
   holy folk would have known,
   where the devil's throwing stones.

Chorus:
   Everybody knows
   that money doesn't grow on trees,
   we keep on craving, feeding
   the desire, the disease.
   We're burning down the grain,
   while the dough is whipping up the flames,
   it's time to wake up,
   'cos the roof's on fire.

3. Where's the money
   they're all talking about,
   go ask the fuel-licking gaslighters,
   truth-twisting go-getters,
   no one is ashamed,
   it's a lifestyle, it's a game,
   the tickets to their show are selling well,
   those crooks should go to hell.

4. Where's the place,
   where the devil spawns a family,
   where it all comes from?
   Where's the fire,
   hey, where did the lightning strike,
   where's the hut,
   where the barn that's ablaze?

Chorus:
   Everybody knows…

Jodlen:
   Heeeeee-a-he-o-hio-ho-ho-ho

Chorus a cappella.

Translation by Hubert von Goisern
& Alicia Edelweiss (2023)

Copyright © Blanko Musik GmbH and Synthakus Musikproduktion GmbH. International Copyright Secured. All rights reserved. Reprinted by permission.

FREEDOM & PEACE   BULGARIA

24
Една българска роза
A Bulgarian Rose

The composer of this song, Dimitar Valchev (1929-95), significantly contributed to the development of Bulgarian popular music in the mid-twentieth century. "A Bulgarian Rose" from 1970 is one of his emblematic songs, reflecting his love for the Motherland through a symbol essential to the Bulgarians – the red rose. The song turned into an evergreen hit and an emblem for the popular – and at the time young – artist Pasha Hristova (1946-71). Nowadays, the song continues to revive, performed at many concerts for the joy of its numerous fans. "A Bulgarian Rose" brings the spirit of the Motherland, regardless how far abroad a person lives today.

By Dr. Jean Pehlivanov, Academy of Music Dance and Fine Arts, Plovdiv, AMDFA

Lyrics: Nayden Valchev (1927-)   Music: Dimitar Valchev (1929-1995)

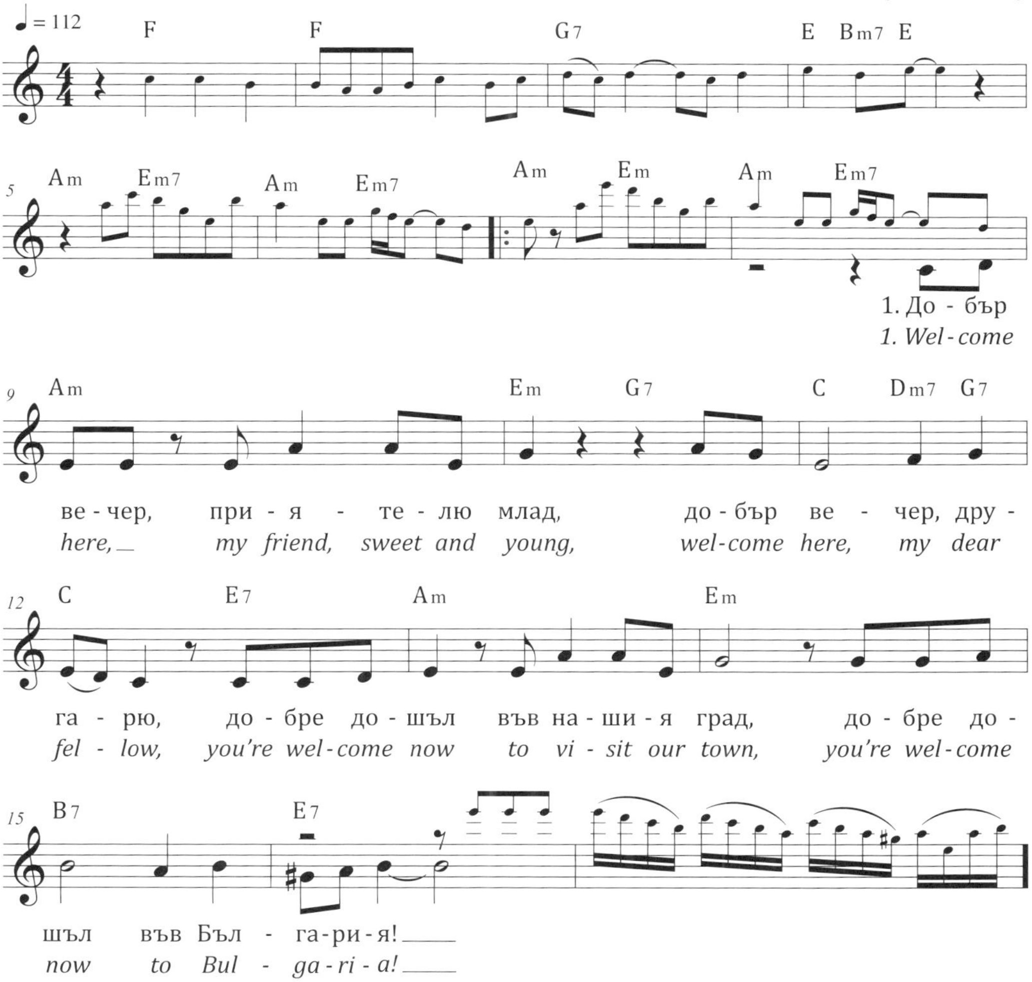

1. До - бър ве - чер, при - я - те - лю млад, до - бър ве - чер, дру - га - рю, до - бре до - шъл във на - ши - я град, до - бре до - шъл във Бъл - га - ри - я!

1. Wel - come here, my friend, sweet and young, wel - come here, my dear fel - low, you're wel - come now to vi - sit our town, you're wel - come now to Bul - ga - ri - a!

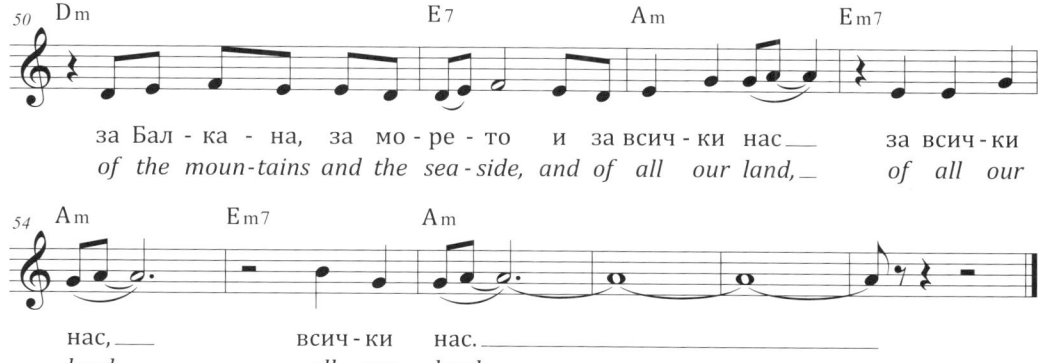

1. Добър вечер, приятелю млад,
   добър вечер, другарю,
   добре дошъл във нашия град,
   добре дошъл във България!

(първи припев):
   Вземи във този хубав ден
   Една българска роза от мен
   Нека тя да ти разкаже
   с ароматния си глас
   За Балкана, за морето
   и за всички нас, всички нас.

2. И когато, приятелю млад,
   и когато, другарю,
   си тръгнеш ти от нашия град,
   си тръгнеш ти от България.

(втори припев):
   Вземи и в този хубав ден
   една българска роза от мен -
   нека тя да ти напомня
   с ароматния си глас
   за Балкана, за морето
   и за всички нас, всички нас.

(трети припев):
   И не забравяй нито ден
   ти таз българска роза …и мен
   Нека тя да ти напомня
   с ароматния си глас
   за Балкана, за морето
   и за всички нас, всички нас…

1. Welcome here, my friend – sweet and young,
   welcome here, my dear fellow,
   you're welcome now to visit our town,
   you're welcome now to Bulgaria!

(First chorus):
   Take this as precious memory -
   a rose, Bulgarian rose here from me.
   Let it whisper tales of wonder
   with its voice so full of scent
   of the mountains and the seaside,
   and of all our land, all our land.

2. And whenever, my friend - sweet and young,
   and whenever, dear fellow,
   it's time for you to leave our town,
   it's time to leave our Bulgaria.

(Second chorus):
   Take this as precious memory -
   a rose, Bulgarian rose here from me.
   Let it whisper and remind you
   with its voice so full of scent
   of the mountains and the seaside,
   and of all our land, all our land.

(Third Chorus)
   And don't forget this memory
   of rose, Bulgarian rose and… of me.
   Let it whisper and remind you
   with its voice so full of scent
   of the mountains and the seaside,
   and of all our land, all our land…

Translation by Desislava Sofranova (2022)

FREEDOM & PEACE   BELGIUM

25
Ik hou van u
Your Love's So Sweet

Written in '95 for Frank Van Passels debut film "Manneken Pis" (Little Pissing Man, like the famous Duquesnoy statue in Brussels). It tells the story of the 28-year old Harry who falls in love with Jeanne, the driver on a tram in Brussels. The song describes the carefree sense of freedom and summer when you are in love: "Open the windows and open the eyes (...)". The unpretentious lyrics use typical Flemish expressions, which makes the song a true hit to use in Dutch courses for non-native speakers. In honor of Belgium's 175th anniversary in 2005, it was re-released in a blend of French and Dutch, the two most spoken languages. A real sing-along song which – thanks to the simple texts as 'doo doo' and 'la la' as well as the 6/8 metre – creates instant happiness.

By Liesbeth Segers, Koor&Stem

Lyrics & Music: Lars Van Bambost, Wim De Wilde & Stijn Meuris (1964-) "Noordkaap"

♩. = 66

doo___ doo doo doo doo___

1. We wa-ren bij-na echt ver-ge-ten hoe
1. We al-most lost this old re-mem-brance a-

schoon de zo-mer wel kan zijn. Zon-der zor-gen en
bout how nice these sum-mers are. Months a-way___from

zon-der re-gen hoe schoon de zo-mer hier kan zijn. 2. We
grey De-cem-ber,___ look how warm these sum-mers are. 2. We

wa-ren uit het oog ver-lo-ren hoe warm een wei-land wel kan zijn.
all lost track of glow-ing na-ture in mead-ows green and warm.___

1. We waren bijna echt vergeten
   hoe schoon de zomer wel kan zijn.
   Zonder zorgen en zonder regen
   hoe schoon de zomer hier kan zijn.

2. We waren uit het oog verloren
   hoe warm een weiland wel kan zijn.
   Open de vensters en open de ogen en
   zie hoe schoon de zomers zijn.

Chorus:
   Ik hou van u, ik hou van u,
   ik hou van u.
   Ja, ik hou van u, ik hou van u,
   ik hou van u.
   Geef me een kus. Geef me een kus.
   Geef me een kus en vlug voor
                         de laatste bus.

3. (repeat verse 1.)

Chorus:
   ||: Ik hou van u, Ik hou van u,
   Ik hou van u.
   Ja, ik hou van u, Ik hou van u,
   Ik hou van u. :||
(slower, accelerando)
   ||: Geef me een kus. Geef me een kus.
   Geef me een kus, en vlug voor
                         de laatste bus. :||

Je t'aime tu sais, je t'aime tu sais,
je t'aime tu sais.
Oui, je t'aime tu sais, oui, je t'aime tu sais,
je t'aime tu sais.

Lalallaalalalaaa...Ik hou van u

Geef me een kus.

1. We almost lost this old remembrance
   about how nice these summers are.
   Months away from grey December,
   look how warm these summers are.

2. We all lost track of glowing nature
   in meadows green and warm.
   Open up the windows, open up your eyes
   to see this beauty just before the storm.

Chorus:
   Your love's so sweet, your love's so sweet,
   your love's so sweet.
   Yes, your love's so sweet, your love's so sweet,
   your love's so sweet.
   Gimme a kiss. Gimme a kiss
   Please let's do this, and be quick;
                         gimme that one last kiss.

3. (repeat 1. verse)

Chorus:
   ||: Your love's so sweet, your love's so sweet,
   your love's so sweet.
   Yes, your love's so sweet, your love's so sweet,
   your love's so sweet. :||
(slower, accelerando)
   ||: Gimme a kiss. Gimme a kiss
   Please let's do this, and be quick;
                         gimme that one last kiss. :||

Je t'aime tu sais, je t'aime tu sais,
je t'aime tu sais.
Oui, je t'aime tu sais, oui, je t'aime tu sais,
je t'aime tu sais.

Lalallaalalalaaa...I love you

Gimme a kiss.

Translation by Stijn Meuris (2022)

FREEDOM & PEACE   POLAND

26
Dziwny jest ten świat
Strange Is This World

Polish singer, multi-instrumentalist and songwriter Czesław Niemen (1939-2004) was among the most outstanding composers of modern Poland. The same year the song was written in 1967, Niemen won the main award at the 5th Song Festival in Opole. A more psychedelic version in English was recorded in 1972. The song is considered to be the first Polish protest song. In its form this soul ballad draws inspiration from hits like James Brown's "It's a Man's, Man's, Man's World", but Niemen's inspiration transcends the theme of passion and explores the universal question of injustice: "A bad word can hurt just like a stab with a knife". The song enjoyed great popularity in the 60's Poland and became an unofficial anthem of Polish youth contesting the establishment. And as long as the world seems strange, this song will remain actualized.

By Dorota Stefaniak, Academy of Music "Stanisław Moniuszko" in Gdańsk

Lyrics: Czesław Niemen (1939-2004)   Music: Czesław Niemen (1939-2004)

1. Dzi - wny jest ten świat, gdzie jesz - cze wciąż mie - ści się wie - le zła. I dziw - ne jest to, że od ty - lu lat czło - wie - kiem gar - dzi czło - wiek. Dziw - ny ten
1. Strange is this world, well, still it seems there is so far so much ev - il. And strange it is that since long a - go man de - spis - es man. Strange this

1. Dziwny jest ten świat,
   gdzie jeszcze wciąż
   mieści się wiele zła.
   I dziwne jest to,
   że od tylu lat
   człowiekiem gardzi człowiek.

2. Dziwny ten świat,
   świat ludzkich spraw,
   czasem aż wstyd przyznać się.
   A jednak często jest,
   że ktoś słowem złym
   zabija tak jak nożem.

Chorus:
   ||: Lecz ludzi dobrej woli jest więcej
   i mocno wierzę w to,
   że ten świat
   nie zginie nigdy dzięki nim.
   Nie! Nie! Nie! Nie!
   Przyszedł już czas,
   najwyższy czas,
   nienawiść zniszczyć w sobie. :||

1. Oh, strange is this world,
   well, still it seems,
   there's so far so much evil.
   And strange it is
   that since long ago
   man despises man.

2. Oh, strange this world
   of human affairs,
   sometimes I'm ashamed to be in it.
   Oh, so often
   a man can kill with a bad word
   or still a knife.

Chorus:
   ||: But most people are of good will,
   I - thanks to them - believe
   that this world
   should never die.
   Never, never die!
   And now, the time has come,
   the final time,
   for hatred to destroy itself. :||

Adaptation by Czesław Niemen (CBS, 1972)

Copyright © EMI Songs Musikverlag GmbH. International Copyright Secured. All Rights Reserved.
Reprinted by permission

FREEDOM & PEACE   SPAIN

27
Libre
Freedom

The music and lyrics come together in an acclamation of freedom, repeating "...free, free..." again and again, free like the sea, the wind, the birds, the sun. The incredible voice of singer Nino Bravo (1944-73) contributed to the songs resounding success in Spain. After dying young in a traffic accident, thus sharing the tragic destiny with the protagonist of the lyrics, the singer became a myth.

By Julio Muñoz & Maria del Carmen García Jiménez, Escuela Superior de Canto de Madrid, ESCM

Lyrics & Music: José Luis Armenteros (1943-2016) & Pablo Herrero (1942-)

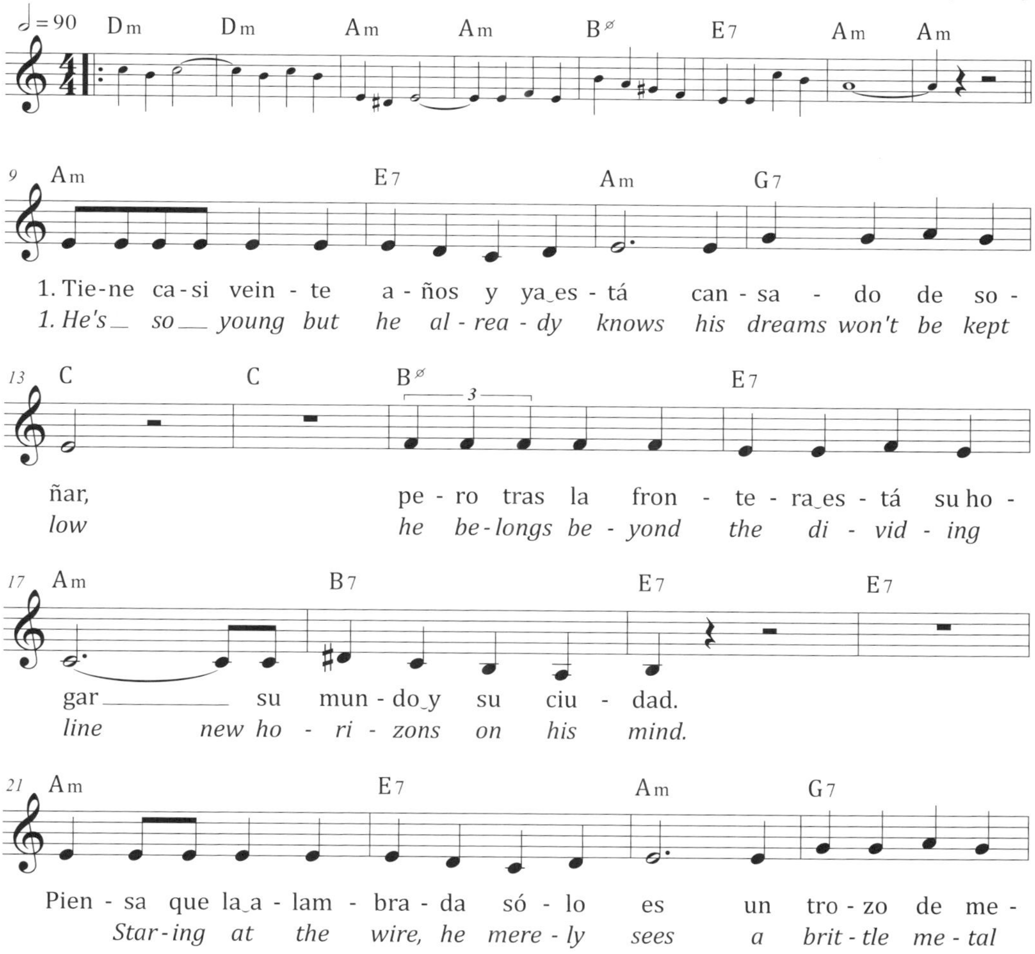

1. Tie-ne ca-si vein-te a-ños y ya_es-tá can-sa - do de so-
1. He's so young but he al-rea-dy knows his dreams won't be kept

ñar,   pe - ro tras la fron - te-ra_es-tá su ho-
low   he be-longs be - yond the di - vid - ing

gar   su mun-do_y su ciu - dad.
line   new ho - ri - zons on his mind.

Pien - sa que la_a-lam - bra-da só - lo   es   un tro-zo de me-
Star-ing at the wire, he mere - ly sees   a   brit-tle me-tal

1. Tiene casi 20 años y ya está
   cansado de soñar,
   pero tras la frontera está su hogar
   su mundo y su ciudad.

   Piensa que la alambrada sólo es
   un trozo de metal,
   algo que nunca puede detener
   sus ansias de volar.

Chorus:
   Libre,
   como el sol cuando amanece, yo soy libre
   como el mar.
   Libre,
   como el ave que escapó de su prisión
   y puede al fin volar.
   Libre,
   como el viento que recoge
   mi lamento y mi pesar,
   camino sin cesar detrás de la verdad
   y sabré lo que es al fin la libertad.

2. Con su amor por bandera se marchó
   cantando una canción
   marchaba tan feliz que no escuchó
   la voz que le llamó

   Y tendido en suelo se quedó
   sonriendo y sin hablar
   sobre su pecho, flores carmesí
   brotaban sin cesar.

Chorus:
   Libre, como el sol ...

1. He's so young but he already knows,
   his dreams won't be kept low,
   he belongs beyond the dividing line
   new horizons on his mind.

   Staring at the wire, he merely sees
   a brittle metal fleece,
   something that will never hold in
   his burning wish to fly.

Chorus:
   Freedom,
   just like the rising morning sun,
   I am free
   as the sea.
   Just free
   as the bird that finally left his cage behind
   and flies to the open sky.
   Freedom,
   as the wind that gently blows
   all my grief and my sorrows
   I'm walking with no end searching for the truth
   just to have the taste of freedom in my life.

2. Filled with joy he bid that fence goodbye,
   love was his ally,
   when leaving he could hardly hear
   the voice calling for him.

   He was left lying on the ground,
   no longer could he make a sound,
   crimson flowers pouring from his chest,
   his smile was all that's left.

Chorus:
   Freedom, just like the rising...

Translation by Joana Serrat (2022)

FREEDOM & PEACE   THE EUROPEAN UNION

28
The European Anthem
Ode an die Freude / Ode to Joy

"The melody used to symbolize the EU comes from the Ninth Symphony composed in 1822-24 by Ludwig Van Beethoven, when he set music to the "Ode to Joy", Friedrich von Schiller's lyrical verse from 1785. The anthem symbolises not only the European Union but also Europe in a wider sense. The poem "Ode to Joy" expresses Schiller's idealistic vision of the human race becoming brothers – a vision Beethoven shared. In 1972, the Council of Europe adopted Beethoven's "Ode to Joy" theme as its anthem. In 1985, it was adopted by EU leaders as the official anthem of the European Union. There are no words to the anthem; it consists of music only. In the universal language of music, this anthem expresses the European ideals of freedom, peace and solidarity. The European anthem is not intended to replace the national anthems of the EU countries but rather to celebrate the values they share. The anthem is played at official ceremonies involving the European Union and generally at all sorts of events with a European character".

The website of the European Commission

Music: Ludwig van Beethoven (1770-1827)

For those who wish to experience Beethoven's inspiration for the melody to the European Anthem, please find on the next page the full version of Friedrich Schiller's (1759-1805) famous poem known as 'Ode an die Freude' (Ode to Joy), a great testament to both the German Enlightenment and the French revolution.

Beethoven adapted the first three verses for the choral part of the final movement of his 9th symphony. However, in the lesser-known verses 4-9 Schiller beautifully interprets 'joy' as the core of nature and axis of the universe, as the driving force in science and faith, as the force to resist tyranny, as well as the root of mercy and reconciliation. Due to the censorship in Vienna in the 1820ies, Beethoven would never have gotten away with including verses eight or nine!

(Thanks to the generous support from the Culture of Solidarity Fund, powered by The European Cultural Foundation, Allianz Foundation and Evens Foundation, the EU Songbook Association is able to present the full poem in all 24 official EU languages (plus Luxembourgish) on our website: www.eu-songbook.org).

An die Freude

1. Freude, schöner Götterfunken,
   Tochter aus Elysium,
   Wir betreten feuertrunken,
   Himmlische, dein Heiligtum!
   Deine Zauber binden wieder,
   Was die Mode streng geteilt;
   Alle Menschen werden Brüder,
   Wo dein sanfter Flügel weilt.

2. Wem der große Wurf gelungen,
   Eines Freundes Freund zu sein,
   Wer ein holdes Weib errungen,
   Mische seinen Jubel ein!
   Ja - wer auch nur eine Seele
   Sein nennt auf dem Erdenrund!
   Und wer's nie gekonnt, der stehle
   Weinend sich aus diesem Bund!

3. Freude trinken alle Wesen
   An den Brüsten der Natur,
   Alle Guten, alle Bösen
   Folgen ihrer Rosenspur.
   Küsse gab sie uns und Reben,
   Einen Freund, geprüft im Tod,
   Wollust ward dem Wurm gegeben,
   Und der Cherub steht vor Gott.

4. Freude heißt die starke Feder
   In der ewigen Natur.
   Freude, Freude treibt die Räder
   In der großen Weltenuhr.
   Blumen lockt sie aus den Keimen,
   Sonnen aus dem Firmament,
   Sphären rollt sie in den Räumen,
   Die des Sehers Rohr nicht kennt.

To Joy (non-singable translation)

1. Joy, beautiful spark of the gods,
   daughter of Elysium,
   fire-drunk we enter
   your holy shrine, oh heavenly one!
   Your magic shall reunite
   that which custom has rigidly divided;
   all humankind shall be brothers
   underneath your gentle wing.

2. All who have achieved the great feat
   of being a true friend,
   all who have won a fair lady,
   come join in our jubilation!
   Yes – even those who can call just one soul
   their own on this earth's sphere!
   While those never able to do so must steal
   away weeping from this company!

3. All creatures drink joy
   at nature's breasts,
   all who are good and all who are wicked
   follow her trail of roses.
   She gave us kisses and grapevines,
   a friend, tested unto death,
   pleasure was granted even to the worm,
   and the cherub stands before God.

4. Joy is the mighty mainspring
   in eternal nature.
   Joy, joy drives the wheels
   in the great universal clock.
   She draws forth the flowers from the seeds,
   suns from the firmament,
   she turns spheres in the spaces
   unknown to the seer's telescope.

5. Aus der Wahrheit Feuerspiegel
   Lächelt sie den Forscher an.
   Zu der Tugend steilem Hügel
   Leitet sie des Dulders Bahn.
   Auf des Glaubens Sonnenberge
   Sieht man ihre Fahnen wehn,
   Durch den Riß gesprengter Särge
   Sie im Chor der Engel stehn.

6. Göttern kann man nicht vergelten,
   Schön ists ihnen gleich zu sein.
   Gram und Armut soll sich melden,
   Mit den Frohen sich erfreun.
   Groll und Rache sei vergessen,
   Unserm Todfeind sei verziehn,
   Keine Träne soll ihn pressen,
   Keine Reue nage ihn.

7. Freude sprudelt in Pokalen,
   In der Traube goldnem Blut
   Trinken Sanftmut Kannibalen,
   Die Verzweiflung Heldenmut.
   Brüder fliegt von euren Sitzen,
   Wenn der volle Römer kreist,
   Laßt den Schaum zum Himmel spritzen:
   Dieses Glas dem guten Geist!

8. Festen Mut in schwerem Leiden,
   Hilfe, wo die Unschuld weint,
   Ewigkeit geschwornen Eiden,
   Wahrheit gegen Freund und Feind,
   Männerstolz vor Königsthronen, –
   Brüder, gält es Gut und Blut –
   Dem Verdienste seine Kronen,
   Untergang der Lügenbrut!

9. Rettung von Tyrannenketten,
   Großmut auch dem Bösewicht,
   Hoffnung auf den Sterbebetten,
   Gnade auf dem Hochgericht!
   Auch die Toten sollen leben!
   Brüder trinkt und stimmet ein,
   Allen Sündern soll vergeben,
   Und die Hölle nicht mehr sein.

5. Out of truth's fiery mirror
   she smiles on the seeker.
   Towards the steep hill of virtue
   she guides the steadfast.
   On the sunlit mountains of faith
   you can see her banners flying,
   through the cracks of shattered coffins,
   standing among the choir of angels.

6. We cannot repay the gods,
   it is splendid to be like them.
   Let sorrow and poverty come forward
   to share good cheer in joyful company.
   Let us forget grudges and revenge,
   forgive our mortal enemy –
   no tears should admonish him,
   no remorse gnaw at him.

7. Joy fizzes in goblets,
   in the golden blood of the grape
   cannibals drink gentleness
   and the despairing take heroic courage.
   Brothers spring up from your seats
   when the brimming glass is passed around,
   spray the foam right up to the sky
   and raise this glass to the good spirit!

8. Resolute courage to the sorely afflicted,
   help where innocence weeps,
   oaths sworn for eternity,
   truth towards both friend and enemy,
   virile pride before the thrones of kings –
   even at the cost of our possessions and blood, brothers!
   Give crowns where crowns are due,
   downfall to the lying brood!

9. Save us from the chains of tyrants,
   show magnanimity even to evil-doers,
   grant hope on our deathbeds,
   mercy before the highest court!
   Even the dead shall join the living!
   Drink, brothers, and join in singing,
   may all sinners be forgiven
   and let hell be no more.

Translation: Kay McBurney (2023)

Chapter II

Love songs

LOVE SONGS   BELGIUM

29
Ne me quitte pas
Do Not Leave Me Now

"Ne me quitte pas", composed in 1959 after a breakup, seems essentially to describe the failure of a broken man. It illustrates the tragedy of a romantic relationship that has no future. Even though the song was originally written to be sung by a woman, Brel, driven by his tremendous conviction as a performer, decided to record it himself. The song became one of the most emblematic works in his repertoire. It has gone far beyond the Belgian borders and has been the subject of many cover versions.

By Reynald Sac, À Coeur Joie Fédération Chorale Wallonie-Bruxelles

Lyrics: Jacques Brel (1929-78)   Music: Jacques Brel (1929-78)
                                              & Gérard Jouannest (1933-2018)

1. Ne me quitte pas, il faut oublier, tout peut s'oublier qui s'enfuit déjà. Oublier le temps des malenten-
1. Do not leave me now, we must just forget, all we can forget, all we did till now, let's forget the cost, of the breath we've

dus et le temps perdu, à savoir comment. Oublier ces
spent, saying words unmeant, and the times we've lost, hours that must des-

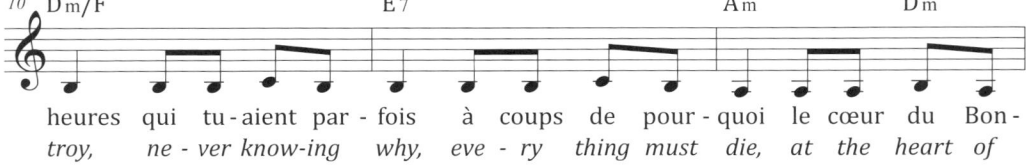

heures qui tuaient parfois à coups de pourquoi le cœur du Bon-
troy, never knowing why, every thing must die, at the heart of

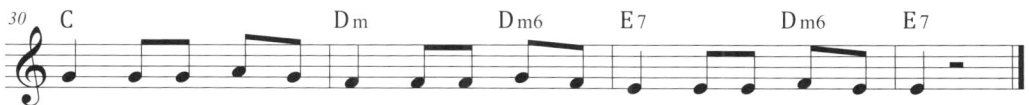

1. Ne me quitte pas
   il faut oublier
   tout peut s'oublier
   qui s'enfuit déjà.
   Oublier le temps
   des malentendus
   et le temps perdu
   à savoir comment.
   Oublier ces heures
   qui tuaient parfois
   à coups de pourquoi
   le cœur du Bonheur.

   Ne me quitte pas,
   ne me quitte pas,
   ne me quitte pas,
   ne me quitte pas.

2. Moi je t'offrirai
   des perles de pluie,
   venues de pays
   où il ne pleut pas;
   je creus'rai la terre,
   jusqu'après ma mort
   pour couvrir ton corps
   d'or et de lumière;
   je f'rai un domaine,
   où l'amour sera roi,
   où l'amour sera loi,
   où tu seras reine.

   Ne me quitte pas,
   ne me quitte pas,
   ne me quitte pas,
   ne me quitte pas.

3. Ne me quitte pas,
   je t'inventerai
   des mots insensés
   que tu comprendras,
   je te parlerai
   de ces amants-là
   qui ont vu deux fois
   leur cœurs s'embrasser.
   Je te raconterai
   l'histoire de ce roi
   mort de n'avoir pas
   pu te rencontrer.

1. Do not leave me now,
   we must just forget
   all we can forget,
   all we did till now.
   Let's forget the cost
   of the breath we've spent,
   saying words unmeant,
   and the times we've lost,
   hours that must destroy,
   never knowing why
   everything must die
   at the heart of joy.

   Do not leave me now,
   do not leave me now,
   do not leave me now,
   do not leave me now.

2. I'll bring back to you
   the clear pearls of rain
   from a distant domain
   where rain never fell,
   and though I grow old
   I'll keep mining the ground
   to deck you around
   in sunlight and gold;
   I'll build you a demesne
   where love's everything,
   where love is the king,
   and you are the queen.

   Do not leave me now,
   Do not leave me now,
   Do not leave me now,
   Do not leave me now.

3. Do not leave me now,
   for you I'll invent
   words and what they meant
   only you will know,
   tales of lovers who
   fell apart and then
   fell in love again
   since their hearts stayed true.
   There's a story too
   that I can confide
   of that king who died
   from not meeting you.

Ne me quitte pas,
ne me quitte pas,
ne me quitte pas,
ne me quitte pas.

*Do not leave me now,
do not leave me now,
do not leave me now
do not leave me now.*

4. On a vu souvent
rejaillir le feu
de l'ancien volcan
qu'on croyait trop vieux.
Il est, paraît-il,
des terres brulées
donnant plus de blé
qu'un meilleur avril.
Et quand vient le soir,
pour qu'un ciel flamboie,
le rouge et le noir
ne s'épousent-ils pas?

*4. And often it's true
that flames spill anew
from ancient volcanos
we thought were too old.
When all's said and done
scorched fields of defeat
could give us more wheat
than the fine April sun.
And when evening is night
with flames overhead,
the black and the red
aren't they joined in the sky?*

Ne me quitte pas,
ne me quitte pas,
ne me quitte pas,
ne me quitte pas.

*Do not leave me now,
do not leave me now,
do not leave me now,
do not leave me now.*

5. Ne me quitte pas,
je ne vais plus pleurer,
je ne vais plus parler,
Je me cacherai là,
à te regarder,
danser et sourire,
et à t'écouter
chanter et puis rire.
Laisse-moi devenir
l'ombre de ton ombre,
l'ombre de ta main,
l'ombre de ton chien.

*5. Do not leave me now,
I will cry no more,
I will talk no more,
hide myself somehow,
and I'll see your smile,
and I'll see you dance,
and I'll hear you sing,
hear your laughter ring.
Let me be for you,
the shadow of your shadow,
the shadow of your hand,
the dog at your command.*

Mais,
ne me quitte pas,
ne me quitte pas,
ne me quitte pas,
ne me quitte pas.

*But,
do not leave me now,
do not leave me now,
do not leave me now,
do not leave me now.*

Translated by Des De Moor (1998)

LOVE SONGS   CYPRUS

30
Το Γιασεμίν
The Jasmine

This beloved traditional Cypriot love song is about a boy praising the beauty of the jasmine flower in the garden of the girl that he loves: His praise is metaphorical since the girls name is – Jasmine. He assures her mother that he has not come to steal her daughter away, but, being a gardener who cares, he is there to prune the jasmine bush.

By Egli Spyridaki, Music Academy ARTE

Lyrics: Traditional   Music: Traditional

Andante molto tranquillo ♩ = 56

1. Το για - σε - μίν στημ πόρ - τα σου, για - σε - μίμ__ μου, Ω!_____ Τζιήρ - τα να το κλα - δέ - ψω, Ω, για - βρίμ__ μου. Τζιε - νό - μι - σεν η μά - να σου, για - σε - μίμ__ μου, Ω!_____ πως ήρ - τα να σε κλέ - ψω, Ω, για - βρίμ__ μου.

1. The jas - mine by your por - tal,__ my jas - mi - ne, Oh!_____ To prune it I had come,__ Oh, my ba - by. But your__ mo - ther thought I came, my jas - mi - ne, Oh!_____ I came to car - ry you a - way,__ Oh, my ba - by.

1. ||: Το γιασεμίν στημ πόρτα σου,
   γιασεμίμ μου, :||
   Ω! Τζ' ήρτα να το κλαδέψω,
   Ω, γιαβρίμ μου.
   ||: Τζι' ενόμισεν η μάνα σου,
   γιασεμίμ μου, :||
   Ω! Πως ήρτα να σε κλέψω,
   Ω, γιαβρίμ μου.

2. ||: Τα μαύραμ μάθκια τα γλυτζιά,
   γιασεμίμ μου, :||
   Ω! Τα φρύθκια τα μεγάλα,
   Ω, γιαβρίμ μου.
   ||: Εκάμαμ με τζι' αρνήθηκα
   γιασεμίμ μου, :||
   Ω! Της μάνας μου το γάλα,
   Ω, γιαβρίμ μου.

3. ||: Το γιασεμίν στημ πόρτα σου,
   γιασεμίμ μου, :||
   Ω! Μοσκοβολούν οι στράτες,
   Ω, γιαβρίμ μου.
   ||: Τζι' η μυρωθκιά του η πολλή,
   γιασεμίμ μου, :||
   Ω! Λαώνει τους δκιαβάτες,
   Ω, γιαβρίμ μου.

1. ||: *The jasmine by your portal,*
   my jasmine, :||
   Oh! To prune it I had come,
   Oh, my baby.
   ||: *But your mother thought I came,*
   my jasmine, :||
   Oh! I came to carry you away,
   Oh, my baby.

2. ||: *Your lovely dark eyes, sweet as honey,*
   my jasmine, :||
   Oh! Your eyebrows so majestic,
   Oh, my baby.
   ||: *And for their sake I must refuse,*
   my jasmine, :||
   Oh! The milk of my good mother,
   Oh, my true love.

3. ||: *The jasmine by your portal,*
   my jasmine, :||
   Oh! Fills all the streets with fragrance
   Oh, my dearest love.
   ||: *Its charming scent, so strong and sweet,*
   my jasmine, :||
   Oh! Beguiles the passers by,
   Oh, my baby.

Translation by Ayis Ioannides (2020)

LOVE SONGS   ESTONIA

31
Tuulevaiksel ööl
Windless Night

Jaan Tätte is a beloved Estonian playwriter and singer-songwriter, whose piece "Tuulevaiksel ööl" was selected as theme song for the Estonian Song and Dance Celebration 2009 (with more than 30.000 participants and 80.000 in the audience), which assisted in making it popular: probably every Estonian knows the song. It was performed as a duet where a woman sings the first verse and a man the latter verse. Jaan Tätte later told on Radio Elmar that, unlike usual, he wrote the melody first: "I chewed on a pen for two weeks and nothing came. Then I took a boat, sailed to a distant stretch of the sea, and as I sat down on a rock, the first pair of words came – "On a windless night" – and then everything else came".

By Kaie Tanner, Sec. General, Estonian Choral Association, ECA

Lyrics: Jaan Tätte (1965-)   Music: Jaan Tätte (1965-)

Tuu - le - vaik - sel ööl   tean, mis - moo - di lööb
On   a wind - less night   there's no boat in sight,

u - du - kell su lae - va - ni - nas. Pai - gal pü - sib aeg.
no fog bell I well re - mem - ber time stands light and still.

Tuu - le - vaik - sel ööl   sü - da kii - relt lööb.
On   a wind - less night   my heart beats, a - light:

Oo - da - nud sind o - len kau - a, vei - di jää - nud veel.
I have wait - ed for so long,___ now there's but a while.

Chorus:

Sul - le tan - han hüü - da ju - ba veel ja veel ja veel,
Hear my call, oh Wind of North, blow more and more and more!

1. Tuulevaiksel ööl
   tean, mismoodi lööb
   udukell su laevaninas.
   Paigal püsib aeg.
   Tuulevaiksel ööl
   süda kiirelt lööb.
   Oodanud sind olen kaua,
   veidi jäänud veel.

   Chorus:
   Sulle tahan hüüda juba
   veel ja veel ja veel,
   tuule suund on nord,
   nüüd on minu kord
   teha tormi sinu südames.

2. Tuulevaikne öö,
   udukell vaid lööb.
   Käed, mis tahtsid rooliratast,
   tahavad nüüd sind.
   Kumer silmapiir
   lahku meid kord viis.
   Sina otsid valget purje,
   mina otsin maad.

   Chorus:
   Sulle tahan...

1. On a windless night
   there's no boat in sight,
   no fog bell I well remember
   time stands light and still.
   On a windless night
   my heart beats, alight:
   I have waited for so long,
   now there's but a while.

   Chorus:
   Hear my call, oh Wind of North,
   blow more and more and more!
   Time has come to start,
   it's my turn in your heart
   raise a storm like never seen before.

2. On a windless night
   the fog bell softly sighs.
   Hands that longed for (the) steering wheel
   now only long for you.
   Dreams of (the) high seas
   once separated us.
   Now you're looking for a sail
   – as I look for landfall.

   Chorus:
   Hear my call...

Translation by Doris Kareva (2020)

LOVE SONGS   POLAND

32
Z tobą chcę oglądać świat
Want to See the World With You

This duo of Zbigniew Wodecki (1950-2017) and Zdzisława Sośnicka (1945-) is considered one of the most interesting collaborations in the history of Polish popular music. This is due not only to both talent and class of both artists, but also to melody and lyrics, which together bring to mind classic American compositions. In the winter of 1986, in a cool room of the Grand Hotel in Sopot, Wodecki very spontaneously composed the dreamy opening of this duo. Shortly after it was completed and arranged. Only the lyrics were missing. While in Wroclaw, Wodecki met with Jonasz Kofta (1942-1988) who within four days returned a ready script: Lyrics capturing how the world can unfold and transform when you are with a loved one.

By Dorota Stefaniak, Academy of Music "Stanisław Moniuszko" in Gdańsk

Lyrics: Jonasz Kofta (1942-1988)   Music: Zbigniew Wodecki (1950-2017)

1. Z to - bą chcę o - glą - dać świat, wśród wy - so - kich błą - dzić traw, wtedy to wszyst-ko to, to co wi - dzę, czu - ję, na-praw-dę jest... Kwit-nie sad, po - wiał wiatr, tak jak śnieg syp-nął kwiat, wszyst-ko to na-praw-dę jest...
2. Z to - bą chcę o - glą - dać świat.

1. Want to see the world with you, wand-er through the gras - sy field, then ev - e - ry sin - gle thing that I feel, is real - ly there... Hear the woods, soft winds sigh, just like snow pet - als fly. All of this is tru-ly real....
2. Want to see the world with you,

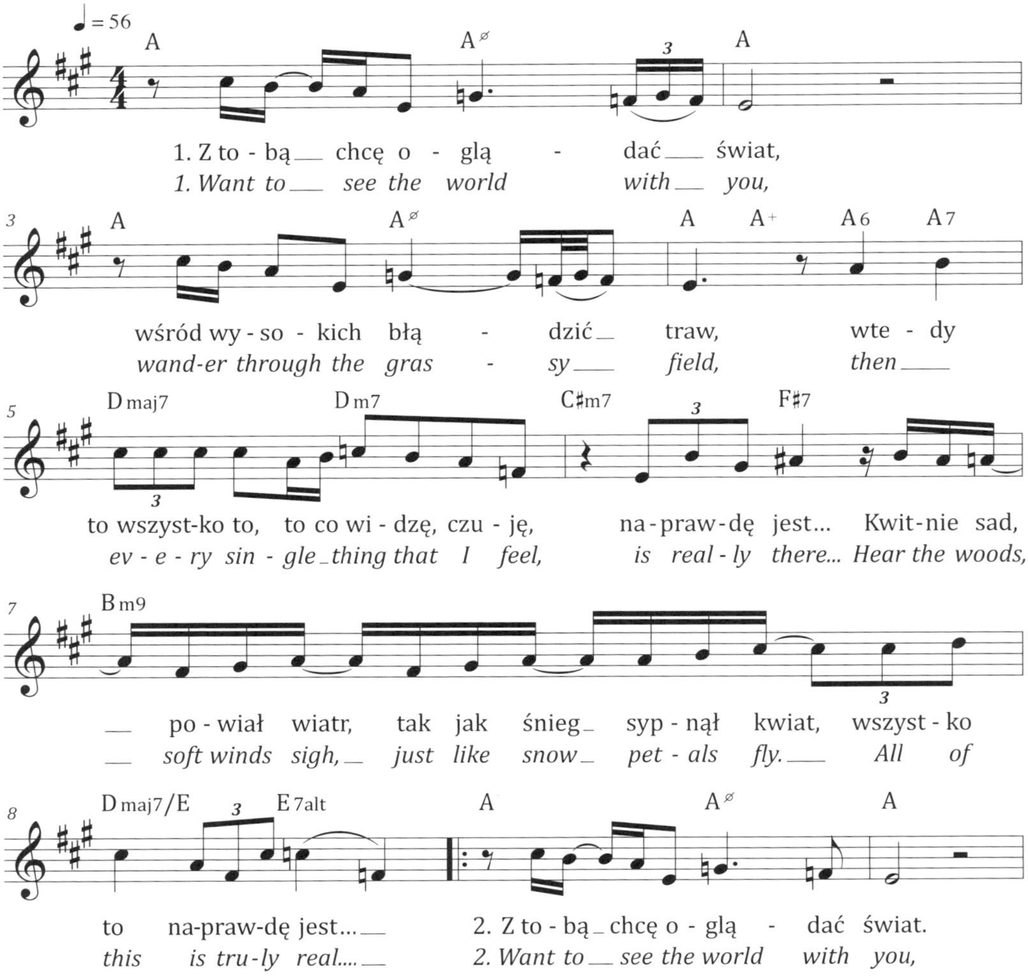

1. Z tobą chcę oglądać świat,
   wśród wysokich błądzić traw,
   wtedy to wszystko to, to co widzę, czuję,
   naprawdę jest…
   Kwitnie sad, powiał wiatr,
   tak jak śnieg sypnął kwiat,
   wszystko to naprawdę jest…

2. Z tobą chcę oglądać świat.
   Jaki piękny księżyc, patrz!
   Widzisz to, to co ja, jakie to jest proste,
   wystarczy być…
   Jaki świt, jaki blask,
   jaki śpiew, jaki ptak,
   wszystko to, to wszystko w nas…

   Gdy ty i ja, cały świat jest dla nas,
   gdy ty i ja…
   Zapach łąk, plaży piach,
   nocy mrok, światło dnia,
   wszystko to, gdy ty i ja…

Chorus:
   Wiem to, czuję, życie mnie nie mija,
   obok Ciebie ważna każda chwila.
   Żyję znów, gdy jesteś tu
   w obłoku snów.
   Piękny świat dziś znów ma sens,
   naprawdę jest to takie proste.

   Spójrz, jak wszystko się niezmiennie zmienia.
   Nigdy dosyć tego zachwycenia.
   Widzisz, spójrz, znów zakwitł bez,
   to wszystko jest…
   Znów widzę sad, kwitnący sad,
   gdy płatków śnieg na nasze głowy spadł.

Repeat verse 2:
   Z tobą chcę oglądać świat….

Outro:
   Z tobą chcę oglądać świat,
   wciąż niezmiennie zmienny…
   Z tobą chcę oglądać świat,
   co dzień niecodzienny świat.

---

1. Want to see the world with you,
   wander through the grassy field,
   then ev-e-ry single thing that I feel,
   is really there…
   Hear the woods, soft winds sigh,
   just like snow petals fly.
   All of this is truly real….

2. Want to see the world with you,
   see the lovely moon above anew.
   What you see, I do too, it's so simply simple,
   simply be…
   What a day, bright as dawn,
   leaves that shake, birds in song,
   all of that - it's all in us…

   With you and me, all the world is for us,
   with you and me…
   Feel the grass, soft white sand,
   evening fades, hand in hand,
   all of that, it's you and me…

Chorus:
   Know it - feel it, life won't miss me out,
   when I'm near you every moment counts.
   I'm alive when you're near,
   dream with you.
   The lovely world makes sense again,
   it really is that simply simple.

   Look at us now, how we're always changing.
   Never enough of this sweet feeling.
   You see, look, the lilacs bloom,
   it's all real…
   I see the woods, the dancing woods,
   when white snow flakes fell on our heads
                                    that time.

Repeat verse 2:
   Want to see the world with you…

Outro:
   Want to see the world with you,
   always changing changing. . .
   Want to see the world with you,
   each day it's a brand new world.

Translation by David & William Malcolm (2021)

LOVE SONGS SWEDEN

33
Så skimrande var aldrig havet
The Sea Did Never Shine So Brightly

Here we have an entire song – a gorgeous declaration of love – in just one sentence! It describes a sunset in a beautiful summer's night and reaches its peak in the memory of the lovers' very first kiss. Evert Taube (1890-1976) was an artist of many forms, a poet who set his own poems to music and often performed them himself, singing and playing the lute. In 1910, as a young travelling artist, he worked on a steam ship sailing to Argentina, where he became a citizen, which is why South American life can be seen in many of his works. Taube's poetic songs have touched many people, and they belong to the Swedish canon of songs. "Så skimrande var aldrig havet" – The Sea Did Never Shine so Brightly – has become one of his most beloved songs; a song for weddings and happiness, but also for funerals and mourning.

By Kerstin Carpvik, head of library, Musikverket

Lyrics: Evert Taube (1890-1976)   Music: Evert Taube (1890-1976)

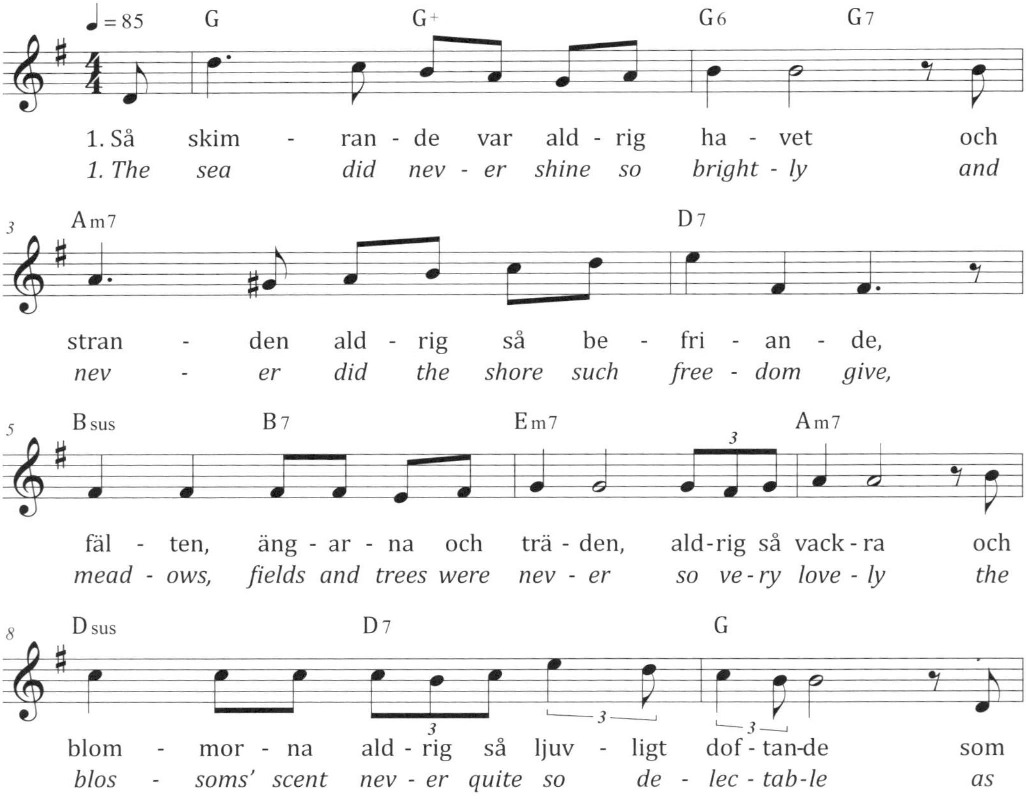

1. Så skim - ran - de var ald - rig ha - vet och
   stran - den ald - rig så be - fri - an - de,
   fäl - ten, äng - ar - na och trä - den, ald-rig så vack - ra och
   blom - mor - na ald - rig så ljuv - ligt dof - tan - de som

1. The sea did nev - er shine so bright - ly and
   nev - er did the shore such free - dom give,
   mead - ows, fields and trees were nev - er so ve - ry love - ly the
   blos - soms' scent nev - er quite so de - lec - tab - le as

Så skimrande var aldrig havet
Och stranden aldrig så befriande,
Fälten, ängarna och träden,
aldrig så vackra
Och blommorna aldrig så ljuvligt doftande
Som när du gick vid min sida
Mot solnedgången, aftonen den underbara
Då dina lockar dolde mig för världen,
Medan du dränkte alla mina sorger,
Älskling,
I din första kyss.

The Sea Did Never Shine So Brightly
and never did the shore such freedom give,
meadows, fields and trees were
never so very lovely,
the blossoms' scent never quite so delectable
as when we two walked side by side there
in to the setting sun, the glory of the evening
from all the world you hid me in your tresses
just as you drowned my each and ev'ry sorrow,
dearest,
in your first sweet kiss.

Translation by Fred Lane (2023)

Copyright © 1948 UNIVERSAL/REUTER-REUTER FORLAG. Copyright Renewed. All Rights in the United States Administered by UNIVERSAL - POLYGRAM INTERNATIONAL PUBLISHING, INC. International Copyright Secured. All Rights Reserved.
Reprinted by Permission of Hal Leonard Europe Ltd.

LOVE SONGS   GREECE

34
Σ' αγαπώ γιατί 'σαι ωραία
I Love You Because You're Beautiful

It is unclear whether this is a traditional song from Asia Minor or composed by Aristeides Moschos (1930-2001), a virtuoso santouri-player, who claimed it but never got the copyright. It is essentially a serenade, meant to be sung by the love-struck man under the – initially closed – window of his beloved. So, in this beloved love song it says "I love you because you are beautiful, I love you because you're you./ And I love the whole world because you exist within./ The window is closed./ Please open one of the shutters 'cause your figure I must see./ And if you don't want to open, they will find me laying dead." Truly a crazy love!

By Thomas Louziotis, president, Hellenic Choirs Association

Lyrics: Traditional   Music: Traditional / or: Aristeides Moschos (1930-2001)

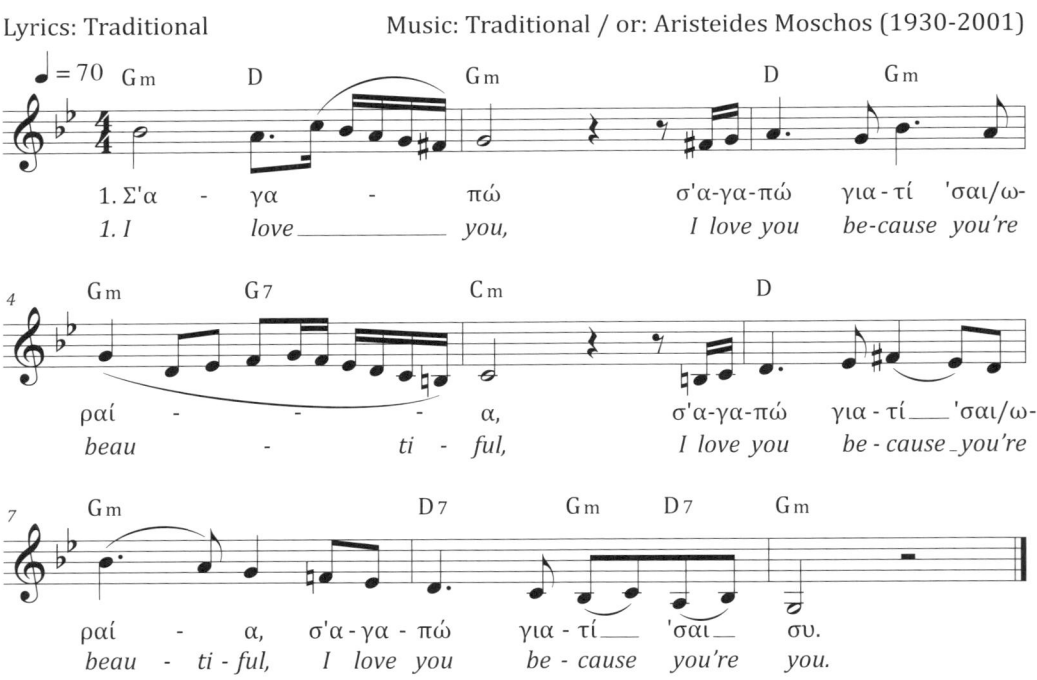

1. Σ' αγαπώ
   σ' αγαπώ γιατί 'σαι ωραία,
   σ' αγαπώ γιατί 'σαι ωραία
   σ' αγαπώ γιατί 'σαι 'σύ.

2. Αγαπώ
   αγαπώ κι όλον τον κόσμο,
   αγαπώ κι όλον τον κόσμο
   γιατί ζεις και 'σύ μαζί.

3. Το παρά
   το παράθυρο κλεισμένο,
   το παράθυρο κλεισμένο
   το παράθυρο κλειστό.

4. Άνοιξε
   άνοιξε το ένα φύλλο,
   άνοιξε το ένα φύλλο
   την εικόνα σου να δω.

5. Κι αν δεν θέ-,
   κι αν δεν θέλεις να μ' ανοίξεις
   κι αν δεν θέλεις να μ' ανοίξεις
   θα με βρουν στη γη νεκρό.

6. Σ' αγαπώ
   σ' αγαπώ γιατί 'σαι ωραία,
   σ' αγαπώ γιατί 'σαι ωραία
   σ' αγαπώ γιατί 'σαι 'σύ.

1. I love you,
   I love you because you're beautiful,
   I love you because you're beautiful,
   I love you because you're you.

2. And I love,
   and I love the whole world,
   and I love the whole world
   because you exist within.

3. The window,
   the window is closed,
   the window is closed,
   the window is shut.

4. Open,
   please open one of the shutters,
   please open one of the shutters,
   'cause your figure I must see.

5. And if you don't,
   and if you don't want to open,
   and if you don't want to open,
   they will find me laying dead.

6. I love you,
   I love you because you're beautiful,
   I love you because you're beautiful
   I love you because you're you.

Translation by Monika & Stavros Xenides (2023)

LOVE SONGS — LITHUANIA

35
Aš mylėjau tave tau nežinant
I Have Loved You and Kept It a Secret

'I have loved you and kept it a secret' is very popular in Lithuania and most likely due to its sincerity, simplicity and subtleness. The most beloved version of this song is in the performance of its author, Olegas Ditkovskis, revered as musician, bard, as well as theatre and film actor. The musician was part of the group 'Trio of actors', popular with the so called 'singing poetry' songs, telling about love and everyday life in an understandable and touching way.

By Dr. Arvydas Girdzijauskas, Lithuanian Choral Union, LCHS

Lyrics: Antanas Jonynas (1923-1976) Music: Olegas Ditkovskis (1955-)

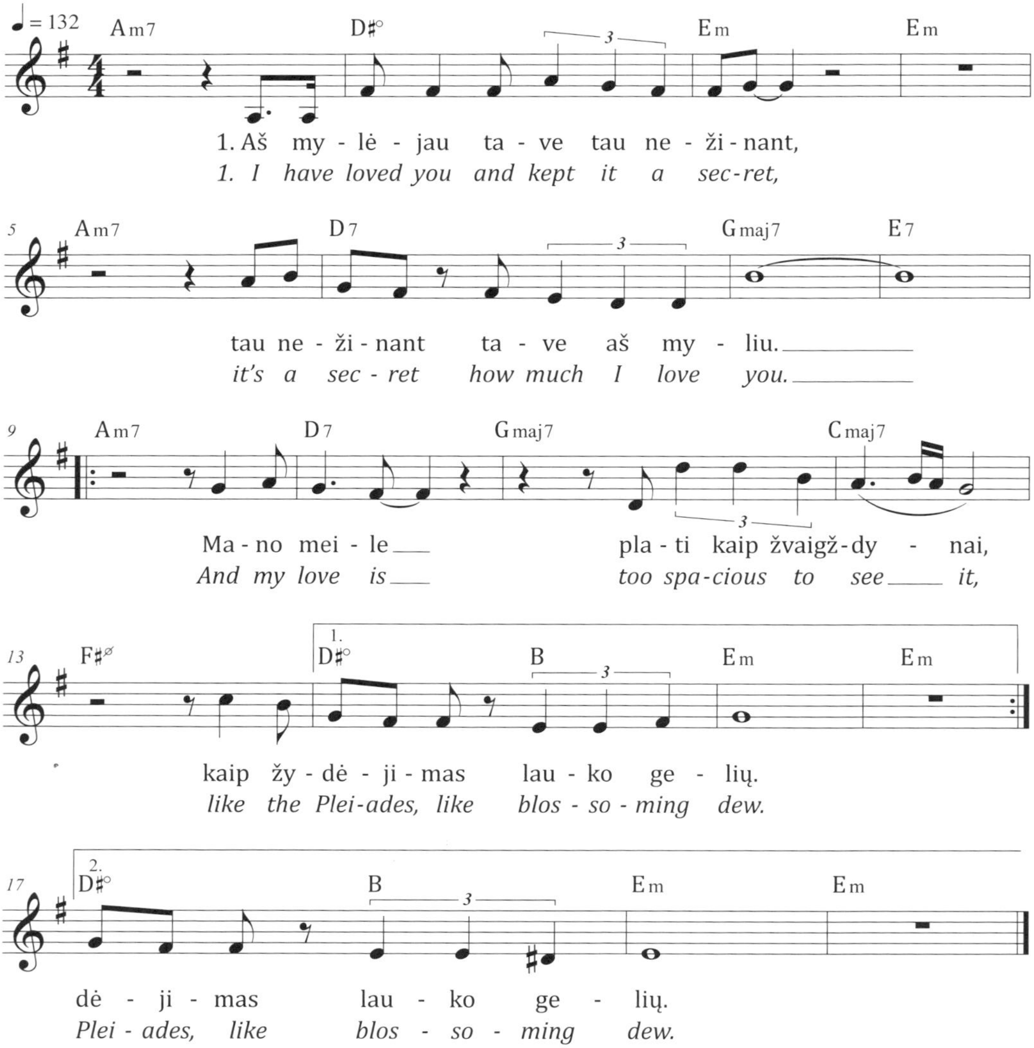

1. Aš my-lė-jau ta-ve tau ne-ži-nant,
1. I have loved you and kept it a sec-ret,

tau ne-ži-nant ta-ve aš my-liu.
it's a sec-ret how much I love you.

Ma-no mei-le pla-ti kaip žvaigž-dy-nai,
And my love is too spa-cious to see it,

kaip ži-dė-ji-mas lau-ko ge-lių.
like the Plei-ades, like blos-so-ming dew.

dė-ji-mas lau-ko ge-lių.
Plei-ades, like blos-so-ming dew.

1. Aš mylėjau tave tau nežinant,
   tau nežinant tave aš myliu.
   ||: Mano meile plati kaip žvaigždynai,
   kaip žydėjimas lauko gelių. :||

2. Ar mylėjai mane nežinojau,
   ar mylėsi paklausti bijau.
   ||: Eisiu eisiu rugsėjui lašnojant,
   į tave kaip ligšiolei ėjau. :||

3. Vėlų vakarą, rudenį pilką,
   tavo balsas per rūką aidės.
   ||: Šauks i kelią, i tolimą ilgą,
   pasitiks ir per naktį lydės. :||

4. Ir mylėsiu tave tau nežinant,
   meile ves tuo dulkėtu keliu.
   ||: Amžina ir plati kaip žvaigždynai,
   kaip žydėjimas lauko geliu. :||

*1. I have loved you and kept it a secret,
   it's a secret how much I love you.
   ||: And my love is too spacious to see it,
   like the Pleiades, like blossoming dew. :||*

*2. Would you love me for ever and ever,
   will you love me I'm too shy to know.
   ||: I'll be walking through drizzling September,
   on and on walking towards you I go. :||*

*3. Late at night, and when autumn brings grey tones,
   your voice echoes through grey misty light.
   ||: Calling me down a long long road alone,
   meeting me to guide me through the night. :||*

*4. I will love you and keep it a secret,
   love will lead me down those dusty roads.
   ||: Wide and endless like a starry night,
   like the blossoming flowers in fields. :||*

Translation by Kerry Shawn Keys & Sonata Paliulytė (2022)

LOVE SONGS   IRELAND

36
Grace

"Grace" was written in 1985 by brothers Frank and Sean O'Meara, and first popularised by the balladeer Jim McCann, a one-time member of the The Dubliners. The title refers to Grace Gifford (1888-1955), an artist and 2nd youngest of twelve children from Rathmines, a suburb of Dublin. Grace Gifford converted to Catholicism in order to marry Joseph Plunkett (1887-1916), an Irish nationalist and revolutionary leader during the 1916 Rising which subsequently led to Ireland's independence. In the song, Plunkett, who had been jailed in Kilmainham Gaol near Dublin painfully describes his love for Grace and reflects on his calling by Patrick Pearse (Pádraig Mac Piaras), a leader of the revolution, to join him in the G.P.O (General Post Office, Dublin), a focal point of the fight. The couple had planned to marry on that same day and, following the jailing of Plunkett, they married in the chapel of the jail just hours before his execution.

By Mark Armstrong, Sing Ireland

Lyrics: Frank & Sean O'Meara   Music: Frank & Sean O'Meara

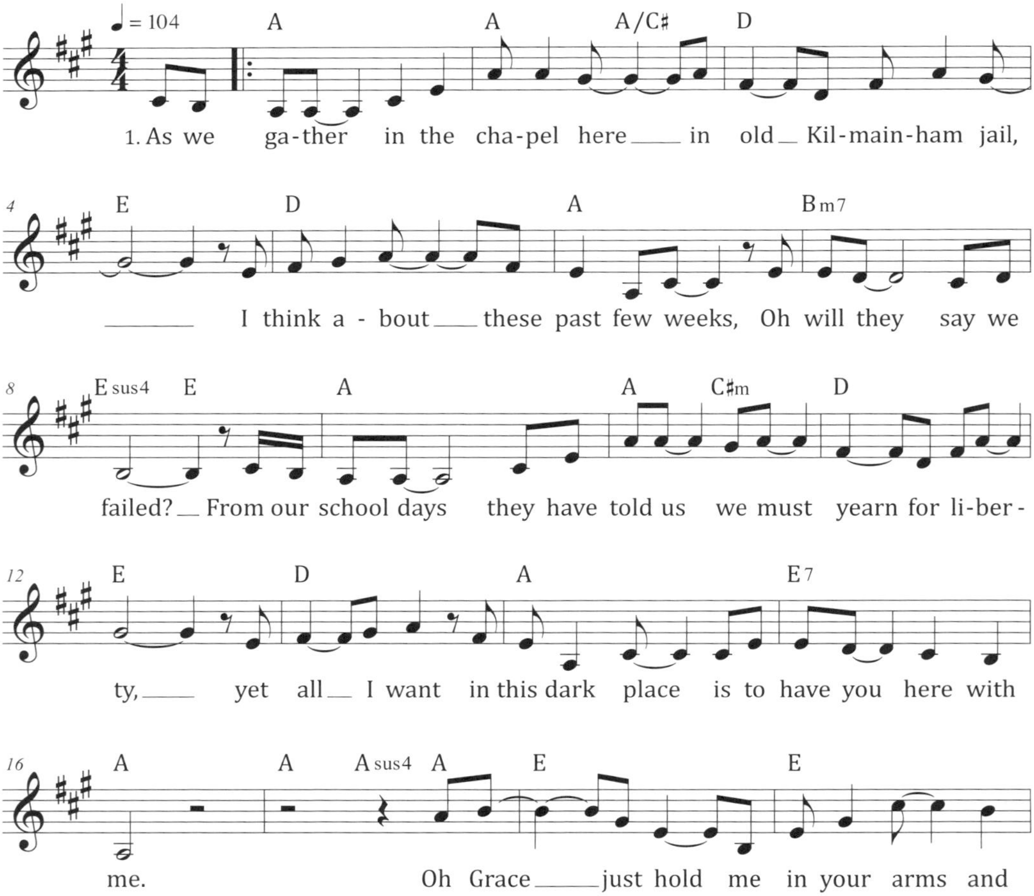

1. As we gather in the chapel here in old Kilmainham jail, I think about these past few weeks, Oh will they say we failed? From our school days they have told us we must yearn for liberty, yet all I want in this dark place is to have you here with me. Oh Grace just hold me in your arms and

1. As we gather in the chapel here in old Kilmainham Jail,
   I think about these past few weeks, oh will they say we've failed.
   From our schooldays they have told us we must yearn for liberty,
   yet all I want in this dark place is to have you here with me.

   Chorus:
   Oh Grace just hold me in your arms and let this moment linger.
   They'll take me out at dawn and I will die.
   With all my love I place this wedding ring upon your finger.
   There won't be time to share our love for we must say goodbye.

2. Now I know it's hard for you, my love, to ever understand
   the love I bear for these brave men, my love for this dear land.
   But when the Padhraic called me to his side down in the GPO,
   I had to leave my own sick bed, to him I had to go.

   Oh Grace just hold me...

3. Now as dawn is breaking, my heart is breaking too,
   on this May morn as I walk out my thoughts well be of you.
   And I'll write some words upon the wall so everyone will know
   I love so much that I could see his blood upon the rose.

   Oh Grace just hold me...

Copyright © 1984 by Asdee Music. All Rights Administered by Peermusic (UK) Ltd. International Copyright Secured.
All Rights Reserved. Reprinted by Permission of Hal Leonard Europe Ltd.

LOVE SONGS FINLAND

37
Sinua, sinua rakastan
You, It Is You, It Is You I Love

"Sinua, sinua rakastan" (You, It Is You, It Is You I Love) was composed for the Mikko Niskanen film 'Asphalt Sheep' (1968) by Kaj Chydenius, one of the pioneers of the Finnish cabaret song and a key figure in the political song movement of the 1960s and 1970s. During his long career, Chydenius has composed political songs, hit songs and classical music, and several of his songs have later become a part of the Finns' common musical heritage. The lyrics were written by Aulikki Oksanen, whose extensive literary output also includes novels, poems, short stories and theatre plays. With both appealing metaphors inspired by Finnish nature and a hint of war angst, and with a dramatic melody, emphasised by short instrumental spacing and tense, suspended long notes over minor-key harmonies, this cherished song has since been interpreted by countless Finnish artists.

By Juha Henriksson, director, Music Archive Finland

Lyrics: Aulikki Oksanen (1944-) Music: Kaj Chydenius (1939-)

1. Si-nu-a, si-nu-a ra-kas-tan, yö pai-naa pää-hä-ni pi-me-än sep-pe-leen, jot-ta en si-nu-a nä-ki-si. Mi-ten tait-ta-vat lin-nut sii-pen-sä, mi-ten
1. You, it is you, it is you I love, the night now lays a dark gar-land up-on my brow, hid-ing your face from my yearn-ing eyes. And I know that the birds now fold their wings; I can

1. Sinua, sinua rakastan,
   yö painaa päähäni pimeän seppeleen,
   jotta en sinua näkisi.
   Miten taittavat linnut siipensä,
   miten vyöryvät vedet kallioitten alla,
   miten nousevat metsät tuulten mukana
   ja pilvien sateet jähmettyvät kiveksi.

2. Sinua, sinua rakastan,
   yö painaa päähäni pimeän seppeleen,
   jotta en sinua näkisi.
   Miten huutaa minulle avaruus,
   miten kirkuvat tähdet ohimoni läpi,
   miten itkevät lapset maailman rannoilla
   ja merien yllä savuavat sydämet.

3. Sinua, sinua rakastan,
   niin liikkuu pehmeä kätesi
   kuin vene varhain aamuisella joella.

1. You, it is you, it is you I love,
   the night now lays a dark garland upon my brow,
   hiding your face from my yearning eyes.
   And I know that the birds now fold their wings;
   I can feel the dark waters rolling under mountains,
   I can see the great forests rising with the wind,
   and falling from grey skies, hard rain turning
                                          into stone.

2. You, it is you, it is you I love,
   the night now lays a dark garland upon my brow,
   hiding your face from my yearning eyes.
   I can hear the call of the universe,
   I can hear the stars scream and shred my soul
                                          in anguish.
   I can hear all the children weeping on the shores,
   and over the oceans all our dreams go up in smoke.

3. You, it is you, it is you I love,
   your hand glides softly across my skin
   like a boat that drifts downstream
   in morning's golden light.

Translation by Jaakko Mäntyjärvi (2021)

Copyright © Warner Chappell Music Finland Oy. Reprinted by permission of Notfabriken Music Publishing AB/Faber Music Ltd.

LOVE SONGS   CZECHIA

38
Lásko má, já stůňu
Oh, My Queen, My Heart Aches

This very popular song by composer Karel Svoboda and lyricist Jiří Štaidl is from the film musical "Night at Karlštejn" from 1973. The film – based on a play from 1884 by Jaroslav Vrchlický – was directed by Zdeněk Podskalský (1923-93) and has a fictional story taking place in 1363 at the court of the Czech King Charles IV at Karlštejn Castle, which was reserved for men only. But his wife Queen Elizabeth (Pomeranian) longs to see her husband and goes to secretly visits the castle. In "Oh, My Queen, My Heart Aches" she sings of her love and the torment of separation. It has undoubtedly become the most popular song of the whole musical.

By Adam Klemens, Copyright Protection Association for Musical Works, OSA

Lyrics: Jiří Štaidl (1943-73)   Music: Karel Svoboda (1938-2007)

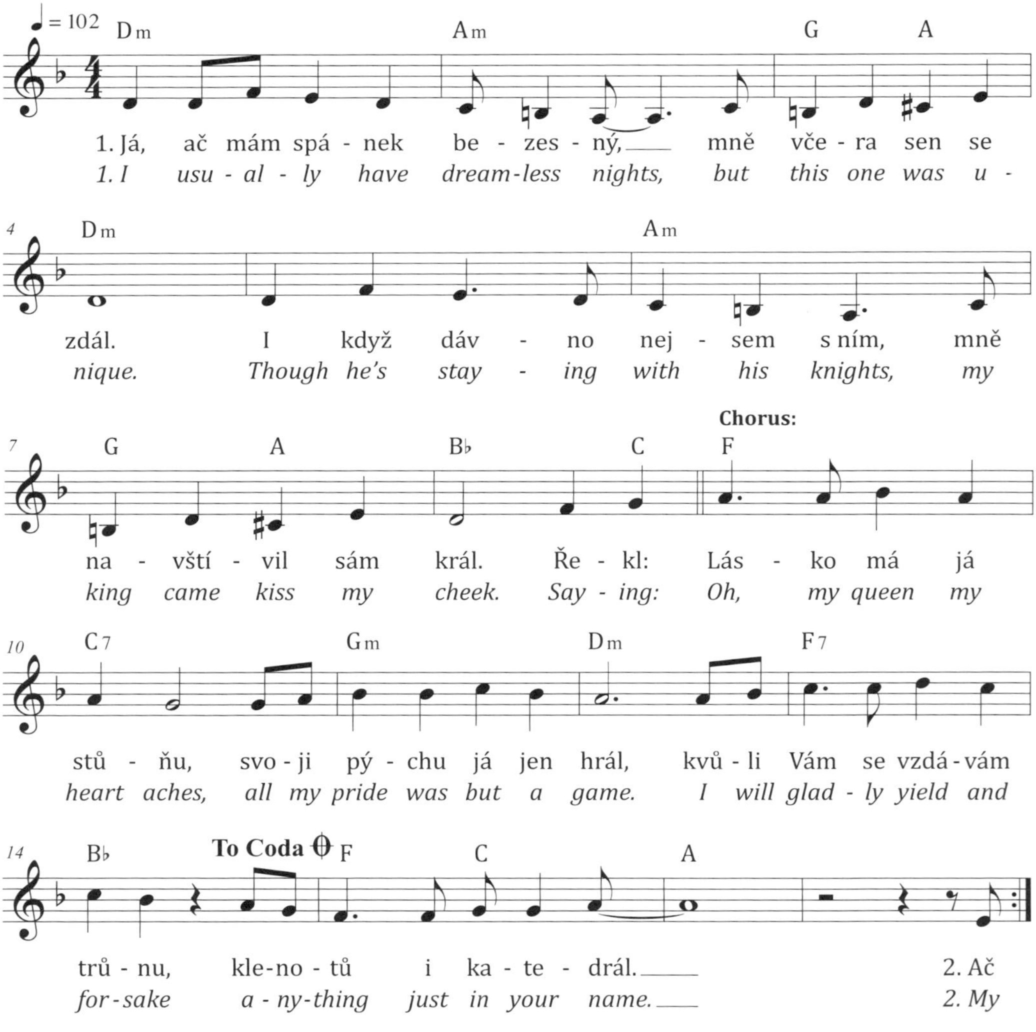

1. Já, ač mám spánek bezesný, mně včera sen se zdál. I když dávno nejsem s ním, mně navštívil sám král. Řekl: Lásko má já stůňu, svoji pýchu já jen hrál, kvůli Vám se vzdávám trůnu, klenotů i katedrál.

1. I usually have dreamless nights, but this one was unique. Though he's staying with his knights, my king came kiss my cheek. Saying: Oh, my queen my heart aches, all my pride was but a game. I will gladly yield and forsake anything just in your name.

2. Ač
2. My

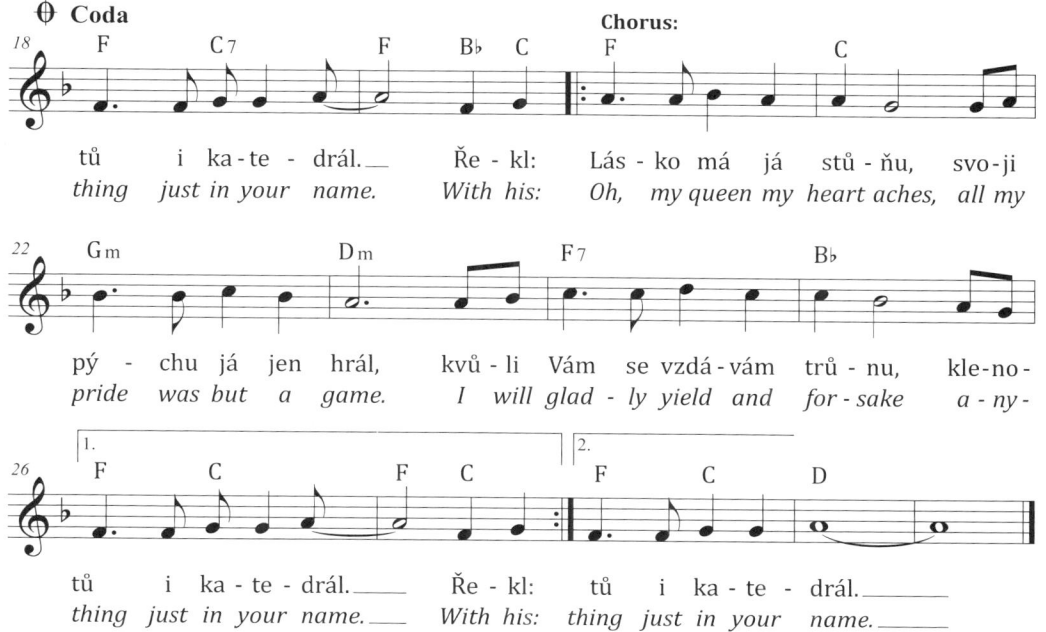

1. Já, ač mám spánek bezesný,
   mně včera sen se zdál.
   I když dávno nejsem s ním,
   mně navštívil sám král.
   Řekl:

Chorus:
||: Lásko má já stůňu,
svoji pýchu já jen hrál,
kvůli Vám se vzdávám trůnu,
klenotů i katedrál. :||

2. Ač den mám jindy poklidný,
   dnes nevím kudy kam.
   Trápí mě sen ošidný
   a trápí mě král sám.
   Řekl:

Chorus:
||: Lásko má já stůňu,
svoji pýchu já jen hrál,
kvůli Vám se vzdávám trůnu,
klenotů i katedrál. :||

1. I usually have dreamless nights,
   but this one was unique.
   Though he's staying with his knights,
   my king came kiss my cheek.
   Saying:

Chorus:
||: Oh, my queen my heart aches,
all my pride was but a game.
I will gladly yield and forsake
anything just in your name. :||

2. My days of royal dignity,
   so hard now to endure.
   This dream of mine troubles me
   and my king even more.
   With his:

Chorus:
||: Oh, my queen my heart aches,
all my pride was but a game.
I will gladly yield and forsake
anything just in your name. :||

Translation by Zuzana Čtveráčková (2022)

LOVE SONGS   GERMANY

39
Sah Ein Knab Ein Röslein Stehen
Rose on the Heath

"Heidenröslein" (Rose on the Heath) is one of the most famous German "folk songs" (although since its origin is known it should be classified as an "art song"). The lyrics are by Germany's most famous poet, Johann Wolfgang Goethe (1749-1832), whos poem first resounded in Heinrich Werner's version in Braunschweig in 1829. In popularity this version surpasses the more challenging versions of Schubert (1815) and Schumann (1840). The meaning of the ambiguous poem is the subject of controversy today: Goethe is being accused of using the lines to describe the rape of a young woman. However, to this day, this interpretation has not detracted from its effect as a – dark – love song: after all, 'the rose' fights back and pricks!

By Ekkehard Klemm, president, Association of German Concert Choirs (VDKC)/
Hochschule für Musik "Carl Maria von Weber" Dresden

Lyrics: JohannWolfgang Goethe (1749-1832)   Music: Henrich Werner (1800-33)

1. Sah ein Knab' ein Röslein stehn, Röslein auf der Heiden, war so jung und morgenschön, lief er schnell es nah zu sehn, sah's mit vielen Freuden. Röslein, Röslein, Röslein rot, Röslein auf der Heiden.

1. Once a boy a rose did view, rose, sweet in the heather. And so young and fair it grew, that to see it near he flew through the summer weather. Rose so fair and rose so red, rose, sweet in the heather.

1. Sah ein Knab' ein Röslein stehn,
   Röslein auf der Heiden,
   war so jung und morgenschön,
   lief er schnell es nah zu sehn,
   sah's mit vielen Freuden.
   Röslein, Röslein, Röslein rot,
   Röslein auf der Heiden.

2. Knabe sprach: ich breche dich,
   Röslein auf der Heiden!
   Röslein sprach: ich steche dich,
   daß du ewig denkst an mich,
   und ich will's nicht leiden.
   Röslein, Röslein, Röslein rot,
   Röslein auf der Heiden.

3. Und der wilde Knabe brach
   's Röslein auf der Heiden;
   Röslein wehrte sich und stach,
   Half ihm doch kein Weh und Ach,
   mußt' es eben leiden.
   Röslein, Röslein, Röslein rot,
   Röslein auf der Heiden.

1. *Once a boy a rose did view,*
   rose, sweet in the heather.
   and so young and fair it grew,
   that to see it near he flew
   through the summer weather.
   Rose so fair and rose so red,
   rose, sweet in the heather.

2. *Said the boy, I shall break you,*
   rose, sweet in the heather!
   Said the rose, I shall prick you,
   this I will not suffer through,
   haunted be forever.
   Rose so fair and rose so red,
   rose, sweet in the heather.

3. *And the boy the rose did break,*
   rose, sweet in the heather.
   Rose did struggle for its sake,
   thorns and cries they could not make
   pain and suff'ring lesser.
   Rose so fair and rose so red,
   rose, sweet in the heather.

Translation by Alicia Edelweiss (2023)

Verse 1, lines 1, 3, 4, 5 are "recycled" from the translation of Eleonore D'Esterre-Keeling (1856-1939)

LOVE SONGS   MALTA

40
Xemx
Sun

Xemx is an iconic love-song composed by Dominic Grech (1950-2005) in 1975, perhaps his best known composition from his time as main singer-songwriter with "The Tramps", Malta's most acclaimed pop band hailing from the island of Gozo. The song is well known locally as it treats the ardent flames of the lover awaiting the day of wedding to his loved one, whom he describes as a sun (xemx).

By Dr. John Galea, School of Performing Arts, University of Malta

Lyrics: Dominic Grech (1950-2005)   Music: Dominic Grech (1950-2005)

1. Jien li-lek__ in-ħob-bok__ bil-wisq mhux fti-it Int dej-jem__ ġo qal-bi____ jien naħ-seb fi-ik.____

1. My dar-ling,__ I love you__ with all my heart, from my heart and my mind__ you're ne-ver far.____

Chorus:

I-va li-lek__ in-ħob-bok, i-va li-lek__ ir-rid.____

How I love you,__ I need you, how I want you,__ I do.____

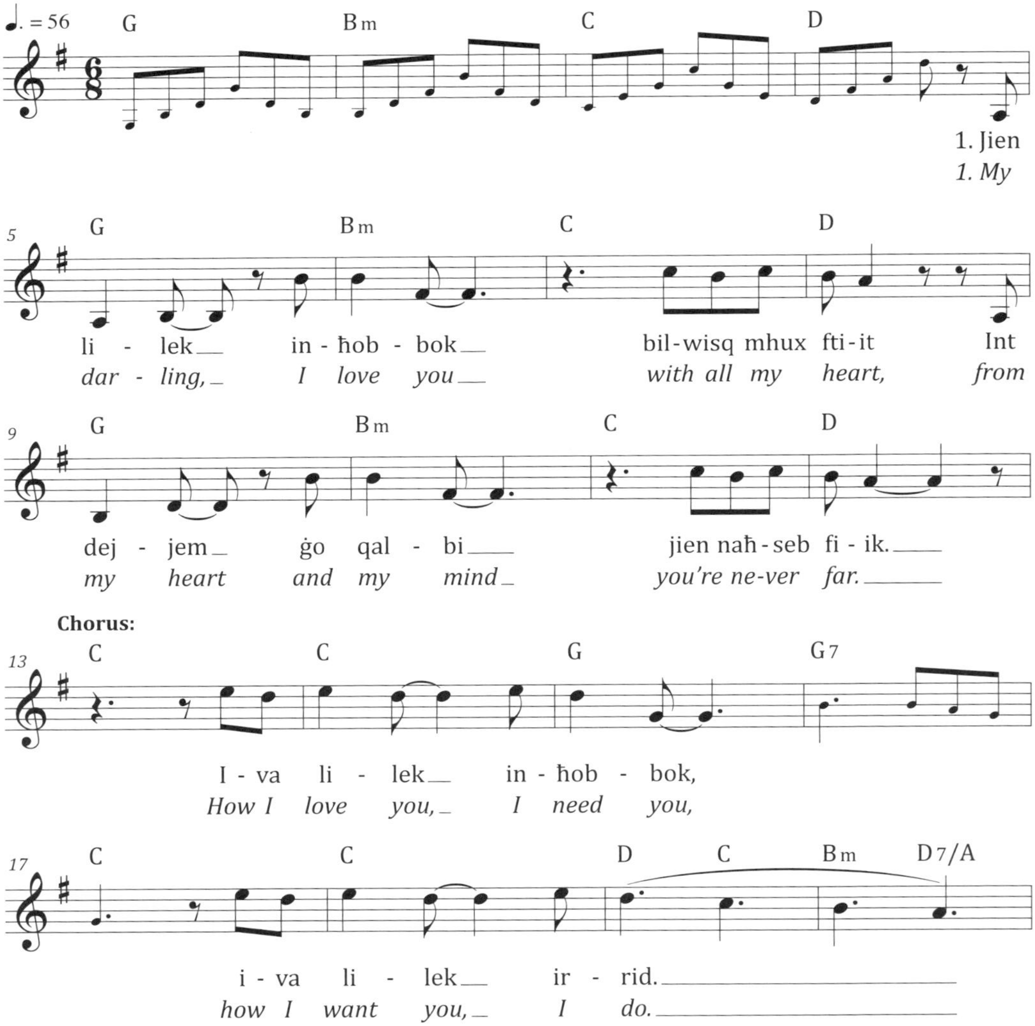

Xemx wisq sabiħa lilek inħobb.
Beautiful sun, you're all I want,

Ġawhra ta' qalbi lilek irrid.
my precious diamond, you're all I need.

1. Lilek inħobbok
   bil-wisq mhux ftit
   int dejjem ġo qalbi
   jien naħseb fik.

   Chorus:
   Iva lilek inħobbok,
   iva lilek irrid.
   Xemx wisq sabiħa
   lilek inħobb.
   Ġawrha ta' qalbi
   lilek irrid.

2. Fin-niket u fl-hena
   niftakar fik,
   għax inti tfarraġni
   nistabar bik.

   Chorus:
   ‖ : Iva lilek inħobbok... :‖

3. Ftit ieħor daqt jasal
   dak il-mument
   li inti tkun tiegħi
   għal-dejjem ħdejk.
   Iva lilek inħobbok,
   iva lilek irrid.

   Chorus:
   ‖: Iva lilek inħobbok... :‖

1. My darling, I love you
   With all my heart
   From my heart and my mind
   You're never far.

   Chorus:
   How I love you, I need you
   How I want you, I do ….
   Beautiful sun,
   you're all I want
   My precious diamond,
   you're all I need.

2. In sorrow, contentment
   I turn to you
   For you are my comfort
   In all fortunes.

   Chorus:
   ‖: *How I love you, I need you..*:‖

3. Can't wait for that moment
   When you'll be mine
   And we'll be together
   'Till end of time.
   How I love you, I need you
   How I want you, I do…

   Chorus:
   ‖: *How I love you, I need you…*:‖

Translation by Richard Grech (2022)

LOVE SONGS   PORTUGAL

41
Amar Pelos Dois
Love for the Both of Us

"Love for the both of us" has become the most popular Portuguese love song nationwide since Salvador Sobral (singer) and his sister Luísa Sobral (composer and lyrics writer) finally won the Eurovision Song Contest in 2017 in a remarkable landslide victory. In this both tender and humble song of consolation, a lover offers "to love for two" in the attempt to heal the broken heart of her/his former partner: "I know you don't love yourself / Maybe slowly, you can learn again". The overall sheer simplicity, the gentle, undulating vocal line of tune and the mild arrangements for essentially a chamber ensemble of classical strings were also key for the national and international popularity of this delightful song of love, intimacy and devotion.

By Manuela Encarnação & Nuno Bettencourt Mendes, Portuguese Music Teacher Association, APEM & Jorge Alves, Association for Choirs in Lisbon, AMLC

Lyrics: Luísa Sobral (b. 1987)   Music: Luísa Sobral (b. 1987)

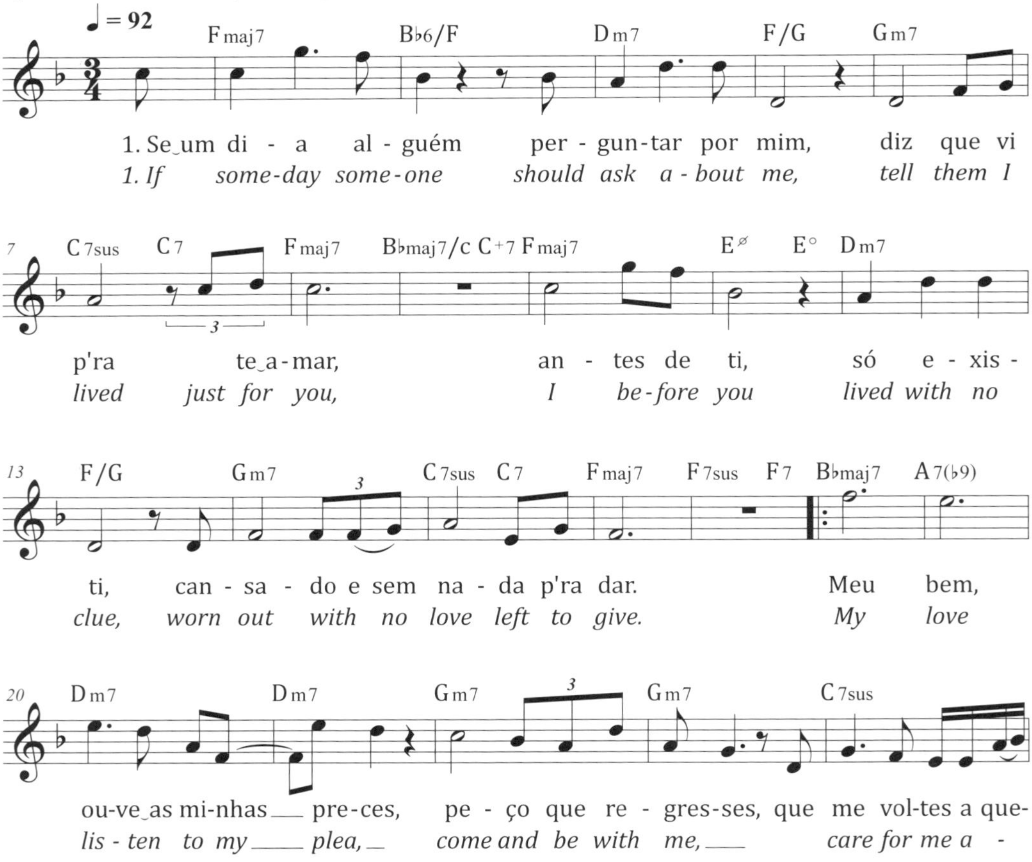

1. Se um di - a   al - guém   per - gun - tar por mim,   diz que vi
1. If   some-day some-one   should ask a - bout me,   tell them I

p'ra   te a - mar,   an - tes de ti,   só   e - xis -
lived   just for you,   I   be-fore you   lived with no

ti,   can - sa - do e sem na - da p'ra dar.   Meu   bem,
clue, worn out   with no love left to give.   My   love

ou - ve as mi - nhas ___ pre - ces,   pe - ço que re - gres-ses, que me vol-tes a que-
lis - ten to my ___ plea, ___   come and be with me, ___   care for me a -

1. Se um dia alguém perguntar por mim,
   diz que vivi para te amar,
   antes de ti, só existi,
   cansado e sem nada para dar.

   ||: Meu bem, ouve as minhas preces,
   peço que regresses,
   que me voltes a querer,
   eu sei que não se ama sozinho
   talvez, devagarinho,
   possas voltar a aprender. :||

2. Se o teu coração, não quiser ceder,
   não sentir paixão, não quiser sofrer,
   sei fazer planos do que virá depois,
   o meu coração pode amar pelos dois.

1. If someday someone should ask about me,
   tell them I lived just for you,
   I before you, lived with no clue,
   worn out with no love left to give.

   ||: My love listen to my plea,
   come and be with me,
   care for me again,
   I know that one can't love alone
   but maybe slowly though,
   you'll learn it all once more :||

2. If your heart decides not to give in,
   no passion allowed, no pain can walk in,
   no need for writing the story that's ahead,
   my heart will feel love for both hearts instead.

Translation by Luísa Sobral (2023)

Copyright © Universal Music Publishing S L. International Copyright Secured. All Rights Reserved.
Reprinted by permission of Hal Leonard Europe Ltd.

LOVE SONGS   SLOVAKIA

42
Vyznanie
Confession

"Vyznanie" – Confession – was written in 1979 for the acclaimed singer Marika Gombitová (b. 1956). Her interpretation was awarded both domestically, for instance Bratislava's Silver Lyre and abroad (Sopot International Song festival in Poland). The song's popularity in Slovakia has continued without interruption until now: prior to being selected for the EU Songbook, its fame was affirmed when the song received the majority of votes in the final round of the musical TV show "Hit storočia" (Hit of the Century), broadcasted by Slovak television in December 2007. A dramatic transformation happens in the song when minor shifts to major and destiny and despair transforms to freedom and hope: "Bring back the tomorrows".

By Dr. Eva Čunderlíková, Slovak Music Teacher Association, AUHS/Academy of Music Bratislava, VŠMU

Lyrics: Kamil Peteraj (1945-)   Music: Janko Lehotský (1947-)

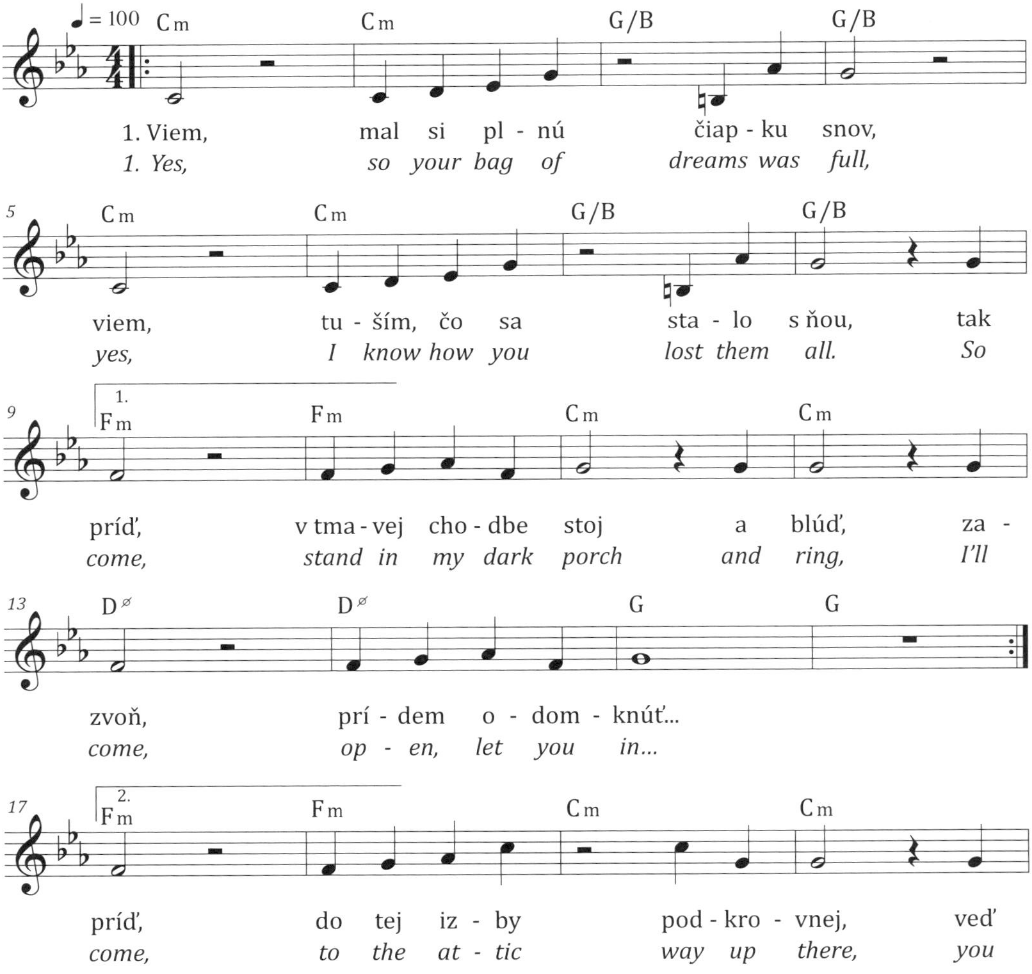

1. Viem, mal si pl - nú čiap - ku snov,
1. Yes, so your bag of dreams was full,

viem, tu - ším, čo sa sta - lo s ňou, tak
yes, I know how you lost them all. So

prídʼ, v tma - vej cho - dbe stoj a blúdʼ, za -
come, stand in my dark porch and ring, I'll

zvoň, prí - dem o - dom - knúť...
come, op - en, let you in...

prídʼ, do tej iz - by pod - kro - vnej, vedʼ
come, to the at - tic way up there, you

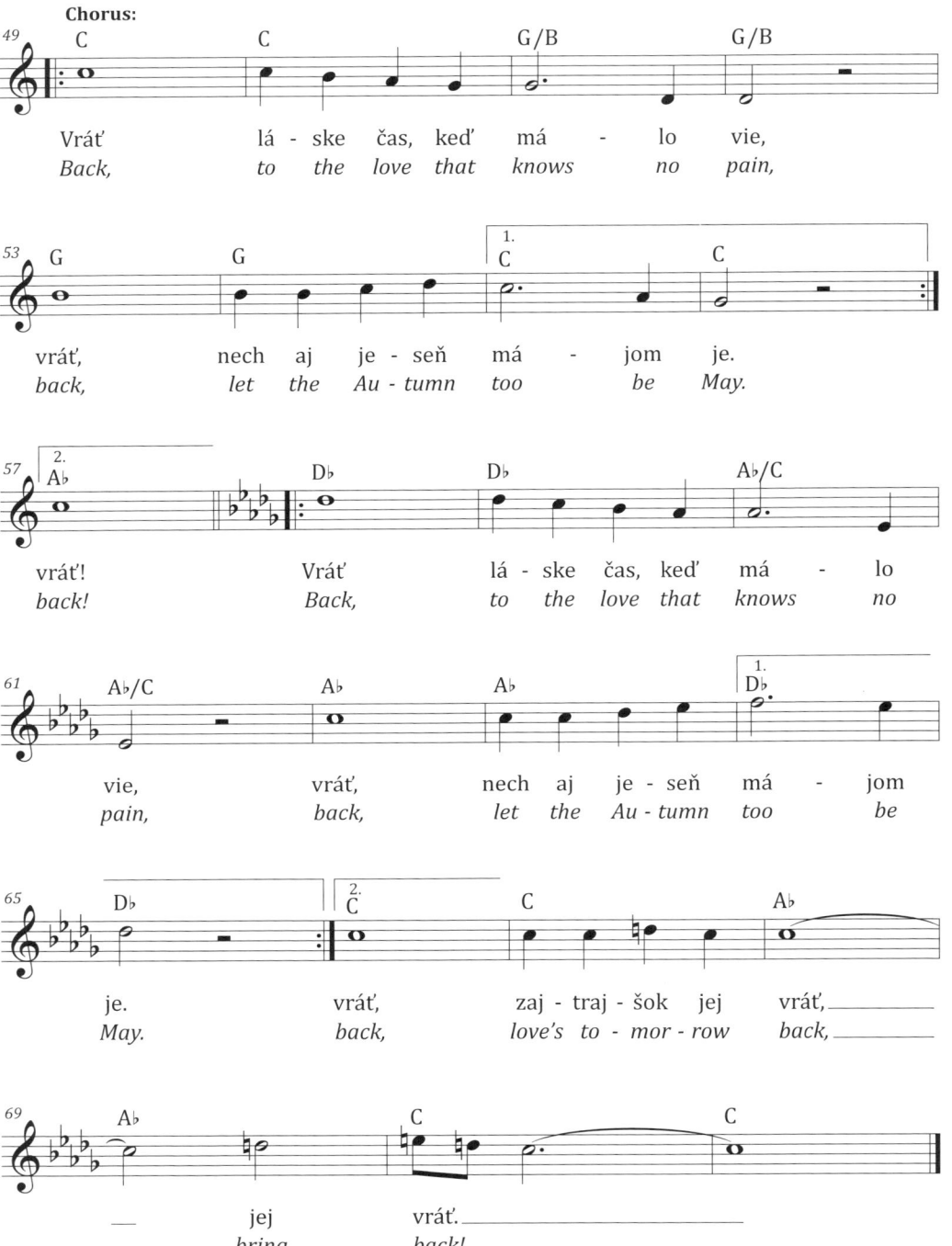

1. Viem, mal si plnú čiapku snov,
   viem, tuším, čo sa stalo s ňou,
   tak príď, v tmavej chodbe stoj a blúď,
   zazvoň, prídem odomknúť...

2. Príď, klavír spí tu pod prachom,
   príď, zahraj mne a oblakom,
   tak príď, do tej izby podkrovnej,
   veď vieš, vyhnali sme lásku z nej.
   Tsratená v púpavách
   stála som tam raz.

3. Seď, seď a do tmy niečo hraj,
   šum letnej lásky privolaj,
   tak hraj o kvitnutí púpav tých,
   raz, raz a navždy sfúknutých.

4. (Drvá polovica slohy
   instrumenta'lma)

   Tak príď, do tej izby podkrovnej,
   veď vieš, vyhnali sme lásku z nej.

Chorus:
   Vráť láske čas, keď málo vie,
   vráť, nech aj jeseň májom je.
   Vráť, nepočítaj týždne strát,
   vráť, zajtrajšok jej vráť!

   Vráť láske čas, keď málo vie,
   vráť, nech aj jeseň májom je.
   Vráť, nepočítaj týždne strát,
   vráť, zajtrajšok jej vráť,
   zajtrajšok jej vráť,
   zajtrajšok jej vráť,
   jej vráť.

1. Yes, so your bag of dreams was full,
   yes, I know how you lost them all.
   So come, stand in my dark porch and ring,
   I'll come, open, let you in…

2. Come, the piano's in a dusty shroud,
   come, play for me and for the clouds,
   so come, to the attic way up there,
   you know, we drove love out in despair,
   to dandelion land,
   where I used to stand.

3. Sit, sit, play something for the gloom,
   call up that love in summer bloom,
   play dandelion blossoms, play,
   here, there, forever blown away!

4. *(The first half of the verse
   instrumental)*

   So come, to the attic way up there,
   you know, we drove love out in despair.

Chorus:
   Back, to the love that knows no pain,
   back, let the Autumn too be May.
   Back, do not count the weeks of lack,
   back, bring tomorrow back!

   Back, to the love that knows no pain,
   back, let the Autumn too be May.
   Back, do not count the weeks of lack,
   back, bring tomorrow back,
   love's tomorrow back,
   love's tomorrow back,
   bring back!

   Translation by John Minahane (2022)

LOVE SONGS   ROMANIA

43
Ce bine că ești
How Lovely You're Here

The musical composition "Ce bine că ești" (How lovely you're here) by Nicu Alifantis (born 1954), is based on the poem by the same title written by Nichita Stănescu (1933-83), one of the most important Romanian poets (nominated for the Nobel Prize in 1980). The love poem, written by the new modernist creator, found its perfect musical match in the melody and chords of Nicu Alifantis, which is why Romanians so selfevidently find this song to be one of their most beloved love songs.

By Alexandra Belibou, Lecturer PhD, Faculty of Music, Transilvania University of Brașov

Lyrics: Nichita Stănescu (1933-83)   Music: Nicu Alifantis (1954-)

1. Du-mă, fericire-n sus, izbește-mi tâmpla de stele, lumea mea prelungă și în nesfârșire se face coloană sau altceva, mult mai înalt și mult mai curând, mult mai înalt și mult mai curând.

1. Happiness takes me up high, knocks me out with the stars, beautiful, unending gift of life twirls into a column or something, much higher up and much sooner too, much higher up and much sooner too.

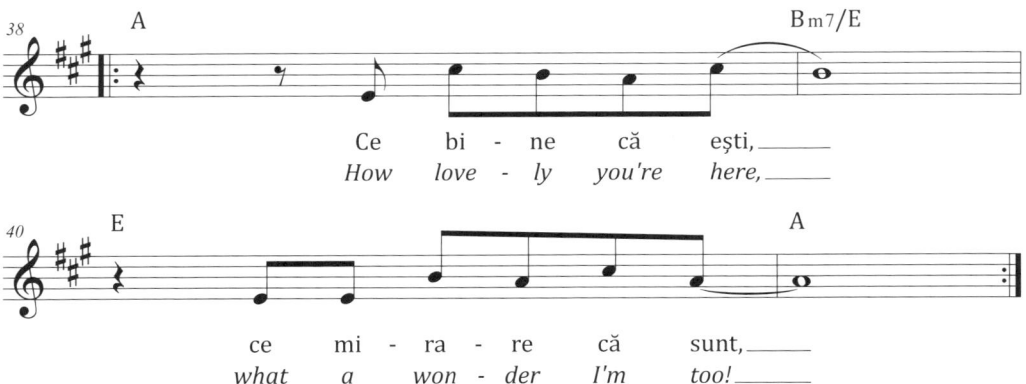

1. Du-mă, fericire'n sus, izbește-mi
   tâmpla de stele,
   lumea mea prelungă și în nesfârșire
   se face coloană sau altceva,
   mult mai înalt și mult mai curând,
   mult mai înalt și mult mai curând.

Chorus:
   Ce bine că ești,
   ce mirare că sunt!
   Două cântece diferite,
   lovindu-se, amestecându-se,
   două culori ce nu s'au văzut niciodată,
   una foarte de jos, întoarsă spre pământ,
   una foarte de sus, aproape ruptă
   în înfrigurata neasemuită luptă
   a minunii că ești,
   a'ntâmplării că sunt.

   ||: Ce bine că ești,
   ce mirare că sunt :||

1. *Happiness takes me up high,*
   knocks me out with the stars,
   beautiful, unending gift of life
   twirls in to a column or something,
   much higher up and much sooner too,
   much higher up and much sooner too.

Chorus:
   How lovely you're here,
   what a wonder I'm too!
   Different couple of tunes
   coming together in harmonies,
   two shades of paint, no one ever seen before,
   one so deep down on the ground,
   and the other, high, one with the light,
   in this crazy twisted unbelievable life.
   I'm so glad that you're here,
   what a wonder I'm too.

   ||: *How lovely you're here,*
   what a wonder I'm too. :||

Translation by Beck Corlan & Alex Szollo (2022)

Copyright © the authors. International copyright secured. All rights reserved. Reprinted by permission

LOVE SONGS HUNGARY

44
Tavaszi szél
Swelling Breezes

It was right 90 years ago, that Sándor Veress (1907-92) composer and collector of folk songs registered this melody in Bogdánfalva, Transylvania. Through the years, it became one of the most well-known love-songs in Hungary. The lyrics evoke the ancient world of „flower songs": the pleasure and delight of free-chosen spouse as well as the rude awakening of a loveless marriage. "Virágom, virágom" means "My flower, my Flower" = my sweetheart! The spring wind makes the waters flow, all the birds choose a mate. "Whom should I choose then? I choose you and you me". The green ribbon ("Zöld pántlika" appearing as "flowing aprons") is a light garment, as the wind blows it playfully. But the bride's veil is burdensome, as sorrow rends it.

By Ágnes C. Szalai, called by the National Association of Hungarian Choirs and Orchestras, KÓTA

Lyrics: folk poem　　　　　　　　　　　　　　　　　　　　　　　Music: folk song

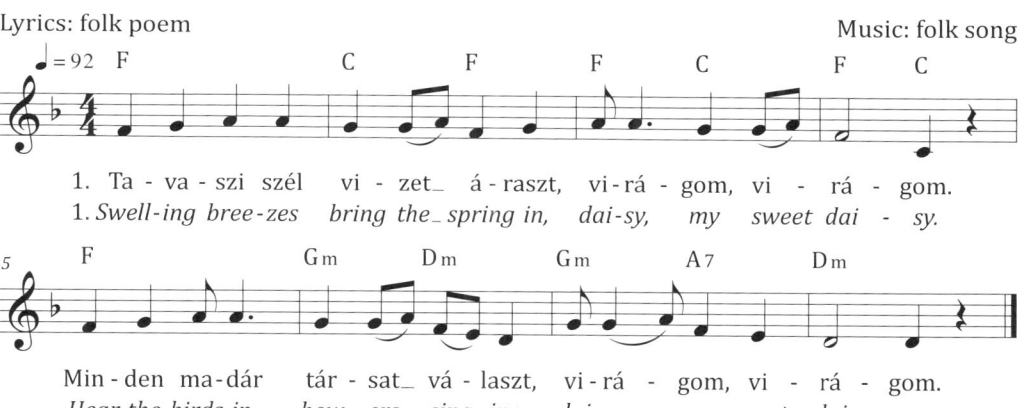

1. Tavaszi szél vizet áraszt,
   virágom, virágom.
   Minden madár társat választ,
   virágom, virágom.

2. Hát én immár kit válasszak,
   virágom, virágom.
   Te engemet, én tégedet,
   virágom, virágom.

3. Zöld pántlika, könnyű gúnya,
   Virágom, virágom.
   Mert azt a szél könnyen fújja,
   Virágom, virágom.

4. De a fátyol nehéz ruha,
   Virágom, virágom,
   Mert azt a bú leszaggatja,
   Virágom, virágom.

1. *Swelling breezes bring the spring in,*
   daisy, my sweet daisy.
   Hear the birds in bowers singing,
   daisy, my sweet daisy.

2. *Will you choose me, early-blooming*
   daisy, my sweet daisy?
   You're the one whom I'll be choosing,
   daisy, my sweet daisy.

3. *I've been wearing flowing aprons,*
   daisy, my sweet daisy,
   lightly danced and laughed at matrons,
   daisy, my sweet daisy.

4. *But this white gown, come tomorrow*
   - daisy, my sweet daisy -
   will be weighed down by my sorrow,
   daisy, my sweet daisy.

Translation by Imre Olivér Horváth (2021)

LOVE SONGS   SPAIN

45
Si tú no estás aquí
If You're Apart From Me

This song by Rosana Arbelo from 1996 is not just a love song, but rather a grieving for the absence of the beloved person that would render life inconceivable. Paradise would turn into hell and even the air she breathes and the beat of her heart would become meaningless. Despite this agony, the song does not convey sadness, but rather the intention to rebel against the grief which the loss of the lover would produce; hence Rosana addresses the lover directly, who bears the burden for everything that would happen "If you are not here ..."

By Julio Muñoz & Maria del Carmen García Jiménez, Escuela Superior de Canto de Madrid, ESCM

Lyrics: Rosana Arbelo Gopar (1963-)   Music: Rosana Arbelo Gopar (1963-)

1. No quie-ro_es-tar sin ti. Si tú no_es-tás a-quí me so-bra_el ai-re. No quie-ro_es-tar a-sí. Si tú no_es-tás la gen-te se_ha-ce na-die.

1. I just be-long with you If you're a-part from me I don't care for breath-ing Don't want to feel this blue. If you're a-part there is no-one ap-pear-ing.

Chorus: Si tú no_es-tás a-quí no sé
If you're a-part there is no more

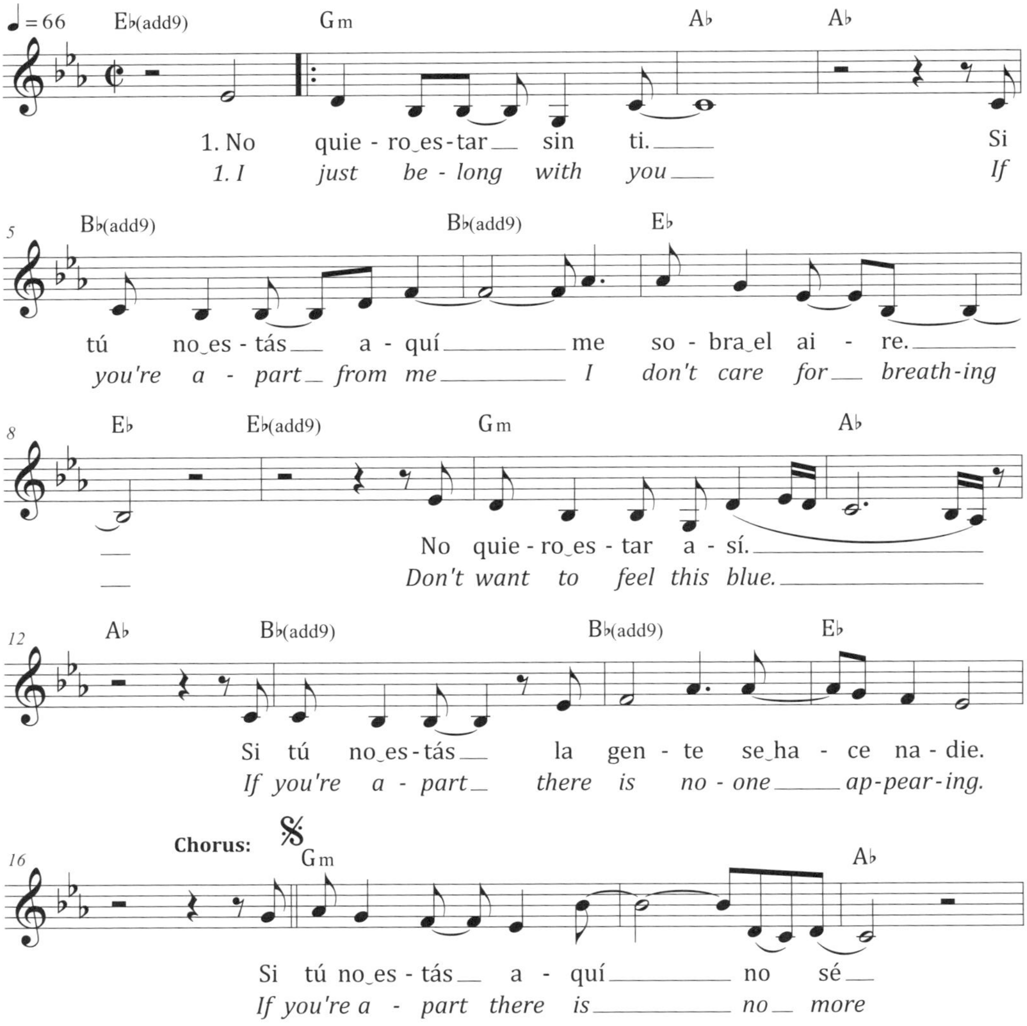

Si tú no_es-tás a - quí.___
If you're a - part from me.___

1.
No quiero estar sin ti.
Si tú no estás aquí me sobra el aire.
No quiero estar así.
Si tú no estás la gente se hace nadie.

Chorus:
Si tú no estás aquí no sé
qué diablos hago amándote.
Si tú no estás aquí sabrás
que dios no va a entender por qué te vas.

2.
No quiero estar sin ti.
Si tú no estás aquí me falta el sueño.
No quiero andar así,
latiendo un corazón de amor sin dueño.

Chorus:
Si tú no estás...

Bridge:
Derramaré mis sueños
si algún día no te tengo.
Lo más grande se hará lo más pequeño.
Pasaré un cielo
        sin estrellas esta vez,
tratando de entender quién hizo
un infierno el paraíso.

No te vayas nunca porque no,
no puedo estar sin ti.
Si tú no estás aquí me quema el aire.

Chorus:
Si tú no estás aquí no sé
qué diablos hago amándote.
Si tú no estás aquí sabrás
que dios no va a entender por qué te vas.

Si tú no estás aquí no sé
qué diablos hago amándote.
Si tú no estás aquí sabrás
que dios no va a entender por qué te vas.

Si tú no estás aquí.

1.
I just belong with you.
If you're apart from me, I don't care for breathing.
Don't wanna feel this blue.
If you're apart, there is no one appearing.

Chorus:
If you're apart, there is no more
hale reasons I should love you so.
If you're apart, you just should know
that even God would ask why you just go.

2.
I just belong with you,
if you're apart from me, I lose my dreaming.
Don't wanna feel this fool,
standing by a love with no returning.

Chorus:
If you're apart, there is no more...

Bridge:
I'll cry out all my illusions
if someday I become lonely.
The big thing will turn out to be just no thing.
I'll walk around on such
        a devastated firmament this time
and wonder who could make a hell from
such a beautifull horizon.

Don't you ever leave 'cause
darling I just belong with you.
If you're apart from me, the air is burning.

Chorus:
If you're apart, there is no more
hale reasons I should love you so.
If you're apart, you just should know
that even God would ask why you just go.

If you're apart, there is no more
hale reasons I should love you so.
If you're apart, you just should know
that even God would ask why you just go.

If you're apart from me.

Translation by Concepción A. Monje Micharet (2013)

Copyright © Sony Music France S A. International Copyright Secured. All Rights Reserved.
Reprinted by permission of Hal Leonard Europe Ltd.

LOVE SONGS   LUXEMBOURG

46
Hey Du
Hey You

A cherised love-song by Luxembourg's most popular rock band of the last 40 years, Cool Feet, founded in 1968. At first Cool Feet sang in English, but since 1980 they solely published music with Luxembourgish lyrics. This song stormed the local charts in the 1980s and has had a solid following ever since.

By Robert Köller, Union Grand-Duc Adolphe, UGDA

Lyrics: Romain Bernard & Cool Feet   Music: Romain Bernard & Cool Feet

1. Hey du, ech muss dir dat e lo soen, Hey du, ech hu laang op dech ge waart, Hey du, loss ni di Zäit ver go en, Hey du, ou ni dech dat wier sou haart. Ech wëll ëm-merbei dir sinn, mat dier maa'n ech meng

1. Hey you, this is the thing to say now, Hey you, I have want-ed you so long, Hey you, don't let time slip a-way now, Hey you, with-out you I feel so wrong. Let me al-ways be with you, and plan my life with

1. Hey du, ech muss dir dat e lo soen,
   Hey du, ech hu laang op dech ge waart,
   Hey du, loss ni di Zaït ver go en,
   Hey du, ou ni dech dat wier sou haart.
   Ech wëll ëmmer bei dir sinn,
   mat dier maa'n ech meng Pläng
   Hey du, loossen dech ni e leng.

2. Hey du, du an ech dat muss dach lafen,
   Hey du, doraus ass nach vill ze maa'n
   Hey du, du däerf Gefiller ni verkafen,
   Hey du, du an ech dat hält nach laang.
   Ech wëll ëmmer bei dir sinn,
   sou laang d'Gefiller reng:
   Hey du, ech loossen dech ni e leng.

   (Instrumental - guitar solo)
   Ech wëll ëmmer bei dir sinn,
   sou laang d'Gefiller reng:
   Hey du, ech loossen dech ni e leng.

3. Hey du, sollt och de Stär mol falen,
   Hey du, dat kann net wierklech sinn,
   Hey du, sollt och déi Bréck net halen.
   Gleef mir, de Wee gëllt dee mir ginn.
   Ech wëll ëmmer bei dir sinn,
   ech brauch déi Kraaft vun dir:
   Hey du, ech kéint dat ni verstoen.
   Hey du, ech kéint dat ni verstoen.

1. Hey you, this is the thing to say now,
   hey you, I have wanted you so long,
   hey you, don't let time slip away now,
   hey you, without you I feel so wrong.
   Let me always be with you,
   and plan my life with you,
   hey you, I'll never become untrue.

2. Hey you, you and I must get things started,
   hey you, there is so much still to do,
   hey you, I know deep down you're tender-hearted,
   hey you, you and I will see this through.
   Let me always be with you,
   if you feel as I do,
   hey you, I'll never become untrue.

   (Instrumental - guitar solo)
   Let me always be with you,
   if you feel as I do,
   hey you, I'll never become untrue.

3. Hey you, if stars to earth should tumble,
   hey you, it can't be really so,
   hey you, if that red bridge should crumble,
   trust me, this is the road to go.
   Let me always be with you,
   just hold you by the hand:
   Hey you, I'll never understand.
   Hey you, I'll never understand.

Translation by Edward Seymour (2021)

Copyright © the author. International copyright secured. All rights reserved. Reprinted by permission

LOVE SONGS   THE NETHERLANDS

47
Mag Ik Dan Bij Jou
Can I Be With You

"Cay I Be With You", from 2009, received nationwide recognition when Dutch cabaret singer Claudia de Breij performed it in a television broadcast in response to the fatal ski accident of the Dutch Prince Johan Friso, who at 44 died from his head injuries after an avalanche. The prince, who gave up his claim to the throne in order to marry against the wish of the government, was survived by two daughters. Since then the song got embraced by the Dutch as a song of comfort when in grief.

By Lieuwe Noordam, Prins Claus Conservatorium, Groningen,
& Christiane Nieuwmeijer, Leiden University of Applied Sciences

Lyrics: Claudia de Breij (1975) Music: Rogier Wagenaar (1946-) & Sander Geboers (1977-)

1. Als de oor-log komt, en als ik dan moet schui-len,
1. When the war breaks out and if I need to shel-ter,

mag ik dan bij jou? Als er een club-je komt, waar
can I be with you? And if they start a club that

ik niet bij wil ho-ren, mag ik dan bij jou? Als
I would hate to be in, can I be with you? And

er een re-gel komt, waar ik niet aan vol-doen kan,
if some rule is made that I can ne-ver play by,

mag ik dan bij jou? En als ik iets moet zijn,
can I be with you? And if my role must be,

1. Als de oorlog komt,
   en als ik dan moet schuilen,
   mag ik dan bij jou?
   Als er een clubje komt,
   waar ik niet bij wil horen,
   mag ik dan bij jou?
   Als er een regel komt,
   waar ik niet aan voldoen kan,
   mag ik dan bij jou?
   En als ik iets moet zijn,
   wat ik nooit geweest ben,
   mag ik dan bij jou?

   Refrein:
   Mag ik dan bij jou schuilen,
   als het nergens anders kan?
   En als ik moet huilen,
   droog jij m'n tranen dan?
   Want als ik bij jou mag,
   mag jij altijd bij mij,
   kom wanneer je wilt,
   'k hou een kamer voor je vrij.

1. When the war breaks out
   and if I need to shelter,
   can I be with you?
   And if they start a club
   that I would hate to be in,
   can I be with you?
   And if some rule is made
   that I can never play by,
   can I be with you?
   And if my role must be
   what I have never been,
   can I be with you?

   Chorus:
   Will you then be my shelter,
   if there's nowhere else to be?
   And when I have to cry,
   wll you then comfort me?
   For if I am with you,
   you can always be with me.
   Come whene'er you want,
   here's a place for you to be.

2. Als het onweer komt,
   en als ik dan bang ben,
   mag ik dan bij jou?
   Als de avond valt,
   en 't is mij te donker,
   mag ik dan bij jou?
   Als de lente komt,
   en als ik dan verliefd ben,
   mag ik dan bij jou?
   Als de liefde komt,
   en ik weet het zeker,
   mag ik dan bij jou?

   Refrein:
   ||: Mag ik dan bij jou schuilen... :||

3. Als het einde komt,
   en als ik dan bang ben,
   mag ik dan bij jou?
   Als het einde komt,
   en als ik dan alleen ben,
   mag ik dan bij jou?

2. *When the storm breaks out
   and if I'm afraid then,
   can I be with you?
   When the evening falls
   and the dark weighs on me,
   can I be with you?
   When the spring arrives
   and if I fall in love then
   can I be with you?
   If our love then grows
   and I know for certain,
   can I be with you?*

   Chorus:
   ||:*Will you then be my shelter...* :||

3. *When the end is near
   and if I'm afraid then,
   can I be with you?
   When the end is near
   and if I'm all alone then,
   can I be with you?*

   Translation by Arnold Mühren (2021)

LOVE SONGS   AUSTRIA

48
Weit, weit Weg
Far Away

With his mix of rock music and elements of traditional folkmusic, Austrian singer-songwriter and world musician Hubert von Goisern has become a prominent exponent of the so-called New Volksmusik and Alpine Rock in Austria, Switzerland and Germany. Born in Bad Goisern in Upper Austria, his stage name "von Goisern" refers to his home town. Hubert von Goisen brings not only traditional Austrian instruments like the Steirische Harmonika (a kind of accordian) into his music, but also instruments from around the world. Hubert von Goisern has been awarded several national and international awards, recently an Amadeus Austrian Music Lifetime Achievement Award in 2024. 'Weit, weit Weg' from 1992 is both a rock ballad full of longing and at the same time quintessentially alpine. The great mountains and the changing seasons serve as a backdrop to descriptions of a great love now distant. Longing and hope resonate in the insurmountable vastness of the Alps.

By Dr. Sarah Weiss, Kunstuniversität Graz

Lyrics & Music: Hubert von Goisern

1. Jetzt sind die tåg schon kür-zer word'n und blat-tln fålln a von die bäum und auf-'m al-ma-så-tl liegt schon schnee,___ a kal-ter wind weht von die berg, die sonn is a___ schon un-ter-gan-gen

1. The days are grow-ing short-er now, the leaves are fall-ing from the trees and snow has fall-en on the moun-tain slopes,___ there's a cold wind blow-ing now, the sun went down a while a-go___

1.
Jetzt sind die tåg schon kürzer word'n
und blattln fålln a von die bäum
und auf'm almasatl liegt schon schnee,

a kalter wind weht von die berg
die sonn is a schon untergangen
und ich hätt di gern in meiner näh.

Chorus:
||: Jetzt bist so weit, weit weg
so weit, weit weg von mir :||
des tuat mir schia und wie.

2.
Du warst wie der sommerwind
der einifahrt in meine haar
als wia a warmer regen auf der haut,

i riech noch deine nassen haar
i spür noch deine händ im g'sicht
und wie du mir ganz tief in d'augen schaust.

Chorus:
Jetzt bist so weit, weit weg...

1.
The days are growing shorter now
the leaves are falling from the trees
and snow has fallen on the mountain slopes,

there's a cold wind blowing now
the sun went down a while ago
and I wish I had you close to me.

Chorus:
||: Now you're so far away,
so far away from me :||
the pain I feel won't leave.

2.
You were like the summer wind
blowing gently through my hair
like warm raindrops falling on my skin,

I can smell your dampened hair,
I feel your hand touching my face
the way you look so deep into my eyes.

Chorus:
Now you're so far away...

3.
Jetzt is bald ein monat her
daß mir uns nach g'halten håbn
und in unsere arm versunken san,

manchmal ist's mir gestern wars
und manchmal wia a ewigkeit
und manchmal håb i angst es war a traum.

Chorus:

Jetzt bist so weit, weit weg...

3.
Soon it will have been a month
since we held each other tight
embracing and forgetting the whole world,

sometimes it's like yesterday
and sometimes like eternity
and sometimes I'm afraid it was a dream.

Chorus:

Now you're so far away...

Translation by Alicia Edelweiss (2024)

LOVE SONGS   BULGARIA

49
Светът е за двама
The World Is for Two

This song, with lyrics by Dimitar Tochev (1930-2006) and music by Maria Neykova (1945-2002), is one of the most striking, emblematic examples of Bulgarian pop music from the '80s. From its debut to the present day it has emotionally captivated a wide audience among all age groups. Subject to lyricism and nostalgia, Neykova is the author of hundreds of works in the Bulgarian popular music: "The World Is for Two" remains as her artistic signature. By managing to give life to both words and melody Orlin Goranov, the beloved Bulgarian singer of both pop and opera, made the song an emblem of his life's work.

By Dr. Jean Pehlivanov, Academy of Music Dance and Fine Arts, Plovdiv, AMDFA

Lyrics: Dimitar Tochev (1930-2006)   Music: Maria Neikova (1945-2002)

1. Не заспивай, когато умират звезди, Не заспивай светът е за двама. Уморен той безсънно за теб ще следи, даже мен даже мен да ме няма. Не сънувай прегръдките нежни на друг,

1. Stay awake when the starlight is starting to fade, stay awake the World is for two hearts. It'll watch over you now so don't be afraid, even when, when I'm gone to the bright stars. Don't go dreaming of somebody's warm tender arms, don't go

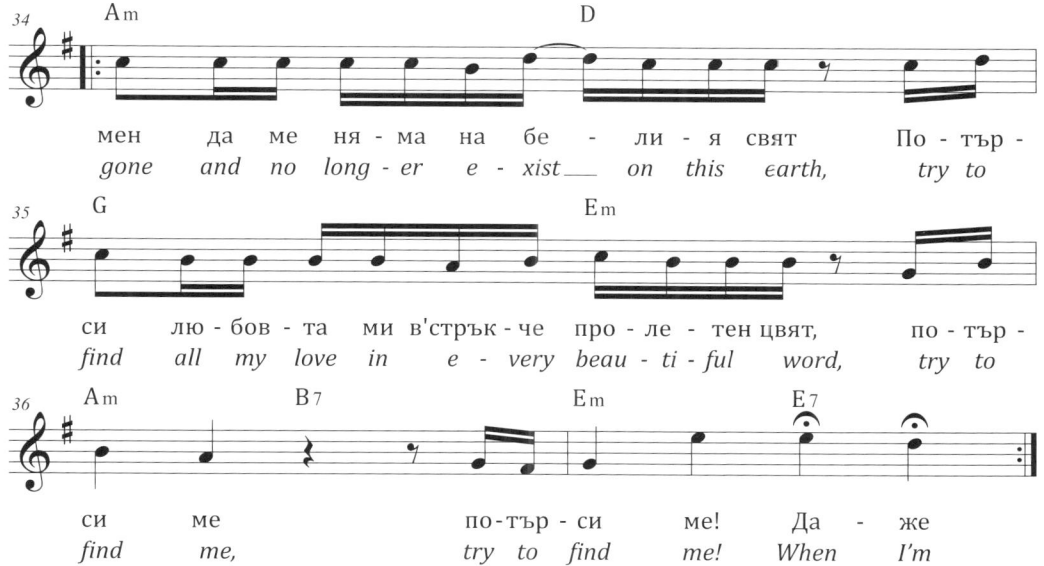

1. Не заспивай, когато умират звезди
   Не заспивай светът е за двама.
   Уморен той безсънно за теб ще следи
   Даже мен, даже мен да ме няма.

   Не сънувай прегръдките нежни
                              на друг,
   Не сънувай, светът е за двама.
   Ще те сгрее морето
                   на топлия юг,
   Даже мен, даже мен да ме няма.

Припев:
   ||: Даже мен да ме няма на белия свят
   Потърси любовта ми
   в стръкче пролетен цвят,
   потърси ме, потърси ме! :||

2. Не посрещай зората без обич за мен,
   Не посрещай светът е за двама.
   Пак ще грее в очите ти приказен ден,
   Даже мен, Даже мен да ме няма.

   Не обиквай ти друг даже сетила зов,
   Не обичай, светът е за двама.
   Ще те грее пак моята нежна любов,
   Даже мен, Даже мен да ме няма.

Припев:
   ||: Даже мен да ме няма... :||

1. Stay awake when the starlight is starting to fade,
   stay awake - the World is for two hearts.
   It will watch over you now, so don't be afraid
   even when, when I'm gone to the bright stars.

   Don't go dreaming of somebody's warm,
                                    tender arms,
   don't go dreaming - the World is for two hearts.
   The embrace of the south sea will keep you
                                         from harm,
   even when, when I'm gone to the bright stars.

Chorus:
   ||: When I'm gone and no longer exist on this earth,
   try to find all my love
   in every beautiful word,
   try to find me, try to find me! :||

2. Never welcome the daybreak with no love for me,
   never welcome - the World is for two hearts.
   And your eyes will be shining again like a dream,
   even when, when I'm gone to the bright stars.

   Show no love or affection to some other man,
   just remember - the World is for two hearts.
   All my love will be warming you gently again,
   even when, when I'm gone to the bright stars.

Chorus:
   ||: When I'm gone and no longer... :||

Translation by Desislava Sofranova (2022)

Copyright © the authors. International copyright secured. All rights reserved. Reprinted by permission

LOVE SONGS   DENMARK

50
Kvinde Min
Lady Oh Lady

'Woman of mine' (in Danish: 'Kvinde min') was released in 1975 by the iconic Danish rock group Gasolin'. The song has ever since been a most beloved song among Danish audiences. Produced by Roy Thomas Baker of Queen fame, the recording has an atmospheric yet uplifting vibe. The melody, which seems in a peculiar contrast to the many assurances of love, reflects the many obstacles – both inner and outer – that must be overcome. The lyrics are confessional and covers a wide spectrum from betrayal and suffering to submission and hope. The song has been perceived as a love song comparable to the most heartfelt songs of the traditional Danish ballad tradition.

By Henrik Marstal, Associate professor, Rhythmic Music Conservatory, RMC

Lyrics: "Gasolin" & Mogens Mogensen (1930-91)   Music: Kim Larsen (1945-2018)

1. Kvin - de min, jeg el - sker dig og jeg ved, du el - sker mig,
1. La - dy oh la - dy, I love you, I know you love me too,

og hvad der så end sker, åh, lad det ske,
and what-e-ver we have to go through, oh let us go,

for jeg er din. Og sel - om vi har
I'll be with you. I know we've had some

skænd - tes tit, og du har grædt og lidt, når
stu - pid fights and you suf - fered lone - ly nights, yes, I

det har væ - ret slemt, så glem det nu, for jeg er din.
know I've been so hard to please, for-give me, for I am yours.

1. Kvinde min, jeg elsker dig
   og jeg ved, du elsker mig,
   og hvad der så end sker,
   åh, lad det ske, for jeg er din.
   Og selvom vi har skændtes tit,
   og du har grædt og lidt,
   når det har været slemt,
   så glem det nu,
   for jeg er din.

   ...Åh, jeg har hustlet
   og spillet tosset
   og jeg har snydt dig, ja,
   og skammet mig
   og stjålet af din kærlighed,
   du ved besked,
   åh ja, åh ja
   wow-wa og ba-ba-li-åh
   og du er stadigvæk akkurat lige så smuk
   som allerførste gang da du kyssede mig
   så inderligt
   så inderligt.

2. Tror du, vi skal følges ad
   til livet det er slut,
   åh, det håber jeg
   ja, jeg gør – ja, jeg gør.
   Så kvinde, kom og drøm med mig
   i den lange nat
   når stjernerne de funkler
   og blinker som besat.

   Nej, bliv ikke bange
   for deres sange.
   Hold bare fast i mig
   når de fortæller dig,
   at der er tusinde mil
   imellem dig og mig
   Nej, nej
   åh, tro det ej
   wau-wa og ba-ba-li-åh
   og du er stadigvæk akkurat lige så smuk
   som allerførste gang, da du kyssede mig
   så inderligt
   så inderligt
   så inderligt.

1. Lady, oh lady, I love you
   I know you love me too
   and whatever we have to go through
   Oh let us go, I'll be with you
   I know we've had some stupid fights
   and you suffered lonely nights
   yes, I know I've been so hard to please
   forgive me,
   for I am yours.

   *...I've been a hustler
   and a clown
   and I've cheated you
   and let you down
   and stolen all your precious love
   I know you know,
   well oh yeah oh yeah.
   wow-wa and ba-ba-li-oh*
   and to me you're beside me just as beautiful
   as the very first day when you kissed me
   so tenderly,
   so tenderly.

2. Woman, I hope you'll stay with me
   'til the end of time,
   and I hope you'll still be mine
   when we drift away the tide.
   So lady, oh lady, won't you dream with me
   dream with me tonight
   when we speak of golden rays
   beneath the stars twinkling so bright.

   *No, don't be afraid
   of what they say,
   it's just to hold you tight
   when they ask you why
   there's a thousand miles
   between you and I,
   no, no,
   it's not so,
   wow-wa and ba-ba-li-oh*
   and to me you're beside me, just as beautiful
   as the the first day when you kissed me
   so tenderly
   so tenderly
   so tenderly.

   Translation by Mick Maloney (1976)

LOVE SONGS   FRANCE

51
Hymne à l'amour
Hymn to Love

Probably the favourite love song of French women. Edith Piaf (1903-61), a popular singer during the post-World War II period, put her emotionally charged voice at the service of a repertoire marked by love passion and the tragedies of life. When in 1949 she wrote this text dedicated to the man of her life, the boxer Marcel Cerdan (1916-49), she made him a promise of eternal love, in which she totally committed herself, body and soul. Marcel Cerdan however, died in October 1949 in a plane crash. From then on, Édith Piaf, shattered by this mourning, expressed her deep despair through this song, until her own demise in 1963.

By Jean Blanchard, Training Center for Teachers of Music, Auvergne Rhône-Alpes, CEFEDEM

Lyrics: Édith Piaf (1915-63)   Music: Marguerite Monnot (1903-61)

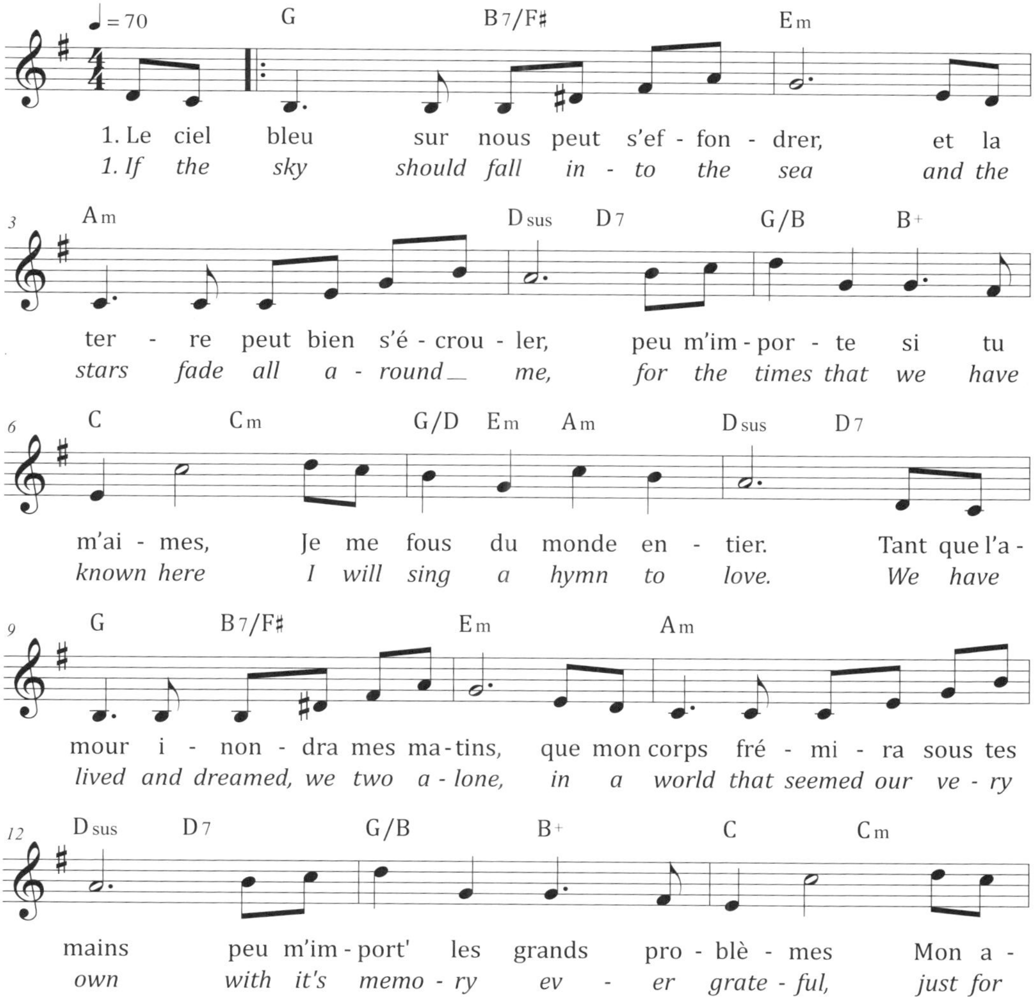

1. Le ciel bleu sur nous peut s'ef-fon-drer, et la ter-re peut bien s'é-crou-ler, peu m'im-por-te si tu m'ai-mes, Je me fous du monde en-tier. Tant que l'a-mour i-non-dra mes ma-tins, que mon corps fré-mi-ra sous tes mains peu m'im-port' les grands pro-blè-mes, Mon a-

1. *If the sky should fall in-to the sea and the stars fade all a-round me, for the times that we have known here I will sing a hymn to love. We have lived and dreamed, we two a-lone, in a world that seemed our ve-ry own with it's memo-ry ev-er grate-ful, just for*

...Dieu ré-u-nit ceux qui s'ai-ment!
He u-nites all those who loved be-fore...

1. Le ciel bleu sur nous peut s'effondrer
   Et la terre peut bien s'écrouler
   Peu m'importe si tu m'aimes
   Je me fous du monde entier
   Tant que l'amour inond'ra mes matins
   Tant que mon corps frémira sous tes mains
   Peu m'importent les problèmes
   Mon amour, puisque tu m'aimes...

   Récitatif:
   J'irais jusqu'au bout du monde
   Je me ferais teindre en blonde
   Si tu me le demandais...
   J'irais décrocher la lune
   J'irais voler la fortune
   Si tu me le demandais...
   Je renierais ma patrie
   Je renierais mes amis
   Si tu me le demandais...
   On peut bien rire de moi,
   Je ferais n'importe quoi
   Si tu me le demandais...

2. Si un jour la vie t'arrache à moi
   Si tu meurs, que tu sois loin de moi
   Peu m'importe, si tu m'aimes
   Car moi je mourrai aussi...
   Nous aurons pour nous l'éternité
   Dans le bleu de toute l'immensité
   Dans le ciel, plus de problèmes
   Mon amour, crois-tu qu'on s'aime ?...

   ... Dieu réunit ceux qui s'aiment !

1. If the sky should fall into the sea
   and the stars fade all around me,
   for the times that we have known here
   I will sing a hymn to love.
   We have lived and dreamed, we two alone
   in a world that seemed our very own
   with it's memory ever grateful,
   just for you, I'll sing a hymn to love...

   Recitation:
   I remember each embrace
   the smile that lights your face
   and my heart begins to sing...
   Your arms, the hands secure
   your eyes that said, "Be sure"
   and my heart begins to sing...

   (This strophe is not part
   of the recording)

2. If one day we had to say goodbye
   and our love should fade away and die,
   in my heart, you will remain, dear,
   and I'll sing a hymn to love.
   Those who love will live eternally
   in the blue, where all is harmony
   with my voice raised high to Heaven
   just for you, I'll sing a hymn to love.

   He unites all those who loved before...

   Translation by Eddie Constantine (1950)

Copyright © 1949 Peter Maurice Music Co. Ltd., EMI Music Publishing Ltd. and Editions Edimarton. Copyright Renewed.
All Rights Administered by Sony Music Publishing (US) LLC, 424 Church Street, Suite 1200, Nashville, TN 37219.
International Copyright Secured. All Rights Reserved. Reprinted by Permission of Hal Leonard Europe Ltd.

LOVE SONGS   ITALY

52
Almeno tu nell'universo
Flame

This love song – living outside the dimension of time – touched the whole country in 1989 where it marked the return of Mia Martini (1947-95), one of the most exciting Italian voices of all time. Written to her in 1972 by two of the greatest Italian songwriters but shelved for 17 years since it was not in tune with the zeitgeist of the era. However, the late '80s, a different decade, individualistic and materialistic, was the ideal moment for this song to surface, since it revives the heart after a exhausting race through the streets of a world gone mad in the grip of consumerism. It has both a sophisticated harmony, an extraordinary melody full of exciting intervals, a range technically difficult to sing (almost two octaves), as well as simple but deeply poetic lyrics that manages to combine personal intimacy and social context: a true masterpiece.

By Alfonso Santimone, National Academy of Jazz, Siena

Lyrics: Bruno Lauzi (1937-2006)   Music: Maurizio Fabrizio (1952 -)

che mi a-me-rai dav-ve-ro, di più, di più, di più.
warmth of your love sur-rounds me and binds my heart to you.

1. Sai, la gente è strana
   Prima si odia e poi si ama
   Cambia idea improvvisamente
   Prima la verità poi mentirà lui
   Senza serietà, come fosse niente.

2. Sai, la gente è matta
   Forse è troppo insoddisfatta
   Lei segue il mondo ciecamente
   E quando la moda cambia,
   Lei pure cambia
   Continuamente, sciocamente.

Chorus:
   Tu, tu che sei diverso
   Almeno tu nell'universo
   Un punto sei,
   che non ruota mai intorno a me
   Un sole che splende per me soltanto
   Come un diamante in mezzo al cuore.

   Tu, tu che sei diverso
   Almeno tu nell'universo
   Non cambierai
   Dimmi che per sempre sarai sincero
   E che mi amerai davvero
   Di più, di più, di più.

3. Sai, la gente è sola
   E come può lei si consola
   Ma non far sì che la mia mente
   Si perda in congetture, in paure
   Inutilmente e poi per niente.

Chorus:
   Tu, tu che sei diverso...

   Non cambierai
   Dimmi che per sempre sarai sincero
   E che mi amerai davvero
   E davvero di più.

1. Smile, a gentle feeling
   sets our love apart,
   you touch me and you're healing
   all of the hurt that's passed, the pain, that's cast
   a shadow on my heart, an echo lost in darkness...

2. Times, when I remember
   all those things I should forget,
   you come to me, and oh so tenderly
   without a single word
   my feelings stir.
   The time is right now, you ignite...

Chorus:
   The flame that becomes a fire,
   the spark that kindles my desire
   to know you're there
   and to share the moments of pain and pleasure,
   to love and to care together.
   The time is right now to ignite...

   The flame that becomes a fire,
   the spark that kindles my desire,
   this dream is real
   and I feel the strength of your arms around me,
   the warmth of your love surrounds me
   and binds my heart to you.

3. Such a gentle feeling
   the beating of my heart
   and the rhythm of your breathing
   comfort my troubled mind, now I find
   the time is right and you ignite...

Chorus:
   The flame that becomes a fire...

   To know you're there
   to share these moments of pain and pleasure,
   who cares if it lasts forever?
   The time is right and you ignite.

   Translation by Bias Boshell (1994)

Copyright © 1994 by Universal Music Publishing Ricordi Srl. International Copyright Secured. All Rights Reserved.
Reprinted by Permission of Hal Leonard Europe Ltd.

LOVE SONGS   SLOVENIA

53
Dan ljubezni
A Day of Love

In 1975, "Dan ljubezni" (A Day of Love) performed by the band Pepel in kri (Blood & Ashes), won the Opatija Festival, one of the leading Yugoslav music events. In an arrangement by Dečo Žgur (b. 1938), the song entered the Eurovision Song Contest the same year. Time didn't stop Slovenes from loving it: its message – appealing to all generations – its country music smoothness and a catchy refrain gave a spirited drive to this evergreen to serve as a hymn of the social movement with the same title since 2012 – The Day of Love (May 23), "a singing event" at different locations throughout Slovenia. The idea, as well as the song, is worth spreading around.

By Dr. Leon Stefanija, Faculty of Arts, University of Ljubljana

Lyrics: Dušan Velkavrh (1943-2016)   Music: Tadej Hrušovar (1945-2020)

1. Pu-sti ti-soč dni in ti-soč no-či, ki jih več ni, če sploh ne veš, da so kdaj bi-li. Vze-mi le en dan, ki skril si ga tja na sr-čno stran, po-za-bil ga ni-ko-li več ne boš. To je bil tvoj dan lju-be-zni, naj-le-pši dan, ki ne mi-ne ni-kdar.

1. Man-y rain-y days could make you be-lieve the sun is gone, your sun-shine world seems so far a-way. Man-y lone-ly nights could make you be-lieve that in your life, there'll nev-er be an-oth-er day of love. Day by day the world will long for a day of love that is drift-ing a-way.

Pre-chorus:

1. Pusti tisoč dni
in tisoč noči,
ki jih več ni,
če sploh ne veš,
da so kdaj bili.
Vzemi le en dan,
ki skril si ga tja
na srčno stran,
pozabil ga
nikoli več ne boš.

Pre-chorus: ||: To je bil tvoj dan ljubezni,
najlepši dan, ki ne mine nikdar.
Svet živi za dan ljubezni,
dan, ki da ti vse
in vse ti vzame.
Tega nikdar ne veš.

Chorus: Kdaj prišel
bo zate spet ta dan,
naj te upanje ne zapusti,
le zaspi,
ko jutro te zbudi
to bo ljubezni dan :||

1. *Many rainy days
could make you believe
the sun is gone,
your sunshine world
seems so far away.
Many lonely nights
could make you believe
that in your life,
there'll never be
another day of love.*

||: *Day by day the world will long for
a day of love that is drifting away.
Everybody knows we live for,
just a simple day
that we'll remember,
until the end of time.*

*Come along,
let's sing a happy song,
this will be a very special day.
Dream away,
we're bringing love your way,
this is a day of love.* :||

Copyright © the authors. International copyright secured. All rights reserved. Reprinted by permission

LOVE SONGS   CROATIA

54
Cesarica
The Queen

As from an earlier time, this striking poetry, evoking feelings of lifelong longing for an unattainable love, is written in selected Dalmatian expressions. The year after being performed for the first time at the festival for popular music "Melodies of the Croatian Adriatic" in 1993, both songwriter (Zlatan Stipišić-Gibonni), singer (Oliver Dragojević) and arranger (Stipica Kalogjera) received the esteemed Porin Music Award. Later Cesarica was named both most performed song of the decade and most successful Croatian song of all time, according to many mainly due to a distinct interpretation of Oliver Dragojević (1947-2018), who rose to the top of the Croatian music scene during his lifetime, winning not only awards but also the hearts of his audience.

By Jasenka Ostojić, professor, University of Zagreb, Music Academy

Lyrics: Zlatan Stipišić-Gibonni (1968-)

Music: Zlatan Stipišić-Gibonni (1968-)
& arr. by Stjepan Stipica Kalogjera (1934-)

1. Zlat - ni kon - ci lit - nje zo - re
1. *Gol - den threads of sum - mer dawn - ing,*

doš - li su u nje - ne dvo - re,
found the throne where she was yarn - ing,

da bi mo - ju ju - bav bu - di - li.
came to wake up my love from her sleep.

2. Svit - lo nek joj ju - bi li - ce
2. *Glo - wing like a queen on du - ty,*

li - po ka' u ce - sa - ri - ce kad je ja ne mo - gu ju - bi -
may the light ca - ress her beau - ty, 'stead of me who wants to kiss her

1. Zlatni konci litnje zore
   došli su u njene dvore,
   da bi moju jubav budili.

2. Svitlo nek joj jubi lice
   lipo ka' u cesarice
   kad je ja ne mogu jubiti.

3. Zlatna mriža njenog tila,
   dušu mi je uvatila
   da je baci nazad u more.

4. Svake noći prije zore
   dolazin u njene dvore,
   bile dvore moje pokore.

Chorus:
   Cilega života ja sam 'tija samo nju
   da do njenog srca nađem put,
   cilega života moje tilo je bez nje
   ka' cviće bez vode.

   Cilega života moje tilo je bez nje
   ka cviće bez vode,
   cilega života moje tilo je bez nje
   ka cviće bez vode.

1. Golden threads of summer dawning,
   found the throne where she was yarning,
   came to wake up my love from her sleep.

2. Glowing like a queen on duty,
   may the light caress her beauty,
   'stead of me who wants to kiss her deep.

3. Golden net rose from her body,
   caught my soul, not anybody's
   and into the deep sea it was sent.

4. Every night before the morning,
   on the shore I watch her crowning,
   on the throne of white, where I repent.

Chorus:
   All I ever wanted was for her, oh, her to stay,
   all I ever searched for was the way,
   when I live without her, oh, I always go astray,
   my heart turns into clay.

   When I live without her, oh, I always go astray,
   my heart turns into clay,
   when I live without her, oh, I always go astray,
   my heart turns into clay.

Translation by Nikola Vranić "J.R. August" (2022)

Copyright © by Croatia Records Music Publishing. Reprinted by permission of ROBA Music Publishing.
International copyright secured. All rights reserved

LOVE SONGS   LATVIA

55
Viņi dejoja vienu vasaru
They Were Dancing for One Sweet Summer

Even prior to being included in the film "Breathe Deeply" (1967), directed by Rolands Kalniņš, and later to be included in the Cannes Classics program (2018), this both tender and dreamy song gained plenty public acclaim and love: Both as winner in the festival "Liepājas dzintars" (1967), and the following 50 years via countless performances by the ensemble "Menuets", via music recordings, balls and concerts of various celebrations, home parties and quiet humming. What is love? For generations now this song has allowed everyone to think about the fragility of love and sometimes shyly tacit or unspoken words and intentions. It tells a story of two people in love – having met, but not stayed together. The fateful question never ceases to sound in their minds: "Kam tad bij' jābūt pēc tam?", – What should've been after?

By Rūta Kanteruka, president, Latvian Music Teachers' Association, LVIIMSA

Lyrics: Māris Čaklais (1940-2003)   Music: Imants Kalniņš (1941-)

[Musical score with lyrics:]

1. Vi - ņi de - jo - ja vie - nu va - sa - ru... Vi - ņi de - jo - ja vie - nu va - sa - ru... Vi - ņi de - jo - ja vie - nu va - sa - ru... Un pēc tam? Pēc tam... Ta - gad kat - rs sa - vam lik - te - nim, Ta - gad kat - rs sa - vam lik - te - nim,

1. They were danc-ing for one sweet sum - mer... They were danc-ing for one sweet sum - mer... They were danc-ing for one sweet sum - mer... And what now, what now...? And now each of them seeks their des - ti - ny, and now each of them seeks their des - ti - ny,

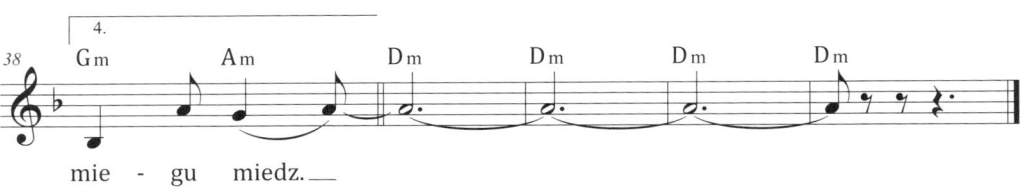

1. Viņi dejoja vienu vasaru...
   Viņi dejoja vienu vasaru...
   Viņi dejoja vienu vasaru...
   Un pēc tam? Pēc tam
   Tagad katrs savam liktenim,
   Tagad katrs savam liktenim,
   Tagad katrs savam liktenim
   prasa: Kam tad bij' jābūt "pēc tam"?

2. Viņi dejoja vienu vasaru...
   Viņi dejoja vienu vasaru...
   Viņi dejoja vienu vasaru...
   Un vēl tagad tās spuldzes skrien,
   Koku galotnēs skaties vai debesīs –
   Koku galotnēs skaties vai debesīs –
   Koku galotnēs skaties vai debesīs –
   Spuldzes skrien, zvaigznes skrien...

Chorus:
   Dienas skrien un sastājas nedēļās,
   top ik mēnesis rāmāks arvien.
   Un tad pienāk tas laiks, kad vairs nedejo
   un kad dienas kā sapītas brien.

3. Tā jau notiek – pāriet un norimst...
   Tā jau notiek – pāriet un norimst...
   Tā jau notiek – pāriet un norimst...
   Bet, kad esi palicis viens,
   Piever acis, un atkal kā toreiz –
   Piever acis, un atkal kā toreiz –
   Piever acis, un atkal kā toreiz –
   Spuldzes skrien, zvaigznes skrien.

Chorus:
   Dienas skrien un sastājas nedēļās...

4. Tā mēs katrs pa vienai vasarai...
   Tā mēs katrs pa vienai vasarai...
   Tā mēs katrs pa vienai vasarai...
   Un pēc tam jau ķīvītes kliedz.
   Kliedz kā jautājums, pārmetums, prasījums,
   Kliedz kā jautājums, pārmetums, prasījums,
   Kliedz kā jautājums, pārmetums, prasījums,
   Kamēr mūžīgu miegu miedz.

1. They were dancing for one sweet summer...
   They were dancing for one sweet summer...
   They were dancing for one sweet summer...
   And what now, what now...?
   And now each of them seeks their destiny,
   And now each of them seeks their destiny,
   And now each of them seeks their destiny,
   Asking: "what comes along for us now?"

2. They were dancing for one sweet summer...
   They were dancing for one sweet summer...
   They were dancing for one sweet summer...
   As the lights whirled away.
   In the tops of the trees and the blushing skies,
   In the tops of the trees and the blushing skies,
   In the tops of the trees and the blushing skies,
   Whirling lights, whirling stars.

Chorus:
   Days flew by, piling up into faded weeks,
   And the months turned a shadowy grey.
   Summer came to an end and the music stopped,
   All the days turned to dreary dismay.

3. That's what happens — all things vanish...
   That's what happens — all things vanish...
   That's what happens — all things vanish...
   But, when you're left alone.
   Close your eyes and go back to the summer
   Close your eyes and go back to the summer
   Close your eyes and go back to the summer
   Whirling lights, whirling stars.

Chorus:
   Days flew by, piling up into faded weeks...

4. Everybody gets one sweet summer...
   Everybody gets one sweet summer...
   Everybody gets one sweet summer...
   Till, at the last, the lapwing cries.
   Cries out questioning, raging and hungering,
   Cries out questioning, raging and hungering,
   Cries out questioning, raging and hungering,
   As eternity shuts your eyes.

Translation by Māra Walsh Sinka (2024)

Chapter III

Nature & Seasons

NATURE & SEASONS   PORTUGAL

56
Canção do Mar
Song of the Sea

If a Portuguese were asked to pick the song which best represents the 'soul' of the people, this just might be it. "Song of the Sea" was first sung in 1951 by Queen of Fado, Amália Rodrigues (1920-99), under the title "Solitude" as the main theme of "Os Amantes do Tejo" (Lovers of the River Tagus). Since then, it has probably become the most circulated Portuguese song worldwide, sung by many brilliant singers in a motley of wonderful covers in different languages. The song is a powerful interpretation of the nature of the seas along Portugal's huge Atlantic coast, their many and changing moods and conditions, from fearfully dark-blue depths and roughness to the gentle breezes and kind rippling on the surface, equating to the wide range of moods and feelings of the people.

By Manuela Encarnação & Nuno B. Mendes, Portuguese Music Teacher Association, APEM
& Jorge Alves, Association for Choirs in Lisbon, AMLC

Lyrics: Frederico de Brito (1894-1977)   Music: Ferrer Trindade (1917-99)

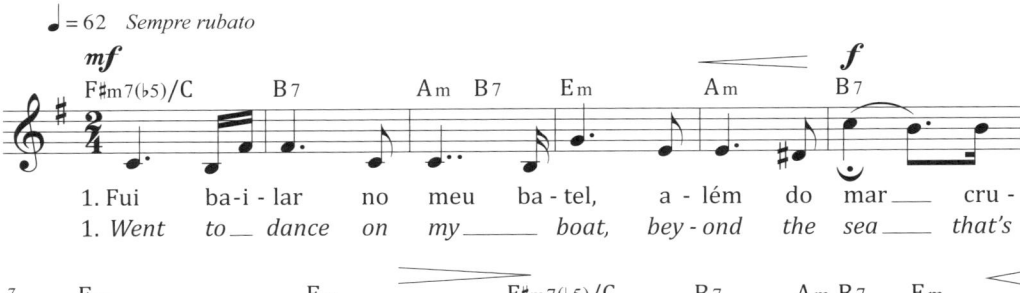

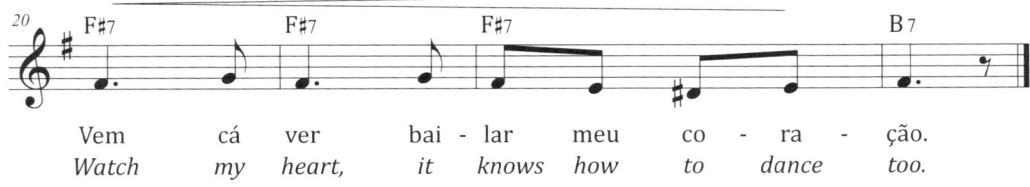

1. Fui bailar no meu batel,
   além do mar cruel
   e o mar bramindo
   diz que eu fui roubar
   a luz sem par
   do teu olhar tão lindo.

   Refrão:
   Vem saber se o mar terá razão.
   Vem cá ver bailar meu coração.

2. Se eu bailar no meu batel
   não vou ao mar cruel
   e nem lhe digo aonde eu fui cantar,
   sorrir, bailar, viver, sonhar contigo.

   Refrão:
   Vem saber se o mar terá razão.
   Vem cá ver bailar meu coração.

   Se eu bailar no meu batel
   não vou ao mar cruel
   e nem lhe digo aonde eu fui cantar,
   sorrir, bailar, viver, sonhar contigo.

1. Went to dance on my boat
   beyond the sea that's cruel,
   the sea that roars
   and says that I took away
   the light that shines
   within those eyes of beauty.

   Chorus:
   Come find out if what it says is true.
   Watch my heart, it knows how to dance too.

2. If I dance on my boat
   no cruel sea will see me
   I wont share the place where I
   went to sing, to smile, to dance, to live,
                       to dream about you.

   Chorus:
   Come find out if what it says is true.
   Watch my heart, it knows how to dance too.

   If I dance on my boat
   no cruel sea will see me,
   I wont share the place where I
   went to sing, to smile, to dance, to live,
                         to dream about you.

   Translation by Luísa Sobral (2022)

Copyright © Warner Chappell Music Spain. Reprinted by permission of Warner Chappell Music Scandinavia AB/
Notfabriken Music Publishing AB/Faber Music Ltd.

NATURE & SEASONS   ESTONIA

57
Põhjamaa ("Laul põhjamaast")
Northern Land

"Põhjamaa", Northern Land, was written in 1969 by Ülo Vinter and Enn Vetemaa as the final chorus of the musical "Pippi Longstocking", based on the rebellious children's book by Swedish Astrid Lindgren (1907-2002). In the scene of Annika and Tommy's departure their mother urges her children never to forget their home, the Nordic Lands. During Soviet occupation this spoke a symbolic truth. Henceforth the song became one of the anthems of Estonian choral music and has been repeatedly performed at the Estonian Song and Dance Celebration, one of the world's largest amateur choral events with more than 30.000 participants. The song was proposed as an Estonian National Anthem candidate.

By Kaie Tanner, president, Estonian Choral Association

Lyrics: Enn Vetemaa (1936-2007)   Music: Ülo Vinter (1924-2000)

singing heartily

1. Põh - ja - maa, me sün - ni - maa, tuul - te ja tui - su - öö - de maa, ran - ge maa ja kan - ge maa, vir - ma - lis - te maa. ma. 2. On lum - me up - pund met - sa - ta - lud, vaik - sed ta - li - teed, nii hel - lad on su ai - sa - kel - lad, lu - mel laul - vad need.

1. North - ern land, my na - tive land, land of the winds and the snow - drift nights, land of stern and land of stone, land of north - ern lights. you. 2. Sno - wy for - ests, co - sy cot - tage, si - lent win - ter road, church bells ring - ing, soft - ly sing - ing sleighs in flee - cy snow..

Fine *f*

D.S. al Fine

1. Põhjamaa, me sünnimaa,
   tuulte ja tuisuööde maa,
   range maa ja kange maa,
   virmaliste maa.

2. Põhjamaa, me sünnimaa,
   iidsete kuuselaante maa,
   lainte maa ja ranna maa,
   sind ei jäta ma.

   On lumme uppund metsatalud,
   vaiksed taliteed,
   nii hellad on su aisakellad,
   lumel laulvad need.

3. Põhjamaa, me sünnimaa,
   karmide meeste kallis maa,
   taplemiste tallermaa,
   püha kodumaa.

4. Põhjamaa, me sünnimaa,
   hinges sind ikka kannan ma,
   kaugeil teil sa kallis meil,
   sind ei jäta ma.

---

1. *Northern land, my native land,*
   land of the winds and the snowdrift nights,
   land of stern and land of stone,
   land of northern lights.

2. *Northern land, my native land,*
   land of sacred groves and woods,
   land of waves and long seastrand,
   I'm never leaving you.

   Snowy forests, cosy cottage,
   silent winter road,
   churchbells ringing, softly singing
   sleighs in fleecy snow...

3. *Northern land, my native land,*
   land of the men with heart and hand,
   who rightly fight with all their might
   for dearest fatherland.

4. *Northern land, my native land,*
   to you, my love, I'm always true –
   may I travel far and wide
   I'm never leaving you.

   Translation by Doris Kareva (2020)

NATURE & SEASONS — BULGARIA

58
Хубава си, моя горо
You Are Beautiful, My Forest

These lyrics were written on the eve before the April Uprising in 1875, the first organised attempt at liberation from the Ottomans, in a poem of the great Bulgarian writer Lyuben Karavelov. In the 1920s, the composer Georgi Goranov added melody to the lyrics, creating one of the most memorable songs of rebirth. "You Are Beautiful, My Forest" is one of the most iconic songs that speaks love for the country, represented in the image of the forest and nostalgia for past times. It is included in the repertoire of many both solo artists and choirs and has become a national anthem for Bulgarians living outside their homeland. When this song starts Bulgarians sing, cry and rejoice together.

By Dr. Jean Pehlivanov, Academy of Music Dance and Fine Arts, Plovdiv, AMDFA

Lyuben Karavelov (1834-79)   Music: Georgi Goranov (1882-1905)

1. Ху - ба - ва си, мо - я го - ро ми - ри - шеш на мла - дост, Ху - дост, Но все - ля - ваш в съ - рца - та ни са - мо скръб и жа - лост. Но - лост.

1. You are beau-ti-ful, oh my fo - rest, scen - ted like my youth-ful glow. You glow, But in - stead of joy, you bring to our hearts on - ly grief and sor - row. But - row.

1. ‖: Хубава си, моя горо
   миришеш на младост, :‖
   ‖: Но вселяваш в сърцата ни
   само скръб и жалост. :‖

2. ‖: Който веднъж те погледне
   той вечно жалее, :‖
   ‖: че не може под твоите
   сенки да изтлее. :‖

3. ‖: А комуто стане нужда
   веч да те остави, :‖
   ‖: Той не може, дорде е жив,
   да те забрави. :‖

1. ‖: *You are beautiful, oh my forest,
   scented like my youthful glow.* :‖
   ‖: *But instead of joy, you bring to our hearts
   only grief and sorrow.* :‖

2. ‖: *Who should just once take a glance at you,
   he'll grieve more than ever,* :‖
   ‖: *Deeply yearning in your shadows
   to be gone forever.* :‖

3. ‖: *When the time comes to go further,
   far away from your story,* :‖
   ‖: *Who could ever in a lifetime
   forget of your glory.* :‖

Translation by Desislava Sofranova (2023)

NATURE & SEASONS   SPAIN

59
Mediterráneo
(Mediterranean)

Water, sun, sand, salt ... the entire Mediterranean Sea embraces this song from start to finish, just as it does with the life of the singer from birth to death. Its lyrics are full of forthright poetry, reminiscent of the fragrances and the play of light familiar to anyone who has gazed at Mediterranean beaches: "I bring with me your light and your scent wherever I go". The melody is uplifting, vibrant, dramatic like that same sea "from Algeciras to Istanbul" which inspired the song. Serrat is considered one of the most important figures of popular music in both the Spanish and Catalan languages and just as this sea unites the region, so this song from 1971 has several times united voters to judge it the best song in Spain.

By Julio Muñoz & Maria del Carmen García Jiménez, Escuela Superior de Canto de Madrid, ESCM

Lyrics: Joan Manuel Serrat (1943-)   Music: Joan Manuel Serrat (1943-)

Moderato ♩ = 100

1. Qui - zas por - que mi ni - nez si - gue ju - gan-do_en tu pla - ya y_es-con - di - do tras las ca - nas duer - me mi pri - mer a - mor, lle-vo tu luz y tu_o - lor por don - de quie - ra que va - ya y_a-mon-to - na - do_en tu_a - re - na guar-do_a - mor, jue - gos y pe - nas yo...

1. May - be 'cause i'm still a kid who keeps play - ing at your wa - ters, and hid - den be - hind your reeds there my first love still beats, your light and scent come with me to wher - e - ver I tra - vel, I keep joy, games and sor - row on this sand that I bor - row.

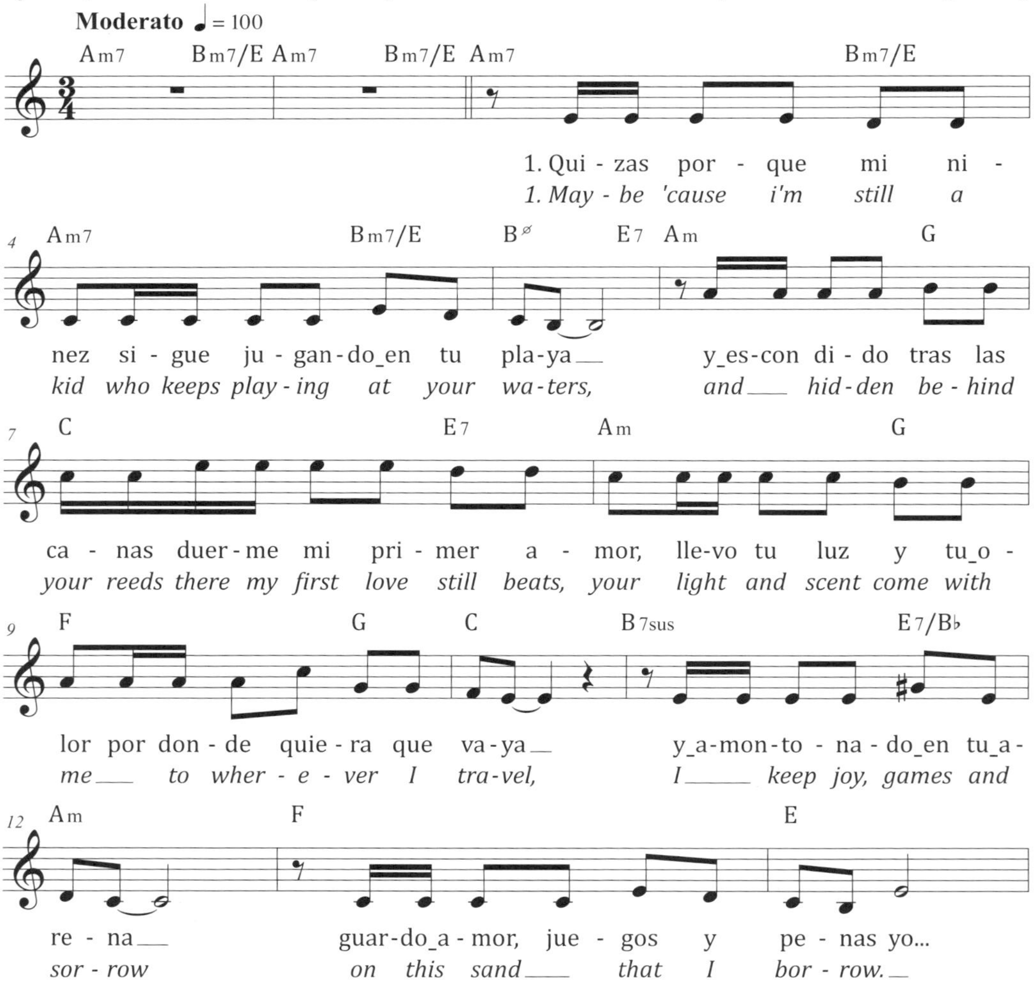

1. Quizá porque mi niñez
   sigue jugando en tu playa,
   y escondido tras las cañas
   duerme mi primer amor,
   llevo tu luz y tu olor
   por donde quiera que vaya,
   y amontonado en tu arena
   guardo amor, juegos y penas.

   Yo, que en la piel tengo el sabor
   amargo del llanto eterno,
   que han vertido en ti cien pueblos
   de Algeciras a Estambul,
   para que pintes de azul
   sus largas noches de invierno.
   A fuerza de desventuras,
   tu alma es profunda y oscura.

1. Maybe 'cause i'm still a kid
   who keeps playing at your waters,
   and hidden behind your reeds
   there my first love still beats,
   your light and scent come with me
   to wherever I travel,
   I keep joy, games and sorrow
   on this sand that I borrow.

   Bitter is the taste of my skin
   flavoured by the eternal wailing
   of those who have fallen in your seas
   from Algeciras to Istanbul,
   for you to be spreading a spark
   in their long dim winter nights.
   Forced to sail in adversity,
   your soul is a big deep dark mystery.

Chorus:
    A tus atardeceres rojos
    se acostumbraron mis ojos
    como el recodo al camino...
    Soy cantor, soy embustero,
    me gusta el juego y el vino,
    tengo alma de marinero...
    Qué le voy a hacer, si yo
    nací en el Mediterráneo,
    nací en el Mediterráneo.

2. Y te acercas, y te vas
    después de besar mi aldea.
    Jugando con la marea
    te vas, pensando en volver.
    Eres como una mujer
    perfumadita de brea
    que se añora y que se quiere,
    que se conoce y se teme.

    Si un día para mi mal
    viene a buscarme la parca,
    empujad al mar mi barca
    con un levante otoñal
    y dejad que el temporal
    desguace sus alas blancas.
    Y a mí enterradme sin duelo
    entre la playa y el cielo...

Chorus:
    En la ladera de un monte,
    más alto que el horizonte,
    quiero tener buena vista.
    Mi cuerpo será camino,
    le daré verde a los pinos
    y amarillo a la genista...
    Cerca del mar, porque yo
    nací en el Mediterráneo,
    nací en el Mediterráneo,
    nací en el Mediterráneo.

Chorus:
    Just like a bend that in the path lies
    framed are my eyes
    in your carmine skies...
    I'm a bard and I'm a liar,
    I like to drink and to gamble,
    The sea is my rolling canvas.
    What can I say if I
    was born in the mediterraneo,
    was born in the mediterraneo.

2. Swelling waters come and go
    after kissing my dear old shore.
    Playing with the tide
    you leave but you'll be back.
    Balmy tar is your smell,
    reminding me of that sweet girl
    that I long for and I love,
    who I know yet have fear of.

    And if in misfortune
    The Dark Angel comes to get me,
    push my boat into the sea,
    the autumn wind will sail she.
    The pouring rain will paint
    white curtains on the open ocean.
    Bury me between the beach and the sky
    with no crying once I die...

Chorus:
    Forever in love with the view
    from the top of the hill
    higher than the horizon.
    My blood be the stream to roam
    I'll colour the pines and the broom
    Yellow and green from my own bloom.
    Close to the sea, because I
    belong to the mediterraneo,
    belong to the mediterraneo,
    belong to the mediterraneo.

Translation by Joana Serrat (2022)

NATURE & SEASONS   CYPRUS

60
Η βρύση των Πεγειώτισσων
The Fountain of Peyia

This song – which is also a folk dance – circles around of a fountain in Peyeia, a village in the Paphos region. The fountain, built in 1907, was a meeting place for the villagers, and it was also a point of acquaintance and meetings of young people of the time. It was there that a great love was created and developed between two young people. The story of the young couple on the way became a song praising the healing powers of the water.

By Egli Spyridaki, Music Academy ARTE

Lyrics: Traditional   Music: Traditional

Moderato ♩ = 96

1. Η βρύ-ση των Πε-γειώ-τισ-σων εμ με το σιε-ντρου-βά-νι, εμ με το σιε-ντρου-βά-νι. Τζια-πό 'σιει πό-νον στην καρ-κιάν ας πα' να πκιει να γιά-νει ας πα' να πκιει να γιά-νει. Τζια-πό 'σιει πό-νον στην καρ-κιάν ας πα' να πκιει να

1. The Pe-yian wo-mens' wa-ter-spring, it has a love-ly foun-tain, it has a love-ly foun-tain. Let him who has an ache in his heart go there to drink and cure it, go there to drink and cure it. Let him who has an ache in his heart go there to drink and

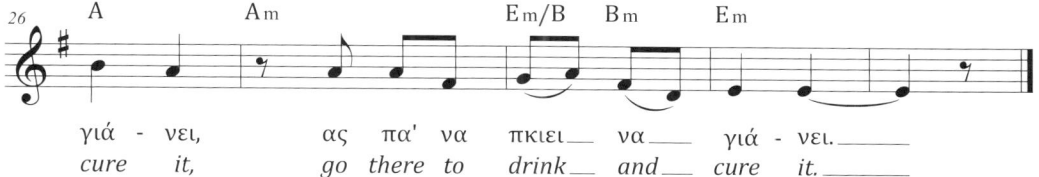

1. Η βρύση των Πεγειώτισσων
   εμ με το σιεντρουβάνι,
   εμ με το σιεντρουβάνι.
   Τζι' από 'σιει πόνον στην καρκιάν
   ας πα' να πκιει να γιάνει,
   ας πα' να πκιει να γιάνει.

2. Η βρύση των Πεγειώτισσων
   εμ με τες καμαρούες,
   εμ με τες καμαρούες,
   που πάσιν τζιαι γεμώνουσιν
   ούλλες οι Πεγειωτούες,
   όμορφες Παφιτούες.

3. Τη βρύσην των Πεγειώτισσων
   εν να την καθαρίσω,
   εν να την καθαρίσω.
   Να πάρω της αγάπης μου
   νερόν να την ποτίσω,
   νερόν να την ποτίσω.

1. The Peyian womens' waterspring,
   it has a lovely fountain,
   it has a lovely fountain.
   Let him who has an ache in his heart
   go there to drink and cure it,
   go there to drink and cure it.

2. The Peyian womens' waterspring
   is built with lovely arches,
   is built with lovely arches,
   where all young and pretty Peyian girls
   collect their water,
   all lovely Pafian lasses.

3. The Peyian womens' waterspring
   shall I go now and clean it,
   shall I go now and clean it,
   to quench the thirst of my love
   with crystal clear, purest water,
   with crystal clear, purest water.

Translated by Ayis Ioannides (2020)

NATURE & SEASONS   FRANCE

61
Le Sud
The South

This song exalts the happiness and calm of a family life, close to nature, an Eden where children and animals can live carefree lives. Nino Ferrer has placed layers of images of his Italian and New Caledonian childhood, a reference to the lost paradise of youth. The clear and calm melodic line admirably supports this tender universe, and the harmonic atmosphere refers to Nino Ferrer's passion for jazz. The many fans of this song are marked by this cosy universe, in spite of the darker end of the text, clouded by thoughts of war and misfortune.

By Jean Blanchard, Training Center for Teachers of Music, Auvergne Rhône-Alpes, CEFEDEM

Lyrics: Nino Ferrer (1934-98)   Music: Nino Ferrer (1934-98)

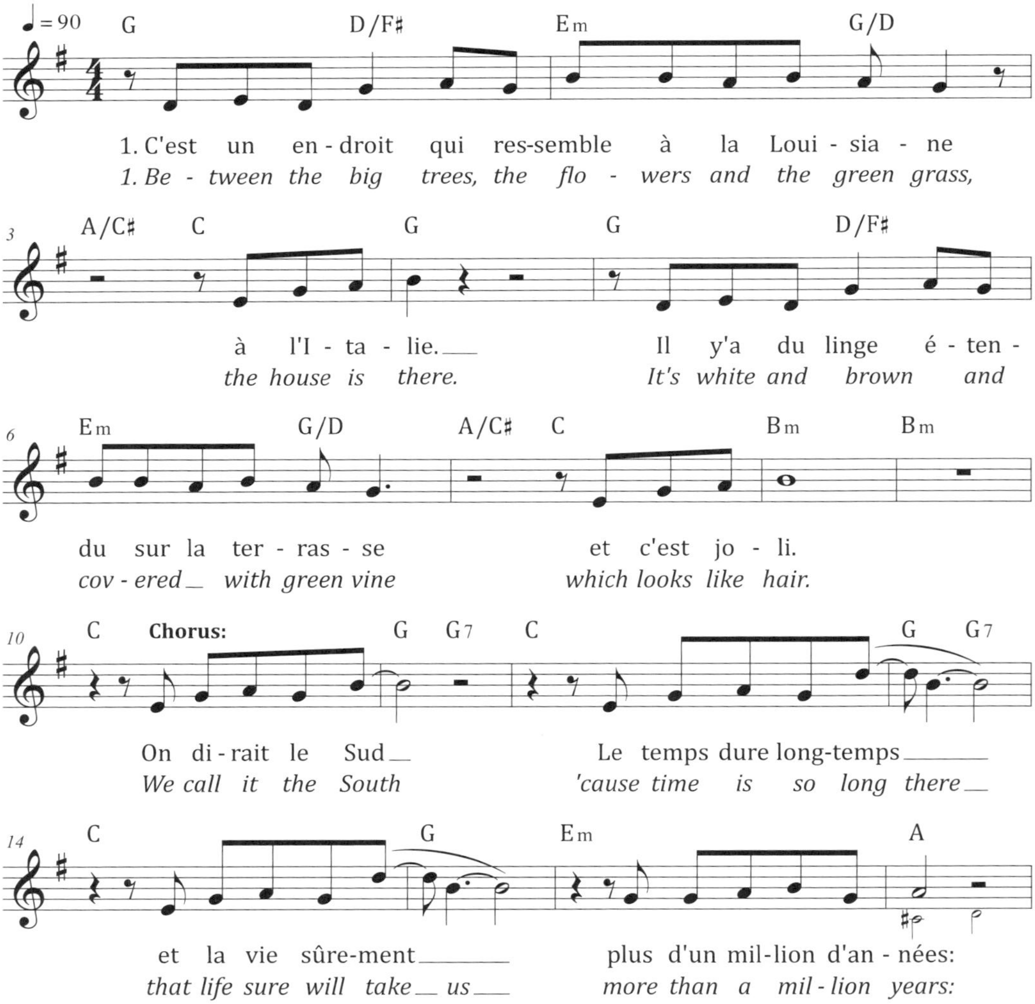

1. C'est un endroit qui ressemble à la Louisiane
   à l'Italie. Il y'a du linge étendu sur la terrasse et c'est joli.

*1. Between the big trees, the flowers and the green grass,
   the house is there. It's white and brown and covered with green vine which looks like hair.*

Chorus:
On dirait le Sud Le temps dure longtemps
et la vie sûrement plus d'un million d'années:

*We call it the South 'cause time is so long there
that life sure will take us more than a million years:*

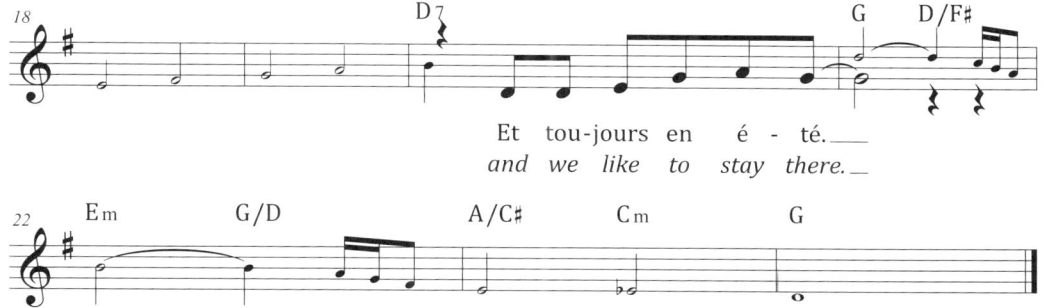

Et tou-jours en é - té.
and we like to stay there.

1. C'est un endroit
   qui ressemble à la Louisiane
   À l'Italie
   Il y a du linge étendu sur la terrasse
   Et c'est joli.

   Chorus:
   On dirait le Sud
   Le temps dure longtemps
   Et la vie sûrement
   Plus d'un million d'années:
   Et toujours en été.

2. Il y a plein d'enfants
   qui se roulent sur la pelouse
   Il y a plein de chiens
   Il y a même un chat, une tortue,
   des poissons rouges
   Il ne manque rien.

   Chorus:
   On dirait le Sud...

3. Un jour ou l'autre il faudra
   qu'il y ait la guerre
   On le sait bien
   On n'aime pas ça,
   mais on ne sait pas quoi faire
   On dit c'est le destin.

   Chorus:
   Tant pis pour le Sud
   C'était pourtant bien
   On aurait pu vivre
   Plus d'un million d'années:
   Et toujours en été.

1. Between the big trees,
   the flowers and the green grass,
   the house is there.
   It's white and brown and covered with green vine
   which looks like hair.

   Chorus:
   We call it the South,
   'cause time is so long there
   that life sure will take us
   more than a million years:
   and we like to stay there.

2. So many children
   are playing in the garden,
   so many dogs.
   There is a cat and a turtle
   and an old well
   but not a frog.

   Chorus:
   We call it the South...

3. I know one day
   I'll have to leave the sweet life
   back to the dark.
   Don't really care
   but they won't ask my opinion,
   as a matter of fact.

   Chorus:
   I hope it's the South
   'cause time is so long there
   that life sure will take us
   more than a million years:
   and we like to stay there.

Translation by Nino Ferrer (1974)

NATURE & SEASONS   HUNGARY

62
Kertész leszek
A Gardener

This lyrical song has been constantly popular for almost 50 years in Hungary, depicting the heartwarming and enviable life of a gardener, who plants and cross-breeds, waters and cherish all trees, plants and flowers, no matter whether it is an oak, rose or stinging nettle. A gardener lives a simple and pure life, setting an example for East and West (not only during the Cold War, but for all times). Why? "For when this world may meet its doom/ Let there be flowers on its tomb." The lyrics are by the one of the greatest Hungarian poets of the 20th century.

By Ágnes C. Szalai, called by the National Association of Hungarian Choirs and Orchestras, KÓTA

Lyrics: József Attila (1905-37)   Music: János Bródy (1946-)

1. Ker-tész le-szek, fát ne-ve-lek, Ke-lő nap-pal én is ke-lek.
1. A gar-de-ner – that's what I'll be, up at sun-rise, nurs-ing a tree.

Lá - lá-lá, Lá - lá-lá lá, lá - lá. Nem tö - rő - döm
Lá - lá-lá, Lá - lá-lá lá, lá - lá. I shall heed or

sem - mi más-sal, Csak a be-ol - tott vi-rág - gal.
care for noth-ing but plants' graft-ing and flow-er - ing.

Lá - lá-lá, Lá - lá-lá lá. Ha már
Lá - lá-lá, Lá - lá-lá lá. For when

el - pusz - tul a vi - lág,____ Le-gyen a sír - já - ra vi-
this world fa-ces its doom,____ let there be flow - ers on its

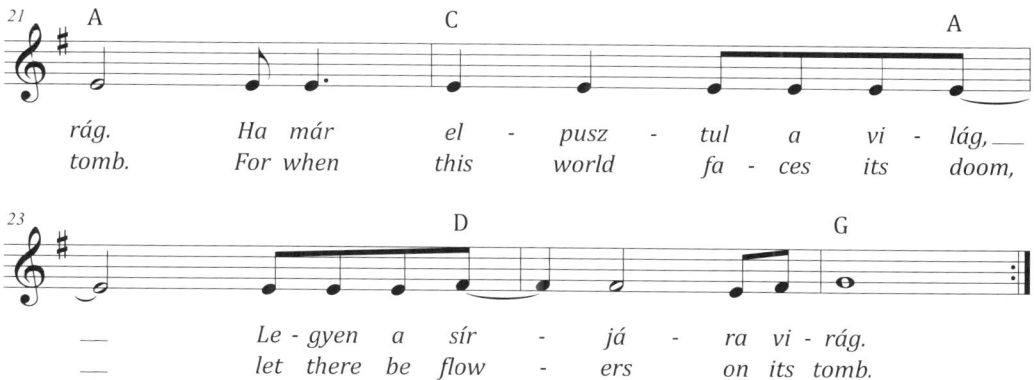

1. Kertész leszek, fát nevelek,
   Kelő nappal én is kelek.
   Lá-lá-lá, Lá-lá-lá lá, lá-lá.
   Nem törődöm semmi mással,
   Csak a beoltott virággal.
   Lá-lá-lá, Lá-lá-lá lá.

2. Minden beoltott virágom
   Kedvesem lesz virág áron.
   Lá-lá-lá, Lá-lá-lá lá, lá-lá.
   Ha csalán lesz, azt se bánom,
   Igaz lesz majd a virágom.
   Lá-lá-lá, Lá-lá-lá lá.

3. Tejet iszok és pipázok,
   Jó híremre jól vigyázok.
   Lá-lá-lá, Lá-lá-lá lá, lá-lá.
   Nem ér engem veszedelem,
   Magamat is elültetem.
   Lá-lá-lá, Lá-lá-lá lá.

Chorus:
   Ha már elpusztul a világ,
   Legyen a sírjára virág.
   Ha már elpusztul a világ,
   Legyen a sírjára virág.

4. Kell ez nagyon, igen nagyon.
   Napkeleten, napnyugaton.
   Lá-lá-lá, Lá-lá-lá lá, lá-lá.
   Ha már elpusztul a világ,
   Legyen a sírjára virág.
   Lá-lá-lá, Lá-lá-lá lá.

Chorus:
   Ha már elpusztul a világ...

1. A gardener – that's what I'll be,
   up at sunrise, nursing a tree.
   Lá-lá-lá, Lá-lá-lá lá, lá-lá.
   I shall heed or care for nothing
   but plants' grafting and flowering.
   Lá-lá-lá, Lá-lá-lá lá.

2. Each engrafted flower of mine
   shall be held dear, for its worth prized,
   Lá-lá-lá, Lá-lá-lá lá, lá-lá.
   Be it nettle - I shall not mind,
   my flow'rs shall be of the true kind.
   Lá-lá-lá, Lá-lá-lá lá.

3. I'll drink milk and I'll smoke my pipe,
   hold on to my good name quite tight,
   Lá-lá-lá, Lá-lá-lá lá, lá-lá.
   No harm will e'er reach me, nor plight,
   I'll sow even myself, that's right.
   Lá-lá-lá, Lá-lá-lá lá.

Chorus:
   For when this world may meet its doom,
   let there be flowers on its tomb.
   For when this world may meet its doom,
   let there be flowers on its tomb.

4. It's much needed, long overdue,
   beneath the sun, east and west, too
   Lá-lá-lá, Lá-lá-lá lá, lá-lá.
   For when this world may meet its doom,
   let there be flowers on its tomb.
   Lá-lá-lá, Lá-lá-lá lá.

Chorus:
   For when this world may meet its doom...

Translation by Arianna Basarić (2021)

Copyright © GrundRecords, Budapest. International copyright secured. All rights reserved. Reprinted by permission

NATURE & SEASONS						IRELAND

63
Song for Ireland

Song for Ireland was written by Phil Colclough (1940-2019) and his wife June (1941-2004), both from North Staffordshire in the midlands of England. Deeply involved in the folk tradition the couple were involved in the establishment of a folk music club in the town of Stoke-on-Trent and were associated in the 1960s with The Critics Group, which was formed to raise the standard of performances of folk and traditional music. The inspiration for Song for Ireland came from a visit by the couple to Ireland's western coast. Dingle is a small town in the County of Kerry in the south-western tip of Ireland renowned for its beautiful scenery and Black Head is a scenic headland in County Clare. The song associates the freedom enjoyed by the falcons flying "silver-winged" around the coast with the meeting of friends, telling of jokes, singing of songs and music-making in the local bars and pubs.

By Mark Armstrong, SING IRELAND

Lyrics & Music: June Colclough (1941-2004) & Phil Colclough (1940-2019)

1. Walking all the day, near tall towers where falcons build their nests. Silver winged they fly, they know the call of freedom in their breasts. Saw Black Head against the sky, where twisted rocks they run to the sea. Living on your western shore, saw summer sunsets, asked for more. I stood by your At-

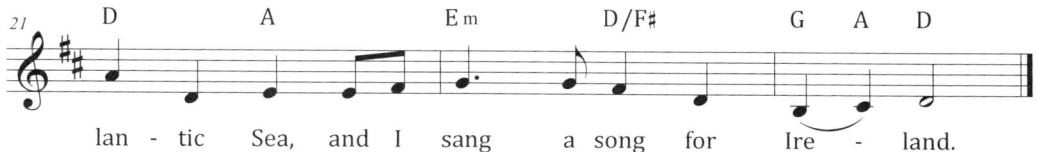

1. Walking all the day
   near tall towers where falcons build their nests.
   Silver winged they fly,
   they know the call for freedom in their breasts.
   Saw Black Head against the sky,
   where twisted rocks they run to the sea.
   Living on your western shore,
   saw summer sun sets, asked for more.
   I stood by your Atlantic Sea,
   and I sang a song for Ireland.

2. Drinking all the day
   in old pubs where fiddlers love to play.
   Saw one touch the bow,
   he played a reel which seemed so grand and gay.
   Stood on Dingle Beach and cast
   in wild foam we found Atlantic bass.
   Living on your western shore,
   saw summer sunsets, asked for more.
   I stood by your Atlantic Sea,
   and I sang a song for Ireland.

3. Talking all the day
   with true friends who try to make you stay.
   Telling jokes and news,
   ainging songs to pass the time away.
   Watched the Galway salmon run
   like silver dancing, darting in the sun.
   Living on your western shore,
   saw summer sunsets, asked for more.
   I stood by your Atlantic Sea,
   and I sang a song for Ireland.

4. Dreaming in the night
   I saw a land where no one had to fight.
   Waking in your dawn
   I saw you crying in the morning light.
   Sleeping where the falcons fly,
   they twist and turn all in your air-blue sky.
   Living on your western shore,
   saw summer sunsets, asked for more.
   I stood by your Atlantic Sea,
   and I sang a song for Ireland.

Copyright © 1981 Leola Music Limited, SGO Music Publishing Ltd. and BMG Rights Management (UK) Limited.
All Rights Administered by BMG Rights Management (US) LLC. International Copyright Secured. All Rights Reserved.
Reprinted by Permission of Hal Leonard Europe Ltd.

NATURE & SEASONS MALTA

64
L-Aħħar Bidwi f'Wied il-Għasel
The Last Farmer in Honey Valley

This folkloristic song tells the story of a farmer who recounts, in a pessimistic manner, the detrimental effects humans have on one of Malta's most popular valleys, found in the limits of Mosta. He describes how its stillness and natural environment are being destroyed due to humans' actions such as hunting and the development of buildings. The farmer expresses his fear that upon his departure, there will not be any farmers left to nurture the lands in this valley.

By Dr. Albert Pace, School of Performing Arts, University of Malta

Lyrics: Alfred C. Sant Music: Paul Abela (1954-)

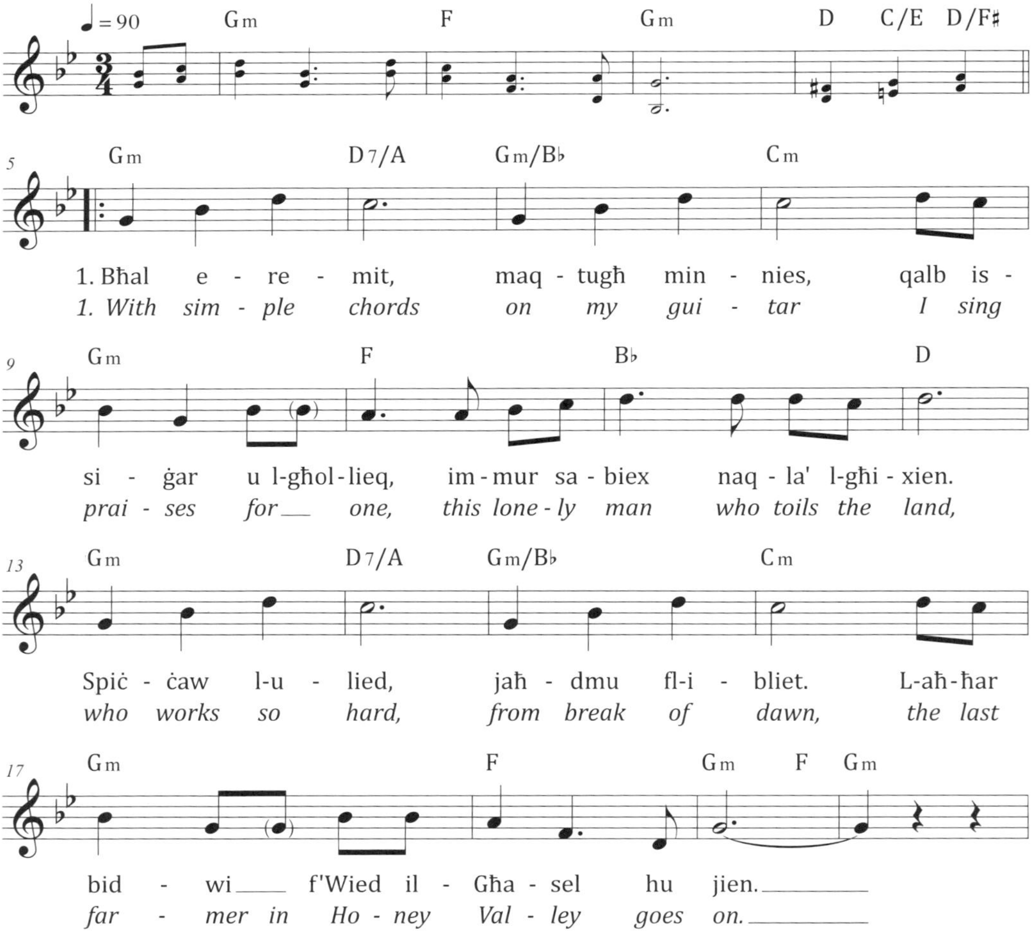

1. Bħal e - re - mit, maq - tugħ min - nies, qalb is-siġar u l-għol-lieq, im-mur sa biex naqla' l-għixien. Spiċ - ċaw l-u - lied, jaħ-dmu fl-i - bliet. L-aħ-ħar bid - wi f'Wied il - Għa - sel hu jien.

1. *With sim - ple chords on my gui - tar I sing prai - ses for one, this lone - ly man who toils the land, who works so hard, from break of dawn, the last far - mer in Ho - ney Val - ley goes on.*

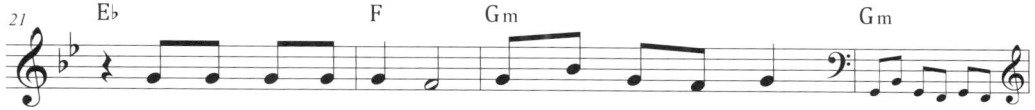

1. Bħal eremit, maqtugħ min-nies,
   qalb is-siġar u l-għollieq,
   immur sabiex naqla' l-għixien.
   Spiċċaw l-ulied, jaħdmu fl-ibliet.
   L-aħħar bidwi f'Wied il-Għasel hu jien.

   Jinżlu f'Wied il-Għasel
   f'dawk il-ġranet sbieħ,
   nies għall-passiġġati,
   jiġu għall-mistrieħ.

2. Raba żdingat, biss riservat
   għall-isnieter w il-klieb tal-kaċċatur -
   Żmien il-gamiem.
   Wara l-moħriet naħdem fis-skiet.
   L-aħħar bidwi f'Wied il-Għasel hu jien.

   Għall-bebbux jew fjuri,
   sagħtar minn ġol-blat,
   jinżlu f'Wied il-Għasel,
   jiġu nhar ta' Ħadd.

3. Kien staġun xott, kemm bata l-frott -
   u għal ħidmieti xi prezz?
   Dawn l-aħħar jiem kont ftit għajjien,
   wara l-moħriet naħdem fis-skiet.
   L-aħħar bidwi f'Wied il-Għasel hu jien.

1. With simple chords on my guitar
   I sing praises for one,
   this lonely man who toils the land,
   who works so hard, from break of dawn,
   the last farmer in Honey Valley goes on.

   Watch out for the hunters
   with their guns and hounds,
   they don't mind the harvest,
   it's their playing ground.

2. Across the fields he's his own chief
   he is holding out with hope
   that he may reap more than he sowed.
   Kids found new jobs, farewell to crops.
   The last farmer in Honey Valley goes on.

   Kinfolk come for picnics,
   sporting painted nails,
   butterflies and flowers,
   picking up a snail.

3. He trusts the soil to bless the plants,
   pray for seasons with rain
   for when it's dry much work is gone,
   and asks the earth, just what I'm worth.
   The last farmer in Honey Valley goes on.

   Translation by Alfred C. Sant (2022)

Copyright © the authors. International copyright secured. All rights reserved. Reprinted by permission

NATURE & SEASONS   POLAND

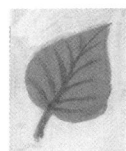

65
Wiosna, ach to ty
Spring, Oh It's You

Written by Marek Grechuta (1945-2006) – a Polish singer, poet, composer, painter, and architect by profession – this original song is a great representation of sung Polish poetry with its slightly erotic, playful, but also – as typical for Grechuta – ironic character. Here the cycle of love is symbolized by the four – shifting! – seasons. The song was the title track of an album from 1987, however the original title was "The Most Beautiful Season of the Year", later changed to "When You Are Here", which indicates it was addressed to his wife. The song offers an atmosphere of undisturbed peace, blissful happiness and subtle shrewdness. In addition to unusual harmonies it is full of passages of sustained lyricism (cantilena). This is a deliberate action, adding space to the music.

By Dorota Stefaniak, Academy of Music "Stanisław Moniuszko" in Gdańsk

Music & Lyrics: Marek Grechuta   Music: Marek Grechuta (1945-2006)

1. Dzi-siaj ra-no nie-spo-dzia-nie za-pu-ka-ła do mych drzwi.
   Wcześ-niej niż o-cze-ki-wa-łem przy-szły te cie-plej-sze dni.
   Zdją-łem z niej zmok-nię-te pal-to, po-sa-dzi-łem vis-à-vis.
   Za-pach-nia-ło, za-ja-śnia-ło wio-sna, ach, to ty.
   (spoken:) Wio-sna, wio-sna, wio-sna, ach, to ty!

2. *In the morn-ing, hear her call-ing, knock-ing un-ex-pec-ted-ly.*
   Soon-er than I thought she'd be here, warm-er days are here with me.
   Throw-ing off her soak-ing coat I sat her down vis-à-vis.
   What a per-fume, the day is bright. Spring you've come to me.
   Spring, spring, spring, you've come to me!

1. Dzisiaj rano niespodzianie
   zapukała do mych drzwi.
   Wcześniej niż oczekiwałem
   przyszły te cieplejsze dni.
   Zdjąłem z niej zmoknięte palto,
   posadziłem vis-à-vis.
   Zapachniało, zajaśniało
   wiosna, ach, to ty!

Spoken:
   Wiosna, wiosna, wiosna, ach, to ty!

Chorus:
   ||: Wiosna, wiosna, wiosna, ach, to ty!
   Wiosna, wiosna, wiosna, ach, to ty! :||

2. Dni mijały coraz dłuższe,
   coraz cieplej było u mnie.
   Coraz lżejsze miała suknie,
   lekko płynął wiosny strumień.
   Wreszcie nocy raz
   czerwcowej zobaczyłem ją, jak śpi.
   Bez niczego, zrozumiałem,
   lato, echże ty!

1. In the morning, hear her calling
   knocking unexpectedly.
   Sooner than I thought she'd be here,
   warmer days are here with me.
   Throwing off her soaking coat
   I sit her down vis-à-vis.
   What a perfume, the day is bright.
   Spring you've come to me.

Spoken:
   Spring, spring, spring, you've come to me!

Chorus:
   ||: Spring, spring, springtime, you've come to me!
   Spring, spring, springtime, you've come to me! :||

2. So the days grew ever longer,
   And the days got even warmer,
   And her frock got ever lighter,
   Softly flowing like a river.
   Then at last one night June,
   I saw her as she dreamed.
   In the nude, I understood
   Summer's come to me!

Spoken:
    Lato, lato, lato, echże ty!

Chorus:
    ||: Lato, lato, lato, echże ty!
    Lato, lato, lato, echże ty! :||

3. Od gorąca twych promieni
    zapłonęły liście drzew.
    Od zieleni do czerwieni
    krążył lata senny lew.
    Mała chmurka nad jej czołem,
    mała łezka, słony smak.
    Pociemniało, poszarzało
     – jesień, jak to tak?

Spoken:
    Jesień, jesień, jak to tak?

Chorus:
    ||: Jesień, jesień, jesień, jak to tak?
    Jesień, jesień, jesień, jak to tak? :||

4. Białe wiatry już zawiały,
    wiosny, lata wszystkie znaki.
    Po niej tylko pozostały
    przymarznięte dwa leżaki.
    Stoję w oknie, wypatruję,
    nagle dzwonek u mych drzwi.
    Zima, zima, wchodźże szybciej,
    ogrzej się na parę chwil.

Chorus:
    ||: Wiosna, wiosna, wiosna,
    ach to ty! :|| (x4)
    ||: Lato, lato, lato, echże ty!
    Wiosna, wiosna, wiosna,
    echże ty! :|| (x2)
    ||: Jesień, jesień, jesień, jak to tak?
    Wiosna, wiosna, wiosna,
    jak to tak? :|| (x2)
    ||: Wiosna, wiosna, wiosna,
                ach to ty! :||

Spoken:
    Summer's come to me!

Chorus
    ||: Summer, summer, summer's, here for me!
    Summer, summer, summer's, here for me! :||

3. From the fire of your beauty
    all the leaves are now aflame
    shiny green to burning red,
    the sleepy summer lion came.
    A tiny cloud above her brow,
    A tear, a salty flow.
    The light grew dark, the light grew gray
     – autumn, how's that so?

Spoken:
    Autumn, autumn, how's that so?

Chorus:
    ||: Autumn, autumn, how's that so?
    Autumn, autumn, how's that so? :||

4. Winds have blown, here to stay,
    spring and summer go away.
    All that's left what we've known
    are the deck chairs in the snow.
    Standing here looking out
    A sudden ringing at my door.
    Winter, winter, come in quick now,
    warm yourself before you go.

Chorus:
    ||: Spring, spring, springtime,
    you've come to me! :|| (x4)
    ||: Summer, summer, summer's, here for me!
    Spring, spring, springtime,
    you've come to me! :|| (x2)
    ||: Autumn, autumn, how's that so?
    Spring, spring, springtime,
    how's that so? :|| (x2)
    ||: Spring, spring, springtime,
                you've come to me! :||

Translation by David & William Malcolm (2021)

NATURE & SEASONS   AUSTRIA

66
In die Berg bin i gern
I Love Mountains

This blissful Alpine song is distributed throughout the Alpine region. Usually it is sung in two voices, like most alpine folk songs. In the early spring someone looks forward to return to the mountains, where he/she can again experience peace of mind and the beauty of the flowers. But will his/hers love, always in his/hers thoughts, still think of him/her when he/she goes away? The third verse of this song is found in a folksong collection of 1884, in collections from 1893 and 1909 all three verses are included. Many Austrians can't remember when they first heard this song, but almost everyone knows it.

By Dr. Eva Maria Hois, Steirische Volksliedwerk & Dr. Sarah Weiss, Kunstuniversität Graz, KUG

Lyrics: folk poem   Music: folk song

1. In die Berg bin i gern,
   und då gfreit si mei Gmiat,
   ||: wo die Ålmröserl wåchsn
   und da Enzian bliaht. :||

2. Und da Schnee geht båld weg,
   und es wird wieder grean,
   ||: und då werd i båld wieder
   auf die Ålm aufi gehn. :||

3. Wo i geh, wo i steh,
   denk i ållweil ån di,
   ||: wirst wohl du, wånn i furtgeh,
   a no denkn ån mi? :||

1. It's my greatest delight,
   I love high mountain air,
   ||: where the flowers are beckoning
   and the gentians bloom fair. :||

2. When spring casts out the snow,
   mountain slopes show their green,
   ||: and again I'll go hiking
   where the world is so clean. :||

3. Where I go, where I am,
   you are close to my heart,
   ||: and I hope you'll remember me,
   though we be far apart? :||

Translation by Lorenz Maierhofer (2020)

NATURE & SEASONS LITHUANIA

67
Kai sirpsta vyšnios Suvalkijoj
When Cherries Ripen in Suvalkija

Vytautas Kernagis (1951-2008) was a pioneer in many ways: he started out as a member of the beat bands Aisčiai ('66–'68) and Rupūs miltai ('69–'72) and recorded this cherized song "Kai sirpsta vyšnios Suvalkijoj" on his first album of "sung poetry" in '78. Kernagis also took part in both the first Lithuanian rock opera Devil's Bride, first Lithuanian musical and first Lithuanian musical for a puppet theatre. Behind the raw lyrics is highly awarded poet Marcelijus Martinaitis (1936-2013), father to the "Kukučio" balades – sung by a trickster, a clown who in a grotesque, ironical way revealed forbidden truths. Songs of Vytautas Kernagis are still very popular after his untimely death in 2008 and his influence on popular music is obvious today.

By Dr. Arvydas Girdzijauskas, Lithuanian Choral Union, LCHS

Lyrics: Marcelijus Martinaitis (1936-2013)   Music: Vytautas Kernagis (1951-2008)

1. Kai sirps-ta vyš-nios Su-val-ki-joj, Rau-do-nos, kad pra-virkt ga-li, Ra-sa ten la-ša nuo le-li-jų Lyg dal-gio aš-me-nys gai-li. Ir pjau-na šir-dį tar-si do-bi-lą Lig gy-vuo-nies, lig pa-šak-nų, O va-ka-rais kaž-ko taip to-li-ma,

1. *When cher-ries ripen in Su-val-ki-ja, turn-ing so red you have to cry, dew drips from lilies in Su-val-ki-ja, sad as the grey blade of a scythe. Cut-ting your heart as if a clo-ver, touch-ing your roots, your spot of pain, long-ing for some-one who is clos-er,*

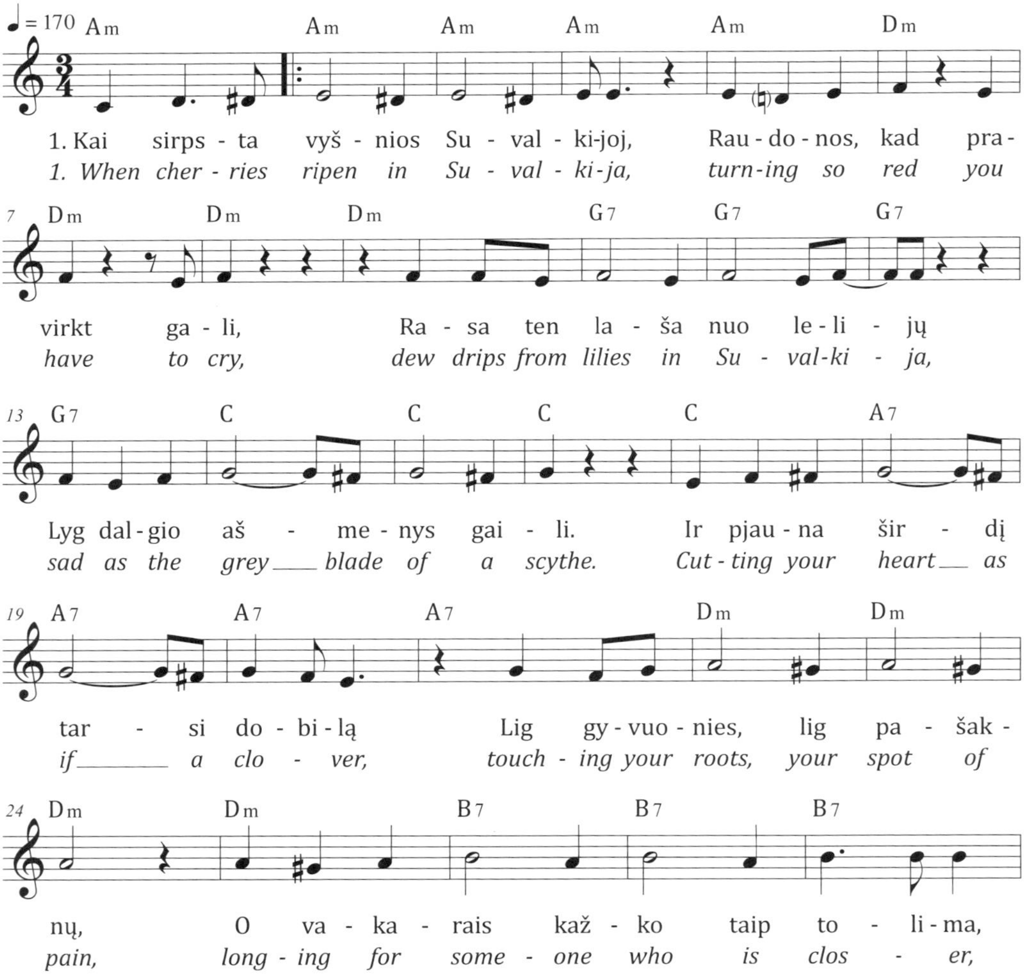

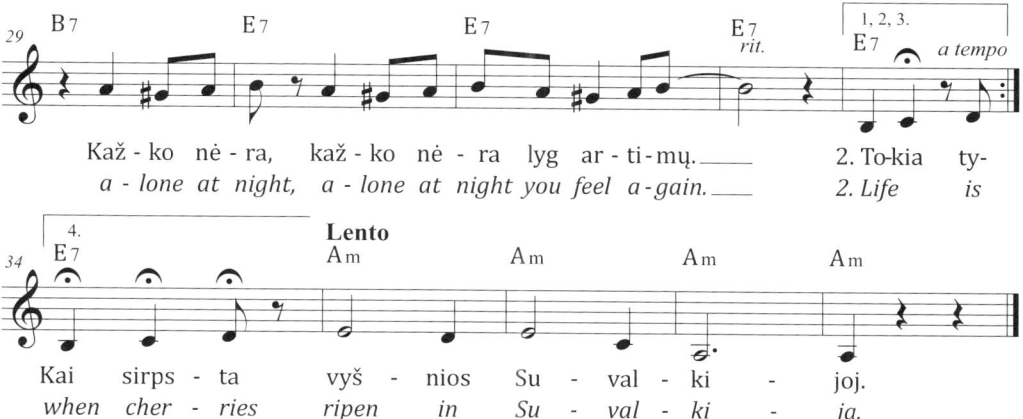

1. Kai sirpsta vyšnios Suvalkijoj,
   Raudonos, kad pravirkt gali, -
   Rasa ten laša nuo lelijų -
   Lyg dalgio ašmenys - gaili.
   Ir pjauna širdį tarsi dobilą
   Lig gyvuonies, lig pašaknų,
   O vakarais kažko taip tolima,
   Kažko nėra, kažko nėra - lyg artimų.

2. Tokia tyla gyvybėn smelkias
   Kasdienio židinio ugnim!
   Tokia daina, kad užsimerkia
   Dainuodami - lyg mirdami!
   Lig pašaknų ten pjauna širdį,
   Ten teka vandenys liūdnai,
   Ir dulkės vieškelių dar šiltos -
   Tarsi sodybų pelenai.

3. La la la …

4. Kai sirpsta vyšnios Suvalkijoj,
   Raudonos, kad pravirkt gali, -
   Rasa ten laša nuo lelijų -
   Lyg dalgio ašmenys - gaili.
   Ir pjauna širdį tarsi dobilą
   Lig gyvuonies, lig pašaknų,
   O vakarais kažko taip tolima,
   Kažko nėra, kažko nėra - lyg artimų.

   Kai sirpsta vyšnios Suvalkijoj.

1. When cherries ripen in Suvalkija,
   turning so red you have to cry, -
   dew drips from lilies in Suvalkija
   sad as the grey blade of a scythe.
   Cutting your heart as if a clover,
   touching your roots your spot of pain,
   longing for someone who is closer,
   alone at night, alone at night - you feel again.

2. Life is overladen by silence
   flames of a simple fireplace!
   A song to sing closing your eyelids
   as if to die here in this place!
   And close to the root your heart is cut there,
   water so sadly flows on and down,
   and dust of roadways is still warm there -
   as if the ash of a farmer's home.

3. La la la …

4. When cherries ripen in Suvalkija,
   turning so red you have to cry, -
   dew drips from lilies in Suvalkija
   sad as the grey blade of a scythe
   cutting your heart as if a clover
   touching your roots, your spot of pain,
   longing for someone who is closer,
   alone at night, alone at night - you feel again.

   When cherries ripen in Suvalkija.

Translation by Kerry Shawn Keys & Sonata Paliulytė (2023)

Reprinted by permission of the author's heirs and Vytauto Kernagio fondas. International copyright secured. All rights reserved

NATURE & SEASONS   GERMANY

68
Geh aus, mein Herz, und suche Freud
Go Forth, My Heart, and Seek Delight

The lyrics of this summer hymn by Baroque poet Paul Gerhardt (1607–76) documents the period shortly after the end of the Thirty Years' War. In these almost 400-year-old lyrics the wonder of trees, flowers, animals, and earth's fertility become an ecological opening to God's creation, an opening through which nature can return spirituality to the observer. As one of the most important poets of his time, Gerhardt created the basis for numerous spiritual songs which are still sung today. August Harder (1775-1813) wrote the melody, still widespread to this day, which the organist Friedrich Eickhoff (1807-86) wove together with the lyrics. In Sweden it has become a popular graduation song ("I denna ljuva sommartid").

By Ekkehard Klemm, president, Association of German Concert Choirs (VDKC)/
Hochschule für Musik "Carl Maria von Weber" Dresden

Lyrics: Paul Gerhardt (1607-76)   Music: August Harder (1775-1813)

1. Geh aus, mein Herz, und suche Freud in
1. Go forth, my heart, and seek delight, while

dieser lieben Sommerzeit an deines Gottes
summer reigns so fair and bright, view God's abundance

Gaben; Schau an der schönen Gärten Zier, und
daily; The beauty of these gardens see, be-

siehe, wie sie mir und dir sich ausgeschmücket
hold how they for me and thee have decked themselves so

ha - ben, sich aus - ge - schmü - cket ha - ben.
gail - y, have decked them - selves so gail - y.

1. Geh aus, mein Herz, und suche Freud
   in dieser lieben Sommerzeit
   an deines Gottes Gaben;
   Schau an der schönen Gärten Zier,
   und siehe, wie sie mir und dir
   sich ausgeschmücket haben,
   sich ausgeschmücket haben.

2. Die Bäume stehen voller Laub,
   das Erdreich decket seinen Staub
   mit einem grünen Kleide;
   Narzissus und die Tulipan,
   die ziehen sich viel schöner an
   als Salomonis Seide,
   als Salomonis Seide.

3. Die Lerche schwingt sich in die Luft,
   das Täublein fliegt aus seiner Kluft
   und macht sich in die Wälder;
   die hochbegabte Nachtigall
   ergötzt und füllt mit ihrem Schall
   Berg, Hügel, Tal und Felder,
   Berg, Hügel, Tal und Felder.

4. Die Glucke führt ihr Völklein aus,
   der Storch baut und bewohnt sein Haus,
   das schwälblein speist die Jungen,
   der schnelle Hirsch, das leichte Reh
   ist froh und kömmt aus seiner Höh
   ins tiefe Graß gesprungen,
   ins tiefe Graß gesprungen.

5. Ich selber kann und mag nicht ruhn,
   des großen Gottes großes Tun
   erweckt mir alle Sinnen;
   ich singe mit, wenn alles singt,
   und lasse, was dem Höchsten klingt,
   aus meinem Herzen rinnen,
   aus meinem Herzen rinnen.

1. Go forth, my heart, and seek delight,
   while summer reigns so fair and bright,
   view God's abundance daily;
   the beauty of these gardens see,
   behold how they for me and thee
   have decked themselves so gaily,
   have decked themselves so gaily.

2. The trees with spreading leaves are blessed,
   the earth her dusty rind has dressed
   in green so young and tender.
   Narcissus and the tulip fair
   are clothed in raiment far more rare
   than Solomon in splendor,
   than Solomon in splendor.

3. The lark soars upward to the skies,
   and from her cote the pigeon flies,
   her way to woodlands winging.
   The silver-throated nightingale
   fills mountain, meadow, hill and dale,
   with her delightful singing,
   with her delightful singing.

4. Here with her brood the hen doth walk,
   there builds and guards his nest the stork,
   the fleet-winged swallows pass;
   the swift stag leaves his rocky home,
   and down the light deer bounding come
   to taste the long rich grass,
   to taste the long rich grass.

5. Thy mighty working, mighty God,
   wakes all my powers; I look abroad
   and can no longer rest:
   I too must sing when all things sing,
   and from my heart the praises ring
   The Highest loveth best,
   the Highest loveth best.

Translation by Catherine Winkworth (1855)

NATURE & SEASONS   GREECE

69
Μες στου Αιγαίου τα νερά
In the Aegean Waters

This traditional folk song from the Greek island of Leros is very popular in all parts of Greece and is danced in the rhythm of Ballos (3,3,2). Most men coming from the islands had to make their living by becoming seamen and thus had to leave their homes for long periods of time. The song says that in the waters of the Aegean Sea, angels flutter and they throw roses in their path. Ah, Aegean Sea please calm your blue waters with the help of Holy Mary, so that the seamen can return to their homes and foreign visitors will come to your longed-for islands.

By Thomas Louziotis, president, Hellenic Choirs Association

Lyrics: traditional   Music: traditional

1. Μες στου Αιγαίου, πρόβαλε να ιδείς
   Μες στου Αιγαίου, Αιγαίου τα νερά
   Α, μες στου Αιγαίου τα νερά
   Αγγέλοι φτερουγίζουν.

2. Και μέσα στο φτε-, βλέπε τους Παναγιά μου
   και μέσα στο φτε-, στο φτερούγισμα
   α, και μέσα στο φτερούγισμα
   τριαντάφυλλα σκορπίζουν.

3. Αιγαίο μου γα-, βόηθα Παναγιά
   Αιγαίο μου γα-, γαλήνεψε
   Α, Αιγαίο μου γαλήνεψε
   τα γαλανά νερά σου.

4. Να 'ρθούνε τα ξε-, βλέπε τους Παναγιά μου
   να 'ρθούνε τα ξε-, τα ξενάκια σου
   Α, να 'ρθούνε τα ξενάκια σου
   στα ποθητά νησιά σου.

5. Ροδόσταμο να, πρόβαλε να ιδείς
   ροδόσταμο να γι-, να γίνουνε
   Α, ροδόσταμο να γίνουνε
   Αιγαίο τα νερά σου.

1. In the Aegean, come out and you will see,
   In the Aegean, Aegean waters,
   Oh, in the Aegean waters
   Angels spread their wings.

2. And when they flutter, hail Mary full of grace,
   And when they flutter with their wings,
   Oh, and when they flutter with their wings
   They spread their way full roses.

3. Oh my Aegean, Mother Mary help
   Oh my Aegean, calm now
   Oh, my Aegean calm now
   your lovely blue waters.

4. For them to come, oh Mother Mary watch over them
   For them to come, your children from abroad
   Oh let your children from abroad
   come to your desired islands

5. Rosewater, come out and you will see,
   Rosewater your water shall become,
   Oh, rosewater shall become
   Your waters my Aegean.

Translation by Monika & Stavros Xenides (2023)

NATURE & SEASONS					ITALY

70
Impressioni di settembre
The World Became the World

In October 1971, when the wave of British progressive rock and psychedelia also swept through Italy, The PFM (Premiata Forneria Marconi) introduced itself with this epochal song that has become a classic. September in central-northern Italy is a month of transition still full of the light, scents and sensations of summer but which, especially at dawn and dusk, foreshadows the fog of the first cold of autumn. The lyrics (co-written by Mogol, one of the greatest Italian lyricists of all time) have almost Dantesque quality as they depict some remote countryside at the break of dawn with the inner transition of a lost man. In the unfolding of a game of shadows and lights, of bewilderment of the self-dissolved in the mystery of nature, comes the explosion of a voiceless chorus that, in a very original way for the time, climbs for an airy melody. In the ending the sun filters through the fog – both an answer and a question.

By Alfonso Santimone, National Academy of Jazz, Siena

Lyrics: Mogol (1936-), Mauro Pagani (1946-)   Music: Franco Mussida (1947-)

1. Quan-te goc - ce di ru - gia - da in - tor - no a me
   cer - co il so - le, ma non c'è
   Dor - me an - co - ra la cam - pa - gna, for - se no,
   è sve - glia, mi guar - da, non so.
   Già l'o - do - re del - la ter - ra, odor di gra - no,

*1. Out-side my win-dow in the court-yard of the world
   the gent-le rain was fall-ing,
   no breath of wind, no cry of beast or bird,
   too qui-et, too still, I turned.
   To see the rain-drops like a thou-sand po-et's words*

1. Quante gocce di rugiada intorno a me
   Cerco il sole, ma non c'è
   Dorme ancora la campagna, forse no
   È sveglia, mi guarda, non so

2. Già l'odore della terra, odor di grano
   Sale adagio verso me
   E la vita nel mio petto batte piano
   Respiro la nebbia, penso a te

3. Quanto verde tutto intorno e ancor più in là
   Sembra quasi un mare l'erba
   E leggero il mio pensiero vola e va
   Ho quasi paura che si perda.

   Chorus: instrumental

4. Un cavallo tende il collo verso il prato
   Resta fermo come me
   Faccio un passo, lui mi vede, è già fuggito
   Respiro la nebbia, penso a te

5. No, cosa sono? Adesso non lo so
   Sono un uomo, un uomo in cerca di sé stesso
   No, cosa sono? Adesso non lo so
   Sono solo, solo il suono del mio passo

   Ma intanto il sole tra la nebbia filtra già
   Il giorno come sempre sarà.

   Chorus: Solo

1. Outside my window
                    in the courtyard of the world
   the gentle rain was falling,
   no breath of wind, no cry of beast or bird,
   too quiet, too still, I turned

2. to see the raindrops like
                    a thousand poet's words
   splash their circles on the stones,
   and seem to wash over everything with love
   and for a moment the courtyard heard

3. until the sun came bursting
                    through the clouds
   hung up his rainbows in the sky,
   and with a laugh of flames said:
                    now go chase the gold,
   and the world became the world.

   Chorus: instrumental

4. Now we're all travellers
                    some seekers and some sought
   who leave the courtyard to be caught
   in nets of self, damned, certainty and choice
   but do you believe our voice?

5. You've got what must belong to me,
   I need, I'll bleed for more possesions,
   you, you've got no right to disagree,
   bow, kneel or fear my aggressions.

   Thank God if sometimes your oyster
                    holds a pearl
   when the world remains the world.

   Chorus: Solo

   Translation by Peter Sinfield (1974)

   *(NB. This is an "authorative adaptation", meaning:
   it is the sole adaptation permitted by the copyright holders)*

NATURE & SEASONS   SLOVENIA

71
Slovenija, od kod lepote tvoje
Slovenia, Where Do Your Splendours Come From?

In the early 1950s, The Avsenik Brothers Ensemble started a musical (even cultural) tectonic movement known as Oberkrainer music: Slovenian-style country music in the polka & waltz genre, a sound that was to inspire Alpine orchestras not only in Slovenia but also in Germany, Austria, Switzerland, and around the world. From both brothers, Vilko Ovsenik and Slavko Avsenik, a number of notable hits were created that were also true patriotic songs. This one was composed in 1974 to the lyrics by Slovene lyricist Marjan Stare (1932-96) and has become one of those songs that are thought of as an unofficial Slovene anthem – a song that has found a permanent place for itself for every Slovene at home and especially abroad.

By Dr. Leon Stefanija, University of Ljubljana, Faculty of Arts

Lyrics: Marjan Stare (1932-96)   Music: Slavko Avsenik (1929–2015)
                                                                                                                                  & Vilko Ovsenik (1928-2017)

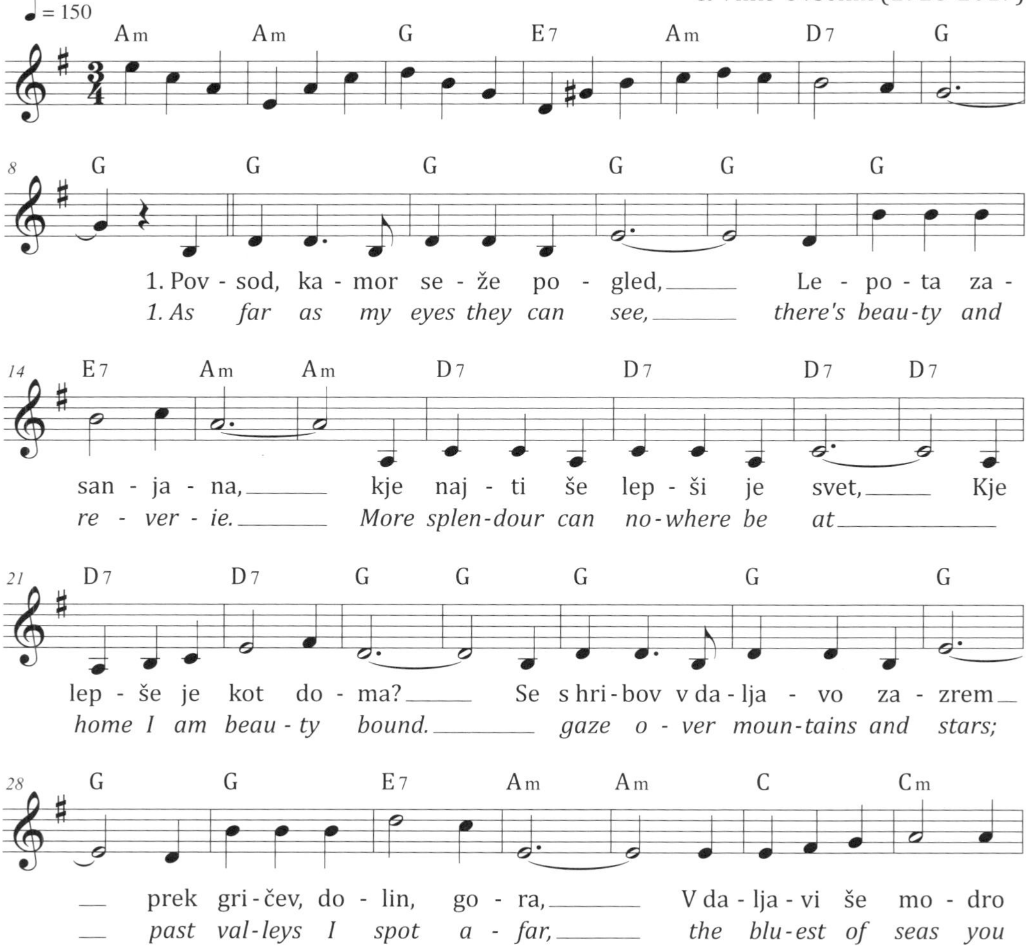

1. Pov - sod, ka - mor se - že po - gled, Le - po - ta za - san - ja - na, kje naj - ti še lep - ši je svet, Kje lep - še je kot do - ma? Se s hri - bov v da - lja - vo za - zrem prek gri - čev, do - lin, go - ra, V da - lja - vi še mo - dro

1. As far as my eyes they can see, there's beau-ty and re - ver - ie. More splen-dour can no-where be at home I am beau - ty bound. gaze o - ver moun-tains and stars; past val-leys I spot a - far, the blu-est of seas you

1. Povsod, kamor seže pogled,
   Lepota zasanjana,
   kje najti še lepši je svet,
   Kje lepše je kot doma?
   Se s hribov v daljavo zazrem prek gričev,
   dolin, gora,
   V daljavi še modro morje uzrem,
   Kje lepše je kot doma?

   Chorus:
   Slovenija - od kod lepote tvoje?
   Pozdravljamo te iz srca
   in srečni tu smo doma,
   Slovenija - naj tebi pesem poje,
   Ne išči sreče drugod kot le doma.

2. Povej še oblaček ti bel,
   Obhodil že ves si svet.
   Je lepša dežela še kje,
   Kot naša kjer sem doma?
   Je vetrič veselo zavel,
   Preletel je prek sveta.
   In takih lepot ni našel nikjer,
   Kot tule, kjer sem doma.

   Chorus:
   Slovenija - naj tebi pesem poje,
   Ne išči sreče drugod kot le doma.

1. As far as my eyes they can see,
   there's beauty and reverie.
   More splendour can nowhere be found -
   at home I am beauty bound.
   I gaze over mountains and stars;
   past valleys I spot afar,
   the bluest of seas you ever have found -
   at home I am beauty bound.

   Chorus:
   Slovenia, where do your splendours come from?
   We sing you praise - you alone,
   the happiest when we're home.
   Slovenia, our song is for you only;
   don't look for happiness far - only at home.

2. Say little white cloud you have been
   across the globe and again;
   and is there a country more fine
   than this wondrous home of mine?
   A breeze that would joyfully blow
   while circling the world we know,
   would not ever find such beauty divine
   like this wondrous home of mine.

   Chorus:
   Slovenia, our song is for you only;
   don't look for happiness far - only at home.

Translation by Steve Klink & Boštjan Malus (2021)

Copyright © the authors. International copyright secured. All rights reserved. Reprinted by permission

NATURE & SEASONS   LUXEMBOURG

72
D'Margréitchen
The Daisy

This song has music by Laurent Menager (1835–1902), a choirmaster, organist and conductor, one of Luxembourg's national composers who founded the national choral association Sang a Klang in 1857. It is based on a poem by Michel Lentz (1820-93), the man behind the lyrics for Luxembourg's national anthem. First published in 1883, at a time when most families barely had enough to eat, this song praises the beauty of the most common of flowers: the daisy.

By Robert Köller, Union Grand-Duc Adolphe, UGDA

Lyrics: Michel Lentz (1820-93)   Music: Laurent Menager (1835–1902)

Allegretto ♩ = 80

1. T'ass Fréi - jor an d'Vul - len déi sinn 'rëm er - waacht, an
1. 'Tis spring-time, the birds are a - wake and a - bout, and

d'Mar - gréit - chen huet sech e - raus och ge - maach. Si
dai - sies have al - so dressed up to come out, a

huet d'wäiss Koll - rett - chen 'rëm frësch u - ge - don, sou -
gleam - ing white neck - lace is what they all bring to

bal si de Pou - fank ge - héi - ert huet schlo'n. Sou -
wel - come the sea - son when chaf - finch - es sing. To

bal si de Pou - fank ge - héi - ert huet schlo'n.
wel - come the sea - son when chaf - finch - es sing.

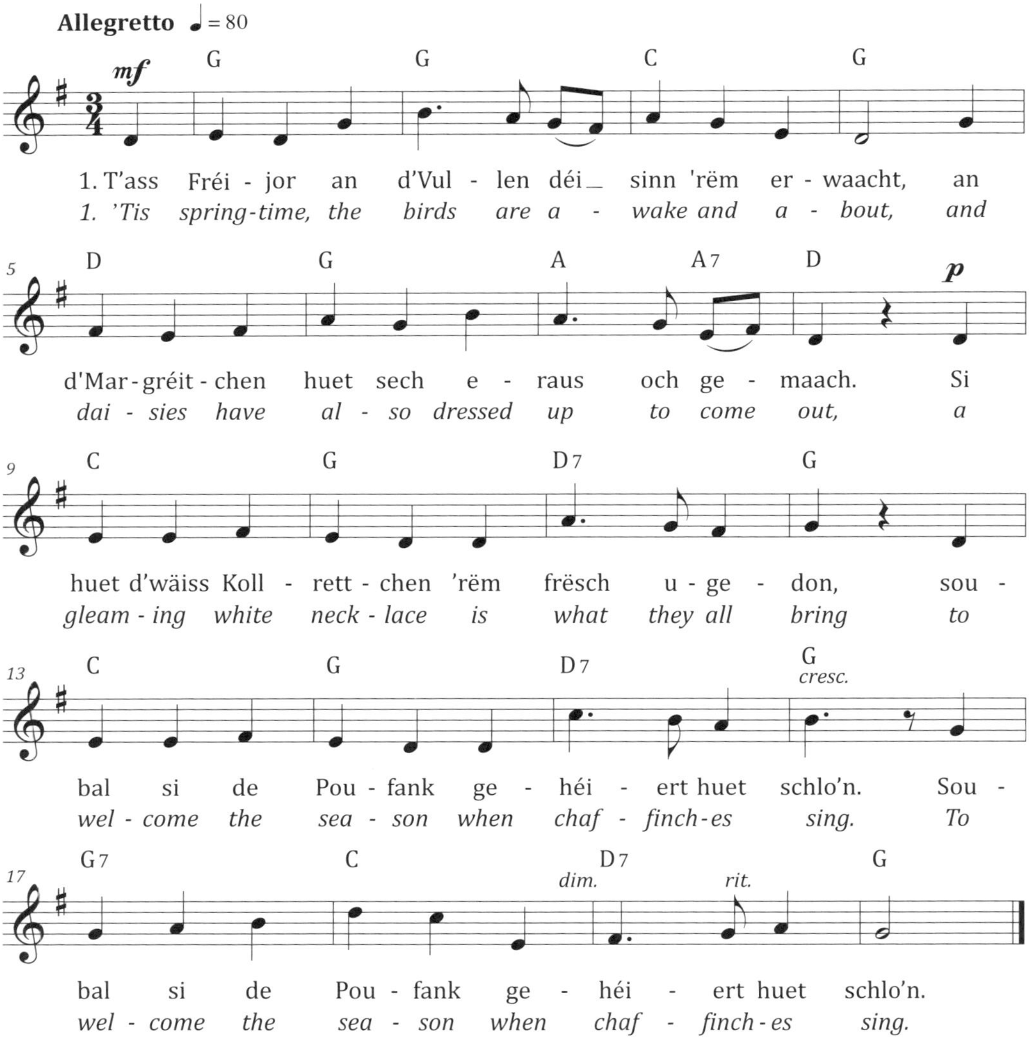

1. T'ass Fréijor an d'Vullen,
   déi sinn rëm erwaacht,
   an d'Margréitchen huet sech
   eraus och gemaacht,
   si huet d'waiss Kolrettche
   rëm frësch ugedoen,
   ||: soubal si de Poufank
   gehéiert huet schlon :||

2. A gréng ginn och d'Wise
   laanscht d'Weeën an d'Pied,
   d'Vioule verstoppen
   sech heemlech am Schied.
   D'Beem kréien nei Blieder,
   den Nuechtegall schléit,
   ||: de Wand séngt duerch d'Bëscher,
   wou d'Meeréische bléit :||

3. An d'Sonn, déi rifft d'Blumme
   schnéi-wäiss, rout a blo,
   wéi d'Stieren um Himmel,
   sou vill sinn der do.
   Si rëschten a botze
   mat Faarwe sech räich,
   ||: a blénken a blëtzen
   duerch Heck a Gesträich :||

4. Dach vun all de Blummen
   am Gaart an um Feld
   ass d'Margréitchen déi mir
   am beschte gefällt.
   Et si wuel méi prächteg,
   méi schéi wuel di meescht,
   ||: mä ech hun eng Freiesch,
   déi Margréitchen heescht :||

1. 'Tis springtime, the birds are
   awake and about,
   and daisies have also
   dressed up to come out,
   a gleaming white necklace
   is what they all bring
   ||: to welcome the season
   when chaffinches sing. :||

2. And green is the meadow,
   the hedgerow or glade,
   where violets modestly
   hide in the shade,
   the trees are in leaf, as
   the nightingale's tune
   ||: is heard in the woodland,
   and May lilies bloom. :||

3. The sun summons flowers
   of red, white and blue,
   like stars in the heavens,
   so many to view;
   they glisten and sparkle,
   and wave in the breeze,
   ||: with colours to brighten
   the bushes and trees. :||

4. Of all the fair flowers
   in bower and lea,
   the daisy's more lovely
   than any to me:
   Some may be much grander,
   but that's all the same -
   ||: for I have a sweetheart,
   and Daisy's her name! :||

Translation by Edward Seymour (2021)

NATURE & SEASONS ROMANIA

73
Au înnebunit salcâmii
Locust Trees Are Going Crazy

"Locust Trees Are Going Crazy" is a song composed and sung by Tudor Gheorghe (born 1945), inspired by the verses of "The Acacia Trees" written by the cultivated Arhip Cibotaru (1935-2010) from Bessarabia (since 1991, Republic of Moldova). Among Romanian singers and composers currently living, Tudor Gheorghe is one of the most loved, well-known for his compositions based on poems written by great Romanian poets. For many years, his musical activity has ensured the survival of folk culture and Romanian poetry, and for many years his thematic concerts have raised and acknowledged sensitive topics of the Romanian people.

By Alexandra Belibou, Lecturer PhD, Faculty of Music, Transilvania University of Brașov

Lyrics: Arhip Cibotaru (1935-2010)   Music: Tudor Gheorghe (1945-)

1. Au în - ne - bu - nit sal - câ - mii
1. Lo - cust trees are go - ing cra - zy,

De a - tâ - ta pri - mă - va - ră,   Um - blă des - pu - iați prin
spring has made them loose their rea - son,   sing - ing wild - ly to the

ce - ruri   Cu tot su - fle - tu'n a - fa - ră.
hea - vens,   of this head - y, fra - grant sea - son!

1. Au înnebunit salcâmii
   De atâta primăvară,
   Umblă despuiați prin ceruri
   Cu tot sufletu-n afară.

   Și l-au scos de dimineață
   Alb și încărcat de rouă
   Cu miresme tari de ceruri
   Smulse dintr-o taină nouă.

   Au înnebunit salcâmii
   Și cu boala lor odată
   S-a-ntâmplat ceva îmi pare
   Și cu lumea asta toată.

2. Păsările aiurite
   Își scot sufletul din ele
   Pribegind de doruri multe,
   Călătoare printre stele.

   S-a-mbătat pădurea verde
   Nu mai e așa de calmă,
   Ține luna lunguiață
   Ca pe-o inimă în palmă.

   Nu-mi vezi sufletul cum iese
   În haotice cuvinte,
   ||: Au înnebunit salcâmii
   Și tu vrei să fiu cuminte? :||

1. *Locust trees are going crazy,*
   spring has made them loose their reason,
   singing wildly to the Heavens,
   of this heady, fragrant season!

   Their souls came out in the morning,
   of the dawn so strongly smelling
   white and dripping with fresh droplets,
   oh, so pure that there's no telling!

   Locust trees are going crazy,
   in their madness ever higher,
   something happened that amazed me
   to this very world entire!

2. *Scatterminded birds are singing,*
   their hearts out in joyful crying,
   all of nature like bells ringing,
   as towards the stars they're flying!

   The intoxicated forest,
   is no longer calm and gentle,
   as she holds the moon the closest,
   with a feeling oh so tender.

   And my soul comes out so hazy,
   in a quick, chaotic mumble,
   ||: locust-trees are going crazy!
   And you want me to be humble? :||

   Translation by Beck Corlan & Alex Szollo (2022)

NATURE & SEASONS SLOVAKIA

74
V dolinách
In the Hills

Every nation has songs that praise their homeland, nature and its people in nice, friendly colors, most of them folk songs treating themes which contemporary artists rarely interpret, why we can only dream of unlocked doors and the hardships of retrieving wood from the mountains. However, the Slovaks did not forget this genre. The song "V dolinách", sung by Karol Duchoň (1950-85), whom the Germans nicknamed "the Slovak Tom Jones", became immensely popular after its release in 1976. And thirty years later, in 2006, the song got a major comeback when the rock band Desmod covered it. A year later it ranked second in the music TV show "Hit Storočia" (Hit of the Century), broadcasted by Slovak television in December 2007. Accordingly, several musicians were inspired to make new adaptations.

By Dr. Eva Čunderlíková, Slovak Music Teacher Association, AUHS/Academy of Music Bratislava, VŠMU

Lyrics: Ľuboš Zeman (1949-)   Music: Peter Hanzely (1947-)

1. V do - li - nách _____ kvit - ne kvet, kto - rý lás - ku nám dá - va, je - ho jas v tma-vom rá - ne vždy svie - ti a - ko briež - de - nie. V do - li - nách _____ les - ný
1. In the hills _____ flow-ers breathe love on each one who pass - es, and their bloom in dark morn - ing shines al - ways in the dawn - ing gloam. In the hills _____ hon-ey's

1.
V dolinách
kvitne kvet, ktorý lásku nám dáva,
jeho jas v tmavom ráne vždy svieti
ako brieždenie.
V dolinách
lesný med vonia viac ako tráva,
na svahoch túlia sa ovčie stáda,
v domoch pieseň znie.

2.
V dolinách
človek sám svoju prírodu chráni,
každý strom, každá lúka na stráni
je náš vzácny liek.
V dolinách
ľudia nemajú zamknuté brány,
majú tam srdcia čisté a vľúdne
ako prúdy riek.

Chorus:
Je to kraj, kde prísne štíty hôr
teplo dolín múdro strážia,
pokým slnka lúč zazvoní
na jarné zvonce ovčích stád.
Je to kraj, kde ráno vstávaš skôr,
kde sa drevo z hory tíško zváža.
Je to Slovensko čarovné, hrdé,
mám ho rád.

Then repeat 1. and 2. verse

1.
In the hills
flowers breathe love on each one who passes,
and their bloom in dark morning shines always
in the dawning gloam.
In the hills
honey's fragrance can blend with the grasses,
down the slopes come the sheep in their masses,
songs are heard from homes.

2.
In the hills
human nature's preserved, it's well-tended,
ev'ry tree, ev'ry meadow is splendid,
our most precious cure.
In the hills
people don't lock their doors when day's ended,
and their hearts are so open and kindly,
like the rivers, pure.

Chorus:
It's a land where watchful mountain crests
wisely guard the heat of hillsides,
while sunbeams go a-ring-a-ding
through flocks of sheep with springtime bells.
It's a land where early rising's best,
where the timber's loaded from the hillsides.
That is magical Slovakia, that I
love so well.

Then repeat 1. and 2. verse

Translation by John Minahane (2022)

NATURE & SEASONS   LATVIA

75
Tik Un Tā
Anyway

Nature's versatility and play of seasonal color! In less than a month after this boldly written song was performed by its composer in an annual radio song competition in 1981, it gained a true and undisguised public love, surviving to the present day. During the Soviet occupation, such declaration of love for Latvia was daring, since anyone could be condemned or punished for it. So it was partly courageous action, partly a coincidence of successful circumstances which enabled the songwriters to publicly invite everyone to feel both care and adoration for their homeland. Still popular among several generations, it is performed on important holidays or national celebrations among families. Every year, the colorful autumn cannot compete with the feeling that dwells in everyone who was born in or lives in Latvia: "Man viņa ir visskaistākā tik un tā", – "She is the most beautiful one to me, anyway".

By Rūta Kanteruka, president, Latvian Music Teachers' Association, LVIIMSA

Lyrics: Māra Zālīte (1952-)   Music: Uldis Stabulnieks (1945-2012)

1. Nāk rudens apglezņot Latviju, bet ne pūlies, necenties tā, man viņa ir visskaistākā tik un tā. Nāk tā.

1. The autumn paints over Latvia, but even without this display, I'd always find her beautiful anyway. The way.

Chorus:
Mazliet par lielu, lai sasildot savu lakatu dotu. Par lielu, lai paņemtu klēpī un apmī-

Just big enough to adventure out and explore all around her. Too big to put her in my lap with my arms a-

1. ||: Nāk rudens apgleznot Latviju,
   bet nepūlies, necenties tā,
   man viņa ir visskaistākā
   tik un tā. :||

Chorus:
   Mazliet par lielu, lai sasildot
   savu lakatu dotu.
   Par lielu, lai paņemtu klēpī
   un apmīļotu.

   Mazliet par mazu, lai palaistu vienu
   pasaules plašajos ceļos,
   par mazu, lai laistu vienu -
   es līdzi ceļos.

1. ||: The autumn paints over Latvia,
   but even without this display,
   I'd always find her beautiful
   anyway. :||

Chorus.
   Just big enough to adventure out
   and explore all around her.
   Too big to put her in my lap
   with my arms around her.

   Slightly too little to leave on her own while
   venturing hither and thither.
   Too little to go without me,
   I'm going with her.

2. ||: Nāk rudens izgreznot Latviju,
   bet nepūlies, necenties tā
   mums viņa ir visskaistākā
   tik un tā. :||

Chorus:
   Mazliet par lielu, lai sasildot
   savu lakatu dotu.
   Par lielu, lai paņemtu klēpī
   un apmīļotu.

   Mazliet par mazu, lai palaistu vienu
   pasaules plašajos ceļos,
   par mazu, lai laistu vienu -
   es līdzi ceļos.

2. ||: *The autumn decorates Latvia,*
   but even without this display,
   we'd always find her beautiful
   anyway. :||

Chorus:
   Just big enough to adventure through
   all the hurdles that face her.
   Too big to put her in my lap
   and fully embrace her.

   Slightly too little to leave on her own while
   venturing hither and thither.
   Too little to go without me,
   I'm going with her.

   Translation by Māra Walsh Sinka (2022)

NATURE & SEASONS　　　　　　　　　　　　　　　　　　　　　　　FINLAND

76
Myrskyluodon Maija
Maya of Storm Islet

Thanks to the TV series "Maya of Storm Islet" (1976), based on Anne Blomqvist's novels set in Åland, for the majority of Finns this song is inextricably linked to Åland's unique and beautiful nature, spread over almost 7,000 islands. The instrumental soundtrack bearing its name became both the best-known composition by jazz musician Lasse Mårtenson and one of the best-selling sheet music publications in its time. The song's original Swedish lyrics by writer Benedict Zilliacus were translated into Finnish by Jukka Virtanen. The lyrics speak of the natural diversity of the archipelago nature while also exposing the harsh life of its inhabitants during the 19th century – specifically the main characters, married couple Maija and Janne. The music is inspired by Mårtenson's love of the Finnish archipelago: The delicate opening section brings to mind calm and beautiful summer days, while the more energetic middle section recalls blowing winds and rumbling waves.

By Juha Henriksson, director, Music Archive Finland

Lyrics: Benedict Zilliacus (1921-2013)　　　　　Music: Lasse Mårtenson (1934-2016)
& Jukka Virtanen (1933-2019)

1. Me - ri jäl - jet lyö luo - toon, va - ot kal - li - on, ne aal - to teh - nyt on. Myös myrs-ky - sää tart - tuu Mai - jan muo - toon, ja Jan - nen sil - miin leu - dot tuu - let kiin - ni jää.
Me - ren an - ka - ra työ, hei - hin merk - kin - sä lyö,

1. Not a word need be spo - ken when I hold his hand as he's come safe to land, home from the sea. But when dawn has brok - en, he will set sail a - gain and leave me on the quay.
Yet we show that we care in the mo - ments we share,

(Maija)
Meri jäljet lyö luotoon,
vaot kallion, ne aalto tehnyt on.
Myös myrskysää tarttuu Maijan muotoon,
ja Jannen silmiin leudot tuulet kiinni jää.
Meren ankara työ,
heihin merkkinsä lyö,
heihin merkkinsä lyö.

Oppii luodolla kielen,
sanat liikaa ois ja joutaa lauseet pois.
Voi aavistaa vaimo toisen mielen,
Hän tuntee tuulen, joka miehen matkaan saa.
Katsoo hän lähtijää,
vielä tyyni on sää,
Vielä tyyni on sää.

(Janne)
Kun saapuu taas saaliineen hän,
on kuin mies naistaan tuntisi enemmän.
Rannalle suurimmat siioistansa tuo huutaen:
"Eivät ne karkaa, suomusta nuo!"
Katsetta arkaa vaimoon hän luo,
karkeaa sarkaa kosketellen
kertoo mies terveiset myrskyjen.

Niin jatkuu tuo yhteinen työ
taas kunnes saapuu tyynenä kesäyö.
Yhdestä katseesta mies ymmärtää vaimoaan,
kuinka hän pelkää
          myrskyävää
pohjoista selkää, yksin kun jää.
"Siis tyynnytelkää huomiset veet
haltiat", mies pyyhkii kyyneleet.

(Maija)
Oppii luodolla kielen,
puhe turhaa on ja lause tarpeeton.
Mies aavistaa liikkeet herkän mielen,
kun nousee aamu, joka miehen
                  matkaan saa.
Katse saattamaan jää,
vielä tyyni on sää,
vielä tyyni on sää.

(Maija)
Not a word need be spoken
when I hold his hand as he's come safe to land,
home from the sea. But when dawn has broken,
he will set sail again and leave me on the quay.
Yet we show that we care
in the moments we share,
not a word need be spoken.

Though the storms rage around us,
I have never cried when he sleeps by my side.
Though to this life Fate has firmly bound us,
it is by choice we're bound together, man and wife.
Weathered skin, smell of brine,
and his warmth close to mine,
though the storms rage around us.

(Janne)
At sunrise I raise up my sail.
She waves farewell, I ride on the autumn gale
seeking the bounty the sea may provide,
I have my nets for the throwing, lines to be cast
paddling and rowing, tied to the mast.
But though I love to fly on the foam,
what I love more is returning home.

Out here in the islands we live,
trusting the gifts the sea promises to give.
Sometimes they're plentiful, sometimes they fail.
We have known hardship and striving,
                      hunger to match,
barely surviving till the next catch.
Yet throughout all the trials we face,
I find my strength in her sweet embrace.

(Maija)
Through each day, through each season
we will live our lives beneath these open skies.
In ice and snow we must hope and reason:
spring will return each year as lifetimes
                      come and go.
I am his, he is mine
to the end of our time,
through each day, through each season.

Translation by Jaakko Mäntyjärvi (2021)

"Lyrics © F-Kustannus (50%). Reprinted by permission of Otava Publishing Company Ltd., Finland.
Music reprinted by permission of the composer's heirs"

NATURE & SEASONS DENMARK

77
Vi elsker vort land (Midsommervise)
We Love Our Land (Midsummer Song)

When the Sun sets at the summer solstice in Denmark, the majority of Danes meet in groups in the countryside or by the coast to light large bonfires and sing the "Midsummer Song" from 1885. The meaning of this ancient social ritual span from lighting up the coming darkness to scaring away evil spirits, witches and trolls. The melody – originally written for solo voice – is as beloved and difficult as the Danish summer: tempo changes three times (!), trying to catch the transition from gratitude and tenderness to celebration and ecstasy.

By Jesper Moesbøl, editor of "Sanghåndbogen"/The Song Handbook

Lyrics: Holger Drachmann (1846-1908)   Music: P. E. Lange-Müller (1850-1926)

1. Vi el-sker vort land, når den sig-ne-de jul tæn-der stjer-nen i træ-et med glans i hvert ø-je, når om vå-ren hver fugl o-ver mark, un-der strand la-der stem-men til hil-sen-de tril-ler sig bø-je: vi syn-ger din lov o-ver vej, o-ver ga-de, vi

1. We love our land when at Christ-mas our prayer lights a star on the tree and a mir-ror in all eyes. When in spring-time the air o-ver sea, o-ver land, brings the wel-come of bird-song from green-woods and blue skies. We sing out your name a-long high-way and by-way. With

1. Vi elsker vort land,
   når den signede jul
   tænder stjernen i træet
   med glans i hvert øje,
   når om våren hver fugl
   over mark, under strand
   lader stemmen til hilsende
                           triller sig bøje:
   vi synger din lov over vej, over gade,
   vi kranser dit navn,
                når vor høst er i lade,
   ||: men den skønneste krans
   bli'r dog din, sankte Hans!
   den er bunden af sommerens hjerter
   så varme, så glade. :||

2. Vi elsker vort land,
   men ved midsommer mest,
   når hver sky over marken
   velsignelsen sender,
   når af blomster er flest,
   og når kvæget i spand
   giver rigeligst gave til flittige hænder;
   når ikke vi pløjer
   og harver og tromler,
   når koen sin middag
   i kløveren gumler:
   ||: da går ungdom til dans
   på dit bud, sankte Hans!
   ret som føllet og lammet,
   der frit over engen sig tumler. :||

3. Vi elsker vort land,
   og med sværdet i hånd
   skal hver udenvælts fjende
   beredte os kende,
   men mod ufredens ånd
   over mark, under strand
   vil vi bålet på fædrenes
                          gravhøje tænde:
   hver by har sin heks,
   og hvert sogn sine trolde,
   dem vil vi fra livet
   med glædesblus holde;
   ||: vi vil fred her til lands,
   sankte Hans, sankte Hans!
   den kan vindes, hvor hjerterne
   aldrig bli'r tvivlende kolde. :||

1. We love our land
   when at Christmas our prayer
   lights a star on the tree
   and a mirror in all eyes.
   When in springtime the air
   over sea, over land,
   brings the welcome of birdsong
                           from greenwoods and blue skies.
   We sing out your name along highway and byway.
   With garlands we thank you
                          for harvests of sweet hay.
   ||: But the finest wreath stands
   in your name Sankte Hans!
   It is woven in joy at the heart of this
   midsummer saint's day. :||

2. We love our land
   on this midsummer's day
   when each cloud showers earth
   with a boon and a blessing.
   When the wildflowers play,
   and each cow knows the hand
   that releases its gift with a careful caressing.
   When evening falls on
   our ploughing and sowing,
   when cattle stand munching
   in clover and lowing,
   ||: then the young long to dance
   to your tune, Sankte Hans!
   as the newly born foal feels
   the freedom of life through it flowing. :||

3. We love our land
   and as one, arm in arm,
   we will ward off invaders
   and fight for our home grounds.
   To preserve us from harm
   over sea, over land
   we will kindle our beacons on
                          ancestors' grave mounds.
   If wizards or witches
   would trouble this shire
   we'll keep them at bay
   with the blaze of our fire!
   ||: We want peace in our land –
   it is ours, Sankte Hans
   and is won by a faith
   that stays warm at the heart of desire. :||

Translation by John Mason (2022)

NATURE & SEASONS   CROATIA

78
Dalmatino povišću pritrujena
Dalmatina, Worn Out by Your History

In 1972, Ljubo Stipišić-Delmata (1938-2011), composer, conductor, ethnomusicologist, poet and tireless collector of traditional treasures, wrote this "klapa song" in his own original way, as an extremely impressive, emotional and picturesque text, strongly based on the Dalmatian dialect. From it's first appearance this song, with its authentic Dalmatian expression, gained respect from both critics and the audience, and rose above other songs as a kind of musical pedestal, an ode to Dalmatia. The distinctive and popular "klapa singing", traditional Croatian polyphonic homophonic a capella singing, was listed on UNESCO's List of the Intangible Cultural Heritage of Humanity. In 2009, the cherished Croatian songwriter Tedi Spalato (born Tadija Bajić, 1954) published an album "Dalmatinska Pismo Moja" (My Dalmatian Letter) with this version for solo voice, which became instantly popular.

By Dr. Jasenka Ostojić, University of Zagreb, Music Academy

Lyrics & Music: Ljubo Stipišić-Delmata (1938-2011)/arranged by Tedi Spalato (1954-)

1. Pu - te, la - ze___ pi - zon du - bli to - va - ri,
1. Beasts of bur-den___ plowed in stones to clear the way,

gu - sti - rne že - dne mi - jun si - ći i la - ti;
wells were drained by buck-ets, count-less eve-ry day;

Chorus:

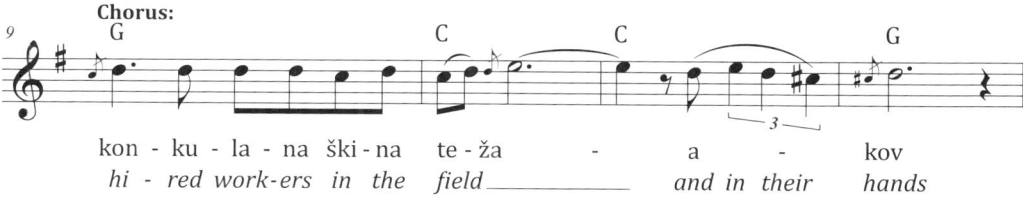

kon - ku - la - na ški - na te - ža - a - kov
hi - red work-ers in the field_____ and in their hands

od mo - tik_____ po žu - rna - a -
mat - tocks,_____ and backs are bent,_____

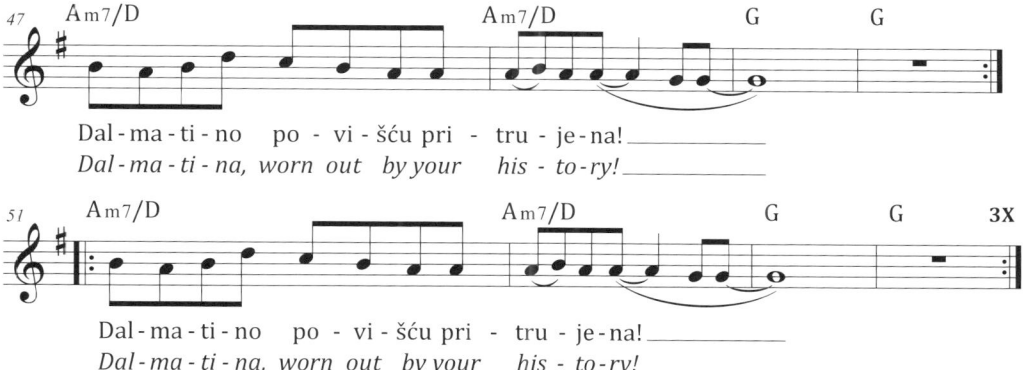

1. Pute, laze pizon dubli tovari,
   gustirne žedne mijun sići i lati;

Chorus:
   konkulana škina težakov, od mo...
   od motik po žurnatin,
   žurnatin pritrujena!

2. Prage kalet žnjutin dubli Puntari,
   naboj dalmatine rebati na drači,

Chorus:
   kroz kadene dicu čičan pasli,
   a judi driti ka kolone;
   Dalmatino povišću pritrujena!

3. Intradu pravice s tilin štrukali
   (Dalmatino povišću pritrujena!)
   Rod puntarski resa na drači;
   (Dalmatino povišću pritrujena!)
   Ditinstvon gladnin povist štukali;
   (Dalmatino povišću pritrujena!)

Chorus:
   ||: Kroz kadene dicu čičan pasli,
   a judi driti ka kolone,
   Dalmatino povišću pritrujena! :||

   Dalmatino povišću pritrujena!
   Dalmatino povišću pritrujena!
   Dalmatino povišću pritrujena!

1. Beasts of burden plowed in stones to clear the way,
   wells were drained by buckets, countless every day;

Chorus:
   hired workers in the field and in their hands
   mattocks, and backs are bent, bent from
   working in the sun all day long!

2. Alleyways plowed with rebel feet and anklebones,
   Dalmatina's blood-sore pulsating from the thorns.

Chorus:
   Chains embraced the bosom nursing their children;
   still, people stand up tall like pillars of stone;
   Dalmatina, worn out by your history!

3. Fruits of labour picked by hands of their own.
   (Dalmatina, worn out by your history!)
   Race of rebels raised in misery;
   (Dalmatina, worn out by your history!)
   their hungry childhoods piling up in memory;
   (Dalmatina, worn out by your history!)

Chorus:
   ||: Chains embraced the bosom nursing their children;
   still, people stand up tall like pillars of stone;
   Dalmatina, worn out by your history! :||

   Dalmatina, worn out by your history!
   Dalmatina, worn out by your history!
   Dalmatina, worn out by your history!

   Translation by Nikola Vranić, a.k.a. J.R. August &
   & Marta Brkljačić (2023)

NATURE & SEASONS   CZECHIA

79
Chválím Tě Země má
I Praise You, Mother Earth

This both majestic and tender hymn of the beloved Czech songwriter duo has become very popular mainly due to the natural lyricism and feeling it carries with it. It tells not only of landscape and nature, but of planet Earth as such. Contrary to most of the songs which the duo created for the TV show "Singing Hour" (1995), this melody was made prior to the lyrics. The composer allegedly first returned the text for reworking, with the words: "This must have been done by either a dumb lyricist or a crowd of people. You are not any of them". This is said to be their only minor creative clash during their 50-year teamwork. The hymn had infact inspired the lyricist into a spiritual call-and-response song: First the spoken adult solo voice is confirmed by the unison children choir, after which roles are reversed – a circle of confirmation. The refrain is sung together. Performed for solo voice, the spoken parts are voluntary.

By Lukáš Prchal, The Czech Choral Union, UČPS

Lyrics: Zdeněk Svěrák (1936-)   Music: Jaroslav Uhlíř (1945-)

♩ = 104

1. Chvá - lím Tě, Ze-mě má, tvůj žár i mráz.
1. I praise You Moth-er Earth, your warmth and cold.

Tvá trá - va ze-le - ná dál vá - bí nás.
You give the green'-ry birth worth more than gold.

Máš zá - voj z ob-la - ků bí - lých, jak sníh,
Your veil of air-y clouds soft, snow - y white.

hvěz-do má, bár-ko zá - zra - ků na ne - be-
Spe-cial cra - dle where won-der sprouts, all hea - ven's

Značí nejdřív recitaci a potom zpěv:

Recitation (in brackets):

1.
(Chválím Tě země má)
Chválím Tě, Země má,
(tvůj žár i mráz)
tvůj žár i mráz.
(Tvá tráva zelená)
Tvá tráva zelená
(dál vábí nás)
dál vábí nás.

(Máš závoj z oblaků)
Máš závoj z oblaků
(bílých, jak sníh)
bílých, jak sníh,
(hvězdo má, bárko zázraků)
hvězdo má, bárko zázraků
(na nebesích)
na nebesích.

1.
(I praise You, Mother Earth)
I praise You Mother Earth,
(your warmth and cold)
your warmth and cold.
(You give the green'ry birth)
You give the green'ry birth
(worth more than gold)
worth more than gold.

(Your veil of airy clouds)
Your veil of airy clouds
(soft, snowy white)
soft, snowy white.
(Special cradle where wonder sprouts)
Special cradle where wonder sprouts,
(all heaven's pride.)
all heaven's pride.

Refrén (společně, unisono):

Ať před mou planetou
hvězdný prach zametou.
Dej vláhu rostlinám,
dej ptákům pít,
prosím svou přízeň dej i nám,
dej mír a klid.

2.
Dej vláhu rostlinám
(Chválím Tě země má)
Dej ptákům pít
(Tvůj žár i mráz)
Svou přízeň dej i nám
(Tvá tráva zelená)
Dej mír a klid
(Dál vábí nás)

(Máš závoj z oblaků)
(Bílých, jak sníh)
(Hvězdo má, bárko zázraků)
(Na nebesích)

Chorus:

Ať před mou
(Ať před mou)
planetou
(planetou)
Hvězdný prach
(Hvězdný prach)
zametou.
Dej vláhu rostlinám
(Dej vláhu rostlinám)
Dej ptákům pít
(Dej ptákům pít)
Prosím svou přízeň dej i nám
(Svou přízeň dej i nám)
Dej mír a klid
(Dej mír a klid).
Svou přízeň dej i nám
Dej mír a klid.

Chorus (together in unison):

Planet mine, holy grail,
every one, come and hail.
Give all the flowers rain,
keep birds at ease.
If I may, in your gracious reign,
give mankind peace.

2.
Give all the flowers rain,
(I praise You, Mother Earth)
keep birds at ease.
(Your warmth and cold)
And in your gracious reign
(You five the green'ry birth)
give mankind peace.
(Worth more than gold)

(Your veil of airy clouds)
(Soft, snowy white)
(Special cradle where wonder sprouts)
(All heavens pride.)

Chorus:

Planet mine,
(Planet mine)
holy grail.
(Holy grail.)
Every one
(Every one)
come and hail.
Give all the flowers rain,
(Give all the flowers rain),
keep birds at ease
(keep birds at ease).
If I may, in your gracious reign,
(And in your gracious reign)
give mankind peace
(Give mankind peace).
And in your gracious name
give mankind peace.

Translation by Zuzana Čtveráčková (2022)

NATURE & SEASONS BELGIUM

80
Mijn vlakke land
My Open Land

Mijn vlakke land (1962) was originally written in French as Le Plat Pays. Brel refers in the song to the landscape of West Flanders, the region his family originates from. Of course, this landscape is rather typical for large parts of the low countries, what clarifies its popularity. Many artists performed the song in French and Dutch. The typical Brel accent, the powerful storytelling, lyric accordion and restless melancholy create a lovely ode to Flanders.

By Liesbeth Segers, Koor&Stem

Lyrics: Jacques Brel (1929-78) Music: Jacques Brel (1929-78)
Translation into Dutch: Ernst van Altena (1933-99)

1. Wan-neer de Noord-zee kop-pig breekt aan ho-ge dui-nen, en wit-te vlok-ken schuim uit-één-slaan op de krui-nen, wan-neer de nor-se vloed beukt aan het zwart ba-salt en o-ver dijk en duin de grij-ze ne-vel valt, wan-neer bij eb het strand woest is als een woes-

1. When the o-cean dark-ens for its cold as-sault, when it beats the dunes with sting-ing spray of salt, when the rocks must face the spring tide's smash-ing reach, when the ebb-ing tide slides hiss-ing on the beach, when the si-lent fog drifts like a face-less

1.
Wanneer de Noordzee koppig breekt aan hoge duinen
En witte vlokken schuim uiteenslaan op de kruinen,
Wanneer de norse vloed beukt aan het zwart basalt
En over dijk en duin de grijze nevel valt,
Wanneer bij eb het strand woest is als een woestijn
En natte westewinden gieren van venijn,
Dan vecht mijn land... Mijn vlakke land...

        1.
        When the ocean darkens for its cold assault,
        when it beats the dunes with stinging spray of salt,
        when the rocks must face the spring tide's smashing reach,
        when the ebbing tide slides hissing on the beach,
        when the silent fog drifts like a faceless ghost,
        when the raging wind tears down the ragged coast,
        my land fights back - my stubborn land...

2.
Wanneer de regen daalt op straten, pleinen, perken,
Op dak en torenspits van hemelhoge kerken,
Die in dit vlakke land de enige bergen zijn,
Wanneer onder de wolken mensen dwergen zijn,
Wanneer de dagen gaan in domme regelmaat
En bolle oostewind het land nog vlakker slaat,
Dan wacht mijn land... Mijn vlakke land...

        2.
        With the drizzle sifting down for days and days,
        draining vivid colours into chilly greys,
        where the mountains are but towering cathedrals,
        and waterfalls drip meekly from its rueful gargoyles,
        where the moaning wind fills man with apprehension
        and makes him tremble feebly, longing for the sun,
        my land must wait - my open land...

3.
Wanneer de lage lucht vlak over 't water scheert,
Wanneer de lage lucht ons nederigheid leert,
Wanneer de lage lucht er grijs als leisteen is,
Wanneer de lage lucht er vaal als keileem is,
Wanneer de noordewind de vlakte vierendeelt,
Wanneer de noordewind er onze adem steelt,
Dan kraakt mijn land... Mijn vlakke land...

3.
With the sky so low it brings humility,
with the sky so low it touches agony,
with the sky so grey it blurs destiny,
with the sky so grey it grows into the sea,
with the freezing wind slicing like a knife,
with the icy wind ripping open life,
my land backs down - my shallow land...

4.
Wanneer de Schelde blinkt in zuidelijke zon
En elke Vlaamse vrouw flaneert in zon-japon,
Wanneer de eerste spin z'n lentewebben weeft
Of dampende het veld in juli-zonlicht beeft,
Wanneer de zuidewind er schatert door het graan,
Wanneer de zuidewind er jubelt langs de baan,
Dan juicht mijn land... Mijn vlakke land...

4.
When the rivers bring in water from the south,
when bouncing children laugh and sing and shout,
when the cobwebs glitter in the dew of spring,
when the summer sun caresses everything,
when the lambs can roll and run in rustic peace,
when the winds play gently with the teasing grass,
my land sings out - my living land...

Adaptation by Morné Coetzer (1997)

Copyright © 1962 Editions Jacques Brel pour la Belgique et les Pays-Bas. © 1962 Editions Musicales Eddie Barclay (Monde sauf pour la Belgique et les Pays-Bas). © Assigned 1964 to Editions Patricia & S.E.M.I., Paris (France) (Le Monde sauf pour la Belgique et les Pays-Bas). Reprinted by permission

NATURE & SEASONS   SWEDEN

81
Öppna landskap
Open Country

"Öppna landskap", Open Country, is a song by singer-songwriter and rock musician, Ulf Lundell, who is beloved by an audience far beyond the domains of rock. It has become a kind of national hymn. It is popular at sing-alongs and school graduations, and even the Royal Guard in Stockholm has featured it. According to Lundell himself, the song was born "in the valley between Genevad and Veinge, along Route 117 from Halmstad to Markaryd", and he says it is "a song about freedom, pride and self-esteem, and it is a very Swedish, not to say Nordic, song."

By Kerstin Carpvik, head of library, Musikverket

Lyrics: Ulf Lundell (1949-)   Music: Ulf Lundell (1949-)

1. Jag trivs bäst i öpp-na land-skap, nä-ra ha-vet vill jag bo,
   1. I feel best in o-pen coun-try, let me live close to the sea,

   någ-ra må-na-der om å-ret, så att
   just a few months eve-ry year will bring some

   sjä-len kan få ro. Jag trivs bäst i öpp-na land-
   in-ner peace to me. I feel best in o-pen coun-

   -skap, där vin-dar-na får fart. Där
   -try where winds blow free and strong. Where

   lär-kor-na står högt i skyn, och sjun-ger un-der-bart.
   larks high in the heav-ens sing so sweet-ly all day long.

1. Jag trivs bäst i öppna landskap
   nära havet vill jag bo
   några månader om året
   så att själen kan få ro.
   Jag trivs bäst i öppna landskap
   där vindarna får fart.
   Där lärkorna står högt i skyn
   och sjunger underbart.
   Där bränner jag mitt brännvin själv
   och kryddar med Johannesört
   och dricker det med välbehag
   till sill och hembakt vört.
   Jag trivs bäst i öppna landskap
   nära havet vill jag bo.

2. Jag trivs bäst i fred och frihet
   för både kropp och själ.
   Ingen kommer i min närhet
   som stänger in och stjäl.
   Jag trivs bäst när dagen bräcker
   när fälten fylls av ljus.
   När tuppen gal på avstånd
   när det är långt till närmsta hus
   Men ändå så pass nära
   att en tyst och stilla natt
   när man sitter under stjärnorna
   kan höra festens skratt.
   Jag trivs bäst i fred och frihet
   för både kropp och själ.

3. Jag trivs bäst när havet svallar
   och måsarna ger skri.
   När stranden fylls av snäckskal
   med havsmusik uti.
   När det klara och det enkla
   får råda som det vill.
   När ja är ja och nej är nej
   och tvivlet tiger still.
   Då binder jag en krans av löv
   och lägger den vid närmsta sten
   där runor ristats för vår skull
   nån gång för länge sen.
   Jag trivs bäst när havet svallar
   och måsarna ger skri.

---

1. *I feel best in open country,*
   let me live close to the sea,
   just a few months every year will bring
   some inner peace to me.
   I feel best in open country
   where winds blow free and strong.
   Where larks high in the heavens sing
   so sweetly all day long.
   That's where my moonshine I distil,
   and flavour it as I require
   with home-baked bread and pickled herring
   it fills my desire.
   I feel best in open country,
   let me live close to the sea.

2. *I feel best when peace and freedom*
   fill my body and my soul.
   They both need a haven where no-one
   can stop me feeling whole
   Let me see the new day breaking,
   as it fills the fields with light.
   As cocks crow from a distance
   with the next house out of sight
   But nonetheless so close that when
   I sit beneath the starry skies
   One quiet night, a party's laughter
   to my haven flies.
   I feel best when peace and freedom
   fill my body and my soul.

3. *Let me hear the cries of seagulls,*
   let me see the ocean's swell.
   The beaches full of shells in which
   the ocean's voices dwell.
   When the clear-cut and the simple
   are at leave to have their say.
   When yes is yes and no is no
   and doubt is far away.
   Then I will bind a wreath of leaves
   and lay it by the nearest stone
   Where runes were carved for our sake,
   sometime in days long gone.
   Let me hear the cries of seagulls,
   let me see the ocean's swell.

   Translation by Fred Lane (2022)

NATURE & SEASONS						THE NETHERLANDS

82
Het regent zonnestralen
It's Raining Sunrays

This song is by the duo Acda and De Munnik. The lyrics tells the story of a man who sits on a terrace in the South of France and reads his obituary in the newspaper! Accordingly he sees this as a great opportunity to escape from his petty-bourgeois existence and choose a different life path. The song is actually a modern variant of "Wanderlust"; the romantic desire to leave one's own ordinary world behind to seek for new paths to wander.

By Christiane Nieuwmeijer, Leiden University of Applied Sciences
& Lieuwe Noordam, Prins Claus Conservatorium, Groningen

Lyrics & Music: Thomas Acda (1967-) & Paul De Munnik (1970)

1. Op een ter-ras er-gens in Fran-krijk in de zon, zit een man die het tot gis-te-ren nooit won. Maar z'n au-to vloog hier vlak-bij uit de bocht, zon-der hem,

1. At a café somewhere in France in the sun, is a man who tried it all but ne-ver won. But his car missing a sharp bend crashed near-by with-out him,

1.
Op een terras ergens in Frankrijk in de zon,
zit een man die het tot gisteren nooit won.
Maar z'n auto vloog hier vlakbij uit de bocht,
zonder hem, zonder Herman...,
want die had hem net verkocht.

2.
Herman in de zon op het terras,
leest in 't AD dat ie niet meer in leven was.
Zijn auto was volledig afgebrand,
en de man die hem gekocht had,
stond onder zijn naam in de krant.

1.
At a cafe somewhere in France in the sun,
is a man who tried it all but never won.
But his car missing a sharp bend crashed nearby
without him, without Herman,
he'd just sold it to some guy.

2.
Herman, in the sunny cafe's hive,
reads in a news report he was no longer alive.
His car had all gone up in fiery flames,
and the poor guy who had bought the thing from him,
got mentioned under Herman's name.

Chorus:
Owohooo... even rustig ademhalen.
Owohooo... lijkt of het regent als altijd.
Maar het regent en het regent zonnestralen...

3.
Een week geleden in een park in Amsterdam,
had ie z'n leven overzien en schrok zich lam.
Hij was een man wiens leven nu al was bepaald
en van al zijn jongensdromen,
was alleen het oud worden gehaald.

Chorus:
Owohooo... even rustig ademhalen...

Bridge:
Op een bankje in het park kwam het besluit.
Noem het dapper, noem het vluchten,
maar ik knijp ertussen uit.
Nu een week geleden
en daar zat ie dan maar weer.
Met meer vrijheid dan hem lief was
en nu wist ie het niet meer.

4.
Herman leest wel honderd keer de krant,
staat het echt pagina achttien zwart omrand?
Hield ie vroeger al z'n meningen
en al z'n dromen stil,
nu was ie niks, niet, niemand, nergens meer...
Kan dus gaan waar ie maar wil!

5.
Herman rekent af en staat dan op,
hij heeft eindelijk de wind weer in z'n kop,
'k Heb een tweede kans gekregen
en dat is meer dan ik verdien.
Maar als dit het is, is dit het...,
als dit het is, is dit het, als dit het is,
is dit het en we zullen het wel zien...

Chorus:
||: Owohooo... even rustig ademhalen... :||
En het regent zonnestralen!

Chorus:
Oh woh oooh... just breathe slowly and lightly.
Oh woh oooh... it's raining as ever before.
But it's raining and it's raining sunrays bright.

3.
A week ago in an Amsterdam park,
he weighed up his life and the future looked dark.
Here was a man whose life had been all foretold,
a man whose only dream come true
would have been his growing old.

Chorus:
Oh woh oooh... just breathe slowly...

Bridge:
Sitting in the park he knew that the game was on
Call it brave, call it flight,
But believe me I am gone.
Only one week - no more -
and he was back for all to see,
with more freedom he could deal with,
not a clue how to be free.

4.
Herman reads the news time and again,
is it really in a black frame on page ten?
Used to keep all his opinions
and all his dreams to himself,
now he reckoned there was no one that knew him...
Can go anywhere he wants!

5.
Herman pays the bill and gets up fast,
a wind of change blowing for him at last.
This is a second chance for me,
more than I deserve I suppose.
But if this is it, this is it,
if this is it, this is it, if this is it,
this is it and we will see how it goes.

Chorus:
||: Oh woh ooh... just breathe slowly... :||
And it's raining sunrays bright!

Translation by Arnold Mühren (2021)

Copyright © 1998 Aedm Music. All Rights Administered by BMG Rights Management (US) LLC. International Copyright Secured. All Rights Reserved. Reprinted by Permission of Hal Leonard Europe Ltd.

Chapter IV

Folksongs & Traditionals

83
Uti vår hage
In Our Meadow

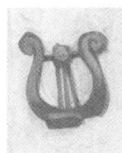

'Uti vår hage' – In Our Meadow – is a Swedish folk song of unknown origin, first written down on the island of Gotland in the 1880s. Accordingly it has become one of the most well-known folk songs, not least thanks to being arranged for choir by Hugo Alfvén (1872-1960) and often performed. Among other things, it is part of the traditional singing at "Valborgsmässoafton" (Mass of Saint Walpurgis Night) on April 30th, when people gather at bonfires to welcome spring. In the first verse of the song, several plants are mentioned: blueberries, lilies, European columbine, sage, mint and lemon balm. These plants have historically been used for medicinal purposes.

By Kerstin Carpvik, head of library, Musikverket

Music & Lyrics: Unknown or Hugo Lutteman (1837-1889)

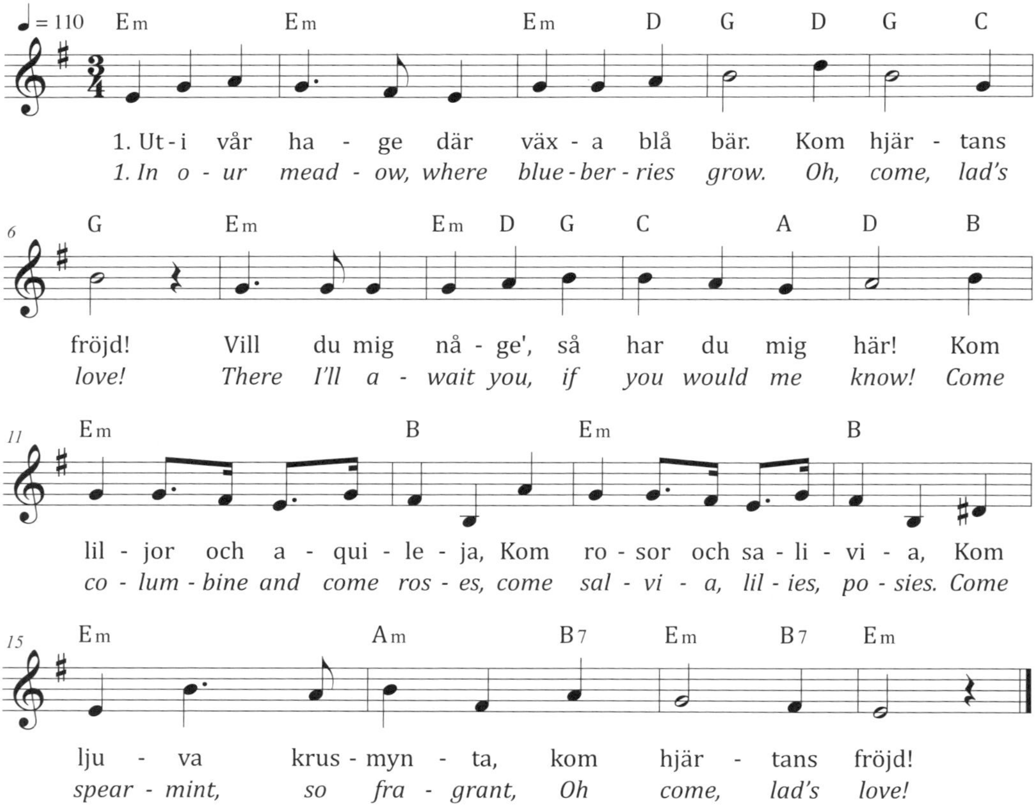

1. Ut-i vår hage där väx-a blå bär. Kom hjär-tans fröjd! Vill du mig nå-ge', så har du mig här! Kom lil-jor och a-qui-le-ja, Kom ro-sor och sa-li-vi-a, Kom lju-va krus-myn-ta, kom hjär-tans fröjd!

1. In o-ur mead-ow, where blue-ber-ries grow. Oh, come, lad's love! There I'll a-wait you, if you would me know! Come co-lum-bine and come ros-es, come sal-vi-a, lil-ies, po-sies. Come spear-mint, so fra-grant, Oh come, lad's love!

1. Uti vår hage där växa blå bär.
    Kom hjärtans fröjd!
    Vill du mig någe', så har du mig här!

Kör:
    Kom liljor och aquileja,
    Kom rosor och salivia,
    Kom ljuva krusmynta, kom hjärtans fröjd!

2. Fagra små blommor där bjuda till dans.
    Kom hjärtans fröjd
    Vill du, så binder jag åt dig en krans!

    Kom liljor och aquileja…

3. Kransen den sätter jag sen i ditt hår,
    Kom hjärtans fröjd
    Solen den dalar men hoppet uppgår!

    Kom liljor och aquileja…

4. Uti vår hage finns blommor och bär,
    Kom hjärtans fröjd
    Men utav alla du kärast mig är!

    Kom liljor och aquileja…

1. In our meadow, where blueberries grow.
    Oh, come, lad's love!
    There I'll await you, if you would me know!

Chorus:
    Come columbine and come roses,
    come salvia, lilies, posies.
    Come spearmint, so fragrant, Oh come, lad's love!

2. Lovely small flowers, they bend in the dew
    Oh, come, lad's love!
    I'll pick them and make a garland for you

    Come columbine and come roses…

3. You'll wear that garland I made as a crown
    Oh, come, lad's love!
    Hope will rise up as the sun it goes down

    Come columbine and come roses…

4. In our meadow, the flowers they bloom
    Oh, come, lad's love!
    We'll be together, a bride and a groom

    Come columbine and come roses…

Translation by Fred Lane (2023)

84
Ljubav se ne trži
Love Is Not for Sale

Međimurska popevka – a type of folk song typical for the Međimurje County in the Northwestern part of Croatia – is listed on UNESCO's List of the Intangible Cultural Heritage of Humanity. The distinctly cantabile tune promotes intense sensibility and is based on pentatonic-like tone scales combined with epic poetry relating to spiritual themes. The poems express love, the natural beauty of Međimurje County, wildlife, homesickness and longing for a loved one, or express some kind of religious sentiment. The songs used to be sung by women, either in solo, or in unison a cappella. Over time, these folk songs developed vocal harmony, various instrumental accompaniment, as well as dance. This well-known Međimurje folk song "Love Is Not for Sale" is popular to this day. It features not only in its authentic, traditional version, but also in various contemporary performances and arrangements.

By Dr. Jasenka Ostojić, University of Zagreb, Music Academy

1. ||: Ljubav se ne trži niti ne kupuje :||
||:Ki ljubiti ne zna, ko ljubiti ne zna
naj se ne hapljuje :||

2. ||: Či pak nam je ljubav iskrena i prava :||
||: Z srca ju ne spere,
                  z srca ju ne spere
Mura niti Drava :||

3. ||: Ljubav ne raspari žbiri ni žandari :||
||: Žbiri ni žandari, žbiri ni žandari
niti poglavari :||

1. ||: *Love is not for sale and love is not for buyin'* :||
||: *Those unable to love, those unable to love shouldn't be even tryin'* :||

2. ||: *If you find a true love, hotter than the lava* :||
||: *'t can't be washed away by,*
                  can't be washed away by
Mura neither Drava :||

3. ||: *Love can't be decoupled by the chiefs or masters* :||
||: *By the chiefs or masters, by the chiefs or masters nor by the policemen* :||

Translation by Nikola Vranić "J.R. August" (2021)

85
Pūt, vējiņi!
Blow, Wind!

First published in 1872, it tells the story of a young man, travelling by boat to the historical region of Kurzeme to meet his bride. Although seemingly reckless he is bravely determined to cross the waters to see his beloved. At the end of the song he assures his bride's mother that everything he owns is his own, earned and saved. Probably this feeling of independence has helped to keep this folk song in the hearts and minds of people from generation to generation. Today, it is performed both in familiar circles and at our giant choir festivals. When the opening line is heard, concert audiences quietly get on their feet to experience with the singers the whole set of emotions of this song – from vigorous conviction to a delicate touch.

By Rūta Kanteruka, president, Latvian Music Teachers' Association, LVIIMSA

Lyrics & music: folk song

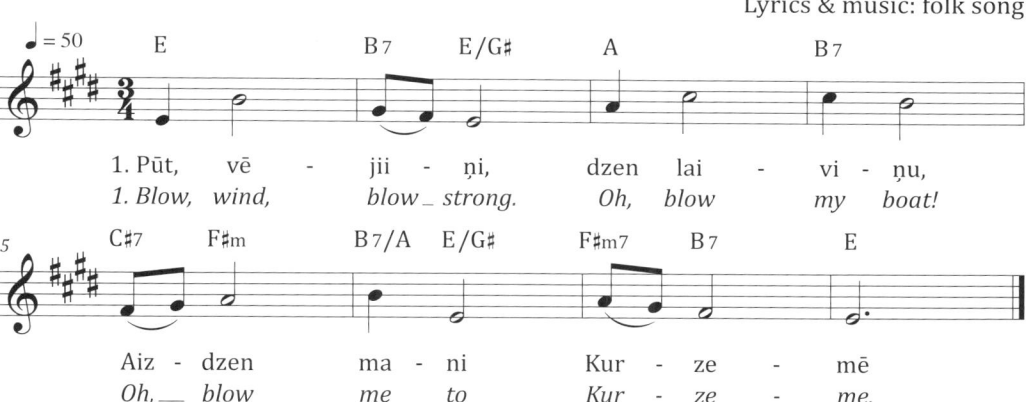

1. Pūt, vējiiņi, dzen laiviņu,
   Aizdzen mani Kurzemē.

2. Kurzemniece man solīja
   Sav' meitiņu malējiņ'.

3. Solīt sola, bet nedeva,
   Teic man lielu dzērājiņ'.

4. Teic man lielu dzērājiņu,
   Kume-liņa skrējējiņ'.

5. Kuru krogu es izdzēru,
   Kam noskrēju kumeliņ'?

6. Pats par savu naudu dzēru,
   Pats skrēj' savu kumeliņ'.

7. Pats paņēmu līgaviņu,
   Tēvam, mātei nezinot.

1. Blow, wind, blow strong. Oh, blow my boat!
   Oh, blow me to Kurzeme.

2. A woman there has promised me
   her daughter's hand in marriage.

3. A promise made, a vow not kept,
   she claims I am a drunkard.

4. She claims I am a drunkard, and
   she claims I am a racer.

5. Whose bar, ask I, did I drink dry?
   Whose horse did I race ragged?

6. I drink with my own salary,
   I race with my own horses.

7. So I took my own bride away
   without her parents knowing.

Translated by MāraWalsh Sinka (2022)

86
Ciuleandra

Originating from the region of Muntenia, "Ciuleandra" is originally an ecstatic folk dance, still danced today. This dance has inspired the famous version recorded in 1956 by one of Romania's greatest voices, Maria Tănase (1913-63). Tănase took over the melodic line of the dance and added lyrics – loud dance commands! – to it. Accompanied by the orchestra conducted by Nicușor Predescu (1919-86), Maria Tănase made "Ciuleandra" one of the best known Romanian folksongs. And just like the Ciuleandra-folk dance, the song opens slowly and has – verse by verse – a progressively accelerated rhythm.

By Alexandra Belibou, Lecturer PhD, Faculty of Music, Transilvania University of Brașov

Lyrics: folk poem   Music: folksong

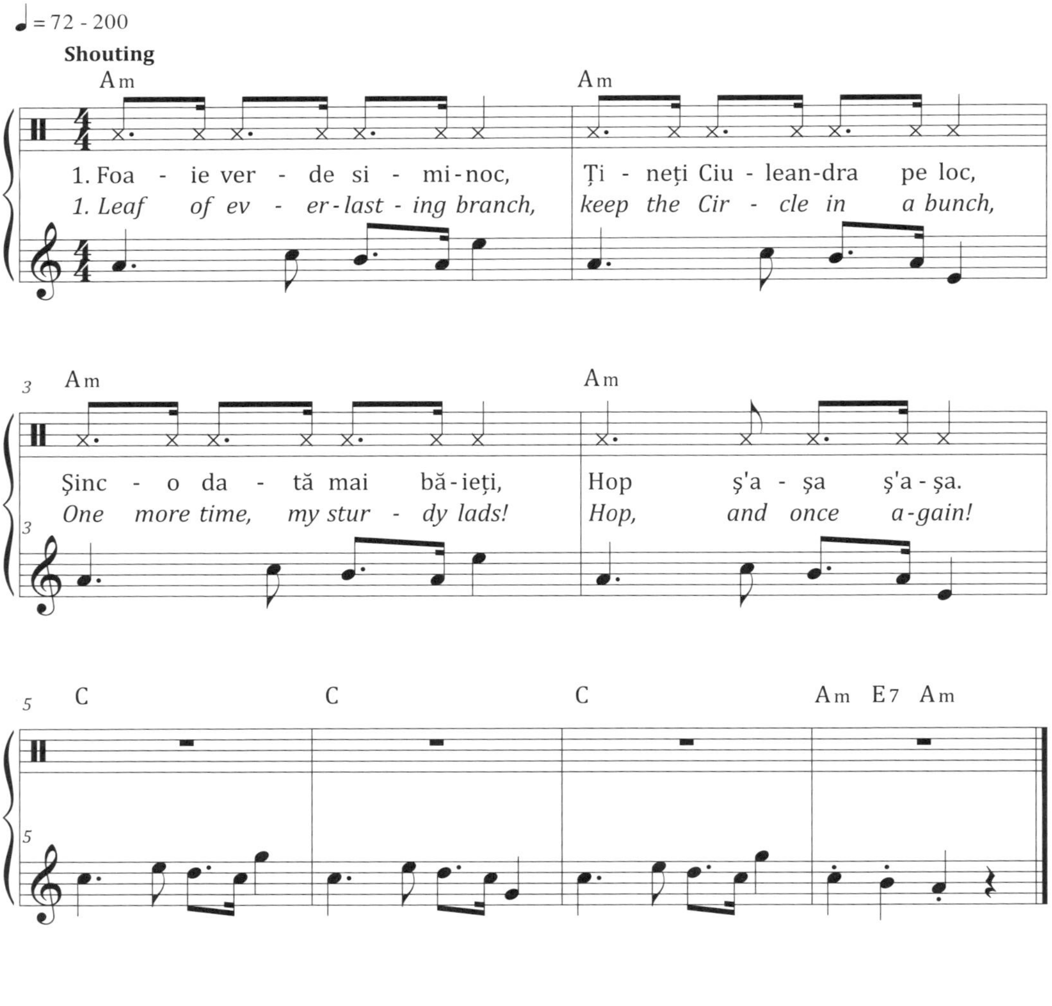

♩ = 72 - 200

Shouting

1. Foa - ie ver - de si - mi - noc, / Ți - neți Ciu - lean - dra pe loc,
   1. Leaf of ev - er - last - ing branch, / keep the Cir - cle in a bunch,

Șinc - o da - tă mai bă - ieți, / Hop ș'a - șa ș'a - șa.
One more time, my stur - dy lads! / Hop, and once a - gain!

1. Foaie verde siminoc,
   Țineți Ciuleandra pe loc,
   Și-nc-o dată, măi băieți,
   Hop ș-așa, ș-așa.

2. Țineți-o, flăcăi așa,
   Până n-ajunge puica,
   Și-nc-o dată, măi băieți,
   Hop ș-așa, ș-așa.

3. Întăriți-o nițeluș,
   C-ajunge acuș-acuș,
   Și-nc-o dată, măi băieți,
   Hop ș-așa, ș-așa.

4. Mai întăriți-o de-un pas,
   C-a ajuns și n-a rămas,
   Și-nc-o dată, măi băieți,
   Hop ș-așa, ș-așa.

5. Două fire, două paie,
   Luați Ciuleandra la bătaie,
   Și-nc-o dată, măi băieți,
   Hop ș-așa, ș-așa.

6. Tot așa, că nu mă las,
   Că sunt cu puica pe-un pas,
   Și-nc-o dată, măi băieți,
   Hop ș-așa, ș-așa.

7. Două fire, două paie,
   Ia ciuleandra la bătaie,
   Și-nc-o dată, măi băieți,
   Hop ș-așa, ș-așa.

---

1. *Leaf of everlasting branch,*
   Keep the Circle in a bunch,
   One more time, my sturdy lads!
   Hop, and once again!

2. *Keep it up, lads, is it clear?*
   'Til my fair maiden gets here!
   One more time, my sturdy lads!
   Hop, and once again!

3. *Kick it up a little bit*
   She'll arrive and then, that's it!
   One more time, my sturdy lads!
   Hop, and once again!

4. *Kick it up, lads, kick away!*
   She arrived and didn't stay!
   One more time, my sturdy lads!
   Hop, and once again!

5. *Straw and blade in bunch of two now*
   Stomp the Circle through and through now!
   One more time, my sturdy lads!
   Hop, and once again!

6. *Keep it up, don't lose your pep,*
   For I matched my maiden's step!
   One more time, my sturdy lads!
   Hop, and once again!

7. *Straw and blade in bunch of two, now,*
   Stomp the Circle through and through now!
   One more time, my sturdy lads!
   Hop, and once again!

Translated by Alex Szollo & Beck Corlan (2023)

POLAND — FOLKSONGS & TRADITIONALS

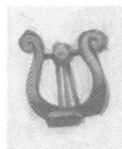

87
Hej sokoły
Hey Falcons!

Whereas the exact origin of the melody is unknown, the author of the lyrics is Tomasz Padura (1801-1871), a Polish-Ukrainian poet and composer. The melody was popular among Polish soldiers during the Polish-Soviet war, and also sung by Home Army guerrillas during World War II. Originally written in Polish, the song "Hey Falcons" (also known as Ukraine) refers to traditional Polish nobility, Polish romanticism and Ukrainian folklore. Today, it is identified with festivities, weddings and feasts, where people hold hands and dance, faster and faster, in couples or in chains. Also popular in other countries like Ukraine (where it is viewed as a native song), Belarus, Slovakia and in the eastern part of Czech Republic.

By Dorota Stefaniak, Academy of Music "Stanisław Moniuszko" in Gdańsk

Lyrics: Tomasz Padura (1801-71)   Music: Ukrainian folksong

♩ = 120-140

1. Hej, tam gdzieś znad czar-nej wo-dy, sia-da na koń ko-zak mło-dy.
1. *Far off where the sea is black, a Coss-ack mounts his hor-se's back.*

Czu-le że-gna się z dziew-czy-ną, jesz-cze czu-lej z U-kra-i-ną.
Fon-dly bids his girl good-bye, fon-der yet for U-kraine he sighs.

Chorus:

Hej, hej, hej so-ko-ły, o-mi-jaj-cie gó-ry, la-sy, do-ły.
Hey, hey, hey, my fal-cons, fly high o-ver fo-rest, val-ley, moun-tain.

Dzwoń, dzwoń, dzwoń dzwo-necz-ku mój ste-po-wy
Ring ring bells are ring-ing. On the steppe a

sko-wro-ne-czku. dzwoń, dzwoń, dzwoń.
lark is sing-ing. ring, ring, ring.

1. Hej, tam gdzieś znad czarnej wody
   siada na koń kozak młody,
   Czule żegna się z dziewczyną,
   jeszcze czulej z Ukrainą.

Chorus:
   Hej, hej, hej, sokoły,
   omijajcie góry, lasy, doły.
   Dzwoń, dzwoń, dzwoń, dzwoneczku,
   mój stepowy skowroneczku.
   Hej, hej, hej sokoły,
   omijajcie góry, lasy, doły.
   Dzwoń, dzwoń, dzwoń, dzwoneczku,
   mój stepowy, dzwoń, dzwoń, dzwoń.

2. Pięknych dziewcząt jest niemało,
   lecz najwięcej w Ukrainie.
   Tam me serce pozostało
   przy kochanej mej dziewczynie.

   Hej, hej, hej, sokoły...

3. Ona biedna tam została,
   przepióreczka moja mała.
   A ja tutaj, w obcej stronie,
   dniem i nocą tęsknię do niej.

   Hej, hej, hej, sokoły...

4. Żal, żal za dziewczyną,
   za zieloną Ukrainą.
   Żal, żal, serce płacze,
   że jej więcej nie zobaczę.

   Hej, hej, hej, sokoły...

5. Wina, wina, wina dajcie,
   a jak umrę – pochowajcie.
   Na zielonej Ukrainie
   przy kochanej mej dziewczynie.

   Hej, hej, hej, sokoły...

1. Far off where the sea is black,
   a Cossack mounts his horse's back.
   Fondly bids his girl goodbye,
   fonder yet for Ukraine he sighs.

Chorus:
   Hey, hey, hey, my falcons,
   fly high over forest, valley, mountain.
   Ring, ring – bells are ringing.
   On the steppe a lark is singing.
   Hey, hey, hey, my falcons,
   fly high over forest, valley, mountain.
   Ring, ring – bells are ringing.
   On the wild steppe – ring, ring, ring.

2. Lots of girls in all the world,
   but most of all in fair Ukraine.
   And my longing, loving heart.
   Shall with my bonny lass remain.

   Hey, hey, hey, my falcons...

3. My sweet poor lass had to stay,
   my wee bird can't fly away.
   Here through foreign lands I go.
   Night and day I miss her so.

   Hey, hey, hey, my falcons...

4. I cry, I cry for my lass,
   for Ukraine's waving grass.
   Sore, sore, my heart is sore,
   for I'll never see you more.

   Hey, hey, hey, my falcons...

5. Bring me, bring me, bring me wine.
   When I'm dead make sure I lie
   in a grave beneath the grass
   side by side with my bonny lass.

   Hey, hey, hey, my falcons...

Translation by David & William Malcolm (2021)

FOLKSONGS & TRADITIONALS   CZECHIA

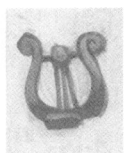

88
Černé oči, jděte spat
Lovely Black Eyes, Time to Sleep

"Lovely Black Eyes, Time to Sleep" is a folk song written in the 19th century. It appears in collections of national songs, the most famous score may be in the collection of Karel Jaromír Erben "Písně národní v Čechách" (The National Songs of Czechia) from the middle of the 19th century. Today it is one of the most famous and popular folk songs in the Czech environment. It is often understood as a lullaby, but the meaning of the song is a little different. This is an important topic of folk literature in the 18th century – a conscription to the war, which for many years meant the end of the life of young men. The song therefore has a tragic subtext.

By Hanuš Bartoň, Academy of Performing Arts in Prague, HAMU

Lyrics: folk poem   Music: folk song

1. Černé oči, jděte spat,
   černé oči jděte spat,
   však musíte ráno vstát,
   však musíte ráno vstát.

2. Ráno, ráno, raníčko,
   ráno, ráno, raníčko,
   dřív než vyjde sluníčko,
   dřív než vyjde sluníčko.

3. Sluníčko už vychází,
   sluníčko už vychází,
   má milá se prochází,
   má milá se prochází.

1. *Lovely black eyes, time to sleep,*
   lovely black eyes, time to sleep,
   in the morning we will meet,
   in the morning we will meet.

2. *Let's say better half way night,*
   let's say better half way night,
   long before the sun shines bright,
   long before the sun shines bright.

3. *Sun is rising fast, beware,*
   sun is rising fast, beware,
   charming maiden waits out there,
   charming maiden waits out there.

4. Prochází se po rynku,
   prochází se po rynku,
   přinesla nám novinku,
   přinesla nám novinku.

5. To novinku takovou,
   to novinku takovou,
   že na vojnu verbujou,
   že na vojnu verbujou.

6. Když verbujou, budou brát,
   když verbujou, budou brát,
   škoda hochů nastokrát,
   škoda hochů nastokrát.

4. She awaits you in the square,
   she awaits you in the square,
   and has vital news to share
   and has vital news to share.

5. News that you would rather miss,
   news that you wou'd rather miss,
   for today you will enlist,
   for today you will enlist.

6. When recruited, there's no choice,
   when recruited, there's no choice,
   I'm so sorry for you boys,
   I'm so sorry for you boys.

Translation by Zuzana Čtveráčková (2021)

FOLKSONGS & TRADITIONALS   IRELAND

89
Whiskey in the Jar

"Whiskey in the Jar", which dates back to the 17th century, tells the story of the exploits of one Patrick Fleming, a famous highwayman from the town of Athlone in the midlands of Ireland. Due to its age the ballad is known in many forms and was exported to the USA by Irish emigrants, where it became well-known in a number of different versions in regions such as the Appalachians and Ozarks in the South. During the American Civil War, the famed Fighting 69th, composed of almost all Irishmen, adopted the song as their own anthem in a version entitled "We'll fight for Uncle Sam". All variants, however, share the common theme of highway robbery, betrayal by a faithless woman (in this version Jenny) and the eventual execution of the hero. It was popularized in recent times by The Dubliners, the Dublin band Thin Lizzy, whose version hit number one in the Irish charts in '73, as well as by Metallica in '99.

By Mark Armstrong, SING IRELAND

Lyrics: folk poem   Music: folksong

1. As I was go-in' o-ver the far famed Ker-ry moun-tains, I met with Cap-tain Far-rell and his mo-ney he was count-ing. I first pro-duced my pis-tol and then pro-duced my ra-pier, saying "Stand and de-li-ver" for he were a bold de-cei-ver. Mush-a ring dumb-a do dumb-a da, wack fall the dad-dy-o,

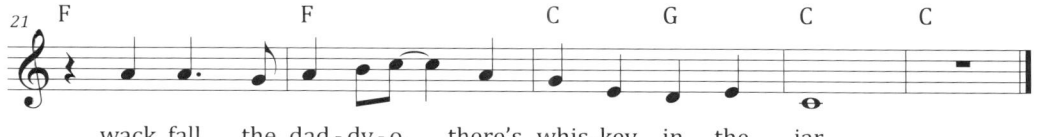

wack fall the dad-dy-o, there's whis-key in the jar.

1. As I was a goin' over the far famed Kerry mountains,
   I met with captain Farrell and his money he was counting,
   I first produced my pistol and I then produced my rapier,
   saying "Stand and deliver" for he were a bold deciever.

   Chorus:
   Mush-a ring dumb-a do dumb-a da,
   wack fall the daddy-o, wack fall the daddy-o,
   there's whiskey in the jar.

2. I counted up my money and it made a pretty penny,
   I took that money home and I gave it to my Jenny,
   she promised and she vowed that she never would deceive me
   but the devil take the women for they never can be easy.

   Mush-a ring dumb-a do dumb-a da...

3. I went into my chamber for to take a little slumber,
   I dreamt of gold and jewels and for sure it was no wonder
   but Jenny took my charges and filled them up with water
   and sent for Captain Farrell to be ready for the slaughter.

   Mush-a ring dumb-a do dumb-a da...

4. It was early in the mornin' before I rose to travel
   surrounded by the footmen and likewise Captain Farrell,
   I went for my old pistol for they'd stolen my old rapier
   but I couldn't shoot the water so a prisoner I was taken.

   Mush-a ring dumb-a do dumb-a da...

5. If anyone can save me it's my brother in the army,
   I think that he is stationed in Cork or in Killarney
   and if he would be here we'd be rovin' in Kilkenny,
   I know he'd treat be better than my darlin' sportin' Jenny.

   Mush-a ring dumb-a do dumb-a da...

6. Now some take delight in the fishin' and the fowlin',
   others take delight in the carriage wheels a rollin,
   I take delight in the juice of the barley
   and countin' pretty women in the mornin' oh so early.

   Mush-a ring dumb-a do dumb-a da...

FOLKSONGS & TRADITIONALS · ESTONIA

90
Kungla Rahvas
People of Kungla

"People of Kungla" is one of the oldest songs in Estonian choral literature, and since almost all Estonians know it, it is often considered a folk song of unknown origin. But it was, in fact, composed by Karl August Hermann in 1874 to lyrics by the poet Friedrich Kuhlbars. It is a part of the first Estonian opera "Estonian gods and peoples" (Uku and Vanemuine) from 1907 and is often sung in the Estonian Song Celebration, since 1869 one of the world's largest amateur choral events held every fifth year in Tallinn with more than 30,000 participants and various parades.

By Kaie Tanner, Sec. General, Estonian Choral Association

Lyrics: Friedrich Kuhlbars (1841-1924)   Music: Karl August Hermann (1851-1909)

1. Kui Kung-la rah-vas kuld-sel a'al kord is-tus ma-ha söö-ma, siis
1. When Kung-la men in good old days sat down to have a nib-ble, then

Va-ne-mui-ne mu-ru-maal läks kand-le-lu-gu löö-ma.
Va-ne-mui-ne, as le-gend goes, came out to play his zi-ther.

Chorus:

Läks a-ga met-sa män-gi-ma, läks a-ga laan-de lau-lu-ga.
Oh hoo-te-nan-ny in the woods, oh hoo-te-nan-ny in the wealds,

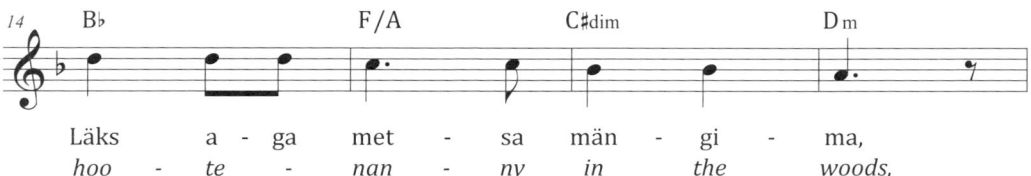

Läks a-ga met-sa män-gi-ma,
hoo-te-nan-ny in the woods,

1. Kui Kungla rahvas kuldsel a'al
   kord istus maha sööma,
   siis Vanemuine murumaal
   läks kandlelugu lööma.

   Chorus:
   Läks aga metsa mängima,
   läks aga laande lauluga.
   Läks aga metsa mängima,
   läks aga laande lauluga.
   Läks lauluga, läks lauluga,
   läks lauluga!

2. Säält saivad lind ja lehepuu
   ja loomad laululugu,
   siis laulis mets ja meresuu
   ja eesti rahva sugu.

   Läks aga metsa mängima …

3. Siis kõlas kaunilt lauluviis
   ja pärjad pandi pähe.
   Ja murueide tütreid siis
   sai eesti rahvas näha.

   Läks aga metsa mängima …

4. Ma mängin mättal, mäe peal
   ja õhtul hilja õues
   ja Vanemuise kandlehääl
   see põksub minu põues.

   Läks aga metsa mängima …

1. When Kungla men in good old days
   sat down to have a nibble,
   then Vanemuine, as legend goes,
   came out to play his zither.

   Chorus:
   Oh hootenanny in the woods,
   oh hootenanny in the wealds,
   hootenanny in the woods,
   hootenanny in the wealds!
   The good old days, the good old days,
   the good old days!

2. The birds, the beasts and even trees
   then joined the song and frolick,
   the forests sang, the seas all sang -
   we know here how to do it.

   Oh hootenanny in the woods...

3. The tune was light, the song was bright
   and girls wore flower-crownes.
   All fairy daughters in a ring
   danced in gossamer gownes.

   Oh hootenanny in the woods...

4. Upon the hill I play alone
   and late at night keep singing,
   as Vanemuine's ancient tune
   still in my heart is ringing.

   Oh hootenanny in the woods...

Translation by Doris Kareva (2021)

FOLKSONGS & TRADITIONALS   BELGIUM

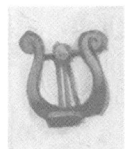

91
Bruxelles
Brussels

In this song, Brel describes the capital of Belgium as in a postcard from the beginning of the 20th century. We find there both the popular side, a little biting humor, the evocation of real places and also the mention of a "Place Sainte-Justine" which never existed. Wound up like a music box, the rhythmic ends up running out of steam at the end of the song as if we were at the end of the spring.

By Reynald Sac, À Coeur Joie Fédération Chorale Wallonie-Bruxelles

Lyrics: Jacques Brel (1929-78)   Music by Jacques Brel (1929-78)
                                                    & Gérard Jouannest (1933-2018)

C'é-tait au temps où Bru-xel-les rê-vait, c'é-tait au temps du ci-né-ma mu-et.
It was the time when Brus-sels could sing, it was the time of the si-lent mo-vies.

C'é-tait au temps où Bru-xel-les chan-tait, c'é-tait au temps où Bru-xelles bru-xel-lait. 1. Place de Brouc-kère on vo-yait des vi-trines a-vec des hommes des femmes en cri-no-line. Place de Brouc-kère on vo-
It was the time when Brus-sels was king, it was the time when Brus-sels brust-led. 1. Pick out a hat so dash-ing and gay, go take a walk, it's a beau-ti-ful day. Put on your spats and your

Chorus:
    C'était au temps où Bruxelles rêvait,
    C'était au temps du cinéma muet,
    C'était au temps où Bruxelles chantait,
    C'était au temps où Bruxelles bruxellait.

1. Place de Brouckère on voyait des vitrines
    Avec des hommes des femmes en crinoline.
    Place de Brouckère on voyait l'omnibus
    Avec des femmes des messieurs en gibus.
    Et sur l'impériale
    Le cœur dans les étoiles.
    Il y avait mon grand-père,
    Il y avait ma grand-mère,
    Il était militaire,
    Elle était fonctionnaire.
    Il pensait pas elle pensait rien,
    Et on voudrait que je sois malin.

Chorus: C'était au temps...

2. Sur les pavés de la place Sainte-Catherine,
    Dansaient les hommes les femmes en crinoline.
    Sur les pavés dansaient les omnibus
    Avec des femmes des messieurs en gibus.
    Et sur l'impériale,
    Le cœur dans les étoiles.
    Il y avait mon grand-père,
    Il y avait ma grand-mère,
    Il avait su y faire,
    Elle l'avait laissé faire,
    Ils l'avaient donc fait tous les deux,
    Et on voudrait que je sois sérieux.

Chorus: C'était au temps...

3. Sous les lampions de la place Sainte-Justine,
    Chantaient les hommes les femmes en crinoline.
    Sous les lampions dansaient les omnibus,
    Avec des femmes des messieurs en gibus.
    Et sur l'impériale,
    Le cœur dans les étoiles.
    Il y avait mon grand-père,
    Il y avait ma grand-mère,
    Il attendait la guerre,
    Elle attendait mon père.
    Ils étaient gais comme le canal,
    Et on voudrait que j'aie le moral.

Chorus (plus lent, comme un train qui s'arrête):
    C'était au temps où Bruxelles rêvait...

Chorus:
    It was the time when Brussels could sing,
    it was the time of the silent movies,
    it was the time when Brussels was king,
    it was the time when Brussels brustled.

1. Pick out a hat so dashing and gay,
    go take a walk, it's a beautiful day,
    put on your spats and your high-buttoned shoes,
    get on the tram, get the gossip and news.
    Not a time for crying,
    how the heart was flying.
    There was my grandfather,
    there was my grandmother.
    He was a young soldier,
    and she was so much bolder.
    He had no brains, neither did she,
    how bright could I turn out to be?

Chorus: Oh, it was the time...

2. Pick out a dress so dashing and gay,
    go take a walk, it's a beautiful day.
    Put on your spats and your high-buttoned shoes,
    get on the tram, get the gossip and news.
    Not a time for crying,
    How the heart was flying.
    There was my grandfather,
    there was my grandmother.
    He knew how to do it,
    and she let him do it,
    they lived in sin, deliciously,
    now they pray for my virginity.

Chorus: Oh, it was the time...

3. Sing out a song so dashing and gay,
    walk hand-in-hand, it's a beautiful day.
    Hop on the tram in your high-buttoned shoes,
    dance on the tram, to the gossip and news.
    Not a time for crying,
    how the heart was flying.
    There was my grandfather,
    there was my grandmother.
    Ten million guns got loaded,
    and World War I exploded.
    It was such fun, wee! What a game!
    They saved the world, but I bring it shame.

Chorus (slower, like a stopping train):
    Oh, it was the time when Brussels could sing...

Translation by Eric Blau (1968) / "Jacques Brel Is Alive and Well and Living in Paris" broadway musical

Copyright © © Copyright 1962, 1968 by EDITIONS MUSICALES CARAVELLE Copyrights Renewed/Éditions Pouchenel/Universal Music Publishing Ltd. International Copyright Secured. All Rights Reserved. Reprinted by permission of Hal Leonard Europe Ltd.

FOLKSONGS & TRADITIONALS   HUNGARY

92
Hull a szilva
Grapes and Plums

This old, pentatonic dance tune was collected in Csíksomlyó, Transylvania, by Péter Pál Domokos (1901-92). Like many Hungarian folksongs, this one melts together scenes from nature and everyday life – farm-work, courtship, weekdays- and holidays etc. "Ej, haj, ruca, ruca, kukorica, derce" – even though these words belong to the farming vocabulary, here the phonetic imitations have more importance, than singing about ducks, maize and cornmeal.

By Ágnes C. Szalai, called by the National Association of Hungarian Choirs and Orchestras, KÓTA

Lyrics: folk poem   Music: folk song

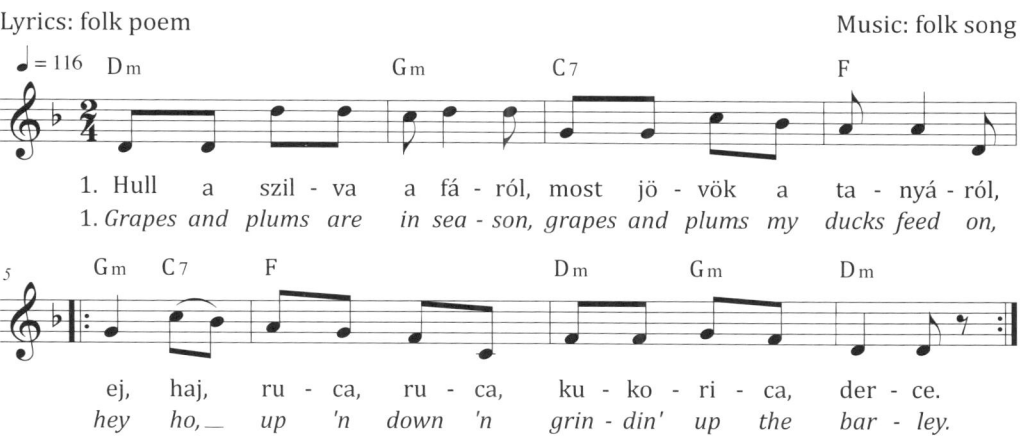

        1. Hull a szilva a fáról,
           most jövök a tanyáról,
           ||: ej, haj, ruca, ruca,
           kukorica, derce. :||

        2. Egyik ága lehajlott,
           az én rózsám elhagyott,
           ||: ej, haj, ruca, ruca,
           kukorica, derce. :||

        3. Kis kalapom fekete,
           pávatollu van benne,
           ||: ej, haj, ruca, ruca,
           kukorica, derce. :||

1. Grapes and plums are in season,
grapes and plums my ducks feed on,
||: hey ho, up 'n down 'n
grindin' up the barley. :||

2. Heavy branches fruit-laden,
Heavy heart and no maiden,
||: hey ho, up 'n down 'n
grindin' up the barley. :||

3. Peacock-feathered hat on head:
this befits a strappin' lad,
||: hey ho, up 'n down 'n
grindin' up the barley. :||

Translation by Imre Olivér Horváth (2021)

93
Malhão, Malhão
Oh Winnower, Winnower

"Malhão, Malhão" is a teasy folk song from the historical province of Douro Litoral, the northern district of port wine, and also a circle dance with clapping, not too hard to learn. Little is known of the origin, though it may date back centuries to the Bohemian musician and improvisor Francisco da Silveira Malhão (1757-1816). From the plain-speaking words of the first verse, it seems to be talking of someone longing for times of leisure, or even a willingness to remain idle: "What is your life like? Strolling down the street". However, the rhymes of the following verses show lack of thematic thread, and some words appear to rhyme rather senselessly or display sheer mockery. This song blends verses and chorus in one single unity, making it even more fun to sing along.

*By Manuela Encarnação & Nuno Bettencourt Mendes, Portuguese Music Teacher Association, APEM
& Jorge Alves, Association for Choirs in Lisbon, AMLC*

Lyrics: folksong / traditional   Music: folksong / traditional

1. Ó Malhão, Malhão, que vid'é a tua? Ò Malhão, Malhão, tua? Comer e beber, ó terim-tim-tim, passear na rua. Comer e beber, rua. Ó Malhão, Malhão, quem te deu as meias? Ó Malhão, Ma-

1. *Oh winnower, winnower, What kind of life is that? Oh winnower, winnower is that? You just drink and eat, dee dee dee dee deet, and walk down the street. You just drink and street. Oh winnower, winnower, Who gave you those socks? Oh winnower, win-*

1. Ó Malhão, Malhão,
   que vid'é a tua?
   Ó Malhão, Malhão
   que vida é a tua?
   Comer e beber,
   ó terim-tim-tim,
   passear na rua.
   Comer e beber,
   ó terim-tim-tim,
   passear na rua.

2. Ó Malhão, Malhão,
   quem te deu as meias?
   Ó Malhão, Malhão,
   quem te deu as meias?
   Foi o caixeirinho,
   ó terrim-tim-tim,
   tem as pernas feias!
   Foi o caixeirinho
   ó terrim-tim-tim,
   tem as pernas feias!

3. Ó Malhão, Malhão,
   quem te deu as botas?
   Ó Malhão, Malhão,
   quem te deu as botas?
   Foi o caixeirinho,
   ó terrim-tim-tim,
   tem as pernas tortas!
   Foi o caixeirinho,
   ó terrim-tim-tim,
   tem as pernas tortas!

1. Oh winnower, winnower
   What kind of life is that?
   Oh winnower, winnower
   What kind of life is that?
   You just drink and eat,
   dee dee dee dee deet,
   and walk down the street.
   You just drink and eat,
   dee dee dee dee deet,
   and walk down the street.

2. Oh winnower, winnower
   Who gave you those socks?
   Oh winnower, winnower
   Who gave you those socks?
   The shopkeeper did
   dee dee dee dee did
   his legs are big as rocks!
   The shopkeeper did
   dee dee dee dee did
   his legs are big as rocks!

3. Oh winnower, winnower
   Who gave you those boots?
   Oh winnower, winnower
   Who gave you those boots?
   The shopkeeper did
   dee dee dee dee did
   The one whose legs are crooked!
   The shopkeeper did
   dee dee dee dee did
   The one whose legs are crooked!

Translation by Luísa Sobral (2023)

FOLKSONGS & TRADITIONALS GREECE

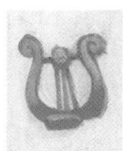

94
Φραγκοσυριανή
Francosyriani

This popular song is one of the most characteristic songs of "the rebetico style". This style, which has its roots on the shores of Asia Minor, came to Greece with the Greek refugees from this area in 1922. The composer Marcos Vamvakaris (1905-1972), born on the island of Syros, was the son of a Catholic family, which is why people nicknamed him "Fragos". The title "Fragosyriani" means "Catholic woman from Syros". He composed this song in 1935 for a complete unknown lady from Syros, who suddenly appeared in front of him while he was playing the bouzouki. Madly in love he wants to take her to all the beautiful places and villages in the island, being prepared to die from the pleasure of being with her...

By Thomas Louziotis, president, Hellenic Choirs Association

Lyrics: Markos Vamvakaris (1905-1972) Music: Markos Vamvakaris (1905-1972)

1. Μία φούντωση, μια φλόγα
   έχω μέσα στην καρδιά
   ||: λες και μάγια μου `χεις κάνει
   Φραγκοσυριανή γλυκιά. :||

   Λα λα λα λα λα λα λα λα...

2. Θα `ρθω να σε αντάμωσω
   κάτω στην ακρογιαλιά
   ||: Θα ήθελα να με χορτάσεις
   όλο χάδια και φιλιά. :||

   Λα λα λα λα λα λα λα...

3. Θα σε πάρω να γυρίσω
   Φοίνικα, Παρακοπή
   ||: Γαλησσά και Ντελαγκράτσια
   και ας μου `ρθει συγκοπή. :||

   Λα λα λα λα λα λα λα...

4. Στο Πατέλι, στο Νυχώρι
   φίνα στην Αληθινή
   ||: και στο Πισκοπιό ρομάντζα
   γλυκιά μου Φραγκοσυριανή. :||

   Λα λα λα λα λα λα λα...

(Finika, Parakopi, Galissa, Delagratsia, Pateli, Nihori, Alithini and Piskopio are all locations on the island of Syros)

1. I can feel a flushing flame
   deep inside my burning heart,
   ||: it's as if you have bewitched me,
   my sweet Francosyriani. :||

   La la la la la la la...

2. I will come again to meet you
   at our dream spot on the beach
   ||: where you'll quench my thirst with kisses
   and caresses by the sea. :||

   La la la la la la la...

3. I will take you around the island
   from the north, south, east to west
   ||: and we'll go on till my heart stops
   or we find our little nest. :||

   La la la la la la la...

4. In every village, in every piazza
   we are going to have a blast,
   ||: my sweet Francosyriani,
   you know this romance's going to last. :||

   La la la la la la la...

Translation by Monika & Stavros Xenides (2022)

Copyright © the author. International copyright secured. All rights reserved. Reprinted by permission

FOLKSONGS & TRADITIONALS   FRANCE

95
À la claire fontaine
Down by the Clearest Fountain

This song is one of the most common themes of the oral tradition in rural French speaking societies. There are over a thousand melodic versions of it in France and Quebec. Its age is evidenced by its poetic form an isometric text with rhymes, a structure already present in medieval times. The text, which is widely used today for children's repertoire, oddly includes the presence of an equally ancient element, the sexually connotative double meaning of the term "bouton de rose" (rosebud) for virginity. Note also the presence of the nightingale, traditionally the messenger of a loving couple.

By Jean Blanchard, Training Center for Teachers of Music, Auvergne Rhône-Alpes, CEFEDEM

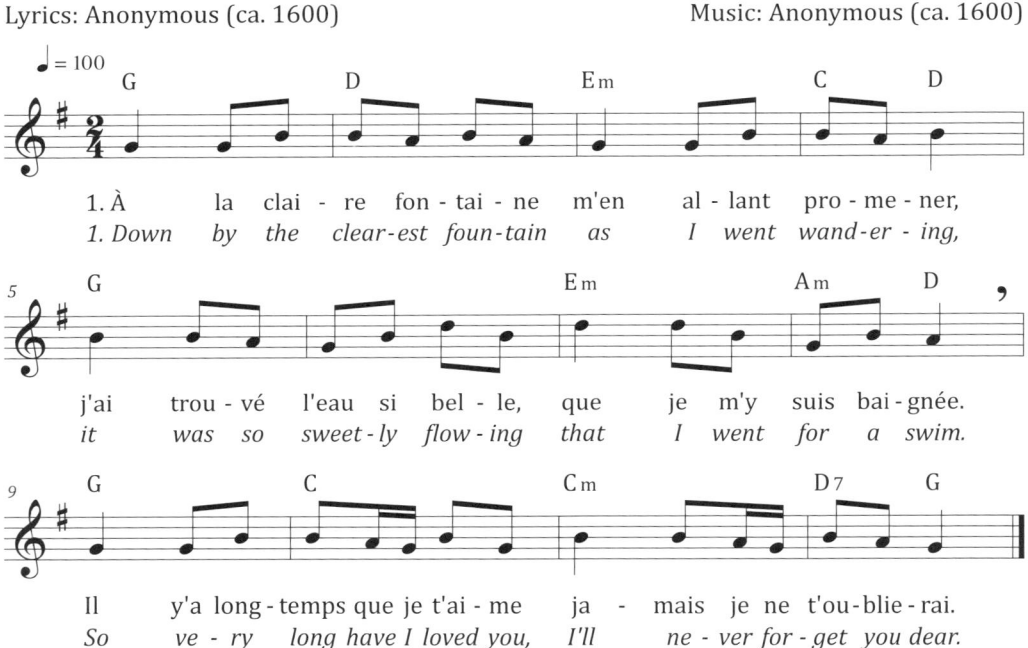

1. À la claire fontaine
   m'en allant promener,
   j'ai trouvé l'eau si belle,
   que je m'y suis baignée.

   Il y a longtemps que je t'aime
   jamais je ne t'oublierai.

*1. Down by the clearest fountain
as I went wandering,
it was so sweetly flowing
that I went for a swim.*

*So very long have I loved you,
I'll never forget you dear.*

2. Sous les feuilles d'un chêne
　 je me suis fait sécher,
　 sur la plus haute branche,
　 un rossignol chantait.

　 Il y a longtemps que je t'aime
　 jamais je ne t'oublierai.

3. Chante, rossignol, chante,
　 toi qui as le coeur gai,
　 tu as le coeur à rire,
　 moi, je l'ai à pleurer.

　 Il y a longtemps que je t'aime
　 jamais je ne t'oublierai.

4. J'ai perdu mon ami
　 sans l'avoir mérité,
　 pour un bouquet de roses
　 que je lui refusai…

　 Il y a longtemps que je t'aime
　 jamais je ne t'oublierai.

5. Je voudrais que la rose
　 fût encore au rosier,
　 et que mon doux ami
　 fût encore à m'aimer.

　 Il y a longtemps que je t'aime
　 jamais je ne t'oublierai.

2. In the shade of a willow
　 I dried off as I lay,
　 perched on the highest branches,
　 there sang a nightingale.

　 So very long have I loved you,
　 I'll never forget you dear.

3. Sing nightingale, keep singing,
　 your heart is full of cheer,
　 your heart does ring with laughter,
　 yet mine is full of tears.

　 So very long have I loved you,
　 I'll never forget you dear.

4. I lost my dearest friend,
　 it was no choice of mine,
　 for a bouquet of roses
　 that I had to decline

　 So very long have I loved you,
　 I'll never forget you dear.

5. How I wish that his roses
　 would have never been picked
　 and that my sweetheart would
　 love me as he once did.

　 So very long have I loved you,
　 I'll never forget you dear.

Translation by Claire Moreau, Lara Tasker
& Amy Winterbotham (2023)

96
Излел е Делю Хайдутин
Once Came Out Delyo the Hajduk

"Once Came Out Delyo the Hajduk" is one of the most famous Bulgarian folk songs, related to the image of the hajduk-fighters for freedom of Bulgaria against the Ottoman yoke. The most striking performance of the song is by the great Rhodopes-singer Valya Balkanska (b. 1942), who with her numerous concerts has been spreading the beauty of the song of the Rhodopes, on as many as five continents. In 1977, Dr. Carl Sagan, chairman of a NASA committee, included the song in the gold plaque containing musical messages from humankind to travel into Space on the American Voyager 1 spacecraft. In 2012, alongside other music from planet Earth, the song "Once Came Out Delyo the Hajduk" left our solar system and floated into interstellar space.

By Dr. Jean Pehlivanov, Academy of Music Dance and Fine Arts, Plovdiv, AMDFA

Lyrics: folk poem   Music: folksong

Bagpipe - prelude **Rubato**

1. Излел йе Делю хайдутин, хайдутин
   Йенкесаджие с Думбовци и Карадджовци.

1. Iz-lel ye De-lyo hay-du-tin, Hay-du-tin
   Yen-ke-sa-dzhi-e, s'Dum-bov-tsi i s'Ka-ra-dzhov-tsi.

1. *Once came out De-lyo the Haj-duk, Great Haj-duk,*
   glo-rious high-land-er, with Dum-bov and Ka-ra-djov men.

Излел е Делю Хайдутин,
Хайдутин Йенкесаджие,
С Думбовци и с Караджовци.

Зароча Делю, пороча
Деридерскинем айене,
Айене кабадайе:

-В селоно имам две лели
Да ми ги не потурчите,
Да ми ги не почорните.

Че кога слеза в селоно,
мночко ща майки разплака,
по-мночко млади невести.

Phonetic version:

Izlel ye Delyo Haydutin,
Haydutin Yenkesadzhie,
S Dumbovtsi i s Karadzhovtsi.

Zarocha Delyo, porocha
Deriderskinem ayene,
Ayene kabadaiye:

- V selono imam dve leli,
Da mi gi ne poturchite,
Da mi gi ne pochornite.

Che koga sleza v selono,
Mnochko shta mayki razplaka,
Po-mnochko mladi nevesti.

*Once came out Delyo the Hajduk,
Great Hajduk, glorious highlander,
with Dumbov and Karadjov men.*

*Ordered then Delyo, he ordered
to the Deridere rulers,
also governors:*

*In the village I have two aunties
don't you dare make them change their faith,
don't you dare make them dress in black.*

*Because when I come back for you,
so many mothers will cry out,
and more so young brides will suffer.*

Translated by Desislava Sofranova (2023)

97
Asturias, patria querida
Asturias, Beloved Homeland

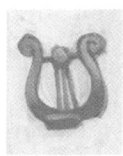 

Although this popular song refers to a region of Spain, it is also an unofficial national anthem which many Spaniards have sung at some point in their lives. As soon as the first notes start to play, many people, whatever their origins. associate this song with celebration with food and drink, with singing in good company and with the nostalgia of homeland. There are two very distinct parts, the second refers to picking a flower for a brunette, and there Spaniards usually lose the thread of the lyrics... Enthusiasm at the beginning and confusion at the end!

By Julio Muñoz & Maria del Carmen García Jiménez, Escuela Superior de Canto de Madrid, ESCM

Lyrics: folk poem   Music: folksong

Moderato ♩ = 66

As - tu - rias, Pa - tria que - ri - da, As - tu - rias de mis a - mo - res; ¡quien es - tu - vie - ra en As - tu - rias en to - das las o - ca - sio - nes! Ten - go de su - bir al ár - bol, ten - go de co - ger la flor, y dár - se - la_a mi mo - re - na, que la pon - ga_en el bal - cón, Que la pon -

As - tu - rias, be - lov - ed home - land, As - tu - rias, home of my true loves, if I could be in As - tu - rias be it for an - y oc - ca - sion! I have to climb up the dear tree, I have to pluck the sweet flow'r and give it to my dear bru - nette to put on her bal - co - ny! She puts it

Asturias, Patria querida,
Asturias de mis amores;
¡quién estuviera en Asturias
en todas las ocasiones!

Tengo de subir al árbol,
tengo de coger la flor,
y dársela a mi morena
que la ponga en el balcón,

Que la ponga en el balcón,
que la deje de poner,
tengo de subir al árbol
y la flor he de coger.

Asturias, beloved homeland,
Asturias, home of my true loves,
if I could be in Asturias
be it for any occasion!

I have to climb up the dear tree,
I have to pluck the sweet flow'r
and give it to my dear brunette
to put on her balcony!

She puts it on her balcony
 or she ceases to do so,
I have to climb up the dear tree,
and the flow'r I have to pluck.

Translation by Nan Maro Babakhanian (2021)

FOLKSONGS & TRADITIONALS   CYPRUS

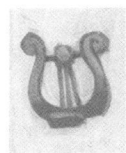

98
Τηλλυρκωτισσα
The Woman from Tillyria

Tillykerottissa, a woman from Tillyria, a region northwest of Cyprus, has magic powers and enchants the elements to cause a storm at sea to prevent the man she wants from sailing abroad. Syllables are constantly repeated to make the text understandable only to those familiar with this code and not to unwanted intruders. In Cyprus this code has acquired a name – 'katsouvellika'.

By Egli Spyridaki, Music Academy ARTE

Lyrics: Traditional   Music: Traditional

1. Ε - σι' έ - βε - ρε - βεν - αν   ά - βα - ρα - βα - στρον   τζι' έ - βε - ρε - βεμ   μι -
1. I   see - vee-ree-vee   a   sta - va-ra-var - let   bri - va-ra-vight and

τσίν,   μες   τους - βου - ρου - βούς   ε - φτά - βα - ρα - βα   πλα -
small,   a - mo - vo - ro - vong   the   se - ve - re - ven   great

νή - βη - ρη - βή - τες   μα - βα - ραυ - ρομ - μά - βα - ρα - τα   μου. ___ Τρια λα λα
pla - va - ra - va - nets, my   da - va - ra - vark-ey - va - ra - veyd   lass. ___ Tria la la

λα   λα λα λα   λα λα λα λα   λα ___   λα λα λα   λα   λα λα λα   λα λα λα λα
la   la la la   la la la la   la ___   la la la   la   la la la   la la la la

λα ___   λα λα λα   λα   λα λα   λα   λα λα λα   λα   λα λα λα   λα λα λα λα
la ___   la la la   la   la la   la   la la la   la   la la la   la la la la

1. Εσι' έβερεβεναν άβαραβαστρον
τζι' έβερεβεμ μιτσίν,
μες τουςβουρουβους εφτάβαραβα
πλανήβηρηβητες,
μαβαραυρομμάβαρατα μου.
Τριαλαλαλα….

2. Τζι' επκιάβαραβασαμ μεβερεβε
μες τηβηρηβην καρκιάν,
τα λόβοροβογια πουβουρουβου μου
είβιριβιπες,
γιαβαραλλουρούβουρουδα μου.
Τριαλαλαλα….

3. Τζι' επήβηρηβηαν τζι' είβηρηβηπαν
τηςβηρηβης πελλής,
πως εβερεβεν να πάβαραβαω
πέβερεβερα,
μουβουρουζουρούβουρουδα μου.
Τριαλαλαλα….

4. Τζι' εμάβαραβαεψεβερεβεν τηθ
θάβαραβαλασσαν,
τζι' εσήβηρηβηκωσεβερεβεν
αέβερεβεραν,
γιαβαραλλουρούβουρουδα μου.
Τριαλαλαλα….

1. *I seeveereevee a stavaravarlet
brivaravight and small,
amovorovong the severeven great
plavaravanets, my
davaravark-eyvaraveyd lass.
Trialalala….*

2. *And avaravall that youvourouvou
have saivairaivaid to me,
has suvuruvunk so deeveereeveep in
my heavaravart, my
sivirivilverspavaravarkling girl.
Trialalala….*

3. *They weverevent and tovorovold
that cravaravazy witch
my plavaravan to govorovo
abrovorovoad, my
chavaravarming, swavaravarthy lass.
Trialalala….*

4. *She cavaravast a speverevell
upovorovon the sea,
and raivairaivaised a mivaravighty
stovorovorm, my
sivirivilverspavaravarkling girl.
Trialalala….*

Translation by Ayis Ioannides (2021)

FOLKSONGS & TRADITIONALS — SLOVAKIA

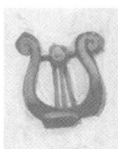

99
A ja taka dzivečka
I'm That Kind of a Girl, You See

"A ja taka dzivečka" – I'm That Kind of a Girl – is a joyous folk dancing song from Eastern Slovakia (Šariš). Like most folk songs, it remained in existence by oral tradition; moreover, this one song has some variants based on the local dialect, for instance, "A ja taká dzivočka". Musically it is related to an Austrian-Hungarian tradition (čardáš). The Eastern part of Slovakia is historically connected with Hungarian culture (in the rest of Slovakia, cultural traces of other countries can be found – Czech, Polish, German but also Turkish, Russian, or French influence). The song is frequently used in the repertoires of folk bands and choirs as well as during popular feasts, weddings, or even at discos.

By Dr. Eva Čunderlíková, Slovak Music Teacher Association, AUHS/Academy of Music Bratislava, VŠMU

Lyrics: folk poem | Music: folksong

1. A ja taka dzivečka, cin-gi lin-gi bom.
   1. I'm that kind of girl, you see, sin-gi lin-gi bom.
   Rada vijem pirečka, cin-gi lin-gi bom.
   I sew feathers prettily, sin-gi lin-gi bom.
   Rada vijem, rada dam cin-gi lin-gi bom, bom, bom,
   I love sewing, I love hats, sin-gi lin-gi bom, bom, bom,
   i za kalap zakladam, cin-gi lin-gi bom.
   when I deck them out like that, sin-gi lin-gi bom.

1. A ja taka dzivečka, cingi lingi bom.
   Rada vijem pirečka, cingi lingi bom.
   ||: Rada vijem, rada dam
   cingi lingi bom, bom, bom,
   i za kalap zakladam, cingi lingi bom. :||

2. A ja taka jak i mac, cingi lingi bom,
   čarne oči mušim mac, cingili lingi bom.
   ||: Čarne oči mac mala,
   cingi lingi, bom, bom, bom,
   ja še na ňu podala, cingi lingi bom. :||

   Instrumental

3. A ty cigan šumňe hraj, cingi lingi bom,
   na dzivčata ňežmurkaj, cingi lingi bom.
   ||: Na dzivčata, na šumne,
   cingi lingi bom, bom, bom,
   naj ňechodza po humňe, cingi lingi bom. :||

1. I'm that kind of girl, you see, singi lingi bom.
I sew feathers prettily, singi lingi bom.
||: I love sewing, I love hats,
singi lingi bom, bom, bom,
when I deck them out like that, singi lingi bom. :||

2. Like my mother, so am I, singi lingi bom.
famous for my jet-black eye, singi lingi bom.
||: Jet-black eyes my mum had too,
singi lingi bom, bom, bom,
I take after her, I do, singi lingi bom. :||

Instrumental

3. Hey, you Roma, sweetly play, singi lingi bom,
don't you tempt the girls away, singi lingi bom.
||: For those girls so full of charms,
singi lingi bom, bom, bom,
don't be going round the barns, singi lingi bom. :||

Translation by John Minahane (2023)

This version and it's translation have been approved by Rómsky inštitút (The Roma Institute, Bratislava).

100
Teka teka šviesi saulė
Rising, Rising, Bright Sun Rising

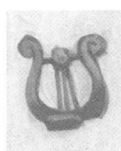 

The traditional Lithuanian song "Teka teka" (Rising, Rising) draws parallels between the life of the soldier, a young boy looking for his girlfriend, and the world of nature. Such parallels are typical of Lithuanian songs, melting together the world of nature – trees, birds, animals and human life. The boy remains lonely, as the girl does not want to give her word to a soldier. The song has a deeply lyrical mood, like the majority of Lithuanian songs.

By Dr. Arvydas Girdzijauskas, Lithuanian Choral Union, LCHS

Lyrics: folk poem

Music: folksongs

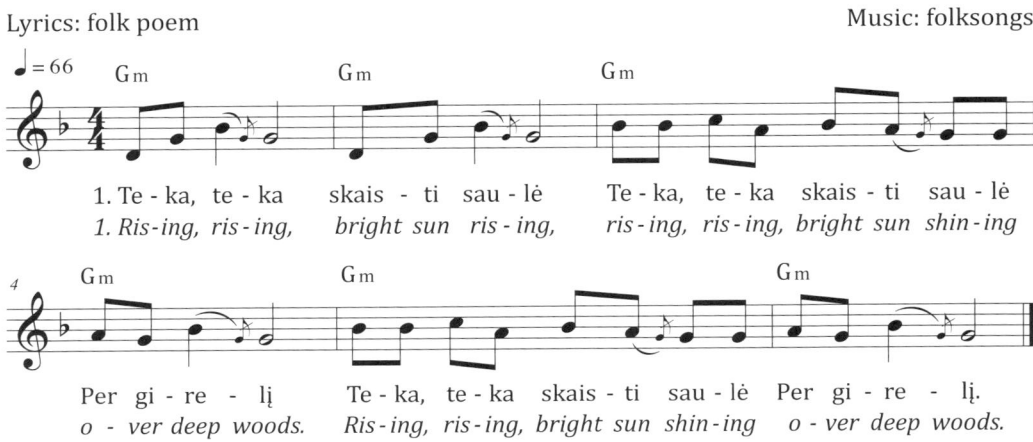

1. Teka, teka skaisti saulė
   Teka, teka skaisti saulė
   Per girelį.

2. Šovė, šovė kareivėlis
   Šovė, šovė kareivėlis
   In liepelį.

3. Atsimušė jo balselis
   Atsimušė jo balselis
   In mergelį.

4. Vai, mergela, lelijėla,
   Vai, mergela, lelijėla,
   Duok žodelį.

1. *Rising, rising, bright sun rising,*
   rising, rising, bright sun shining
   over deep woods.

2. *Shot the soldier, the young soldier,*
   opened fire, brave young soldier
   at the linden.

3. *Voice did echo, sounding loudly,*
   voice did echo, resonating
   at the maiden.

4. *Oh, fair maiden, lovely flower,*
   oh, dear maiden, fairest flower,
   give me your word.

5. Oi, berneli, dobilėli,
   Aš neduosiu tau žodelio
   Kareivėliui.

6. Sunku augti stabarėliui
   Sunku augti stabarėliui
   Žalion girion.

7. Tep man jaunam bernužėliui
   Tep man jaunam bernužėliui
   Be mergelės.

5. *Oh, sweet young boy, oh, my dearest,*
   I will never make a promise
   to a soldier.

6. *One stalk can't grow, as a green tree,*
   one stalk can't grow, as a green tree
   in the deep woods.

7. *So too, I can't, a young laddie,*
   so too, I can't, a young laddie,
   have no maiden.

Translation by Gabriella Žičkienė (2022)

FOLKSONGS & TRADITIONALS   GERMANY

101
Der Mond ist aufgegangen (Abendlied)
The Moon Is Risen, Beaming (Evening Song)

The beautiful poem behind this peace-loving song was first published in 1779 and clearly refers to the song "Nun ruhen alle Wälder" (Now All Forests Rest) from 1647 by Baroque poet, Paul Gerhardt (1607-76), who at the time lived during the Thirty Years War. Philosopher Johann Gottfried Herder (1744-1803) added it to his collection of folksongs with the great title The Voices of Peoples in Songs (1807). The melody was created in 1790 by J.A.P. Schulz. The view of nature and deep faith go back to ideas of the Reformation. Since then, it has been one of the most cherished and widespread pieces of music in Germany; even today, almost every child is sung to sleep with it.

By Ekkehard Klemm, president, Association of German Concert Choirs (VDKC)/
Hochschule für Musik "Carl Maria von Weber" Dresden

Lyrics: Matthias Claudius (1740-1815)   Music: J. A. Peter Schulz (1747-1800)

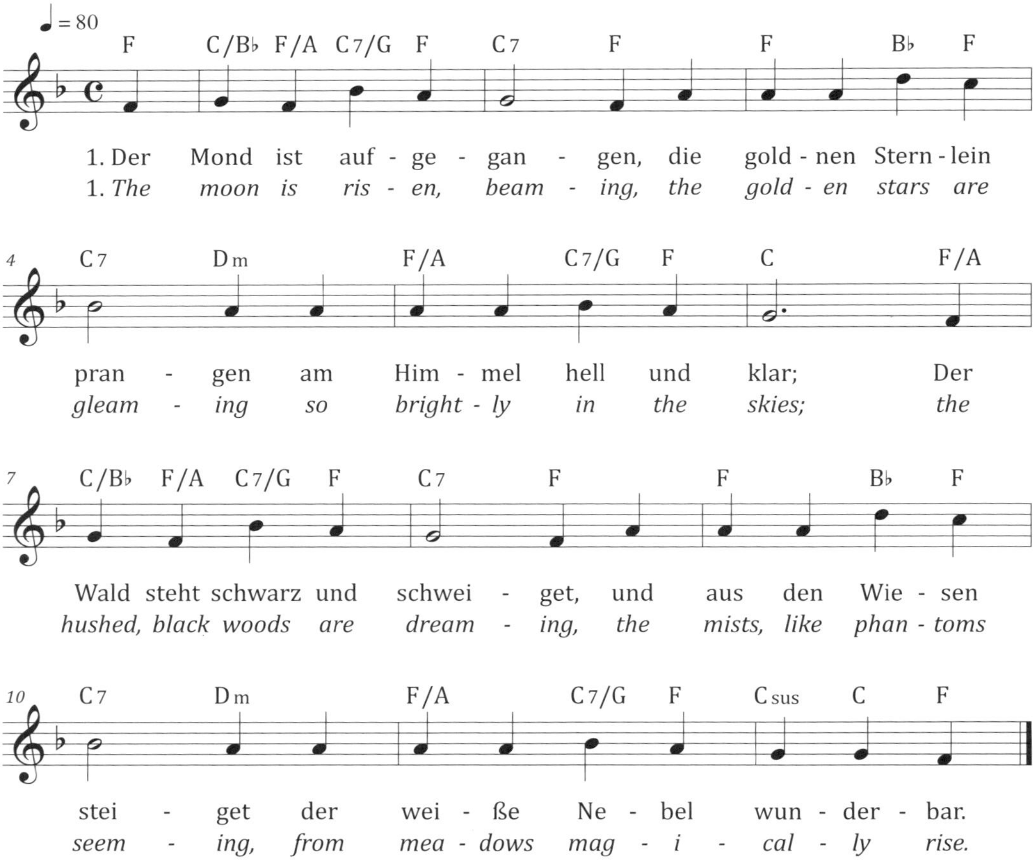

1. Der Mond ist auf-ge-gan-gen, die gold-nen Stern-lein
1. *The moon is ris-en, beam-ing, the gold-en stars are*

pran-gen am Him-mel hell und klar; Der
gleam-ing so bright-ly in the skies; the

Wald steht schwarz und schwei-get, und aus den Wie-sen
hushed, black woods are dream-ing, the mists, like phan-toms

stei-get der wei-ße Ne-bel wun-der-bar.
seem-ing, from mea-dows mag-i-cal-ly rise.

1. Der Mond ist aufgegangen,
   Die goldnen Sternlein prangen
   Am Himmel hell und klar;
   Der Wald steht schwarz und schweiget,
   Und aus den Wiesen steiget
   Der weiße Nebel wunderbar.

2. Wie ist die Welt so stille,
   Und in der Dämmrung Hülle
   So traulich und so hold!
   Als eine stille Kammer,
   Wo ihr des Tages Jammer
   Verschlafen und vergessen sollt.

3. Seht ihr den Mond dort stehen?
   Er ist nur halb zu sehen,
   Und ist doch rund und schön!
   So sind wohl manche Sachen,
   Die wir getrost belachen,
   Weil unsre Augen sie nicht sehn.

4. Wir stolze Menschenkinder
   Sind eitel arme Sünder
   Und wissen gar nicht viel;
   Wir spinnen Luftgespinste
   Und suchen viele Künste
   Und kommen weiter von dem Ziel.

5. Gott, laß uns dein Heil schauen,
   Auf nichts Vergänglichs trauen,
   Nicht Eitelkeit uns freun!
   Laß uns einfältig werden
   Und vor dir hier auf Erden
   Wie Kinder fromm und fröhlich sein!

6. Wollst endlich sonder Grämen
   Aus dieser Welt uns nehmen
   Durch einen sanften Tod!
   Und, wenn du uns genommen,
   Laß uns in Himmel kommen,
   Du unser Herr und unser Gott!

7. So legt euch denn, ihr Brüder,
   In Gottes Namen nieder;
   Kalt ist der Abendhauch.
   Verschon uns, Gott! mit Strafen,
   Und laß uns ruhig schlafen!
   Und unsern kranken Nachbar auch!

---

1. The moon is risen, beaming,
   the golden stars are gleaming
   so brightly in the skies;
   The hushed, black woods are dreaming,
   the mists, like phantoms seeming,
   from meadows magically rise.

2. How still the world reposes,
   while twilight round it closes,
   so peaceful and so fair!
   A quiet room for sleeping,
   into oblivion steeping
   the day's distress and sober care.

3. Look at the moon so lonely!
   One half is shining only,
   yet she is round and bright;
   thus oft we laugh unknowing
   at things that are not showing,
   that still are hidden from our sight.

4. We, with our proud endeavour,
   are poor vain sinners ever,
   there's little that we know.
   Frail cobwebs we are spinning,
   our goal we are not winning,
   but straying farther as we go.

5. God, make us see Thy glory,
   distrust things transitory,
   delight in nothing vain!
   Lord, here on earth stand by us,
   to make us glad and pious,
   and artless children once again!

6. Grant that, without much grieving,
   this world we may be leaving
   in gentle death at last.
   And then do not forsake us,
   but into heaven take us,
   lord God, oh, hold us fast!

7. Lie down, my friends, reposing,
   your eyes in God's name closing.
   How cold the night-wind blew!
   Oh God, Thine anger keeping,
   now grant us peaceful sleeping,
   and our sick neighbour too.

Translation by Margarete Münsterberg (1916)

FOLKSONGS & TRADITIONALS   DENMARK

102
I Danmark er jeg født
In Denmark I Was Born

The lyrics of this unofficial national anthem are written in 1850 by the world-famous Danish fairytale writer Hans Christian Andersen, who, due to his travels and surprisingly for his era, spent more time abroad than in his homeland ("to travel is to live"). Denmark had just finished a violent civil war, the southern part fighting in vain to unify with Germany. It was a time of nationalism and anti-German sentiment. However, despite this, the poem is a declaration of love for nature, history and language. Also the melody seems free from pathos. It is simple and straightforward – ending with a surrendering sigh.

By Jesper Moesbøl, editor of "Sanghåndbogen"/The Song Handbook

Lyrics: H.C. Andersen (1805-1875)   Music: Poul Schierbeck (1888-1949)

1. I Danmark er jeg født, dér har jeg hjemme, dér har jeg rod, derfra min verden går; du danske sprog, du er min moders stemme, så sødt velsignet du mit hjerte når. Du danske, friske strand, hvor oldtids kæmpe-

1. In Denmark I was born, that's where my home is. It's where my world is rooted, where it grows. The music of my tongue is mama's love song, so sweet and tender longing, free of woes. Our beaches are so fresh, with giant graves, of

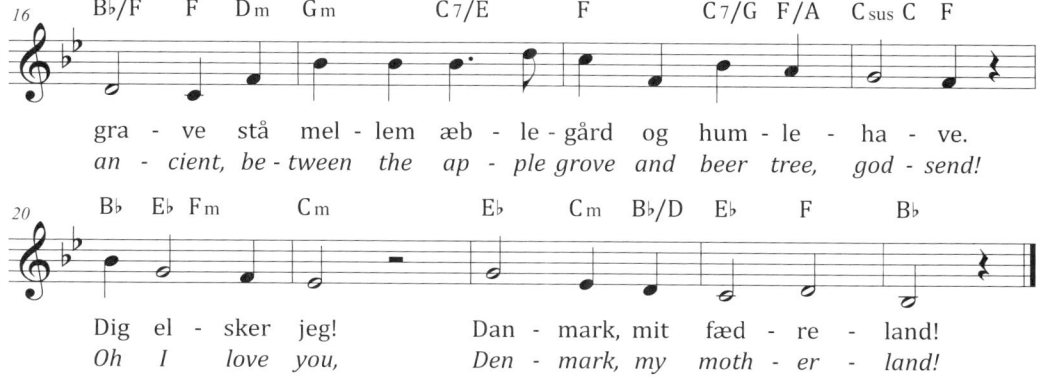

1.
I Danmark er jeg født, dér har jeg hjemme,
dér har jeg rod, derfra min verden går,
du danske sprog, du er min moders stemme,
så sødt velsignet du mit hjerte når.
Du danske, friske strand,
hvor oldtids kæmpegrave
stå mellem æblegård og humlehave.
Dig elsker jeg! Danmark, mit fædreland!

2.
Hvor reder sommeren vel blomstersengen
mer rigt end her, ned til den åbne strand?
Hvor står fuldmånen over kløverengen
så dejlig som i bøgens fædreland?
Du danske, friske strand,
hvor Dannebrogen vajer.
Gud gav os den, Gud giv den bedste sejer!
Dig elsker jeg! Danmark, mit fædreland!

3.
Engang du herre var i hele Norden,
bød over England, nu du kaldes svag,
Et lille land, og dog så vidt om jorden
end høres danskens sang og mejselslag.
Du danske, friske strand,
plovjernet guldhorn finder,
Gud giv dig fremtid, som han gav dig minder!
Dig elsker jeg! Danmark, mit fædreland!

4.
Du land, hvor jeg blev født,
hvor jeg har hjemme,
hvor jeg har rod, hvorfra min verden går,
hvor sproget er min moders bløde stemme
og som en sød musik mit hjerte når.
Du danske, friske strand
med vilde svaners rede,
I grønne ø'r, mit hertes hjem hernede!
Dig elsker jeg! Danmark, mit fædreland!

1.
In Denmark I was born, that´s where my home is.
It´s where my world is rooted, where it grows.
The music of my tongue is mama´s love song,
so sweet and tender longing, free of woes.
Our beaches are so fresh -
with giant graves, of ancient –
between the apple grove and beer tree, god-send!
Oh I love you, Denmark, my motherland!

2.
Where else are flower meadows spread so richly,
as summer´s sand towards the open beach?
Where else does moonlight shine above the clover,
as in our dearest country of the beech?
Our beaches are so fresh -
a thousand flags are flying,
God gave it, may he make my love undying.
Oh I love you, Denmark, my motherland!

3.
You once were king the Nordic ruling master,
you conquered England - now they call you weak.
A tiny land, yet Danish tongue and chisel
are widely heard for we are not that meek.
Our beaches are so fresh
where ancient treasure burrows,
your memories turn into bright tomorrows.
Oh I love you, Denmark, my motherland!

4.
In Denmark I was born,
that´s where my home is,
it´s where my world is rooted, where it grows.
The music of my mama´s love song moves me.
My heart so sweet and swelling, free of woes.
Our beaches are so fresh –
the wild swans nestle yonder,
our isles of green, the home of heartfelt wonder!
Oh I love you, Denmark, my motherland!

Translation by Isam Bachiri & Suzanne Brøgger (2023)

103
'O Sole Mio
It's Now or Never

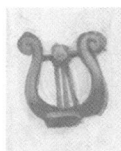

Composed in 1898, this song is a classic that, especially internationally, overlaps in the collective perception the very idea of Italy, thanks to the famous version of the great tenor Caruso (1873-1921). It is mistakenly thought to be a popular traditional melody but in reality it is what Hungarian Béla Bartók would define as a "popularesque" song since it has known authors who are part of the great tradition of Neapolitan song, firmly intertwined with the great and refined Neapolitan "cultured" school. The call to the sun strongly links the song to the beautiful city of Naples, pearl of the Mediterranean and territory of crossroads of cultures. The poetic invention of the lyrics in the Neapolitan language is realized in the parallel between the beauty of a sunny day and the even more wonderful sunshine that seems to emanate from the face of the beloved woman.

By Alfonso Santimone, National Academy of Jazz, Siena

Lyrics: G. Capurro (1859-1920)

Music: E. Di Capua (1865-1917) & A. Mazzucchi (1878-1972)

1. Che bel-la co-sa na jur-na-ta 'e so-le,___ n'a-ria se-re-na dop-po na tem-pe-sta!___ Pe' ll'a-ria fre-sca pa-re già na fe-sta...___ Che bel-la co-sa na jur-na-ta 'e so-le.___ Ma n'a-tu so-le___ cchiù bello, oi ne',___

1. When I first saw you with your smile so ten-der,___ my heart was cap-tured,___ my soul sur-ren-dered!___ I spent a life-time wait-ing for the right time...___ Now that you're near the time is here at last.___ It's now or ne-ver,___ come hold me tight,___

Chorus:

1. Che bella cosa na jurnata 'e sole,
   n'aria serena doppo na tempesta!
   Pe' ll'aria fresca pare già na festa...
   Che bella cosa na jurnata 'e sole.

   Chorus
     Ma n'atu sole cchiù bello, oi ne',
     'o sole mio sta nfronte a te!
     'o sole, 'o sole mio
     sta nfronte a te, sta nfronte a te!

2. Lùceno 'e llastre d''a fenesta toia;
   'na lavannara canta e se ne vanta
   e pe' tramente torce, spanne e canta,
   lùceno 'e llastre d''a fenesta toia.

   Chorus
     Ma n'atu sole cchiù bello, oi ne'...

3. Quanno fa notte e 'o sole se ne scenne,
   me vene quasi 'na malincunia;
   sotto 'a fenesta toia restarria
   quanno fa notte e 'o sole se ne scenne.

   Chorus
     Ma n'atu sole cchiù bello, oi ne'...

1. When I first saw you with your smile so tender,
   my heart was captured, my soul surrendered!
   I spent a lifetime waiting for the right time...
   Now that you're near the time is here at last.

   Chorus
     It's now or never, come hold me tight,
     kiss me, my darling, be mine tonight!
     Tomorrow will be too late,
     it's now or never, my love won't wait!

2. Just like a willow we would cry an ocean,
   if we lost true love and sweet devotion.
   Your lips excite me, let your arms invite me.
   For who knows when we'll meet again this way.

   Chorus
     It's now or never, come hold me tight...

Adaptation by Wally Gold & Aaron H. Schroeder (1960)

(This adaptation - Elvis' bestselling single ever - is the sole English version authorized for print)

Copyright © 1960 by Universal Music Publishing Ricordi Srl and Gennarelli Bideri Editori Srl. International Copyright Secured.
All Rights Reserved. Reprinted by Permission of Hal Leonard Europe Ltd.

FOLKSONGS & TRADITIONALS   AUSTRIA

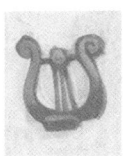

104
Kein schöner Land in dieser Zeit
No Better Land

In Austria the popularity of this tune was cemented with its inclusion in the book of songs, published in 1912, for the Austrian branch of the Wandervogel Movement, a back-to-nature, anti-industrialization Central European youth movement popular at the beginning of the twentieth century. Lyrics were written in 1838 by German writer and song collector Anton Wilhelm Florentin Zuccalmaglio, whereas the origin of the melody is unknown. It was first published in Berlin in 1840 with the title 'Abendlied' (Evening Song).

By Dr. Eva Maria Hois, Steirische Volksliedwerk & Dr. Sarah Weiss, Kunstuniversität Graz

Lyrics: Anton Wilhelm Florentin Zuccalmaglio (1803-69)   Music: Unknown

1. Kein schö-ner Land in die-ser Zeit, als hier das uns-re weit und breit, wo wir uns fin - den wohl un - ter Lin - den zur A - bend - zeit. wo wir uns fin - den wohl un - ter Lin - den zur A - bend - zeit.

1. No land is bet - ter, near or far, more charm-ing than here, where we are, where with friends we can be be - neath the lin - den tree when day is done, where with friends we can be be - neath the lin - den tree when day is done.

1. Kein schöner Land in dieser Zeit,
   als hier das unsre weit und breit,
   ||: wo wir uns finden
   wohl unter Linden
   zur Abendzeit. :||

2. Da haben wir so manche Stund'
   gesessen da in froher Rund'
   ||: und taten singen;
   die Lieder klingen
   im Eichengrund. :||

3. Dass wir uns hier in diesem Tal
   noch treffen so viel hundertmal,
   ||: Gott mag es schenken,
   Gott mag es lenken,
   er hat die Gnad. :||

4. Jetzt, Brüder, eine gute Nacht,
   der Herr im hohen Himmel wacht,
   ||: in seiner Güten
   uns zu behüten,
   ist er bedacht. :||

---

1. No land is better, near or far,
   more charming than here, where we are,
   ||: where with friends we can be
   beneath the linden tree
   when day is done. :||

2. Many a joyful hour we spend,
   sitting together, hand in hand,
   ||: merrily singing
   and goodwill bringing
   in groves of oak. :||

3. May we all meet with joy and grace
   one hundred times in this fair place.
   ||: May the Lord grant this,
   in His great goodness,
   splendour and grace. :||

4. Now, to all friends, a pleasant night,
   bathed in the Saviour's gentle light,
   ||: who will with kindness
   always protect us,
   so His intent. :||

Translation by Lorenz Maierhofer (2020)

FOLKSONGS & TRADITIONALS　　　　　　　　　　　　　　　　　　　　　　　　　　　MALTA

105
Viva Malta
Viva Malta

Viva Malta is an iconic song penned by Freddie Portelli, considered as Malta's Rock 'n Roll legend. Through this song, Portelli and the 'Malta Bums' beat group achieved international recognition and up till the present day Viva Malta is still the most widely played Maltese song, at home and abroad. Written back in 1967, this song explores the national sentiment, exalting the natural wonders of the country while extolling the heroic and resilient character of the Maltese nation when coming face to face with adversity throughout its checkered history. Due to the contours of its highly infectious tune, this song has ensured that audiences from every generation sing along while answering antiphonally the main vocal line hailing 'Viva Malta' – 'Long Live Malta'.

By Dr. John Galea, School of Performing Arts, University of Malta

Lyrics: Freddie Portelli (1944-)　　　　　　　　　　　　　　　Music: Freddie Portelli (1944-)

♩ = 132

1. Vi - va Mal - ta　u l- Mal - tin　Din l-art hi tal- qal - be - nin
1. Vi - va Mal - ta　my home-land　I will love you till the end,

Din l-art ħel - wa　kol - lha xemx　Żgur fid - din - ja　bħal - ha m'hemmx
ancient is - land　e - ver smart,　you've known his - tory　from the start.

Chorus:

— Mel' ej - jew ngħi - du vi - va Mal - ta　Mal - ta wil - Mal -
— Oh lit - tle is - land full of sun - shine,　a land of fun you

tin.　Għal din l-art aħ - na nagħm - lu kol - lox,
are.　Oh you're a land of friend - ly peo - ple,

1. Viva Malta u l-Maltin
   Din l-art hi tal qalbenin
   Din l-art ħelwa kollha xemx
   Żgur fid-dinja bħala m'hemmx.

   Chorus:
   Mela ejjew ngħidu viva Malta
   Malta w il-Maltin
   Għal din l-art aħna nagħmlu kollox
   Kollox u bil-qalb Viva din l-art
   L-art tal-Maltin
   Viva din l-art
   L-art tal-Maltin
   Viva din l-art.

2. Glied u gwerer din l-art rat
   Izda rebħet kull kumbat
   Għanda swar sodi w għoljin
   Li qatt ma ġew mirbuħin.

   Chorus:
   Mela ejjew ngħidu viva Malta
   Malta w il-Maltin
   Għal din l-art aħna nagħmlu kollox
   Kollox u bil-qalb Viva din l-art
   L-art tal-Maltin
   Viva din l-art
   L-art tal-Maltin
   Viva din l-art.

*1. Viva Malta my homeland
   I will love you till the end,
   ancient island ever smart
   you've known history from the start.*

   *Chorus:
   Oh little island full of sunshine,
   a land of fun you are.
   Oh you're a land of friendly people,
   a land of song and wine
   where a sky of blue,
   and a sea of green
   will hit your eyes
   just like a dream....*

*2. Gallantry and bravery
   ranks you high in history,
   been through battles, been through wars
   victory's been always yours.*

   *Chorus:
   So let me sing Viva Malta,
   Malta you're a dream.
   That's why the whole world calls you sunshine,
   a land of warmth you are.
   No wonder why
   I sing this song,
   Malta you're nice
   and beautiful.*

   Translation by Freddie Portelli (2022)

Copyright © the author. International copyright secured. All rights reserved. Reprinted by permission

FOLKSONGS & TRADITIONALS LUXEMBOURG

106
Kättche, Kättche bréng mer nach e Pättchen
Rita, Rita, Bring Another Litre

These lyrics by Willy Goergen (1867-1942) praise the virtues and qualities of Luxembourg's Moselle wines. One hundred years later, there is still not a single wine festival or harvest celebration in the country that could afford to leave out this song!

By Robert Köller, Union Grand-Duc Adolphe, UGDA

Lyrics: Willy Goergen (1867-1942)   Music: Jean Eiffes (1889-1961)

Cheerful ♩ = 120

1. Et wues-sen an de frie-me Län-ner, vill schwéi-er Wäi-ner roud a wäiss. Si si ge-sicht vu vil-le Ken-ner, vum Rhäin bis déi-säit vu Pa-räis, ech ha-le mech un d'Mis-ler-blimm-chen, dat ass de Wéng-che fir onst Land, e geet dem Jonk-tem wéi dem Éim-chen, wann si en

1. The vines they grow in oth-er plac-es make heav-y wine, some peo-ple see this is the best, and or-der cas-es from up the Rhine or from Pa-ree. I'd rath-er have a Mo-sel-flow-er, that is the wine for our coun-try; For young and old, if they've the pow-er to hold their

1. Et wuessen an de frieme Länner,
   vill schwéier Wäiner roud a wäiss.
   Si si gesicht vu ville Kenner,
   vum Rhäin bis déi säit vu Paräis,
   ech hale mech un d'Mislerlblimmchen,
   dat ass de Wéngche fir onst Land,
   e geet dem Jonktem wéi dem Éimchen,
   wann si en drénke mat Verstand.

   Chorus:
   ||: Kättche, Kättche bréng mer nach e Pättche,
   vun der Musel a soss keen.
   Ei, wéi schmaacht mer dee Kadettchen,
   t'ass en Dronk fir Broscht a Been. :||

2. Wou kënnt Dir nach e Wéngche fannen,
   esou gemittlech a sou frësch,
   t'gëtt een sou liicht dervun heibannen,
   dir gitt gesond ewéi e Fësch.
   Vill Wäiner maachen d'Leit wéi rosen,
   d'Gesiichter glouse wéi eng Schmelz.
   Mä dat muss een dem Misler loossen,
   hie suergt datt s du de Kapp behäls.

   Kättche, Kättche bréng mer nach e Pättche...

3. Ob dir bedreift sidd oder lëschteg,
   en deet seng Fliicht zu jidder Stonn.
   En ass vun heem aus fromm a chrëschtlech,
   e krut de Seege vun der Sonn.
   Bleift him ewech mat Zockerwaaser,
   e brauch net méi gedeeft ze ginn,
   e séngt mam Lentz fir net ze spaassen:
   „Mir wëlle bleiwe wat mir sinn!"

   Kättche, Kättche...

1. The vines they grow in other places
   make heavy wine, some people see,
   this is the best, and order cases
   from up the Rhine or from Paree.
   I'd rather have a Mosel-flower,
   that is the wine for our country;
   for young and old, if they've the power
   to hold their drink responsibly.

   Chorus:
   ||: Rita, Rita, bring another litre,
   only Mosel, fill the bowl,
   what a treat, a happiness-completer,
   that's the drink for heart and soul. :||

2. There can you find a wine to beat it,
   to cheer you up and keep you fresh?
   This lets you have your cake and eat it,
   you'll be as lively as a fish!
   Some wines will set your face on fire,
   they fill you up with rage and flame.
   But Mosel wine is not so dire,
   your state of mind remains the same.

   Rita, Rita, bring another litre...

3. If you are sad or if you're merry,
   it does the trick for ev'ryone.
   It is by nature kind and friendly,
   with benediction from the sun.
   So take away that sugar-water,
   no need to leave it on the bar,
   the poet Lentz has put it better,
   'We want to stay the way we are'.

   Rita, Rita...

   Translation by Edward Seymour (2021)

FOLKSONGS & TRADITIONALS   SLOVENIA

107
Kje so tiste stezice
Where Are The Footpaths

As with all folksongs that are classic in a certain culture, the theme here is existential. The hero(ine) of this song from the region of Koroška (Carinthia) observes what time has changed: "Where have the footpaths gone that once have been around / overgrown with the bushes and grasses abound. / I will weed out all the bushes, reap the green grass, / rebuild all the footpaths that once were around. / All footpaths are beautiful, yet the most beautiful one / is the footpath leading to the house of my mom." Mom is, of course, a catchword for a utopian completion, the surplus of every human being. And it is evasive; just as the melody wanders around and seeks its completion in a subtle series of attempts to reach a peak that is always falling down...

By Dr. Leon Stefanija, University of Ljubljana, Faculty of Arts

Lyrics: folk poem   Music: folk song

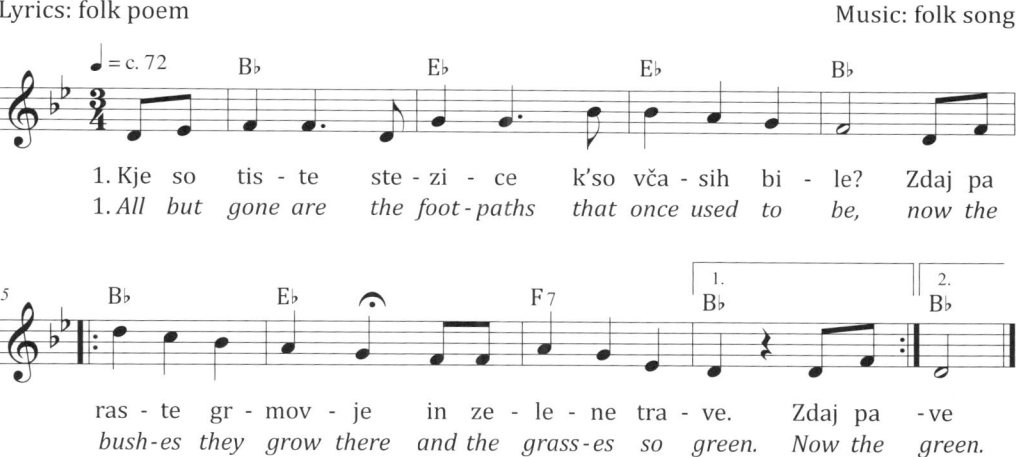

1. Kje so tiste stezice k'so včasih bile?
   ||: Zdaj pa raste grmovje
   in zelene trave. :||

2. Bom grmovje posekal trevice požel,
   ||: bom naredil stezice,
   ki so včasih bile. :||

3. Vse stezice so lepe, najlepša je ta,
   ||: ki me vodi do doma,
   kjer so mamca moja. :||

1. All but gone are the footpaths that once used to be,
   ||: now the bushes they grow there
   and the grasses so green. :||

2. I will cut down the bushes and harvest the grass,
   ||: and then walk down the footpaths
   that there once used to be. :||

3. All the footpaths are lovely - the best one for me
   ||: leads me right to the house
   of my mother so dear. :||

Translation by Steve Klink & Boštjan Malus (2021)

FOLKSONGS & TRADITIONALS   THE NETHERLANDS

108
Brabant

Brabant is the name of one of the 12 Dutch provinces and also the title of this hit from 2003 by the Dutch singer-songwriter Guus Meeuwis. According to the singer, the lyrics were written during a winter in Moscow, where he felt so homesick and nostalgic that he not only missed the warmth and coziness of the cafés in his home province, but even "the whining about everything for nothing". Soon after its appearance the song became – and still is – popular in both Brabant and beyond.

By Christiane Nieuwmeijer, Leiden University of Applied Sciences
& Lieuwe Noordam, Prins Claus Conservatorium, Groningen

Lyrics: Guus Meeuwis (1972-)   Music: Jan Willem Rozenboom (1974-)

1. Een muts op mijn hoofd, m'n kraag staat om-hoog. Het is hier ijs-koud, maar ge-lukkig wel droog. De da-gen zijn kort hier, de nacht be-gint vroeg. De men-sen zijn stug en er is maar één kroeg. Als ik naar m'n ho-

1. A cap on my head, my col-lar flipped high. The wea-ther's ice-cold, but thank hea-ven it's dry. The days here are short-er, and ear-ly the night. The peo-ple look stern, not a pub in sight. Walk-ing back to my

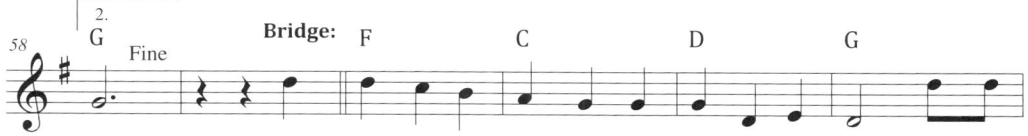
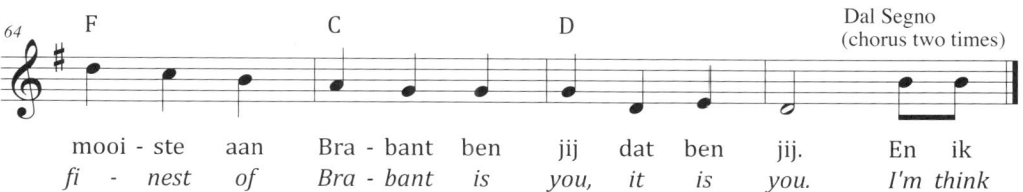

1. Een muts op mijn hoofd,
   m'n kraag staat omhoog.
   Het is hier ijskoud,
   maar gelukkig wel droog.
   De dagen zijn kort hier,
   de nacht begint vroeg.
   De mensen zijn stug en
   er is maar één kroeg.
   Als ik naar m'n hotel loop,
   na een donkere dag.
   Dan voel ik m'n huissleutel
   diep in m'n zak.

   Refrein:
   En ik loop hier alleen in een te stille stad.
   Ik heb eigenlijk nooit last van heimwee gehad.
   Maar de mensen ze slapen,
   de wereld gaat dicht.
   En dan denk ik aan Brabant,
   want daar brandt nog licht.

2. Ik mis hier de warmte
   van een dorpscafé.
   De aanspraak van mensen
   met een zachte 'G'.
   Ik mis zelfs het zeiken
   op alles om niets.
   Was men maar op Brabant
   zo trots als een Fries.
   In het zuiden vol zon
   woon ik samen met jou
   't Is daarom dat ik zo
   van Brabanders hou.

   Refrein:
   En ik loop hier alleen in een te stille stad...

   Bridge:
   De Peel en de Kempen en de Meierij,
   maar het mooiste aan Brabant
   ben jij dat ben jij.

   Refrein:
   En ik loop hier alleen in een te stille stad...

---

1. A cap on my head,
   my collar flipped high.
   The weather's ice-cold,
   but thank heaven it's dry.
   The days here are shorter,
   and early the night.
   The people look stern,
   not a pub in sight.
   Walking back to my lodgings
   on a long and dark road,
   I then feel my house-key
   deep down in my coat.

   Chorus:
   And I'm here all alone in too quiet a town.
   Cannot say I have ever felt homesick and down.
   But with people all sleeping,
   life shuts for the night.
   And I'm thinking of Brabant,
   for there is still light.

2. I do miss the warmth
   of a village cafe,
   The chatting with folks
   and the games we play.
   Miss even their whining
   how nothing is good.
   Wish we felt for Brabant
   the pride that we should.
   In the south full of sun
   I'm together with you
   That is why folks in Brabant
   have all my love too.

   Chorus:
   And I'm here all alone in too quiet a town...

   Bridge:
   There's beautiful nature for people to view
   but the finest of Brabant
   is you, it is you.

   Chorus:
   And I'm here all alone in too quiet a town...

   Translation by Arnold Mühren (2021)

FOLKSONGS & TRADITIONALS **FINLAND**

109
On suuri sun rantas autius
I Long for the Shore So Bleak and Bare

Aksel Törnudd, a lecturer at a teacher training college in Rauma, published a songbook for primary schools in 1913. His idea was to use traditional folk tunes and furnish them with patriotic lyrics. In one of the songs Törnudd combined the poem 'Rannalta' (From the Shore), by the young Finnish poet Veikko Antero Koskenniemi, with a folk tune from South Ostrobothnia. The result was a masterpiece in which the melancholic lyrics successfully merge with a simple melody in a minor key. The song captured the hearts of Finns and soon became a classic in the national choral repertoire.

By Dr. Vesa Kurkela, Sibelius Academy

Lyrics: Veikko Antero Koskenniemi (1885-1962)   Music: Folk song

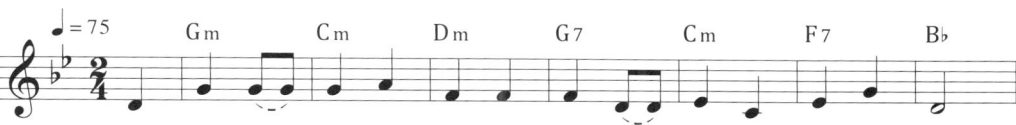

1. On suuri sun rantas autius,
   sitä sentään ikävöin:
   Miten villisorsan valitus
   soi kaislikossa öin.

2. Joku yksinäinen, eksynyt,
   joka vilua vaikeroi,
   jok' on kaislikossa kierrellyt
   eik' emoa löytää voi.

3. Sun harmajata aaltoas
   olen katsonut kyynelein:
   Ens' surunsa itkenyt rannallas
   mun on oma nuoruutein.

4. On syvään sun kuvasi painunut,
   ja sitä ikävöin.
   Olen villisorsaa kuunnellut
   mä siellä monin öin.

1. *I long for the shore so bleak and bare*
   where I wandered long ago,
   where the wild duck's call on the frozen air
   would echo on the snow.

2. *'Twas the cry of a lost and lonesome soul*
   in the rushes said to roam
   once gone astray in the winter cold
   never found its way back home.

3. *The image deep in my mind I've kept*
   of those waters dark and slow.
   'Twas there for my first true loss I wept
   in my youth so long ago.

4. *I've longed for that shore all through each year*
   in times both good and ill.
   The wild duck's call in my mind I hear,
   and the memory haunts me still.

Translation by Jaakko Mäntyjärvi (2021)

Copyright © Fennica Gehrman Oy, Helsinki. Reprinted by permission.

FOLKSONGS & TRADITIONALS   UNITED KINGDOM

110
Auld lang syne
Should Old Acquaintance Be Forgot

'Auld lang syne' dates from the 1660s and was noted down in 1788 by Robert Burns (1759-96), widely regarded as the national poet of Scotland. It is traditionally sung on New Year's Eve at midnight, and marks both the end of the old year and the beginning of the new one. When singing, it is de rigeur for everyone to cross arms and hold hands with the nearest people, moving hands and arms up and down to the beat. Bearing in mind the celebrations which will have preceded the midnight bell, it is perhaps not surprising that usually only the first verse and chorus are sung, the chorus being repeated molto accelerando until it collapses! Nonetheless, the text is more nostalgic than celebratory. The three words of the title refer to 'days gone by' and the song is one of nostalgia for good times long past and a call never to forget long-standing friendships.

By David Saint, former rector, Birmingham Conservatoire

Lyrics: Robert Burns (1759-96)   Music: folksong

1. Should auld ac-quain-tance be for-got, and nev-er brought to mind? Should auld ac-quain-tance be for-got, and auld lang syne?
1. Should old ac-quaint-ance be for-got, and nev-er brought to mind? Should old ac-quaint-ance be for-got, and days of long a-go?

Chorus:
For auld lang syne, my jo, for auld lang syne, we'll tak' a cup o' kind-ness yet for auld lang syne.
For days of long a-go, my dear, for days of long a-go, we'll drink a cup of kind-ness yet, for days of long a-go.

1. Should auld acquaintance be forgot,
    and never brought to mind?
    Should auld acquaintance be forgot,
    and auld lang syne?

Chorus:
    For auld lang syne, my jo,
    for auld lang syne,
    we'll tak' a cup o' kindness yet,
    for auld lang syne

2. And surely ye'll be your pint-stoup!
    and surely I'll be mine!
    And we'll tak' a cup o' kindness yet,
    for auld lang syne.

    For auld lang syne...

3. We twa hae run about the braes,
    and pou'd the gowans fine;
    But we've wander'd mony a weary fit,
    sin' auld lang syne.

    For auld lang syne...

4. We twa hae paidl'd in the burn,
    frae morning sun till dine;
    But seas between us braid hae roar'd
    sin' auld lang syne.

    For auld lang syne...

5. And there's a hand, my trusty fiere!
    and gie's a hand o' thine!
    And we'll tak' a right gude-willie waught,
    for auld lang syne.

    For auld lang syne...

*1. Should old acquaintance be forgot,
    and never brought to mind?
    Should old acquaintance be forgot,
    and days of long ago?*

*Chorus:
    For days of long ago, my dear,
    for days of long ago,
    we'll drink a cup of kindness yet,
    for days of long ago.*

*2. And surely you'll buy your pint cup!
    and surely I'll buy mine!
    And we'll take a cup of kindness yet,
    for days of long ago.*

    For days of long ago...

*3. We two have run about the hills,
    and picked the daisies fine;
    But we've wandered many a weary foot,
    since days of long ago.*

    For days of long ago...

*4. We two have paddled in the stream,
    from morning sun till dine;
    But seas between us broad have roared
    since days of long ago*

    For days of long ago...

*5. And there's a hand my trusty friend!
    And give me a hand of yours!
    And we'll take a right good-will draught,
    for auld lang syne.*

    For days of long ago...

*This fine song, one among the six chosen in our association's public song
vote in the UK prior to Brexit in 2016, got to "remain" in the EU Songbook:
May it be symbollic of UK's future relationship to the EU and vice versa:
"And there's a hand my trusty friend! / And give me a hand of yours!".*

Chapter V

Faith & Spirituality

(religious, pantheist & atheist songs)

FAITH & SPIRITUALITY   AUSTRIA

111
Stille Nacht, heilige Nacht
Silent Night

The creation of this world-famous song was described in the composer's diary. On Christmas Eve 1818, priest Josef Mohr (1792-1848) visited the newly build parish church of St Nicola in Oberndorf, where the schoolmaster Franz Xaver Gruber (1787-1863) was the organist. Mohr presented a poem and asked Gruber to write a piece for two voices with guitar accompaniment. Later, on that same evening, Mohr and Gruber performed the piece together during the midnight mass to much applause. Since World War One, it has become iconic for peace, as on Christmas Eve 1914 it was sung from the trenches on both sides, in German, French and English, an event which led to the Christmas Truce, where soldiers met in "no-man's land" and played soccer. Today, it exists in over 300 languages, three stanzas of the original six being most usually sung: the first, the second, and the sixth.

By Dr. Eva Maria Hois, Steirische Volksliedwerk & Dr. Sarah Weiss, Kunstuniversität Graz

Lyrics: Joseph Franz Mohr (1792-1848)   Music: Franz Xaver Gruber (1787-1863)

1. Stil - le Nacht, hei - li - ge Nacht! Al - les schläft,
1. Si - lent night, ho - ly night! All is calm,

ein - sam wacht nur das trau - te hoch hei - li - ge Paar.
all is bright, 'round yon Vir - gin Mo - ther and child,

Hol - der Kna - be im lo - cki - gen Haar, schla - fe in himm - li - scher
ho - ly in - fant so ten - der and mild, sleep in hea - ven - ly

Ruh, schla - fe in himm - li - scher Ruh!
peace, sleep in hea - ven - ly peace!

1. Stille Nacht, heilige Nacht!
   Alles schläft, einsam wacht
   nur das traute hoch heilige Paar.
   Holder Knabe im lockigen Haar,
   schlafe in himmlischer Ruh,
   schlafe in himmlischer Ruh!

2. Stille Nacht, heilige Nacht!
   Gottes Sohn, o wie lacht
   Lieb aus deinem göttlichen Mund,
   da uns schlägt die rettende Stund.
   Jesus in deiner Geburt,
   Jesus in deiner Geburt.

3. Stille Nacht, heilige Nacht!
   Hirten erst kundgemacht
   durch der Engel Alleluja,
   tönt es laut von ferne und nah:
   Jesus, der Retter ist da,
   Jesus, der Retter ist da!

1. Silent night, holy night!
   All is calm, all is bright,
   'round yon Virgin Mother and child,
   holy infant so tender and mild,
   sleep in heavenly peace,
   sleep in heavenly peace!

2. Silent night, holy night!
   son of God, love's pure light,
   radiant beams from thy holy face
   with the dawn of redeeming grace,
   Jesus, Lord, at thy birth,
   Jesus, Lord, at thy birth!

3. Silent night, holy night!
   Shepherds quake at the sight,
   glories stream from Heaven afar,
   heavenly hosts sing Alleluia:
   Christ the Saviour is born,
   Christ the Saviour is born!

Translation by John Freeman Young (1820-85)

FAITH & SPIRITUALITY   ITALY

112
Il testamento di Tito
The Testament of Tito

In Italy, Fabrizio 'Faber' De Andrè (1940-99) is considered by several generations as the singer-songwriter par excellence of the last forty years of the 20th century. As a cultural protagonist of the '60s and '70s, De Andrè's poetry in music embodies a political idea of art that wants to ignite the sensitivity of listeners towards the need for a more just world. This folk ballad, typical of his style, appeared in the concept album 'La buona novella' (The Good News, 1970). It develops an original and decidedly anarchist reading of the Ten Commandments through the voice of Tito, one of the two thieves crucified next to Jesus of Nazareth. Through the voice of the thief, the poet unveils the revolutionary message linked to the earthly experience of the figure of Jesus. In the final two stanzas, Tito turns to a mother (his own or Maria?) and puts love at the center of the whole meaning of human existence.

By Alfonso Santimone, National Academy of Jazz, Siena

Lyrics: Fabrizio De André (1940-99)

Music: Fabrizio De André (1940-99) & Corrado Castellari (1945-2013)

1. "Non avrai altro Dio all' in-fuo-ri di me" spes-so mi ha fat-to pen-sa-re: gen-ti di-ver-se, ve-nu-te dall' Est di-ce-van che in fon-do era u-gua-le: cre-de-va-no a un al-tro di-ver-so da Te, e non mi han-no fat-to del

1. *"You shall worship no gods other than me" I of-ten looked at this claim: dif-fer-ent peo-ples, who came from the East, said in the end it's the same: they prayed to an-oth-er they could-n't see, but did-n't cause me no*

1. "Non avrai altro Dio all'infuori di me"
   spesso mi ha fatto pensare:
   genti diverse, venute dall'Est
   dicevan che in fondo era uguale:
   ||: credevano a un altro diverso da Te,
   e non mi hanno fatto del male. :||

2. "Non nominare il nome di Dio,
   non nominarlo invano".
   Con un coltello piantato nel fianco
   gridai la mia pena e il suo nome:
   ma forse era stanco, forse troppo occupato,
   e non ascoltò il mio dolore:
   ma forse era stanco, forse troppo lontano,
   davvero lo nominai invano.

3. Onora il padre, onora la madre,
   e onora anche il loro bastone:
   bacia la mano che ruppe il tuo naso
   perché le chiedevi un boccone.
   ||: Quando a mio padre si fermò il cuore,
   non ho provato dolore :||

4. Ricorda di santificare le feste;
   facile per noi ladroni,
   entrare nei templi che rigurgitan salmi
   di schiavi e dei loro padroni.
   ||: Senza finire legati agli altari,
   sgozzati come animali. :||

5. Il quinto dice "non devi rubare",
   e forse io l'ho rispettato
   vuotando, in silenzio, le tasche già gonfie
   di quelli che avevan rubato:
   ||: Ma io, senza legge, rubai in nome mio
   quegli altri nel nome di Dio :||

1. *"You shall worship no other gods than me"*
   I often looked at this claim:
   different peoples, who came from the East,
   said - in the end it's the same:
   ||: they prayed to another they couldn't see,
   but didn't cause me no pain. :||

2. *"You shall not take the name of the Lord,*
   you shall not name it in vain".
   With a knife in my side, I cried out my pain
   I cried out my heart and his name:
   perhaps he was tired or busy somewhere
   'cause he didn't hear me begging:
   perhaps he was tired or deaf to my pain,
   it's true that I called him in vain.

3. *Honor your father and honor your mother,*
   and also honor their cane:
   give a kiss to the hand that bumped your head
   just because you asked for bread.
   ||: When the heart of my father ended its strain
   I didn't feel sorrow nor pain. :||

4. *"Remember the days you've to sanctify"*
   ...easy to do for us thieves
   to walk into temples filled to their brims
   with slaves, their masters, and hymns
   ||: without becoming an animal to slaughter
   - tied up upon the alter. :||

5. *The fifth one forbids, forbids you to steal,*
   perhaps I've respected this one,
   emptying the pockets of those who had much
   because they had stolen from us:
   ||: but I only stole what was actually mine,
   they stole while serving the divine :||

6.
"Non commettere atti che non siano puri",
cioè non disperdere il seme…
Feconda una donna ogni volta che l'ami
così sarai uomo di fede.
Poi la voglia svanisce e il figlio rimane
E tanti ne uccide la fame.
Io, forse, ho confuso il piacere e l'amore
Ma non ho creato dolore.

7.
Il settimo dice "non ammazzare".
se del cielo vuoi essere degno
Guardatela oggi, questa legge di Dio,
tre volte inchiodata nel legno.
||: Guardate la fine di quel nazzareno:
e un ladro non muore di meno. :||

8.
"Non dire falsa testimonianza",
e aiutali a uccidere un uomo.
Lo sanno a memoria il diritto divino,
e scordano sempre il perdono.
||: Ho spergiurato su Dio e sul mio onore
e no, non ne provo dolore :||

9.
"Non desiderare la roba degli altri,
non desiderarne la sposa".
Ditelo a quelli, chiedetelo ai pochi
Che hanno una donna e qualcosa
Nei letti degli altri, già caldi d'amore,
non ho provato dolore.
L'invidia di ieri non è già finita:
stasera vi invidio la vita.

10.
Ma adesso che viene la sera ed il buio
mi toglie il dolore dagli occhi,
e scivola il Sole al di là delle dune
a violentare altre notti,
io nel vedere quest'uomo che muore
Madre, io provo dolore;
nella pietà che non cede al rancore
Madre, ho imparato l'amore.

6.
Do not commit any adultery at all,
which means do not spill seed in vain.
Impregnate the woman every time you make love,
so you'll be a true man of faith.
Then desire disappears, but the children remain
and hunger kills so many of them.
I might have made love and pleasure the same
but I did not cause any pain.

7.
The seventh one says "You shall not kill"
if you want to be worthy of God's Heaven.
Is this the strange fruit of His divine will?
Three humans are nailed to three crosses.
||: Look at the Nazarene with his pierced chest
- a thief does not die any less :||

8.
"Don't bear false witness, tell us all you can,"
and help them to murder a man.
They keep on their lips the justice of God,
but know not forgiveness and mercy.
||: I perjured God with my heart drunk with rain
that's why I don't feel any pain.:||

9.
"You shall not covet the wife of your neighbor,
you shall not lust for his house".
Tell this to those, tell the lucky few
who indeed have a home and a spouse.
In the warm beds of others I felt no shame
nor did I feel any pain.
The envy I've felt hasn't faded away:
It's life that I envy today.

10.
But now, as evening falls, darkness wipes way
the burning sensation from my eyes,
the sun sets behind the far desert dunes
to have his way with more nights.
I turn to look at this man dying slain.
and, Mother, I now feel his pain;
in feeling compassion for all who are scorned,
Mother, I've learned what love is.

Translated by Francesco Ciabattoni
& Massimo Bubola (2023)

FAITH & SPIRITUALITY   HUNGARY

113
Erdő mellett estvéledtem
Night fell Upon the Willow Grove

Kodály, Zoltán (1882-1967), the great composer and determining reformer of music education in Hungary and worldwide collected this folksong in Pásztó (Nógrád county) in 1922. It is beautiful in its severity, but even more moving when the arrangement of Kodály himself, "Esti dal"(Evening Song), is sung. The lyrics are a prayer formed in a tired, lonesome exile to the Lord, at first asking for an outlaw to find a night shelter, then the way back to his beloved homeland. The third verse is from the region of Szeged: "May he fill our hearts with hope's light, May God give you peaceful good night."

By Ágnes C. Szalai, called by the National Association of Hungarian Choirs and Orchestras, KÓTA

Lyrics: folk poem   Music: folk song

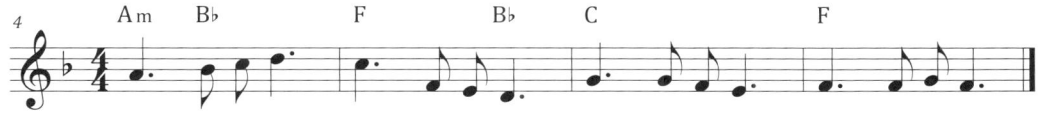

1. Erdő mellett estvéledtem,
   Subám fejem alá tettem,
   Összetettem két kezemet,
   úgy kértem jó Istenemet.

2. Én Istenem, adjál szállást,
   Már meguntam a járkálást,
   A járkálást, a bujdosást,
   Az idegen földön lakást.

3. Adjon Isten jó éjszakát,
   Küldje hozzánk szent angyalát,
   Bátorítsa szívünk álmát,
   Adjon Isten jó éjszakát.

1. *Night fell 'pon the grove of willow,*
   lamb fur coat was my soft pillow,
   I joined my hands, said a brief prayer,
   hoping my God hears me up there.

2. *Oh, my good Lord, give me lodging,*
   I feel weary of wandering,
   I've been roving, I've been hiding,
   in foreign lands I've been striving.

3. *May God give you peaceful good night,*
   angels help you with your hard plight.
   May he fill our hearts with hope's light,
   may God give you peaceful good night.

Translation by Gyula Hegedűs (2021)

FAITH & SPIRITUALITY   CROATIA

114
Zdravo Djevo
Virgin Mary

Peter Perica, a Catholic priest (1881-1944), is remembered particularly as the revered author of one of the favorite church songs in Croatia, regularly sung during church ceremonies and mass celebrations. In the words "Rajska Djevo, kraljice Hrvata, naša Majko, naša zoro zlata" (Paradise Virgin, Queen of Croats, our Mother, our Dawn of Gold), Perica highly expresses the love and confidence of the Croatian Christians towards the Virgin, a confidant and protector on their thorny historical path.

By Dr. Jasenka Ostojić, University of Zagreb, Music Academy

Lyrics: Petar Perica (1881-1944)   Music: from the sacred Czech folksong
                                                                                 „Tisickrate pozdravujem Tebe".

1. Zdra - vo, Dje - vo, svih mi - los - ti pu - na, vječ-nog sun - ca o - gr - nu te sjaj. O - ko če - la zvje-zda-na ti kru - na, iz - pod no - gu ste - nje pa - kla zmaj. Raj - ska Dje - vo, kra - lji - ce Hr - va - ta, na - ša Maj - ko, na - ša zo - ro zla - ta, o - da - nih ti sr - ca pri - mi dar, pri - mi

1. Vir - gin Mar - y, full of grace and glo - ry, may the Sun shine bright-er when You two meet. May the stars in heav - en tell your sto - ry, growl-ing drag - on's hell be - neath your feet. Bless - ed Vir - gin, heav-en - ly our Moth - er, take this pres - ent from your sons and daugh - ters, Queen of Cro - ats, o - ur gold-en dawn, take this

1. Zdravo, Djevo, svih milosti puna,
vječnog sunca ogrnu te sjaj.
Oko čela zvjezdana ti kruna,
izpod nogu stenje pakla zmaj.

Chorus:
Rajska Djevo, kraljice Hrvata,
naša Majko, naša zoro zlata,
||: odanih ti srca primi dar,
primi čiste ljubavi nam žar :||

2. Blažena si, jerbo sva si čista,
zmijin dah ne okuži ti grud!
Zvijezda sreće i nama da blista,
noći grijeha mrak rasprši hud!

Chorus:
Rajska Djevo, kraljice Hrvata...

*1. Virgin Mary, full of grace and glory,
may the Sun shine brighter when You two meet.
May the stars in heaven tell your story,
growling dragon's hell beneath your feet.*

*Chorus:
Blessed Virgin, heavenly our Mother,
take this present from your sons and daughters,
||: Queen of Croats, our golden dawn,
take this ardor of our true pure love. :||*

*2. You are blessed for you are so pure,
may the snakes around you breathe in fear!
Make the star of happiness our cure,
make the dark nights of sin disappear!*

*Chorus:
Blessed Virgin, heavenly our Mother,...*

Translation by Nikola Vranić "J.R. August" (2022)

FAITH & SPIRITUALITY — CYPRUS

115
Τ' 'Αϊ Γιωρκού
Saint George's Day

The stanzas of this song are selected from a long ballad that tells the story of St. George and the dragon, which would only let water reach the city in exchange for humans as food! When it is the princess' turn to sacrifice herself, Saint George comes to the rescue and kills the dragon. As reward, he wants neither the princess' hand nor all the wealth of the kingdom. His only wish is for the king to build a small church in his name and to celebrate his day on April 23rd. The melody is a variation on similar melodies often used in Cyprus for the narration of ballads with typical 15-syllable verses.

By Egli Spyridaki, Music Academy ARTE

Lyrics: Traditional   Music: Traditional

Moderato ♩ = 76

1. Δευ - τέ - ρα 'τουν της Κα - θα - ράς που κά - μνουν την νο - μά - δαν, μες
1. It was that first Mon - day in Lent, the sac - red day of feast-ings, the

το κα - ρά - βιν έ - μπη - κεν την πρώ - την ε - φτο - μά - δαν.
Saint em - barked his sail - ing craft, that first of weeks of fast - ing.

Τζιαι τρεις η - μέ - ρες έ - κα - μεν να ρέ - ξει το Βε - ρούτιν, ψου-
And three whole days he spent at sea to sail a - cross from yon - der, no

μίν, νε - ρόν εν ε - βρέ - θη - κεν μέ - σα στην χώ - ραν τού - την. 2. Ψου
crumb of bread, no drop of wa - ter was there in this cor - ner. 2. But

λί - ου, που έρ - κε - ται η μέ - ρα του 'κοσ - τρείς του Απ - ριλ - λί - ου.
A - pril, and ce - le - brate his me - mo - ry the twen - ty - third of A - pril.

1. Δευτέρα 'τουν της Καθαράς
   που κάμνουν την νομάδαν,
   μες το καράβιν έμπηκεν
   την πρώτην εφτομάδαν.
   Τζιαι τρεις ημέρες έκαμεν
   να ρέξει το Βερούτιν,
   ψουμίν, νερόν εν εβρέθηκεν
   μέσα στην χώραν τούτην.

2. Ψουμίν, νερόν είσιεν πολλύν
   κάτω μακράν στο πλάτος,
   τζιειμέσα εκατώκησεν
   ένας μεγάλος δράκος.
   Τζιαι δεν αφήνει το νερόν
   στηχ χώραν τους να πάει,
   ταΐνιν του εκάμνασιν
   'πό 'ναν παιδιν να φάει.

3. "Ώρα καλή σου λυερή,
   ώρα καλή τζιαι γειά σου,
   μούσκους τζιαι ροδοπέταλα
   στα καμαρόβρυά σου.
   Τζ' ίντα γυρεύκεις λυερή
   στου δράκου το λειβάδιν,
   στου δράκοντα του πονηρού
   να βκει τζιαι να σε φάει;"

4. Μιαν χαρζιαρκάν του χάρισεν
   τζι' η πόλις ούλλη εσείστην
   τζιαι το σκαμνίν του βασιλιά
   εσείστην τζιαι ραΐστιν.
   Βκάλλει που το δισάτζιν του
   μεγάλον αλυσίδιν
   τζι' έπκιασεν τζιαι χαλίνωσεν
   τζιειν το μεγάλον φίδιν.

5. Άνταν τους βλέπει ο βασιλιάς
   κρυφές χαρές παθθαίνει,
   "ποιός είν' αυτός που μούκαμεν
   τούτην την καλωσύνην;
   Να δώκω το βασίλειόν μου
   τζι' ούλλον τον θησαυρόν μου,
   να δώκω τζιαι την κόρην μου
   τζιαι να γινεί γαμπρός μου".

6. Τζι' επολοήθην Άγιος
   τζιαι λέει τζιαι λαλεί του,
   "έθ θέλω το βασίλειόν σου
   μήτε τοθ θησαυρόν σου.
   Μιαν εκκλησιάν να κτίσετε
   μνήμην του Άϊ Γιωρκίου,
   που έρκεται η μέρα του
   'κοστρείς του Απριλλίου,
   που έρκεται η μέρα του
   'κοστρείς του Απριλλίου."

1. *It was that first Monday in Lent,*
   the sacred day of feastings,
   the Saint embarked his sailing craft,
   that first of weeks of fasting.
   And three whole days he spent at sea
   to sail across from yonder,
   no crumb of bread, no drop of water
   was there in this corner.

2. *But bread and water plent' enough*
   was there across the valley,
   wherein resided a great dragon
   in a feaful gully.
   He does not let the water pass
   beyond his dreadful lair,
   unless he's offered for his food
   boys young and maidens fair.

3. *"My graceful lady, fine and lithe,*
   I greet and I salute thee,
   your eyes be sprayed with perfumes sweet
   of roses and of lillies.
   Whatever are you seeking, lady,
   at the dragon's region?
   The evil monster will appear
   and eat you like a pigeon."

4. *A mighty blow he gives the beast*
   and all the land was shaken,
   and ev'n the king's throne shook so strongly
   that was cracked and broken.
   Out of his travel bag he pulls
   a sturdy chain of iron,
   and with that chain he wraps and drags
   along that fearful satan.

5. *The king sees them as they approach*
   and feels such joy replete,
   "who is this saviour of my realm
   who has performed this feat?
   My kingdom shall I give to him
   and all my precious treasure,
   my daughter too shall marry him
   and that will be her pleasure.

6. *The Saint gives answer to the king*
   and utters words of wisdom,
   "neither your treasures do I need,
   nor do I want your kingdom.
   Build me instead a little church
   Saint George to honour veril',
   and celebrate his memory
   the twenty-third of April,
   and celebrate his memory
   the twenty-third of April.

Translation by Ayis Ioannides (2021)

FAITH & SPIRITUALITY   CZECHIA

116
Ktož jsú boží bojovníci
All You Mighty Warriors of God

The song is originally a Hussite chorale from the 15th century. Later it became one of the unofficial Czech national symbols and is mostly updated in times of political oppression, restrictions on freedom, uncertainty, etc. Its tune was used in works by many composers as a symbol or as a latent element of compositional material, the best-known quote being in the cycle of symphonic poems by Bedřich Smetana (1824-84) "Má vlast" (My Country) in the poem "Tábor", but Antonín Dvořák (1841-1904) and Karel Husa (1921-2016) also quoted the chant. The chorale also found its way into Czech pop music. However modern sung versions do not fully coincide with the original inscription from the "Jistebnice Hymn Book", mainly with deviations from the original melody and especially the rhythm.

By Dr. Hanuš Bartoň, Academy of Performing Arts in Prague, HAMU

Lyrics: Hussite chorale   Music: Hussite chorale

♩ = 120 **Verse 1, 3, 4 and 5**

1. Ktož jsú boží bojovníci a zákona jeho,
1. All you mighty warriors of God, His ardent disciples,

prostež od Boha pomoci a ufajte v něho,
pray for His help and do fear not, believe in His guidance.

že konečně vždycky s ním svítězíte.
Follow this path and you'll know but a triumph.

Verse 2

2. Tenť pán velíť se nebáti záhubcí tělesných,
2. Do not dread death, fight in His name, should you die, then be it.

velíť i život složiti pro lásku svých bližních.
In God live, for your fellow men, do whatever's needed.

1. Ktož jsú boží bojovníci
   a zákona jeho,
   prostež od Boha pomoci
   a ufajte v něho,
   že konečně vždycky s ním svítězíte.

2. Tenť pán velíť se nebáti
   záhubcí tělesných,
   velíť i život složiti
   pro lásku svých bližních.

3. Kristusť vám za škody stojí,
   stokrát viec slibuje.
   Pakli kto proň život složí,
   věčný mieti bude;
   blaze každému, ktož na pravdě sende.

4. Protož střelci, kopiníci
   řádu rytieřského,
   sudličníci a cepníci
   lidu rozličného,
   pomnětež všichni na Pána štědrého!

5. Nepřátel se nelekajte,
   na množstvie nehleďte,
   pána svého v srdci mějte,
   proň a s ním bojujte
   a před nepřáteli neutiekajte!

1. *All you mighty warriors of God,*
   His ardent disciples,
   pray for His help and do fear not,
   believe in His guidance.
   Follow this path and you'll know but a triumph.

2. *Do not dread death, fight in His name,*
   should you die, then be it.
   In God live, for your fellow men,
   do whatever's needed.

3. *Be assured that Christ is worth it*
   all your pain and struggle.
   Should He decide that you are fit
   you will live forever.
   Blessed be he who walks in His way, truth and life!

4. *Whether noble, whether humble,*
   armed or just with bare hands.
   Keep your head up, hear the rumble,
   fight mountains and wastelands.
   But always make sure that you keep God in mind.

5. *Never fear your enemies and*
   never count their numbers.
   Cherish His name, never pretend.
   With Him you'll do wonders.
   You should your faith, land and God proudly defend!

Translation by Zuzana Čtveráčková (2023)

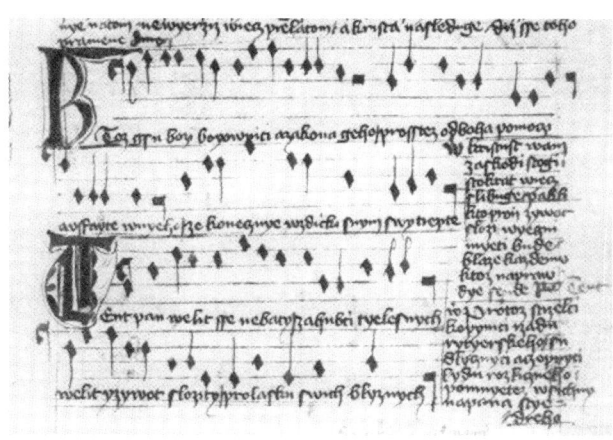

The Jistebnice hymn book (Czech: Jistebnický kancionál), ca. 1430

FAITH & SPIRITUALITY   DENMARK

117
I østen stiger solen op
In Eastern Skies the Sun Climbs Up

When, in 1837, poet Ingemann (1789-1862) and composer Weyse (1774-1842) – two of the most cherished Danish artists in the 1900 century – were commissioned by a group of philanthropists to write a set of morning songs for the poorest children in the first kindergardens in Copenhagen. They were to touch the feelings of many generations to come. Even today the simple psalms are known to most Danes, both children and adults. In order to make God's love and mercy present, the songs find inspiration in everyday life. In this specific psalm the light from the sunrise symbolizes a glimpse of paradise.

By Jesper Moesbøl, editor of "Sanghåndbogen"/The Song Handbook

Lyrics: B.S. Ingemann (1789-1862)   Music: C.E.F. Weyse (1774-1842)

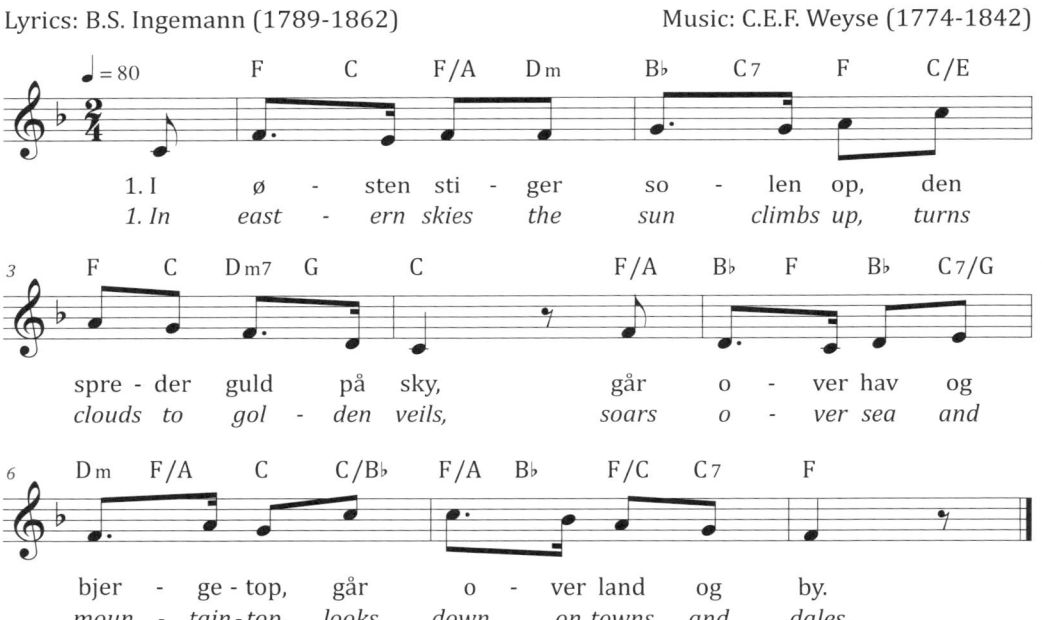

    1. I østen stiger solen op,   *1. In eastern skies the sun climbs up,*
       den spreder guld på sky,   *turns clouds to golden veils,*
       går over hav og bjergetop,   *soars over sea and mountaintop,*
       går over land og by.   *looks down on towns and dales.*

    2. Den kommer fra den favre kyst,   *2. It comes to us from heav'n above,*
       hvor Paradiset lå;   *from paradisal halls;*
       den bringer lys og liv og lyst   *it brings us light and life and love*
       til store og til små.   *to all, both great and small.*

3. Den hilser os endnu så smukt
fra Edens morgenrød,
hvor træet stod med evig frugt,
hvor livets væld udflød.

4. Den hilser os fra lysets hjem,
hvor størst Guds lys oprandt
med stjernen over Bethlehem,
som Østens vise fandt.

5. Og med Guds sol udgår fra øst
en himmelsk glans på jord,
et glimt fra Paradisets kyst,
hvor livets abild gror.

6. Og alle stjerner neje sig,
hvor østens sol går frem:
Den synes dem hin stjerne lig,
der stod ved Bethlehem.

7. Du soles sol fra Bethlehem!
Hav tak og lov og pris
for hvert et glimt fra lysets hjem
og fra dit Paradis!

3. *It greets us now from beauty's root*
in Eden's distant dawn,
the tree that bore eternal fruit,
life's overflowing horn.

4. *It springs from where all blessings stem*
when God created day –
the star that shone on Bethlehem
that lit the wise men's way

5. *God's sun from eastern realms will pour*
a heavenly glow on earth,
a glimpse of paradise's shore
which first brought life to birth.

6. *And one by one the stars incline*
as dawn o'ershadows them;
it brings another star to mind
that shone on Bethlehem.

7. *You, sun of suns from Bethlehem!*
We praise you to the skies,
for every glimpse of light's true gem
and of your paradise.

Translation by John Mason (2022)

FAITH & SPIRITUALITY   PORTUGAL

118
Foi Deus
It was God

Some of the finest Fado-songs performed by the famous singer Amalia Rodrigues' in the 50s and 60s were written by Alberto Janes (1909-71), a pharmacist most of his lifetime living in rural Alentejo. He had a positive passion for music and dedicated much of his output of popular songs to her. "Foi Deus", (It Was God) is surely the best case in point. Indeed, it rapidly became a signature song for Amalia' s musical personality. In the verses and melody of "Foi Deus", the composer and lyricist deeply expressed his religious faith in God as well as his great admiration for the Diva of Fado, thereby attributing Amalia' s talent and unsurpassed vocal perfection to heavenly creation, only comparable to the 'wondrous miracles' of sublime nature.

By Manuela Encarnação & Nuno B. Mendes, Portuguese Music Teacher Association, APEM
& Jorge Alves, Association for Choirs in Lisbon, AMLC

Lyrics: Alberto Janes (1909-71)   Music: Alberto Janes (1909-71)

1. Não sei, não sabe ninguém porque canto o fado neste tom magoado de dor e de pranto. E neste tormento todo o sofrimento, eu sinto que a alma cá dentro se acalma nos versos que

1. Don't know and no one else knows why I do sing fado with this hurtful tone of pain and mourning. And in this torment, all that I'm suffering, I feel that my soul gains peace above all from the words that I

1. Não sei,
   Não sabe ninguém
   porque canto o fado
   nesse tom magoado
   de dor e de pranto.
   E neste tormento,
   todo o sofrimento
   Eu sinto que a alma
   cá dentro se acalma
   com os versos que canto.

1. Don't know,
   and no one else knows
   why I do sing fado
   in this hurtful tone
   of pain and mourning.
   And in this torment,
   all that I'm suffering,
   I feel that my soul
   gains peace above all
   from the words that I sing.

Foi Deus que deu luz aos olhos, perfumou as rosas, deu oiro ao sol e prata ao luar.	´Twas God, He gave light to my eyes, He scented the roses, gave gold to the sun, silver to the moon.
Foi Deus que me pôs no peito o rosário de penas que vou desfiando e choro a cantar.	´Twas God, that around my neck placed a feathered rosary that I unravel while I cry and sing.
E pôs as estrelas no céu, e fez o espaço sem fim, deu o luto as andorinhas, ai, e deu-me esta voz a mim.	He put the stars in the sky, made space spread endlessly, taught swallow birds how to grieve, ah, and gave this voice to me.

2. Se canto,
   não sei o que canto.
   Misto de ventura,
   saudade, ternura
   e talvez amor.
   Mas sei que cantando,
   sinto o mesmo quando
   se tem um desgosto
   e o pranto no rosto
   nos deixa melhor.

2. If I sing,
   don't know what I'm singing.
   Something between joy,
   longing and tenderness
   and even love.
   I know when I sing,
   I feel the same thing
   when my heart is broken
   and all that I cry
   brings peace to my soul.

Foi Deus,
que deu voz ao vento,
luz ao firmamento
e deu o azul às ondas do mar.

´Twas God,
He gave voice to the wind,
He lit up the sky and
colored blue the waves in the sea.

Ai foi Deus,
que me pôs no peito
um rosário de penas
que vou desfiando
e choro a cantar.

´Twas God,
that around my neck
placed a feathered rosary
that I unravel
while I cry and sing.

Fez poeta o rouxinol,
pôs no campo o alecrim,
|: deu flores à primavera, ai!,
e deu-me esta voz a mim. :|

Taught nightingales poetry,
filled the field with rosemary,
||: gave many flowers to spring, ah!,
and He gave this voice to me :||

Translation by Luísa Sobral (2022)

FAITH & SPIRITUALITY — GREECE

119
Αι γενεαί πάσαι
All the Generations

This is one of the most sacred hymns of the Greek Orthodox Church, sung during the Service of Good Friday. It is a lament for Jesus Christ, who is taken off the cross and buried by the women carrying myrrh. It says that all generations offer to Jesus Christ a hymn for his death. Following the descent from the cross, Christ is put in the grave. Women came very early in the morning to put myrrh on Christ and in the grave, while Holy Mary is wondering where the beauty of Christ has gone. These are 5 of 48 verses of the hymn.

By Thomas Louziotis, president, Hellenic Choirs Association

Lyrics: Byzantine song (330-1453)   Music: Byzantine song (330-1453)

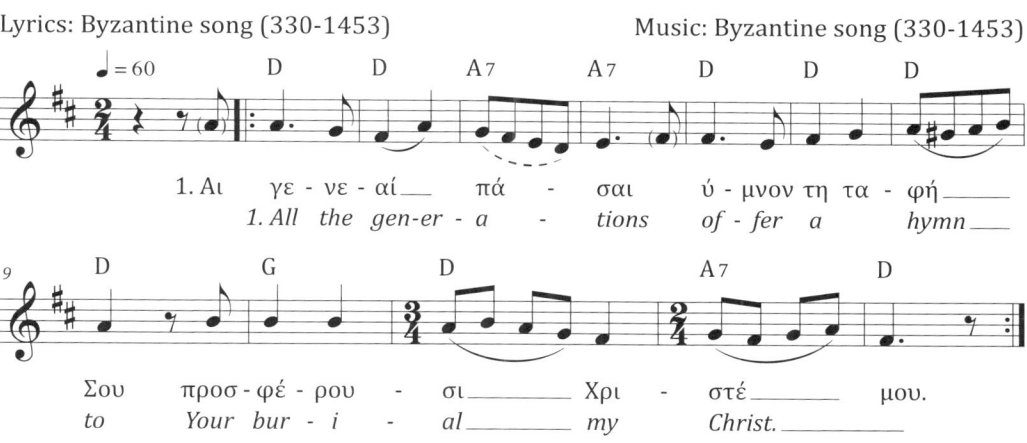

1. Αι γενεαί πάσαι,
   ύμνον τη Ταφή Σου,
   προσφέρουσι Χριστέ μου.

2. Καθελών του ξύλου,
   ο Αριμαθείας,
   εν τάφω Σε κηδεύει.

3. Μυροφόροι ήλθον,
   μύρα σοι, Χριστέ μου,
   κομίζουσαι προφρόνως.

4. Ερραναν τον τάφον
   αι Μυροφόροι μύρα,
   λίαν πρωί ελθούσαι.

5. Ω γλυκύ μου έαρ,
   γλυκύτατόν μου Τέκνον,
   πού έδυ σου το κάλλος;

1. All the generations
   offer a hymn to
   Your burial my Christ.

2. Down from the cross
   the Arimathean
   layed You in your tomb.

3. Women came with myhhr
   to prepare Your body
   for Your burial (my Christ).

4. They sprinkled Your tomb
   with myhhr and perfumes
   at the break of dawn.

5. Oh my sweet spring
   my sweetest Child
   where does Your beauty fade?

Translation by Monika & Stavros Xenides (2023)

FAITH & SPIRITUALITY   FRANCE

120
Ave Maria

This religious Latin text, stemmed from the Catholic liturgy, was adapted by Charles Gounod (1818-93) in the 1850s on the first prelude of the 1st book of Préludes and Fugues, 'The well-tempered piano, book 1 (BWV 846)' by Johann-Sebastian Bach (1685-1750) in 1722. The story, reported by the historian Alain Duault, tells us that this melody was initially improvised by Charles Gounod on the prelude in question, then transformed by him into a love poem to address of one of his students, before being finally "purified" by this religious text allegedly sent to him by the student's mother. Curiously, this detour allows us find the principle dear to J-S. Bach for the Protestant Chorales: a religious text on a simple melody that the whole world can sing as well.

By Jean Blanchard, Training Center for Teachers of Music, Auvergne Rhône-Alpes, CEFEDEM

Lyrics: Catholic prayer (1400 ac)   Music: Johann Sebastian Bach (1685-1750)
                                                               & arr. by Charles Gounod (1818-93)

A - ve Ma - ri - a   Gra - ti - a ple - na
A - ve ma - ri - a,   Toi____ qui fus mè - re
A - ve Ma - ri - a,   boun - ti-ful and full of grace,

Do - mi-nus te - cum   Be - ne - dic - ta
Sur____ cet-te ter - re, Tu____ souf - fris____ com - me
walk - ing with the Lord him-self, oh____ heav-en-ly moth-er of us

tu   In mu - li - er - bus   Et____ be - ne - dic - tus
nous, Tu par - ta-geas nos chaî - nés, Al - lè-ge nos pei - nes,
all, bless - ed____ a-bove all wo - men, hon - ored with a chi - ild,

fruc - tus____ Ven - tri____ tu - i Je - sus
Vois,____ nous som-mes tous,____ Nous som-mes tous à tes ge - noux,
your____ womb bore the fruit____ of Ba-by Je - sus.

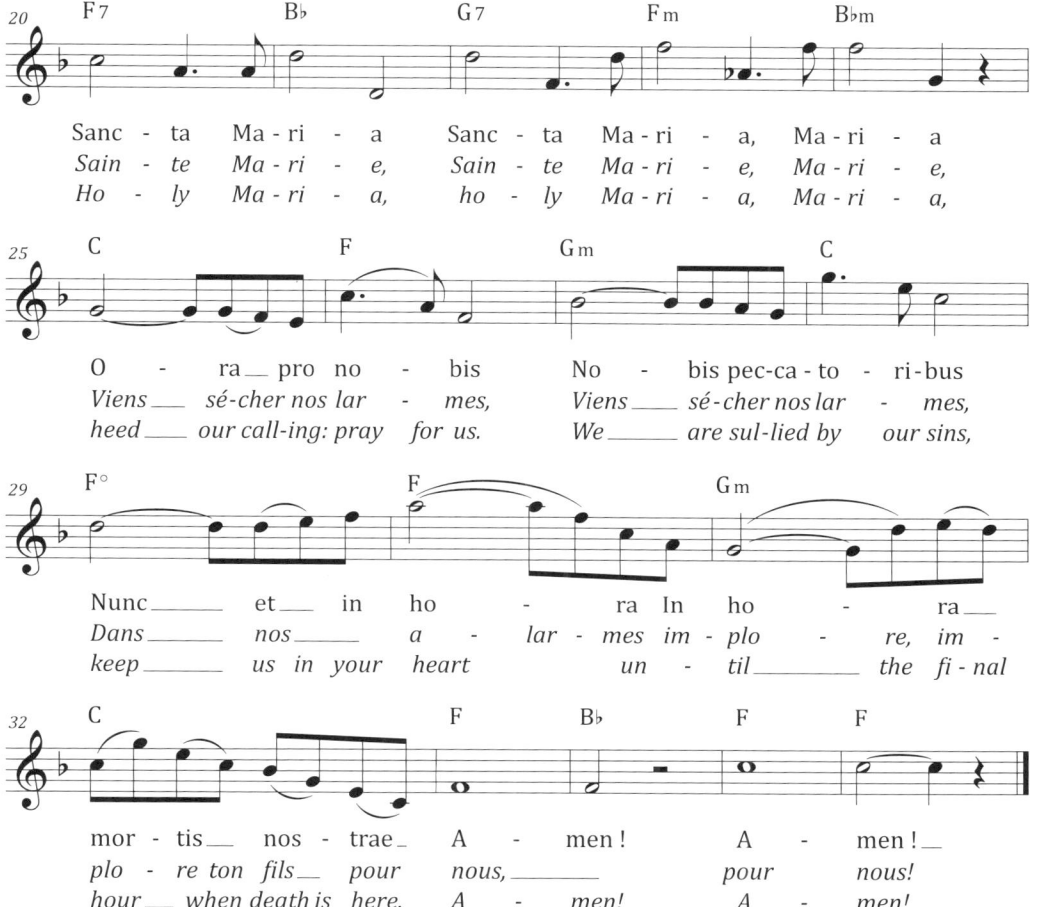

Ave Maria	Ave maria,	Ave Maria,
Gratia plena	Toi qui fus mère	bountiful and full of grace,
Dominus tecum	Sur cette terre,	walking with the Lord himself,
Benedicta tu	Tu souffris comme nous,	oh heavenly mother of us all,
In mulierbus	Tu partageas nos chaines,	bless-ed above all women,
Et benedictus fructus	Allège nos peines,	honored with a child,
Ventri tui Jesus	Vois, nous sommes tous,	your womb bore the fruit of Baby Jesus.
Sancta Maria	Nous sommes tous à tes genoux,	Holy Maria,
Sancta Maria, Maria	Sainte Marie,	holy Maria, Maria,
Ora pro nobis	Sainte Marie, Marie,	heed our calling: pray for us.
Nobis peccatoribus	Viens sécher nos larmes,	We are sullied by our sins,
Nunc et in hora	Viens sécher nos larmes,	keep us in your heart
In hora mortis nostrae	Dans nos alarmes implore,	until the final hour when death is here.
Amen ! Amen !	implore ton fils pour nous,	Amen! Amen!
	pour nous !	

First existing adaptation into French by Paul Bernard (1857)

Translation by Claire Moreau & Lara Tasker (2023)

FAITH & SPIRITUALITY   GERMANY

121
Von guten Mächten
By Gentle Powers

German priest Dietrich Bonhoeffer (1906-45) wrote this poem "Von guten Mächten wunderbar geborgen" in a Gestapo prison in late December 1944 in a letter to his fiancée, her parents and siblings. The text is one of the most poignant documents of a horrific time, since Bonhoeffer was arrested by the Nazis as an opponent to the regime and associated with the German Resistance and executed at age 39 in Flossenbürg concentration camp in the last month of the war. In the poem, Bonhoeffer surrenders his fate into God's hands. The first musical version by Otto Abel was followed by approximately another 70 variations from various composers. The most famous of these is the one from 1970 by Siegfried Fietz.

By Ekkehard Klemm, president, Association of German Concert Choirs (VDKC) /
Hochschule für Musik "Carl Maria von Weber" Dresden

Lyrics: Dietrich Bonhoeffer (1906-45)   Music: Siegfried Fietz (1946-)

1. Von gu-ten Mäch-ten treu und still um-ge-ben, be-hü-tet und ge-trös-tet wun-der-bar so will ich die-se Ta-ge mit euch le-ben und mit euch ge-hen in ein neu-es Jahr.

1. Sur-roun-ded by such true and gen-tle pow-ers. So won-drous-ly con-soled and with-out fear. Thus will I spend with you these fi-nal ho-urs and then to-geth-er en-ter a new year.

Chorus:
Von gu-ten Mäch-ten wun-der-bar ge-bor-gen, er-war-ten
By gen-tle pow-ers lov-ing-ly sur-roun-ded. With pa-tience

1. Von guten Mächten treu und still umgeben,
   behütet und getröstet wunderbar,
   so will ich diese Tage mit euch leben
   und mit euch gehen in ein neues Jahr.

Chorus:
   Von guten Mächten wunderbar geborgen,
   erwarten wir getrost, was kommen mag.
   Gott ist bei uns am Abend und am Morgen
   und ganz gewiss an jedem neuen Tag.

2. Noch will das Alte unsre Herzen quälen,
   noch drückt uns böser Tage schwere Last.
   Ach Herr, gib unsern aufgeschreckten Seelen
   das Heil, für das du uns geschaffen hast.

Chorus:
   Von guten Mächten wunderbar geborgen...

3. Doch willst du uns noch einmal Freude schenken
   an dieser Welt und ihrer Sonne Glanz,
   dann wolln wir des Vergangenen
   gedenken, und dann gehört dir unser Leben ganz.

Chorus:
   Von guten Mächten wunderbar geborgen...

1. Surrounded by such true and gentle powers.
   So wondrously consoled and without fear.
   Thus will I spend with you these final hours
   and then together enter a new year.

Chorus:
   By gentle powers lovingly surrounded.
   With patience we'll endure, let come what may.
   God is with us at night and in the morning,
   and certainly on every future day.

2. The worries of the old year still torment us,
   we're troubled still by long and wicked days.
   Oh Lord give our frightened souls the healing,
   for which you've chastened us in many ways.

Chorus:
   By gentle powers lovingly surrounded...

3. And should it be your will once more to grant us
   to see the world and to enjoy the sun,
   then we will all the past events remember
   and finally, our life with you is one.

Chorus:
   By gentle powers lovingly surrounded...

Translation by Ulrich Schaffer (1986)

Copyright © ABAKUS Musik Barbara Fietz. Reprinted by permission

FAITH & SPIRITUALITY   FINLAND

122
En etsi valtaa loistoa
Give Me no Gems nor Gifts of Gold

This song was composed by Jean Sibelius in 1909 and has become one of the most beloved Christmas carols in Finnish families. The original Swedish version ('Giv mig ej glans, ej guld, ej prakt') was taken from Zachris Topelius' collection of poems from 1889. The author of the Finnish version of the lyrics (published in 1909) is unknown. The song emphasizes the message of the Christian Christmas, a moment of peace and settling down in the midst of the world's controversies. It asserts that Christmas is not a celebration of consumption but a time of silence. The song was also the favorite Christmas carol in Sibelius's own family.

By Dr. Vesa Kurkela, Sibelius Academy

Lyrics: Zachris Topelius (1818-98)   Music: Jean Sibelius (1865-1957)
Finnish translation: unknown

1. En et-si val-taa, lois-to-a, en kai-paa kul-taa-kaan; ma
1. *Give me no gems nor gifts of gold when Christ-mas comes to call; give*

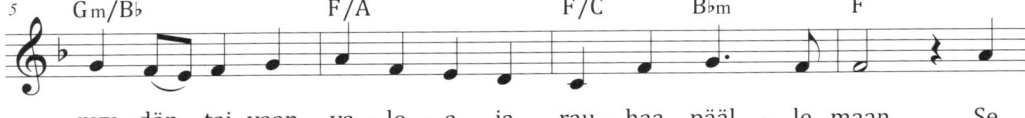

pyy-dän tai-vaan va-lo-a ja rau-haa pääl-le maan. Se
me the an-gels' song of old and peace on earth for all; a

jou-lu suo, mi on-nen tuo ja mie-let nos-taa Luo-jan luo. Ei
gath'-ring blessed, my heart at rest, the King of Heav'n as hon-oured guest. Give

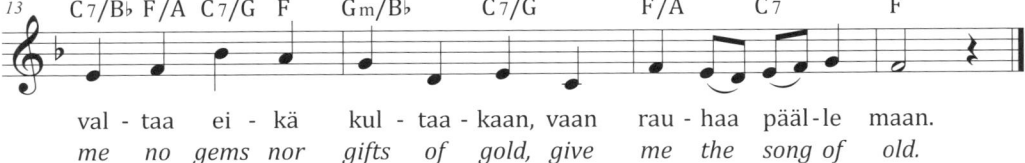

val-taa ei-kä kul-taa-kaan, vaan rau-haa pääl-le maan.
me no gems nor gifts of gold, give me the song of old.

1. En etsi valtaa, loistoa,
   en kaipaa kultaakaan;
   ma pyydän taivaan valoa
   ja rauhaa päälle maan.
   Se joulu suo, mi onnen tuo
   ja mielet nostaa Luojan luo.
   Ei valtaa eikä kultaakaan,
   vaan rauhaa päälle maan.

2. Suo mulle maja rauhaisa
   ja lasten joulupuu,
   Jumalan sanan valoa,
   joss' sieluin kirkastuu!
   Tuo kotihin, jos pieneenkin,
   nyt joulujuhla suloisin,
   Jumalan sanan valoa,
   ja mieltä jaloa.

3. Luo köyhän niinkuin rikkahan,
   saa joulu ihana!
   Pimeytehen maailman
   tuo taivaan valoa!
   Sua halajan, Sua odotan,
   sa Herra maan ja taivahan.
   Nyt köyhän niinkuin rikkaan luo
   suloinen joulus tuo!

1. *Give me no gems nor gifts of gold*
   when Christmas comes to call;
   give me the angels' song of old
   and peace on earth to all;
   a gath'ring blessed, my heart at rest,
   the King of Heav'n as honoured guest.
   Give me no gems nor gifts of gold,
   give me the song of old.

2. *Give me a home where may be found*
   a children's Christmas tree,
   a light that shines through darkness round
   that home, for all to see;
   in quiet night by candlelight
   the Word of God that burns most bright.
   Give me a home where may be found
   a light that shines around.

3. *To all and sundry, rich or poor,*
   may Yuletide grant its grace.
   May we with childlike joy endure
   the winter's long embrace.
   My Lord, my King, your blessings bring,
   for which with thanks your praise we sing!
   With all and sundry, rich or poor,
   may childlike joy endure.

   Translation by Jaakko Mäntyjärvi (2021)

FAITH & SPIRITUALITY   BULGARIA

123
Ако си дал
If You Have Shared

"If You Have Shared" has music and lyrics by Emil Dimitrov, one of the most emblematic Bulgarian composers in the field of light, fun-loving and popular music from the second half of the twentieth century. He is the author of over 280 Schlager songs that are still popular today. Emil Dimitrov is known not only as an author but also as a performer of his work. For his 39-year music career, his albums have been distributed in 65 million copies in many countries around the world and taken together they highlight both kindness and compassion for the human character. Among his songs "If You Have Shared" has both a lyrical character and a vividly memorable melody.

By Dr. Jean Pehlivanov, Academy of Music Dance and Fine Arts, Plovdiv, AMDFA

Lyrics: Ilya Borisov Velchev (1947-)   Music: Emil Dimitrov (1940-2005)

1. А - ко си дал на глад - ни - я до - ри тро - ши - ца хляб от сво - я хляб. А - ко си дал на скит - ни - ка до - ри ис -

1. If you have shared with the poor one a sin - gle crumb of bread from your own bread. If you have shared with the home - less one a sin - gle

1.
Ако си дал на гладния
дори трошица хляб от своя хляб.
Ако си дал на скитника
дори искрица огън от своя огън.
Ако си дал на милата
от своето сърце.
Ако си дал на чуждите
живот от себе си.

Bridge:
||: Ако си дал, ако си дал,
ако си дал от себе си,
не си живял, не си живял напразно. :||

Chorus:
Никой не може да ти отнеме
обичта, обичта на хората.
Никой не може да ти я вземе
любовта, любовта към хората.
И никой и нищо не ще
　　　　　　　ти отнема
вярата в тях, вярата в тях, вярата в тях.
Ти закъсняваш понякога истинно,
но винаги идваш, идваш при нас.

2. *(spoken)*
Ако си взел от славата на някой друг
дори една частица.
Ако си чул от клюката
и я повториш
дори една секунда.
Ако си враг на подлия,
но го послушаш
дори един единствен път.
Ако си ял от залъка на свой приятел
и го забравиш.

Bridge:
||: Дали е трябвало, дали е трябвало,
дали е трябвало изобщо,
дали е трябвало изобщо
да се раждаш. :||

Chorus:
Никой не може да ти отнеме…

1.
*If you have shared with the poor one
a single crumb of bread from your own bread.
If you have shared with the homeless one
a single spark of hope from your own hope.
If you have shared with someone dear
a true love from your heart.
If you have shared with a stranger
a piece of your own life.*

Bridge:
||: *If you have shared, if you have shared,
if you have shared a piece of you,
you haven't lived, you haven't lived in vain.* :||

Chorus:
*No one can take this, not in a lifetime,
all the love, all the love received.
No one can steal this, not in a lifetime,
all the love, all the love you've given.
And nothing and no one can take this
　　　　　　　　　from your heart,
your true belief, your true belief, your true belief.
We know that sometimes the truth is belated,
but it's always coming, coming to us.*

2. *(spoken)*
*If you have stolen the glory of someone else
even just a bit.
If you have heard the gossip
and repeat it
even for a second.
If you resist the evil one,
but listen to a word he says
even just for once.
If you have broken bread with a friend
and yet forget them.*

Bridge:
||: *I wonder if you should, I wonder if you should
I wonder if you should for real,
I wonder if you should for real
be on this earth.* :||

Chorus:
No one can take this, not in a lifetime…

Translation by Desislava Sofranova (2022)

FAITH & SPIRITUALITY   IRELAND

124
Ag Críost an Síol
Christ's Is the Seed

This Irish hymn is composed by the celebrated Irish composer Sean Ó Riada (1931-71) with lyrics believed to be written by Father Michael Sheehan (1870-1945), a strong proponent of the Irish language from Waterford. The imagery is drawn from nature with the poet comparing the embrace of God with the harvest gathered into grain-stores and the fish being gathered in the nets of fishermen. In his later years Ó Riada settled in an Irish-speaking area in west Cork and immersed himself in the local language and culture. Here he composed two settings of the Mass for a local male voice choir, Cór Chúil Aodha. Ag Críost an Síol appears as an Offertory Hymn in Ó Riada's 1968 setting of the mass, Ceol an Aifrinn (Music of the Mass). This short unison hymn is written in an Irish traditional style and has become one of the most popular pieces of sacred music written in the Irish language, performed at both weddings and funerals.

By Mark Armstrong, SING IRELAND

Lyrics: Father Michael Sheehan (1870-1945)   Music: Sean Ó Riada (1931-1971)

1. Ag Críost an síol, ag Críost an fomhar, i n'ioth-lainn Dé, go dtugtar sinn. Ag Críost an mhuir, ag Críost an tiasc, i líontaibh Dé go gcastar sinn. Ó fhás go haois, is ó aois go bhás, Do dhá láimh a Chríost, anall tharainn. Ó

1. The seed is Christ's, the harvest his. Into his store he gathers us in. The sea is Christ's, the fish within. The nets of God they bring us in. We grow through age, and from age to death. Your two hands, O Christ, surround us tight. Death is

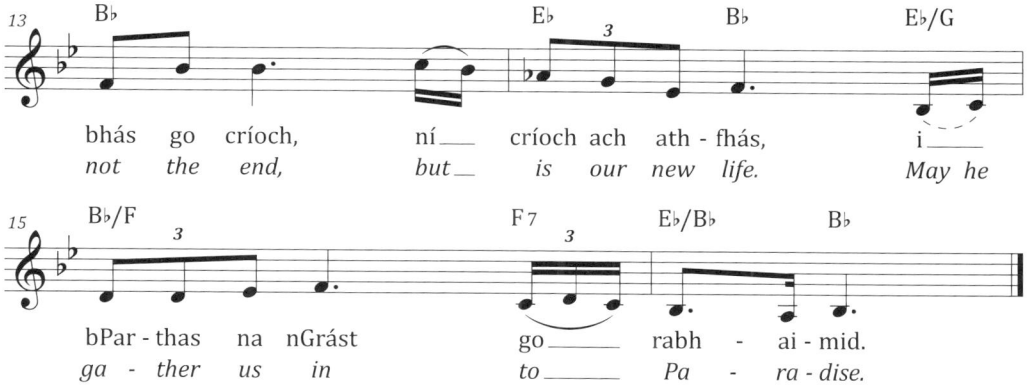

1. Ag Críost an síol, ag Críost an fómhar;
   in iothlainn Dé go dtugtar sinn.
   Ag Críost an mhuir, ag Críost an t-iasc;
   i líonta Dé go gcastar sinn.

2. Ó fhás go h-aois, is ó aois go bás,
   do dhá láimh, a Chríost, anall tharainn.
   Ó bhás go críoch, ní críoch ach athfhás,
   i bParthas na nGrást go rabhaimid.

1. The seed is Christ's, the harvest his;
   into his store he gathers us in.
   The sea is Christ's, the fish within;
   the nets of God they bring us in.

2. We grow through age, and from age to death.
   Your two hands, O Christ, surround us tight.
   Death is not the end, but is our new life.
   May he gather us in to Paradise.

Translation by Mark Armstrong (2021)

Copyright © 1968 Real World Works Ltd. Copyright Renewed. All Rights Administered by Sony Music Publishing (US) LLC, 424 Church Street, Suite 1200, Nashville, TN 37219. International Copyright Secured. All Rights Reserved. Reprinted by Permission of Hal Leonard Europe Ltd.

FAITH & SPIRITUALITY   MALTA

125
Iddeċidejt
I've Decided

This religious song from 1989 is one amongst the many composed by Tiziana Grech, and is played frequently in prayer groups and other religious gatherings in Malta. The lyrics of the song speak about the decision to devote oneself wholly to God.

By Dr. Albert Pace, School of Performing Arts, University of Malta

Lyrics: Tiziana Grech   Music: Tiziana Crech

1. Id - de-ċi-dejt Mu - lej li ħaj - ti rrid nagħ-tik Jien nof -
1. I've made the choice oh Lord to lis - ten to your voice and to

fri-lek li-li nnif-si kif jien. Hud - ni f'i-dejk u agħ-mel
of - fer all I am un - to you. In - to your hands, I give my -

bi - ja dak li trid Kun int Mu-lej is-Sid ta' ħaj - ti. Hawn
self just as I am that you may be my Lord and Sav - iour. Lord

jien Mu-lej, jien lest għa - lik u għal kull ma trid. Hawn
here I am, I come that I may do your will. Lord

jien Mu-lej, b'im-ħab - ba kbi - ra għa-lik. Hawn
here I am, my heart just can - not be still. Lord

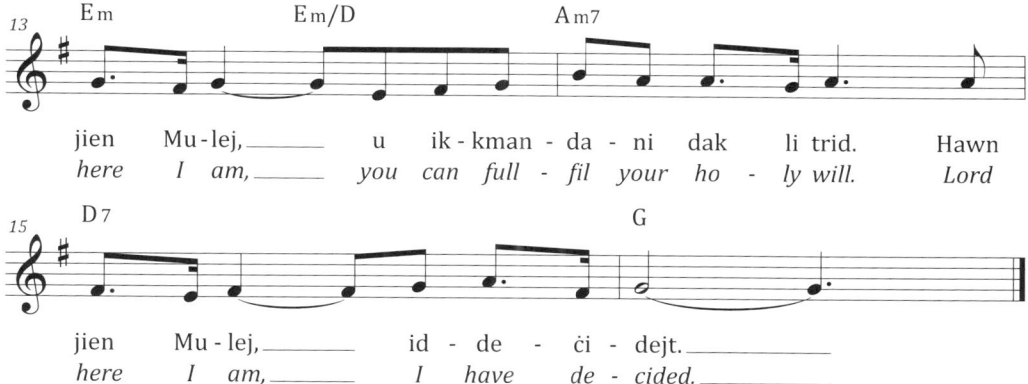

Iddeċidejt Mulej li ħajti rrid nagħtik
Jien noffrilek lili nnifsi kif jien.
Ħudni f' idejk u agħmel bija dak li trid
Kun int Mulej is-Sid ta' ħajti.
Hawn jien Mulej,
jien lest għalik u għal kull ma trid.
Hawn jien Mulej, b'imħabba kbira għalik.
Hawn jien Mulej, u ikkmandani dak li trid.
Hawn jien Mulej, iddeċidejt.

*I've made the choice oh Lord to listen to your voice
and to offer all I am unto you.
Into your hands, I give myself just as I am
that you may be my Lord and Saviour.
Lord here I am,
I come that I may do your will.
Lord here I am, my heart just cannot be still.
Lord here I am, you can fullfil your holy will.
Lord here I am, I have decided.*

Translation by Andrew Cauchi (2022)

FAITH & SPIRITUALITY   LATVIA

126
Pie Dieviņa gari galdi
Dieviņš Keeps a Lavish Table

In Latvian culture, this folk song is a message of a person's place in the world. In Latvian mythology, deities of different levels and manifestations relate to anyone who is born, grows and lives, here or in the afterworld. One honors and acts with them and asks for advice. Each deity has its own symbol, which followers manifest in costume details, jewelry and tools. In this folk song all the deities sit at the table with God (the deity of heaven, father and creator) and the beloved Māra (the goddess of fertility, mother of the world), who takes care of the tangible world. It is still sung today with great reverence and love, both in happy and sad times.

By Rūta Kanteruka, president, Latvian Music Teachers' Association, LVIIMSA

Lyrics: folk poem   Music: folksong

1. Pie Die-vi-ņa ga-ri gal-di, ga-ri gal-di,
1. Die-viņš keeps a lav-ish ta-ble, lav-ish ta-ble,

Tur sēž pa-ti mī-ļā Mā-ra, mī-ļā Mār'
Mā-ra takes the seat of hon-our, takes the seat.

Pie Die-vi-ņa ga-ri gal-di, ga-ri gal-di
Die-viņš keeps a lav-ish ta-ble, lav-ish ta-ble,

Tur sēž pa-ti mī-ļā Mā-ra, mī-ļā Mār'
Mā-ra takes the seat of hon-our, takes the seat.

1. ||: Pie Dieviņa gari galdi, gari galdi
   Tur sēž pati mīļā Māra, mīļā Mār' :||

2. ||: Tur sēž pati mīļā Māra, mīļā Māra
   Villainītes rakstīdama, rakstīdam'. :||

3. ||: Izrakstīja, saskaitīja, saskaitīja,
   Dod Dieviņa rociņās, rociņās. :||

4. ||: Nu, Dieviņi, Tava vaļa, Tava vaļa,
   Nu Tavās rociņās, rociņās. :||

5. ||: Nu Tavās rociņās, rociņās
   Pašas laimes atslēdziņa, atslēdziņ'. :||

6. ||: Dod, Dieviņi, kalnā kāpt, kalnā kāpt,
   Ne no kalna lejiņā, lejiņā. :||

7. ||: Dod, Dieviņi, otram dot, otram dot,
   Ne no otra mīļi lūgt, mīļi lūgt. :||

1. ||: *Dieviņš keeps a lavish table, lavish table,*
   Māra takes the seat of honour, takes the seat. :||

2. ||: *Māra takes the seat of honour, seat of honour,*
   there she sits embroidering, embroidering. :||

3. ||: *Māra gathers up her sewing, takes her sewing,*
   puts it in the hands of Dieviņš, in his hands. :||

4. ||: *Dieviņš, it is up to you now, up to you now,*
   everything is in your hands, is in your hands. :||

5. ||: *Now you hold within your hands,*
                              within your hands,
   the key to perfect happiness, to happiness. :||

6. ||: *Dieviņš, let me climb the mountain,*
                              climb the mountain,
   not descend into the valley, not descend. :||

7. ||: *Dieviņš, let me give to others, give to others,*
   not receive from other people, not receive. :||

Translation by Māra Walsh Sinka (2023)

FAITH & SPIRITUALITY						LITHUANIA

127
Tyliąją naktį
On That Silent Night

Composer Juozas Nasujalis (1869-1934) was one of the forefathers of Lithuanian professional music in the period of the first liberation of Lithuania in the early 20th century. He worked as an organist in the Kaunas Cathedral, which let him to create and compose numerous sacred songs and hymns. "Tyliąją naktį" – On That Silent Night – remains popular to this day and is sung during Christmas season.

By Dr. Arvydas Girdzijauskas, Lithuanian Choral Union, LCHS

Lyrics: unknown					Music: Juozas Naujalis (1869-1934)

1. Ty - lią - ją nak - tį bal - sas su - gau - dė:
   Pie - me - nys, kel - kit: Die - vas už - gi - mė!
   Grei - tai ren - ki - tės ir bė - kit, Į Bet - lie - jų
   pa - sku - bė - kit svei - kint Vieš - pa - ties!

1. Bells on that fate - ful si - lent night did ring,
   shep - herds a - rise: born our Lord, our King!
   Don your robes, and hur - ry fast, to Beth - le - hem
   at long last, ye praise our Lord!

1. Tyliąją naktį balsas sugaudė:
   Piemenys, kelkit: Dievas užgimė!
   Greitai renkitės ir bėkit,
   Į Betliejų paskubėkit sveikint Viešpaties!

2. Nuėję rado Jėzų ėdžiose,
   Kaip pranašauta Dievo knygose.
   Jį Dievu jie pripažino,
   Kaip juos angelas mokino ir pasveikino.

3. O Atpirkėjau, seniai laukiamas,
   Tūkstančius metų žmonių meldžiamas!
   Laukė pranašai, karaliai,
   O Tu šią tiktai naktelę tepasirodei.

4. Mes irgi laukiam, Viešpatie, Tavęs;
   O kai ateisi pas mus per Mišias,
   Pulsim prieš Tave ant kelių,
   Gyvą kiekvienoj dalelėj šventos Ostijos.

1. Bells on that fateful silent night did ring,
   shepherds arise: born our Lord, our King!
   don your robes, and hurry fast,
   to Bethlehem at long last, ye praise our Lord!

2. Found in the manger sweet baby Jesus,
   as God's good book then did teach us.
   They made Him our only God
   as the angel He did laud, and adore, extol.

3. O great Redeemer, long-awaited King,
   Ye who all did pray for the peace He'd bring!
   Royals and wise prophets amassed
   and You came to us at long last, on this silent
                                              night.

4. We long for You now, our blessed Lord;
   and when You come to us at Mass, adored,
   on our knees we all shall fall
   for You are alive in all, each taste of the Host.

Translation by Gabriella Žičkienė (2022)

FAITH & SPIRITUALITY   LUXEMBOURG

128
O Mamm, léif Mamm do uewen
O Mother, Up Above Us

This poem became a song, also called 'Ons Himmelsmamm' (Our Heavenly Mother), dedicated to the Virgin Mary, the patron saint of the Grand-Duchy of Luxembourg, at the end of the 19th century. It has come to be sung as the closing hymn at every church service dedicated to her in Luxembourg, but has also been sung as an expression of patriotism at times when the independence of the country was at stake.

By Robert Köller, Union Grand-Duc Adolphe, UGDA

Lyrics: Charles Müllendorff (1830-1902)   Music: Pierre Barthel (1852-1923)

1. O Mamm, léif Mamm do ue - wen, ech hunn Dech een - zeg gär: Däi Numm ass mir ge - grue - wen an d'Häerz bis an der Kär. Däi Numm ass mir ge - grue - wen an d'Häerz bis an der Kär.

1. O Mo - ther up a - bove us, I love you more and more, your name, O Ho - ly Mo - ther, rests in my deep heart's core. Your name, O Ho - ly Mo - ther, rests in my deep heart's core.

1. O Mamm, léif Mamm do uewen,
   ech hunn Dech eenzeg gär:
   ||: Däi Numm ass mir gegruewen
   an d'Häerz bis an der Kär. :||

2. Ech sinn, sou wäit ech denken,
   e Muttergotteskand.
   ||: Wie soll séch hier nët schenken
   am Lëtzebuerger Land? :||

3. Wa méch méng Sënnen drécken,
   bei Gott a bei de Leit,
   ||: kënns du méch gläich erquécke
   mat Jesus, dee verzeiht. :||

4. Wann ech, vu Leed a Suergen,
   mäin Hierz hu schwéi'r an déck,
   ||: da bleiwt Dir näischt verbuergen,
   méng Mamm, mäin Trouscht, mäi Gléck! :||

5. Héi'r onst Gebiet, onst Kloen,
   gutt Mamm, um Kräiz gewonn,
   ||: an hëllef d'Kräiz ons droen
   mat Déngem léiwe Sonn. :||

6. O Gléck, Dech Mamm, ze ierwen!
   Ons Hand an Dénger Hand,
   ||: am Liewe wéi am Stierwen,
   gi mir an d'Heemechtsland! :||

1. O Mother up above us,
   I love you more and more,
   ||: your name, O Holy Mother,
   rests in my deep heart's core. :||

2. I am, I must believe it,
   a Holy Mother's child,
   ||: for Luxembourgers think it
   is true of all the world. :||

3. When I offend my Maker,
   or those with whom I live,
   ||: with you I reawaken,
   for Jesus to forgive. :||

4. When pain and sorrow burden
   my heart, and take their toll,
   ||: from you no hurt is hidden,
   my Mother, you console. :||

5. Hear our lament, dear Mother,
   who knew the cross's pain,
   ||: help us to bear our crosses,
   with your dear Son again. :||

6. O joy to call you Mother,
   go with you, hand-in-hand,
   ||: through life and, at our dying,
   enter our native land. :||

Translation by Edward Seymour (2021)

FAITH & SPIRITUALITY   BELGIUM

129
Dominique

The composer and performer, Jeanne Paule Marie (Jeannine) Deckers (1933-85), was a Dominican nun – "Soeur Sourire" (Sister Smile) – when she wrote and recorded the song. The structure is very classic: it alternates a refrain that easily stays in mind with verses describing certain facts from the life of Saint Dominic, founder of the religious order of the Dominicans to which Sister Sourire belonged. The song became a hit across Europe and, quickly, internationally known. The tone is light and fresh. However, the composers own destiny ended in minor. Both, literature, a play and a film are made about her tragic story.

By Reynald Sac, À Coeur Joie Fédération Chorale Wallonie-Bruxelles

Lyrics & Music: "Soeur Sourire", Jeanne Paule Marie (Jeannine) Deckers (1933-85)

Do-mi-ni-que, ni-que, ni-que s'en al-lait tout sim-ple-ment, rou-
Do-mi-ni-que, ni-que, nique, o-ver the land he plods a-long and

tier, pauv-re et chan-tant.____ En tous che-mins, en tous lieux, il ne
sings a lit-tle song.____ Nev-er ask-ing for re-ward, he just

parle que du Bon Dieu, il ne parle que du Bon Dieu.
talks a-bout the Lord, he just talks a-bout the Lord.

1. À l'é-poque où Jean Sans Ter-re, D'An-gle-ter-re é-tait roi Do-mi-
1. At a time when John-ny Lack-land o-ver Eng-land was the King, Do-mi-

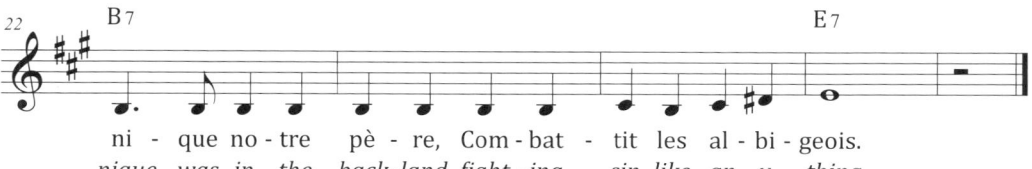

ni-que no-tre pè-re, Com-bat-tit les al-bi-geois.
nique was in the back-land fight-ing sin like an-y-thing.

Chorus:
    Dominique, nique, nique
    S'en allait tout simplement,
    Routier, pauvre et chantant
    En tous chemins, en tous lieux,
    Il ne parle que du Bon Dieu,
    Il ne parle que du Bon Dieu.

1. À l'époque où Jean Sans Terre,
   D'Angleterre était le roi
   Dominique notre père,
   Combattit les albigeois.
   Dominique, nique, nique...

2. Certains jours un hérétique,
   Par des ronces le conduit
   Mais notre Père Dominique,
   Par sa joie le convertit.
   Dominique, nique, nique...

3. Ni chameau, ni diligence,
   Il parcourt l'Europe à pied
   Scandinavie ou Provence,
   Dans la sainte pauvreté.
   Dominique, nique, nique...

4. Enflamma de toute école
   Filles et garçons pleins d'ardeur
   Et pour semer la parole,
   Inventa les Frères-Prêcheurs.
   Dominique, nique, nique...

5. Chez Dominique et ses frères,
   Le pain s'en vint à manquer
   Et deux anges se présentèrent,
   Portant de grands pains dorés
   Dominique, nique, nique...

6. Dominique vit en rêve,
   Les prêcheurs du monde entier
   Sous le manteau de la Vierge,
   En grand nombre rassemblés.
   Dominique, nique, nique...

7. Dominique, mon bon Père,
   Garde-nous simples et gais
   Pour annoncer à nos frères,
   La vie et la vérité.
   Dominique, nique, nique...

Chorus:
    Dominique, nique, nique,
    over the land he plods along
    and sings a little song.
    Never asking for reward
    he just talks about the Lord,
    he just talks about the Lord.

1. *At a time when Johnny Lackland*
   over England was the King,
   Dominique was in the backland
   Fighting sin like anything.
   Dominique, nique, nique...

2. *Now a heretic, one day*
   among the thorns forced him to crawl,
   Dominique with just one prayer
   made him hear the good Lord's call.
   Dominique, nique, nique...

3. *Without horse or fancy wagon*
   he crossed Europe up and down,
   poverty was his companion
   as he walked from town to town.
   Dominique, nique, nique...

4. *To bring back the straying liars*
   and the lost sheep to the fold,
   he brought forth the Preaching Friars,
   Heaven's soldier's, brave and bold.
   Dominique, nique, nique...

5. *One day, in the budding Order*
   there was nothing left to eat,
   suddenly two angels walked in
   with a loaf of bread and meat.
   Dominique, nique, nique...

6. *Dominique once, in his slumber*
   saw the Virgin's coat unfurled
   over Friars without number
   preaching all around the world.
   Dominique, nique, nique...

7. *Grant us now, oh Dominique,*
   the grace of love and simple mirth
   that we all may help to quicken
   Godly life and truth on Earth.
   Dominique, nique, nique...

Translation by Noël Regney (1922 –2002)

Copyright © 1963 Primavera Editions Musicales (Nv). Warner Chappell Overseas Holdings Ltd, London, W8 5DA.
Reprinted by permission of Faber Music Ltd. All rights reserved

FAITH & SPIRITUALITY   THE NETHERLANDS

130
Midden in de winternacht
See, Amid the Winter Night

This Dutch Christmas carol is based on the 17th century Catalan carol, "El desembre congelat" (The Cold December), with a melody that – due to the circulation of ideas in the musical melting pot – is based on a joyous French drinking song "Quand la mer Rouge apparut" (When the Red Sea appeared) dating from as early as the 16th century. Whereas the Catalan lyrics evolves around flowers and spring, the Dutch lyrics, written during WW2 by Harry Prenen (1915-92), tell of the shepherds' joy of the birth of Christ. They dance, sing and make music. The catchy chorus, in which the various music instruments are being sung about, probably contributed to the popularity of the song.

By Christiane Nieuwmeijer, Leiden University of Applied Sciences
& Lieuwe Noordam, Prins Claus Conservatorium, Groningen

Lyrics: Harry L. Prenen (1915-92)   Music: old French melody

1. Mid - den in de win - ter - nacht, ging de he - mel o - pen;
1. See, a - mid the win - ter night, hea - ven's door has o - pened;

die ons't Heil der we - reld bracht, ant - woord op ons ho - pen.
bring - ing us our Sa - viour's light, this is what we hoped for.

Chorus:
El - ke vo - gel zingt zijn lied; her - ders, waar - om zingt gij niet? Laat de
Eve - ry bird shall sing its song, shep - herds please do sing a - long. On the

ci - thers slaan, blaast de flui - ten aan, laat de bel, laat de trom, laat de
zith - ers strum, blow the flutes' warm hum, ring the bell, beat the drum, sound the

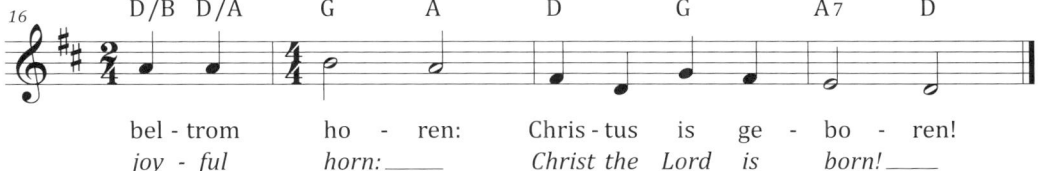

bel - trom ho - ren: Chris - tus is ge - bo - ren!
joy - ful horn: Christ the Lord is born!

1. Midden in de winternacht,
   ging de hemel open;
   die ons 't Heil der wereld bracht,
   antwoord op ons hopen.

   Refrein:
   Elke vogel zingt zijn lied;
   herders, waarom zingt gij niet?
   Laat de cithers slaan,
   blaast de fluiten aan,
   laat de bel, laat de trom,
   laat de beltrom horen:
   Christus is geboren!

2. Vrede was het overal,
   wilde dieren kwamen
   bij de schapen in de stal
   en zij speelden samen.

   Refrein:
   Elke vogel zingt zijn lied…

3. Ondanks winter, sneeuw en ijs
   bloeien alle bomen,
   want het aardse paradijs
   is vannacht gekomen.

   Refrein:
   Elke vogel zingt zijn lied…

4. Ziet reeds staat de morgenster,
   stralend in het duister,
   want de dag is niet meer ver,
   bode van de luister,

   Refrein:
   Die ons weldra op zal gaan,
   herders blaast uw fluiten aan
   laat de bel, bim-bam
   laat de trom, rom-bom
   kere om, kere om,
   laat de beltrom horen:
   Christus is geboren!

1. See, amid the winter night,
   Heaven's door has opened,
   bringing us our Saviour's light,
   this is what we hoped for.

   Chorus:
   Every bird shall sing its song,
   shepherds please do sing along.
   On the zithers strum,
   blow the flutes' warm hum,
   ring the bell, beat the drum,
   sound the joyful horn:
   Christ the Lord is born!

2. Everywhere a peaceful world,
   bears and wolves come hither
   in the field they join the sheep,
   frolicking together.

   Chorus:
   Every bird shall sing its song…

3. Under winter snow and ice
   all the trees are growing,
   for the earthly paradise
   has their lifeblood flowing.

   Chorus:
   Every bird shall sing its song…

4. See the morning star up there
   shining in the dark night,
   for the day it does prepare,
   waking us to bright light.

   Chorus:
   Let us join in morning song,
   shepherds play your flutes along
   ring the bell ding-dong
   beat the drum dum-dum
   turn around, turn around,
   sound the joyful horn:
   Christ the Lord is born!

Translation by Arnold Mühren (2021)

Copyright © Universal Music Publishing. International Copyright Secured. All Rights Reserved.
Reprinted by permission of Hal Leonard Europe Ltd.

FAITH & SPIRITUALITY　　　　　　　　　　　　　　　　　　　SWEDEN

131
En vänlig grönskas rika dräkt
The Earth Adorned in Verdant Robe

Waldemar Åhlén (1894-1982), organist and composer, wrote the beautiful melody for "Sommarpsalm" – Summer Hymn – probably better known as "En vänlig grönskas rika dräkt" (The Earth Adorned in Verdant Robe) for a school graduation in 1933. The words were written in 1895 by Carl David af Wirsén (1842-1912), secretary of the Swedish Academy of Letters. The hymn is one of the most loved and is also a popular choir piece.

By Kerstin Carpvik, head of library, Musikverket

Lyrics: Carl David af Wirsén (1842-1912)　　　　Music: Waldemar Åhlén (1894-1982)

1. En vän - lig grön - skas ri - ka dräkt har smyc - kat dal och äng - ar. Nu sme - ker vin - dens ljum - ma fläkt de fa - gra ör - te - säng - ar. Och so - lens ljus och lun - dens sus och vå - gens sorl bland vi - den för - kun - na som - mar - ti - den.

1. *The earth a - dorned in ver - dant robe sends prais - es up - ward surg - ing, while soft winds breathe on fra - grant flow'rs from win - ter now e - merg - ing. The sun - shine bright gives warmth and light to budd - ing blos - soms ten - der, pro - claim - ing sum - mer splen - dour.*

1. En vänlig grönskas rika dräkt
   har smyckat dal och ängar.
   Nu smeker vindens ljumma fläkt
   de fagra örtesängar.
   Och solens ljus
   och lundens sus
   och vågens sorl bland viden
   förkunna sommartiden.

2. Sin lycka och sin sommarro
   de yra fåglar prisa.
   Ur skogens snår, ur stilla bo
   framklingar deras visa.
   En hymn går opp
   av fröjd och hopp
   från deras glada kväden,
   från blommorna och träden.

3. Men du, o Gud som gör vår Jord
   så skön i sommarns stunder:
   Giv att jag aktar främst ditt ord
   och dina nådesunder.
   Allt kött är hö
   och blomstren dö
   och tiden allt fördriver,
   blott Herrens ord förbliver.

4. Allt kött är hö, allt flyktar här
   och snart förvissna gräsen.
   Hos dig allena, Herre, är
   ett oförgängligt väsen.
   Min ande giv
   det nya liv,
   som aldrig skall förblomma,
   fast äng och fält stå tomma.

5. Då må förblekna sommarns glans
   och vissna allt fåfängligt;
   min vän är min och jag är hans,
   vårt band är oförgängligt.
   I paradis
   han huld och vis,
   mig sist skall omplantera,
   där inget vissnar mera.

---

1. The earth adorned in verdant robe
   sends praises upward surging,
   while soft winds breathe on fragrant flow'rs
   from winter now emerging.
   The sunshine bright
   gives warmth and light
   to budding blossoms tender,
   proclaiming summer splendour.

2. From out the wood the birds now sing
   and each its song now raises,
   to join with all the universe
   in voicing thankful praises.
   With hope and joy
   their songs employ
   a rapturous exultation
   in praise of God's creation.

3. O God, amid these joys of life,
   creation's glory beaming,
   grant us the grace to keep Your word
   and live in love redeeming.
   All flesh is grass,
   the flowers fade,
   and time is fleeting ever;
   God's word remains forever.

4. All flesh is grass. All things will fade,
   and soon will winter harden.
   With You, our Lord, in healthy shade
   the plants adorn Your garden.
   My heart, come through
   with life anew
   that never can go sunder,
   for heav'n awaits me yonder.

5. The summer splendour fades away
   and goes like evening shadows.
   My Friend is mine, and He will stay
   with me past death's grim meadows.
   In Paradise
   He will me rise
   and let me stay forever.
   No graves will be there, never.

Translation by Carolyn & Kenneth Jennings (v. 1-3);
Folmer E. Johansen (v. 4-5) - (1974)

FAITH & SPIRITUALITY   SLOVENIA

132
Glej zvezdice božje
Behold the Little Stars of God

Leopold Belar, the author of this song, died in 1899. We do not have all the details of his compositions. However, among the ca. 100 pieces known to be by him, 'Glej zvezdice božje' ('Behold the Little Stars of God') has certainly a special meaning for every religious soul in Slovenia. This Christmas carol is indispensable for Slovene church choirs and the music is a charming example of bel canto as it echoed in the Slovenian church music of the 19th century. This song radiates the benevolent stance toward the universe in which we live: the more we give in to the simplicity of its message and the loveliness of its melodic articulation, the more it entices and captivates us.

By Dr. Leon Stefanija, University of Ljubljana, Faculty of Arts

Lyrics: Leopold Belar (1828-99)   Music: Leopold Belar (1828-99)

1. Glej, zve - zdi - ce bo - žje mi - glja - jo le - po, od -
1. Be - hold, stars of God twink-ling beau - tif - 'lly nigh, wide

pr - to ši - ro - ko je sve - to ne - bo. Du -
o - pen and ho - ly they shine 'cross the sky. The

ho - vi ne - beš - ki se zra - ja vr - ste, pre -
spi - rits from hea - ven make mer - ri - ly in turn, they

pe - va - jo sla - vo, na zem - ljo hi - te. Du - - te
sing of the glo - ry, to earth they re - turn. The - turn.

1. Glej, zvezdice božje migljajo lepo,
   odprto široko je sveto nebo.
   ||: Duhovi nebeški se z raja vrste,
   prepevajo slavo, na zemljo hite. :||

2. Obljuba predavna postala je res,
   zveličar je rojen ljudem iz nebes.
   ||: Pri ubogih pastircih na slam'ci leži,
   si revščino izvoli, ponižnost uči. :||

3. O, srečne dušice, ki njega časte,
   z nebeško tolažbo jim polni srce.
   ||: Le k njemu hitimo,
                   saj rad nas ima,
   zaupno odkrijmo mu rane srca. :||

1. *Behold, stars of God twinkling beautif'lly nigh,*
   wide open and holy they shine 'cross the sky.
   ||: The spirits from paradise make merrily in turn,
   they sing of the glory, to earth they return. :||

2. *A promise most ancient has now come to pass:*
   the Saviour from Heaven's been born unto us.
   ||: He teaches us humility, impov'rished he shall stay;
   befriended by shepherds, asleep on the hay. :||

3. *Oh happy the souls that accepted his call!*
   With heavenly solace he comforts us all.
   ||: In confidence we rush to him,
                   he's loved us from the start;
   to Him we're revealing the wounds of our hearts. :||

Translation by Steve Klink & Boštjan Malus (2021)

FAITH & SPIRITUALITY   ROMANIA

133
O, ce veste minunată!
Wondrous Tiding, Joyful Feeling

Although sung differently in many regions of Romania, this old carol, loved by all Romanians wherever they are, has remained emblematic after being performed so exceptionally by the Madrigal Choir in the 1970's in a remake by the composer Dumitru Georgescu Kiriac (1866-1928), one of the founders of the Romanian Composers Society (1920). This Christmas carol is distinguished both by its melodic delicacy and the unmodified modal formula, which preserve its originality, even if traces of tonal harmony can be found. Throughout the entire vocal and choral conception, the composer makes use of folkloric and modal features to fully enhance the carol's values.

By Dr. Grigore Cudalbu, National University of Music, Bucharest, UNMB/ Romanian National Association of Choral Music, ANCR

Lyrics & Music: Dumitru Georgescu Kiriac (1866-1928)

1. O, ce veste minunată! În Betleemni sarată, Că a născut prunc, prunc din Duhul Sfânt Fecioara curată.
   Fecioara curată.

1. Wondrous tiding, joyful feeling, unto Bethlehem revealing, in that very place, born with Heaven's grace, he who brings us healing!
   he who brings us healing!

1. O, ce veste minunată!
   În Betleem ni s-arată,
   ||: Că a născut prunc,
   prunc din Duhul Sfânt
   Fecioara curată. :||

2. Că la Betleem Maria
   Săvârsind călătoria,
   ||: În sărac lăcas,
   lâng-acel oras,
   A născut pe Messia. :||

3. Pe Fiul cel din vecie
   Ce l-a trimis Tatăl mie,
   ||: Să se nască
   Si să crească,
   Să ne mântuiască. :||

1. *Wondrous tiding, joyful feeling,*
   unto Bethlehem revealing,
   ||: *In that very place,*
   born with Heaven's Grace,
   He who brings us healing! :||

2. *For in Bethlehem did Mary*
   from her troubled journey weary
   ||: *Into this world bring,*
   oh, a newborn King,
   Lord Messiah very! :||

3. *Oh, the Son as there's no other,*
   sent by the Eternal Father
   ||: *Through His Godly birth,*
   to increase our worth,
   every man a brother! :||

Translation by Beck Corlan & Alex Szollo (2022)

FAITH & SPIRITUALITY   SLOVAKIA

134
Daj Boh šťastia tejto zemi
Lord, Oh Let This Earth Be Happy

A melody of this song is a variant of a widely known Christmas carol "Hore vstavajťe Valasi a posluchaje" (Shepherds, Wake Up and Listen) from the songbook of teacher and organist Gašpar Drozd (1805-74), who lived in the village of Chrenovec. It was first discovered in 1989, but the carol was spread in various variants throughout Slovakia and also became the anthem of the Union of Slovaks in Hungary. The version presented here has lyrics by Viliam Ján Gruska (1936-2019), one of the founders of the "Dni kolied kresťanov", the Christian Caroling Days festival, where it was first heard. The song gained popularity mainly thanks to the interpretation of Pavol Habera (b. 1962). However currently it is popular in Christmas programs of several other singers of various genres.

By Dr. Eva Čunderlíková, Slovak Music Teacher Association, AUHS/Academy of Music Bratislava, VŠMU

Lyrics: Viliam Ján Gruska (1936-2019)   Music: folksong

1. Daj, Boh, šťas-tia tej-to ze-mi, všet-kým ľu-ďom v nej,
   1. Lord, oh let this earth be hap-py, all the peo-ple there!

nech im sln-ko jas-ne svie-ti kaž-dý Bo-ží deň.
May the sun shine on them bright-ly, eve-ry bless-ed day.

Nech ich su-sed v lás-ke má, nech im pria-zeň, po-koj dá.
May their neigh-bours love them well, ev-er peace-ful may they dwell.

Daj, Boh, šťas-tia tej-to ze-mi, všet-kým ľu-ďom v nej.
Lord, oh let this earth be hap-py, all the peo-ple there!

1. Daj, Boh, šťastia tejto zemi,
   všetkým ľuďom v nej,
   nech im slnko jasne svieti
   každý Boží deň.

   ||: Nech ich sused v láske má,
   nech im priazeň, pokoj dá.
   Daj, Boh, šťastia tejto zemi,
   všetkým ľuďom v nej. :||

2. Daj, Boh, šťastia celej zemi,
   všetkým národom.
   Nech im svetlo hviezdy lásky
   ožiaruje dom.

   ||: Hladným chleba dobrého,
   chorým zdravia pevného.
   Daj, Boh, šťastia celej zemi,
   všetkým národom. :||

3. Dopraj, Bože, svojmu dielu
   večné trvanie.
   Nech sa samo nezahubí
   všetci prosíme.

   ||: Rybám čistej vody daj,
   vtáctvo a zver zachovaj.
   Dopraj, Bože, svojmu dielu
   večné trvanie. :||

1. Lord, oh let this earth be happy,
   all the people there!
   May the sun shine on them brightly,
   every blessed day.

   ||: May their neighbours love them well,
   ever peaceful may they dwell.
   Lord, oh let this earth be happy,
   all the people there! :||

2. Lord, oh let this earth be happy,
   nations all have light!
   May the star of love shine always,
   make their houses bright.

   ||: Give the hungry decent bread,
   let the sick have health instead.
   Lord, oh let this earth be happy,
   nations all have light! :||

3. Grant, O Lord, that your creation
   lasts for ever more.
   May it not be self-destroying,
   humbly we implore.

   ||: Give the fish their water pure,
   lives of birds and beasts secure.
   Grant, O Lord, that your creation
   lasts for ever more. :||

Translation by John Minahane (2022)

FAITH & SPIRITUALITY POLAND

135
Zegarmistrz światła purpurowy
Clock Master of the Purple Light

Tadeusz Woźniak (1947-), privately a fan of old clocks, recorded this existential song with the Polish female vocal band "Alibabki" on their debut album in 1972. In the same year, the song won the main prize at the 10th National Polish Song Festival in Opole. The author of the lyrics, Bogdan Chorążuk (1934-), is a poet, painter and philosopher. With a clear text and an unusual metaphor, Tadeusz Woźniak considers this composition "a triptych", where the whole is greater than the sum of its parts. The song touches on the theme of readiness to leave, when time has come. The title, Watchmaker, is treated as an allegory of death, maybe also as God, destiny or fate.

By Dorota Stefaniak, Academy of Music "Stanisław Moniuszko" in Gdańsk

Lyrics: Bogdan Chorążuk (1934-) Music: Tadeusz Woźniak (1947-)

1. A kie-dy przyj-dzie także po mnie zegarmistrz świa-tła pur-pu-ro-wy,
1. And when he comes to get me too clock master of the purple light,

by mi za-beł-tać błękit w gło-wie, to będę ja-sny i go-to-wy.
to make my brain boil wild with blue, I'll be ready and robed in white.

Spły-ną prze-ze mnie dni na prze-strzał,
The days will slice right through me.

||: A kiedy przyjdzie także po mnie
zegarmistrz światła purpurowy,
by mi zabełtać błękit w głowie,
to będę jasny i gotowy.

Spłyną przeze mnie dni na przestrzał,
zgasną podłogi i powietrza.
Na wszystko jeszcze raz popatrzę
i pójdę nie wiem gdzie na zawsze. :||

||: And when he comes to get me too,
clock master of the purple light,
to make my brain boil wild with blue,
I'll be ready and robed in white.

The days will slice right through me.
Floor and air will vanish surely.
Give it all one last long stare
and go for ever – don't know where. :||

Translation by David & William Malcolm (2021)

FAITH & SPIRITUALITY ESTONIA

136
Palve (Looja, hoia Maarjamaad)
Prayer

Palve (Prayer), composed in 1988 by Estonian singer-songwriter Tõnis Mägi and with lyrics by Villu Kangur, became one of the anthems of the Estonian Singing Revolution, which was essential for the independence of Estonia from the Soviet Union in 1991. Lasting over four years, this bloodless protest movement unfolded in all three Baltic States, where protesters gathered in defiance to express liberty and national unity through singing. This song is well-known to every Estonian, and its choral arrangements have been sung in several Song Celebrations ever since.

By Kaie Tanner, Sec. General, Estonian Choral Association, ECA

Lyrics: Villu Kangur (1957-) Music: Tõnis Mägi (1948-)

1. Looja, hoia Maarjamaad ja andesta meile me vead. Looja, kaitse Eestimaad, peod selleks palveks nüüd sean. 2. Looja, hoia hiiepuid, sest ladvad neil langu on maas. Looja, kaitse kodutuid, kord nad ehk tulevad

1. Lord, guard Estonia, forgive and forget our flaws. Lord, guard my homeland's holy ground for this prayer I pause. 2. Lord, protect the sacred groves, all the tall trees weighed down. Harbour, Lord, the homeless souls, until they're healed a-

1. Looja, hoia Maarjamaad
   ja andesta meile me vead.
   Looja, kaitse Eestimaad,
   peod selleks palveks nüüd sean.

2. Looja, hoia hiiepuid,
   sest ladvad neil längu on maas.
   Looja, kaitse kodutuid,
   kord nad ehk tulevad taas.

3. Kirjas on Aegade Raamatus:
   õndsad on need, kes ei näe.
   Uskudes, et see on saamatus,
   kui keegi läeb.

4. Loon ja hoian Maarjamaad,
   loon ja loodan, sest tean,
   milleks need ladvad on kaarjamad,
   ja peod selleks palveks ma sean -

   et Looja hoiaks Maarjamaad,
   hoiaks Maarjamaad.

1. Lord, guard Estonia,
   forgive and forget our flaws.
   Lord, guard my homeland's holy ground –
   for this prayer I pause.

2. Lord, protect the sacred groves,
   all the tall trees weighed down.
   Harbour, Lord, the homeless souls,
   until they're healed again.

3. In the Scriptures it's said:
   blessed are those who are blind.
   I firmly believe what I have read:
   true wisdom is to be kind.

4. I'm devoted to this land,
   at heart is a song for her cause -
   a breeze in the trees I understand.
   For this prayer I pause:

   Lord, guard Estonia...
   Estonia...

   Translation by Doris Kareva (2021)

FAITH & SPIRITUALITY — SPAIN

137
La Saeta
The Chant

The combination of Antonio Machado's (1875-1939) poem and Joan Manuel Serrat's (1943-) music is overwhelming in this chant that evokes Holy Week in Seville, the birthplace of the poet. Serrat's audacity in putting processional music to the lyrics of Machado continues to reap a surprising success and thrills anyone who listens to it, regardless of one's religious sentiment.

By Julio Muñoz & Maria del Carmen García Jiménez, Escuela Superior de Canto de Madrid, ESCM

Lyrics: Antonio Machado (1875-1939)   Music: Joan Manuel Serrat (1943-)

1. Oh, la sa-e-ta_el can-tar al Cris-to de los gi-ta-nos siem-pre con san-gre_en las ma-nos, siem-pre por des-en-cla-var. Can-tar del pue-blo_an-da-luz que to-das las pri-ma-ve-ras an-da pi-dien-do_es-ca-le-ras pa-ra su-bir a la cruz. Can-tar de la tie-rra mí-a, que e-cha

1. Oh the psalm of la sa-e-ta that sings to the gyp-sies' Christ, al-ways blood on his hands, al-ways bound to the nails. The song of An-da-lu-cians, who each and e-ve-ry spring claim for that lad-der to clam-ber the cross. Songs from my home-land that wor-ship with

RESITADO: Dijo una voz popular:
¿Quién me presta una escalera
para subir al madero
para quitarle los clavos
a Jesús el Nazareno?

1. Oh, la saeta, el cantar
al Cristo de los gitanos
siempre con sangre en las manos,
siempre por desenclavar.

Cantar del pueblo andaluz
que todas las primaveras
anda pidiendo escaleras
para subir a la cruz.

Cantar de la tierra mía,
que echa flores
al Jesús de la agonía
y es la fe de mis mayores.

(3x) ||: ¡Oh, no eres tú mi cantar,
no puedo cantar, ni quiero,
a este Jesús del madero
sino al que anduvo en la mar! :||

¡Oh, no eres tú mi cantar...!

SPOKEN: A wistful voice said:
Who can lend me a ladder
to climb up the timber
to take the nails out
from the Jesus The Nazarene?

1. Oh the psalm of la saeta
that sings to the gypsies' Christ,
always blood on his hands,
always bound to the nails.

The song of Andalucians
who each and every spring
claim for that ladder
to clamber the cross.

Songs from my homeland
that worship with flowers
a tormented Jesus
and the faith of my ancestors.

*(3x) ||: Oh you are not my melody,
and I'm not willing to sing
to that Jesus king
but to the one that sailed at sea! :||*

Oh you are not my melody...!

Translation by Joana Serrat (2022)

Copyright © Universal Music Publishing S L. International Copyright Secured. All Rights Reserved.
Reprinted by permission of Hal Leonard Europe Ltd.

Chapter VI

Children's songs

CHILDREN'S SONGS   FRANCE

138
Au clair de la lune
Lit up by the Moonlight

This song is a representation of ancient texts whose double-sense have been lost in the course of the centuries. Transcribed in the 19th century in Ile-de-France as a part of the oral tradition. It was then published in some collections intended for children, limited to the two first verses. The full text is more naughty especially when we understand the meaning of old sayings and ancient expressions. "Beat the lighter" meant "make love" in the 18th century and the verses 3 and 4 describe obviously Pierrot, our hero, in search of a gallant occasion, "for the God of love".

By Jean Blanchard, Training Center for Teachers of Music, Auvergne Rhône-Alpes, CEFEDEM

Lyrics: unknown (18th century)   Music: unknown (18th century)

       1. Au clair de la lune,   *1. Lit up by the moonlight,*
          mon ami Pierrot,   *Pierrot friend of mine,*
          prête moi ta plume   *lend a quill so I might*
          pour écrire un mot.   *write a little line.*
          Ma chandelle est morte,   *My candle has gone out,*
          je n'ai plus de feu;   *I am now at odds;*
          Ouvre-moi ta porte,   *open up your door now,*
          pour l'amour de Dieu !   *for the love of God!*

2. Au clair de la lune,
   Pierrot répondit:
   "Je n'ai pas de plume,
   je suis dans mon lit:
   Va chez la voisine,
   je crois qu'elle y est,
   car dans la cuisine
   on bat le briquet."

3. Au clair de la lune,
   l'aimable Lubin
   frappe chez la brune,
   ell' répond soudain:
   "Qui frapp' de la sorte?"
   Il dit à son tour:
   "Ouvrez votre porte
   pour le Dieu d'amour!"

4. Au clair de la lune,
   on n'y voit qu'un peu.
   On chercha la plume,
   on chercha du feu.
   En cherchant d'la sorte,
   je n'sais c'qu'on trouva;
   Mais j'sais que la porte
   sur eux se ferma...

2. Lit up by the moonlight
   Pierrot shook his head:
   "I don't have a quill and
   I am tucked in bed:
   Go and see the neighbour
   I think she's at home,
   heard her in the parlour
   she is not alone".

3. Lit up by the moonlight
   Lubin made his way
   the brunette was in sight,
   'answered straight away:
   "Who knocks at this hour?"
   He said, as one does:
   "Open up your door now
   for the God of Love!"

4. Lit up by the moonlight
   they could hardly see.
   No match nor quill in sight,
   where could they both be?
   No one in the world knows
   what the pair did find;
   But I know the door closed
   with them both inside...

   Translation by Claire Moreau,
   Lara Tasker & Amy Winterbotham (2023)

CHILDREN'S SONGS   POLAND

139
Na Wojtusia z popielnika
For My Wojtuś From the Ashes

Definitely the most popular Polish lullaby, this is a song full of magic, both simple and melodious. It is well known in Polish homes and kindergartens and used to put children to sleep. The author of the lyrics is Polish writer Janina Porazińska (1882-1971). The poem of the lullaby appeared in 1925 in a collection of children's poetry. It is inspired by the lives of children during the author's childhood (late 19th century). The traditional melody, taken from rural folklore, has several titles in English: "For Wojtuś From the Ashes" and "Spark's Tale". The title refers to a spark telling a child (called Wojtuś) a fairytale. Unfortunately, it is short because the spark goes out and does not end the stories! So the child can fall asleep – and dream the endings...

By Dorota Stefaniak, Academy of Music "Stanisław Moniuszko" in Gdańsk

Lyrics: Janina Porazińska (1888-1971)   Music: folksong

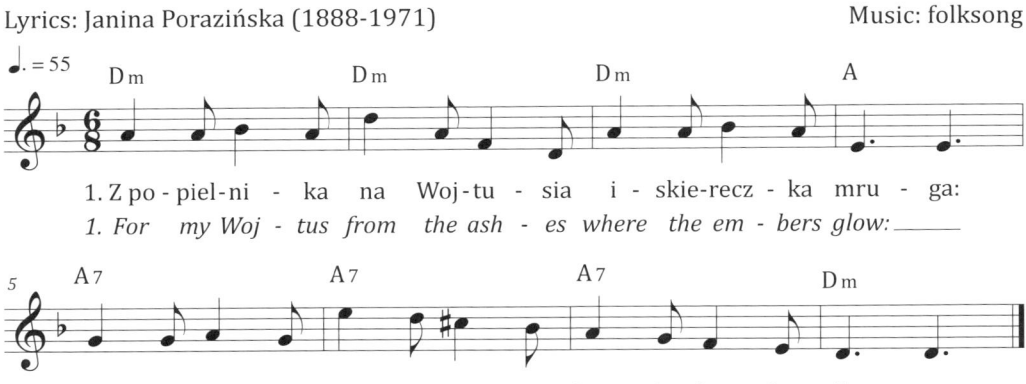

1. Z popielnika na Wojtusia
   iskiereczka mruga:
   „Chodź, opowiem ci bajeczkę,
   bajka będzie długa.

2. Była sobie raz królewna,
   pokochała grajka,
   król wyprawił im wesele
   i skończona bajka.

3. Była sobie Baba Jaga,
   miała chatkę z masła,
   a w tej chatce same dziwy...".
   Psst... iskierka zgasła.

1. *For my Wojtuś from the ashes*
   where the embers glow:
   "Come, and I will tell a tale
   but I will tell it slow.

2. *Once there was a princess fine*
   who loved a fiddler so,
   the king threw them a wedding feast,
   or so the story goes.

3. *Once there was a Baba Yaga*
   with a house of bread.
   In the house were wonders so..."
   Hush...now, the fire's dead.

4. Z popielnika na Wojtusia
   iskiereczka mruga:
   „Chodź, opowiem ci bajeczkę,
   bajka będzie długa.

5. Już ci Wojtuś nie uwierzy,
   iskiereczko mała.
   Chwilę błyśniesz, potem zgaśniesz,
   ot i bajka cała".

4. *For my Wojtuś from the ashes*
   where the embers glow:
   "Come, and I will tell a tale
   but I will tell it slow.

5. *I can never trust in you,*
   my little spark so bold.
   First you sparkle then you splutter,
   so the story's told".

Translation by David & William Malcolm (2021)

CHILDREN'S SONGS　　　　　　　　　　　　　　　　　　　　　　　　BULGARIA

140
Детство мое
My Sweet Childhood

The song "My Childhood" has lyrics by Bogomil Gudev and music by Vili Kazasyan – a prominent Bulgarian composer and conductor in the field of popular, film and jazz music – and originates from the movie "Unexpected Vacation". In a radio poll it was announced as the favorite children's song in Bulgaria. Today, the song remains a favorite for Bulgarian children and is marked as mandatory at school as part of the music program curriculum. It is recognised for the vividly memorable melody and lively rhythm, provoking the empathy in children with choreographed dance moves and use of children's musical instruments. The lyrics speak of the most joyful and brightest period of a person's life – the happy and carefree childhood.

By Dr. Jean Pehlivanov, Academy of Music Dance and Fine Arts, Plovdiv, AMDFA

Lyrics: Bogomil Gudev (1935-93)　　　　　　　　Music: Vili Kazasyan (1934-2008)

1. Дет - ство мо - е, ре-ал - но и въл-шеб - но, дет - ство
1. My sweet child - hood, so real and so en - chan - ted, my sweet

мо - е, та - ка си ми по - треб - но. Все се
child - hood, I need you once more gran - ted. I'm still

мъ - ча све - та да об - ър - на ях нал
tur - ning the world up - side down, ri - ding

1. Детство мое, реално и вълшебно,
   детство мое, така си ми потребно.
   Все се мъча света да обърна
   яхнал пръчка при тебе да се върна.

2. Пак в юмруче ръждив петак да скрия
   пак със кучето да вдигна олелия,
   пак с пипер да поръся филия
   от хляба чер.

3. Детство мое, на ръст едноетажно,
   детство мое, за мен така е важно,
   щом студено ми стане да мога
   да си взема от детския огън.

4. Все се мъча света да обърна,
   яхнал пръчка при теб да се върна,
   всеки ден по една дяволия
   да е от мен.

1. My sweet childhood, so real and so enchanted,
   my sweet childhood, I need you once more granted.
   I'm still turning the world upside down,
   riding broomstick, returning to you now.

2. Once more hiding a rusty little nickel,
   once more me and doggy making fuss and tickle,
   once more chomping a slice with a pickle -
   from pumpernickel.

3. My sweet childhood, in height you're single storey,
   my sweet childhood, you help me to be more me.
   When I'm cold, I just try to remember,
   feeling true glow from your fire's embers.

4. I'm still turning the world upside down,
   riding broomstick, returning to you now,
   every day one mischief or another -
   it is on me.

Translation by Desislava Sofranova (2023)

CHILDREN'S SONGS — GERMANY

141
Guten Abend, gut' Nacht (Wiegenlied)
A Good Evening, a Good Night (Lullaby)

This gentle lullaby is one of the world famous art songs of German origin and is still sung at children's bedtimes every evening. In 1868 Brahms dedicated it to his friend, Bertha Faber, with whom he had been in love in her youth, and who had just given birth to a son. The first verse appeared in 1808 in "Gute Nacht, mein Kind!" (Good Night, My Child!) in the collection "Des Knaben Wunderhorn" (The Boy's Magic Horn). The second verse was by folk song collector Georg Scherer (1824-1909), when in 1849 he included the lullaby in "Alte und neue Kinderlieder" (Old and New Children's Songs). Roses are mentioned because they are supposed to form a protective roof, whereas the "Näglein" refer to cloves, which were supposed to keep disease and vermin away by means of their scent and essential oils.

By Ekkehard Klemm, president, Association of German Concert Choirs (VDKC)/
Hochschule für Musik "Carl Maria von Weber" Dresden

Lyrics: folk poem/ Georg Scherer (1824-1909)   Music: Johannes Brahms (1833-97)

1. Guten Abend, gut' Nacht, mit Rosen bedacht, mit Näglein besteckt, schlupf unter die Deck: Morgen früh, wen Gott will, wirst du wieder geweckt, morgen früh, wenn Gott will, wirst du wieder geweckt.

1. A good evening, a good night, with the stars shining bright, cloves and roses for you, and the moon's smiling too. You will wake up again, you'll be safe in God's hand, you will wake up again, you'll be safe in God's hand.

1. Guten Abend, gut' Nacht,
   mit Rosen bedacht,
   mit Näglein besteckt,
   schlupf unter die Deck:
   ||: Morgen früh, wenn Gott will,
   wirst du wieder geweckt. :||

2. Guten Abend, gut' Nacht,
   von Englein bewacht,
   die zeigen im Traum
   dir Christkindleins Baum.
   ||: Schlaf nun selig und süß,
   schau im Traum 's Paradies. :||

1. A good evening, a good night,
   with the stars shining bright,
   cloves and roses for you
   and the moon's smiling too.
   ||: You will wake up again,
   you'll be safe in God's hand. :||

2. A good evening, a good night,
   bathed in heavenly light,
   angels guarding your sleep
   bring you dreams sweet and deep.
   ||: Rest in peace, close your eyes
   and you'll see Paradise. :||

Translation by Heinz Rudolf Kunze (2022)

English translation: Copyright © 2022 Weltverbesserer Musikverlag.

CHILDREN'S SONGS SLOVENIA

142
Kekčeva pesem
Kekec's Song

Josip Vandot (1884-1944) wrote three stories about Kekec after the Great War. The character still remains popular, especially since Kekec was featured in three youth adventure movies (one was awarded the Golden Lion at the Venice International Film Festival). The stories of Kekec focus on a wholehearted boy shepherd from the Julian Alps who spiritedly overcomes the dangers he stumbles upon. Kekec is a synonym for a brave, positive, future-oriented, nature-loving man with a Robin-Hood-like aura and abilities. Both music and lyrics were very successful in both the 1951 version (Kozina/Ježek) as well as in this masterly crafted march from 1963, and they still convey the same optimistic message that was so typical for Socialist Yugoslavia: utopia. To this day Kekec continues "to sow the seed of 'good mood' to people" and spreads the joy of climbing mountains.

By Dr. Leon Stefanija, University of Ljubljana, Faculty of Arts

Lyrics: Kajetan Kovič (1931-2014)   Music: Marjan Vodopivec (1920-1977)

1. Kdor vesele pesmi poje, gre po svetu lahkih nog. Če mi kdo nastavi zanko, ga uženem v kozji rog! Jaz pa pojdem in zasejem dobro voljo pri lju-

1. He who's singing merry songs he roams the world with feet so light. If someone then tries to trick him, he outwits them: table's turned! I go onward and I'm spreading my good-will to all the

1. Kdor vesele pesmi poje
   gre po svetu lahkih nog,
   če mu kdo nastavi zanko,
   ga užene v kozji rog.

   Chorus:
   Jaz pa pojdem in zasejem
   dobro voljo pri ljudeh.
   V eni roki nosim sonce,
   vdrugi roki zlati smeh.

2. Bistri potok, hitri veter,
   bele zvezde vrh gora,
   gredo z mano tja do konca
   tega širnega sveta.

   Chorus:
   Jaz pa pojdem in zasejem…

1. He who's singing merry songs
   he roams the world with feet so light.
   If someone then tries to trick him,
   he outwits them: table's turned!

   Chorus:
   I go onward and I'm spreading
   my goodwill to all the land!
   In my one hand is the sunshine,
   in the other laughter grand!

2. Gusting wind, the clearest river,
   whitest stars on mountain tops,
   follow me on my adventures
   to the ends of this wide world!

   Chorus:
   I go onward and I'm spreading…

Translation by Steve Klink & Boštjan Malus (2021)

CHILDREN'S SONGS   FINLAND

143
Päivänsäde ja menninkäinen
The Sunbeam and the Goblin

Even though 'The Sunbeam and the Goblin' can be considered a children's song, for the past 70 years this song about hopeless love between light and darkness has had its place in the hearts of Finns of all ages. Reino Helismaa, perhaps Finland's best-known performer-songwriter of all time, wrote the magical lyrics of which Tapio Rautavaara (1915-79), a charismatic hit singer, popular film actor and Olympic javelin champion, recorded a famous interpretation. It tells the story of a fairy of the sunlight and a goblin wandering in the darkness whose love can never be requited. Like most Finnish hits, the song is in a minor key. However, each stanza ends upliftingly in the parallel major key – a sign of hope. As a lullaby, when day is departing and children have to surrender to sleep, it genially offers a universal explanation of the impossible love of the light.

By Juha Henriksson, director, Music Archive Finland

Lyrics: Reino Helismaa (1913-65)   Music: Reino Helismaa (1913-65)

1. Au - rin - ko kun päät - ti ret - ken, sis - kois - taan jäi jäl - keen het - ken
1. Day to dusk was soon de - clin - ing, sun - beam - sis - ters bright - ly shin - ing

päi - vän - sä - de vii - mei - nen.   Hä - mä - rä jo mail - le hii - pi,
fled the sky as dark - ness fell.   Twi - light shades were slow - ly creep - ing

päi - vän - sä - de kul - ta - sii - pi ai - koi juu - ri len - tää ees - tä sen, kun
ov - er for - ests soft - ly sleep - ing; one last sun - beam ling - ered in the dell. Sur-

men - nin - käi - sen pie - nen nä - ki vas - taan tu - le - van: mi
prised she was to see a wood - land gob - lin on the ground, now

1. Aurinko kun päätti retken,
   siskoistaan jäi jälkeen hetken
   päivänsäde viimeinen.
   Hämärä jo maille hiipi,
   päivänsäde kultasiipi
   aikoi juuri lentää eestä sen,
   kun menninkäisen pienen näki
              vastaan tulevan:
   mi juuri oli noussut luolastaan.
   Kas, menninkäinen ennen päivän
              laskua ei voi
   milloinkaan elää päällä maan.

2. Katselivat toisiansa:
   menninkäinen rinnassansa
   tunsi kummaa leiskuntaa.
   Sanoi: "Poltat silmiäni,
   mutten ole eläissäni
   nähnyt mitään yhtä ihanaa!
   Ei haittaa, vaikka loistosi mun
              sokeaksi saa;
   on pimeässä helppo taivaltaa.
   Jää luokseni, niin kotiluolaan
              näytän sulle tien,
   ja sinut armaakseni vien.

3. Säde vastas: "Peikko kulta,
   pimeys vie hengen multa,
   enkä toivo kuolemaa.
   Pois mun täytyy heti mennä.
   Ellen kohta valoon lennä,
   niin en hetkeäkään elää saa!"
   Niin lähti kaunis päivänsäde,
              mutta vieläkin,
   kun menninkäinen yksin tallustaa,
   hän miettii, miksi toinen täällä
              valon lapsi on
   ja toinen yötä rakastaa.

1. Day to dusk was soon declining,
   sunbeam-sisters brightly shining
   fled the sky as darkness fell.
   Twilight shades were slowly creeping
   over forests softly sleeping;
   one last sunbeam lingered in the dell.
   Surprised she was to see a woodland
              goblin on the ground,
   now cautiously emerging from his lair:
   for creatures of the night avoid the day
              and won't be found
   by sunlight in the open air.

2. At each other they stood gazing,
   soon the goblin's heart was blazing
   with an aching thrill most keen.
   He said: "Though my eyes are burning,
   I have never felt such yearning;
   you're the fairest thing I've ever seen!
   You make me blind, but I don't mind,
              I now feel less alone.
   Would you be mine and let me take you home?
   It's safe down in the dark, and there you
              could call me your own,
   together in the world we'd roam."

3. She said kindly: "Night is falling,
   and I hear my sisters calling,
   to the sun I must return.
   In the dark I'd surely perish,
   and my life in light I cherish,
   in your world my flame would never burn."
   She left, but ever after, as the goblin
              walks by night,
   he ponders on the bliss he never found.
   Why should it be that some of us are
              children of the light
   and others to the dark are bound?

Translation by Jaakko Mäntyjärvi (2021)

Copyright © Warner Chappell Music Finland Oy. Reprinted by permission of Notfabriken Music Publishing AB/Faber Music Ltd.

CHILDREN'S SONGS DENMARK

144
Jeg ved en lærkerede
I Know Two Larks Are Nesting

A child has discovered a nest with vulnerable bird chicks on the ground and by keeping it a secret it keeps the defenseless safe. Outside Denmark, Carl Nielsen (1865-1931) is mostly known for his symphonies, but at home his simple melodies have become a treasury of song. He intentionally made them simple so that all people – regardless of social class – could play and sing them. Parallel to its lyrics, this melody is humble and seems to express the flight of the lark, the soft movements safely and gently circling the basis chords. This is probably a song which most Danes know by heart.

By Jesper Moesbøl, editor, "Sanghåndbogen"/The Song Handbook

Lyrics: Harald Bergstedt (1877-1965)   Music: Carl Nielsen (1865-1931)

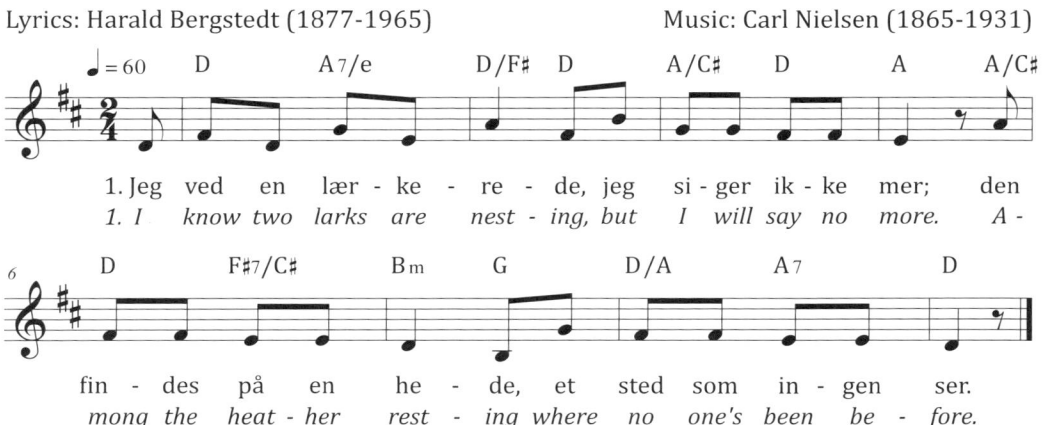

1. Jeg ved en lærkerede,
   jeg siger ikke mer;
   den findes på en hede,
   et sted som ingen ser.

2. I reden er der unger,
   og ungerne har dun.
   De pipper, de har tunger,
   og reden er så lun.

3. Og de to gamle lærker,
   de flyver tæt omkring.
   Jeg tænker nok de mærker,
   jeg gør dem ingenting.

1. I know two larks are nesting,
   but I will say no more.
   Among the heather resting
   where no one's been before.

2. With warm and downy feathers
   the nest is full of young;
   small voices chirp together –
   each baby has a tongue.

3. Their parents fly so near me –
   I hear their eager song.
   I know they do not fear me
   or think I'll do them wrong.

4. Jeg lurer bag en slåen.
   Der står jeg ganske nær.
   Jeg rækker mig på tåen
   og holder på mit vejr.

5. For ræven han vil bide
   og drengen samle bær,
   men ingen skal få vide,
   hvor lærkereden er.

4. I hide behind a dog-rose –
   I'm close enough to touch.
   I raise myself on tiptoes,
   I hold my breath and watch.

5. Some boys are good at guiding
   the fox to find his prey.
   But where my larks are hiding
   I'll never ever say.

Translation by John Mason (2022)

Lyrics reprinted by permission of the Harald Bergstedt Foundation

CHILDREN'S SONGS SWEDEN

145
Idas sommarvisa
Ida's Summer Song

The children's song lyrics of Astrid Lindgren (1907-2002) – Sweden's world famous children's book writer – are amazing; the lyrics combined with music composed by some of Sweden's best jazz musicians are a treasure trove! 'Idas sommarvisa' (Ida's Summer Song), set to music in 1973 by Georg Riedel (1934-2024), is a favorite of all children at school graduations. This song is from the film about Emil, where Emil's little sister Ida sings her song with the lyrics "I make the flowers flower". Summer itself explains – both to and through – the child, which signs of life to look for in nature, as a confirmation of its own magical arrival. This ecological song will surely remain a part of the Swedish cultural heritage of children's songs.

By Kerstin Carpvik, head of library, Musikverket

Lyrics: Astrid Lindgren (1907-2002)   Music: Georg Riedel (1934-2024)

1. Du ska inte tro det blir sommar i fall inte nån sätter fart på somarn och gör lite somrigt, då kommer blommorna snart. Jag gör så att blommorna blommar, jag gör hela kohagen grön. Och

1. Believe me, there will be no summer unless some-one gives it a nudge and makes lots of sum-mer-y things turn up with-out that, the sum-mer won't budge. I make all the flow-ers start bloom-ing, I make all the green mea-dows grow. And

1. Du ska inte tro det blir sommar
   ifall inte nån sätter fart
   på sommarn och gör lite somrigt,
   då kommer blommorna snart.
   Jag gör så att blommorna blommar,
   jag gör hela kohagen grön.
   Och nu så har sommaren kommit
   för jag har just tagit bort snön.

2. Jag gör mycket vatten i bäcken
   så där så det hoppar och far.
   Jag gör fullt med svalor som flyger
   och myggor som svalorna tar.
   Jag gör löven nya på träden
   och små fågelbon här och där.
   Jag gör himlen vacker om kvällen
   för jag gör den alldeles skär.

3. Och smultron det gör jag åt barna
   för det tycker jag dom kan få
   och andra små roliga saker
   som passar när barna är små.
   Och jag gör så roliga ställen
   där barna kan springa omkring.
   Då blir barna fulla med sommar
   och bena blir fulla med spring.

1. Believe me, there will be no summer
   unless someone gives it a nudge
   and makes lots of summery things turn up
   without that, the summer won't budge.
   I make all the flowers start blooming,
   I make all the green meadows grow.
   And see now, the summer has come to us,
   'cos I took away all the snow.

2. I fill up the river with water
   to make it all jumpy and fleet.
   I make lots of swallows that fly around
   and midges for swallows to eat.
   I make the leaves new on the trees again
   and little bird's nests, in a wink.
   I make the sky lovely each evening
   'cos I make it totally pink.

3. For children I make some wild strawberries
   so that they can eat up them all.
   And all sorts of other small funny things
   that suit children when they are small.
   And lots of fun places I make for them
   where children can run and be free,
   that fills up the children with summer
   and legs full of running, you see.

Translation by Fred Lane (2023)

Music: Copyright © Georg Riedel. Reprinted by permission of Desert Business Service AB.
Lyrics: Copyright © The Astrid Lindgren Company AB/Universal Music Publishing AB.
Reprinted by permission of Hal Leonard Europe Ltd.

CHILDREN'S SONGS   CZECHIA

146
Vadí, nevadí (Není nutno)
Worry or Not

This song is titled 'Vadí, nevadí' (Worry or Not) but has become engraved in the public consciousness with its first words, 'Není nutno' (Not Necessary). It was created in 1983 as main song for the fairytale film 'The Three Veterans', directed by Oldřich Lipský (1924-86). Jaroslav Uhlíř told how he was especially impressed by the verses "Have no money? Don't be sad. Have no feelings? That's bad". Due to its highly optimistic mood, this song was also chosen for the online happening 'No need not to sing', during which on March 25, 2020, at the very beginning of the COVID-19 crisis, tens of thousands of Czechs joined their voices to sing as an expression of support for paramedics, rescuers, and all workers in the so-called 'first line'.

By Lukáš Prchal, The Czech Choral Union, UČPS

Lyrics: Zdeněk Svěrák (1936-)   Music: Jaroslav Uhlíř (1945-)

(musical score)

1. Ne - ní nut - no, ne - ní nut - no, a - by by - lo pří - mo ve - se - lo,
1. Keep on smil - ing, keep on smil - ing, e - ven if you are not o - ver - joyed.

hla - vně nes - mí bý - ti smut - no, na - tož a - by se bre - če -
but in case you feel like cry - ing, well, I am beg - ging you, please,

lo. 2. Chceš - li, trap se, že ti v kap - se zla - té min - ce ne - chřes -
don't. 2. I am sor - ry if you wor - ry there's no for - tune in your

tí, ne - mít žád - né ka - ma - rá - dy, to - mu já ří - kám ne - štěs -
purse, hav - ing no real friends at all, in my o - pin - ion, that's much

tí. *Fine* Chorus: Ne - mít pra - chy ne - va - dí, ne - mít srd - ce
worse. Have no mon - ey? Don't be sad. Have no feel - ings?

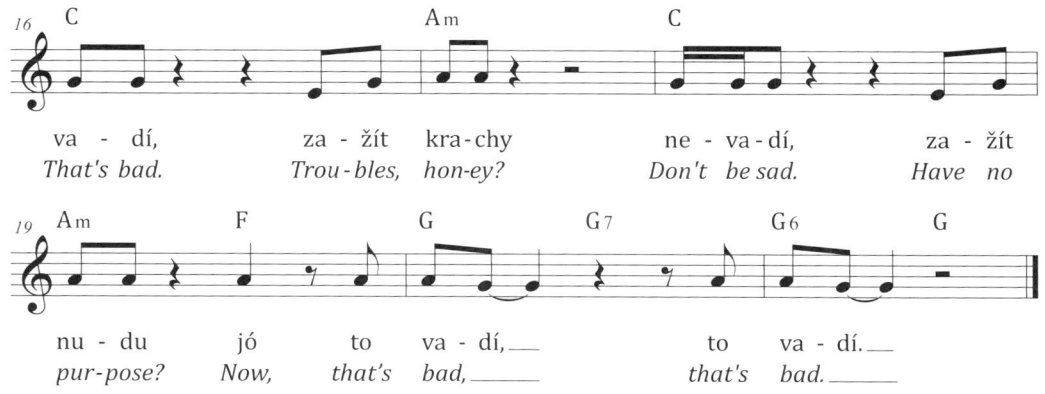

1. Není nutno, není nutno,
   aby bylo přímo veselo,
   hlavně nesmí býti smutno,
   natož aby se brečelo.

2. Chceš-li, trap se, že ti v kapse
   zlaté mince nechřestí,
   nemít žádné kamarády,
   tomu já říkám neštěstí.

   Chorus:
   Nemít prachy - nevadí,
   nemít srdce - vadí,
   zažít krachy - nevadí,
   zažít nudu - jó to vadí, to vadí.

1. ||: Není nutno, není nutno,
   aby bylo přímo veselo,
   hlavně nesmí býti smutno,
   natož aby se brečelo. :||

1. Keep on smiling, keep on smiling,
   even if you are not overjoyed,
   but in case you feel like crying,
   well, I am begging you, please, don't.

2. I am sorry if you worry
   there's no fortune in your purse,
   having no real friends at all,
   in my opinion, that's much worse.

   Chorus:
   Have no money? Don't be sad.
   Have no feelings? That's bad.
   Troubles, honey? Don't be sad.
   Have no purpose? Now, that's bad, that's bad.

1. ||: Keep on smiling, keep on smiling,
   even if you are not overjoyed,
   but in case you feel like crying,
   well, I am begging you, please, don't. :||

Translation by Zuzana Čtveráčková (2021)

CHILDREN'S SONGS AUSTRIA

147
Åba Heidschi bumbeidschi, schlåf långa
Sleep Well

In 1905, in Friedberg near the Bohemian forest (formerly in the Habsburg monarchy, today in the Czech Republic), the folk song collectors Franz Friedrich Kohl and Josef Reiter recorded a two-verse version of this sad song as sung by Mila Moherndl. In 1924-25, it found its way into collections of children's and Christmas songs. This lullaby is known throughout Austria today. Lullabies with syllabic texts and invented, rhyming words were common in the region from at least the beginning of the nineteenth century. This same song appears with different invented syllables – 'haidl bubaidl in guada Rua' and other variants – in collections from southern Lower Austria from at least 1819. What does "Heidschi bumbeidschi" mean? In the first two verses it seems to mean "fall sleep". A fourth verse often sung was omitted here. It seems to be too little child-friendly, since it is probably sung by death.

By Dr. Eva Maria Hois, Steirische Volksliedwerk & Dr. Sarah Weiss, Kunstuniversität Graz

Lyrics: Traditional Music: Traditional

1. Å-ba hei-dschi, bum-bei-dschi, schlåf lån-ga, es is jå dei Muat-ta aus-gån-ga, sie is jå aus-gån-ga und kimmt neam-ma hoam und låsst dås kloa Büa-ba-le gånz al-loan. Å-ba hei-dschi, bum-bei-dschi, bum bum! Å-ba

1. My darling, sleep well and sleep long, your mother has left, she has gone. She really has gone and will never come home, alas, leaving her baby all a-lone. Sleep sound-ly, my darling, sleep well! Sleep

hei - dschi, bum - bei - dschi, bum bum!
sound - ly, my dar - ling, sleep well!

1. Åba heidschi, bumbeidschi, schlåf långa,
   es is jå dei Muatta ausgånga,
   sie is jå ausgånga und kimmt neamma hoam
   und låsst dås kloa Büabale gånz alloan.
   Åba heidschi, bumbeidschi, bum bum!
   Åba heidschi, bumbeidschi, bum bum!

2. Åba heidschi, bumbeidschi, schlåf süaße!
   Die Engelan låssn di grüaße,
   sie låssn di grüaßn und låssn di frågn,
   ob du in Himml spaziern willst fåhrn.
   Åba heidschi, bumbeidschi, bum, bum!
   Åba heidschi, bumbeidschi, bum bum!

3. Åba heidschi, bumbeidschi, in Himml,
   då fåhrt di a schneeweißer Schimml,
   drauf sitzt a kloans Engerl mit oaner Latern,
   drin leucht vom Himml der ållerschenst Stern.
   Åba heidschi, bumbeidschi, bum, bum!
   Åba heidschi, bumbeidschi, bum, bum!

1. My darling, sleep well and sleep long,
   your mother has left, she has gone.
   She really has gone and will never come home,
   alas, leaving her baby all alone.
   Sleep soundly, my darling, sleep well,
   sleep soundly, my darling, sleep well.

2. My darling, sleep well and dream sweet,
   in dreams kindly angels will greet.
   They'll greet you and ask you with heavenly love,
   if you'd like to wander in heaven above.
   Sleep soundly, my darling, sleep well,
   sleep soundly, my darling, sleep well.

3. My darling, sleep well without sorrow,
   you'll ride a white horse to the morrow.
   A star in your lantern, though far away,
   will show you the way to a bright new day.
   Sleep soundly, my darling, sleep well,
   sleep soundly, my darling, sleep well!

Translation by Lorenz Maierhofer (2020)

CHILDREN'S SONGS   CROATIA

148
Kad se male ruke slože (Himna zadrugara)
When The Little Come Together

Children's feature film "The Train in the Snow" (1976), based on a novel of the same name by Croatian children's writer Mate Lovrak (1899-1974), is still a joy to watch. Equally loved is this song from the film, "When Little Hands Are Put Together", composed by the respected Croatian poet, translator and singer-songwriter Arsen Dedić to the lyrics of acclaimed songwriter and poet Drago Britvić. The words of this children's song speak of the importance and power of fellowship, and this cheerful tune is still sung today by all generations of Croatians.

By Dr. Jasenka Ostojić, University of Zagreb, Music Academy

Lyrics: Drago Britvić (1935-2005)   Music: Arsen Dedić (1938-2015)

1. Kad se mno-go ma-lih slo-ži, tad se sna-ga sto-put mno-ži, a to zna-či da smo ja-či, kad se sku-pi-mo u zbor. 2. Ma-la ka-o vrap-ci, živ, živ, živ. Kad se male ruke slo-že, sve se mo-že, sve se mo-že! Kad se ka-o vrap-ci, živ, živ, živ.

1. When the lit-tle come to-geth-er, then we fly like birds of feath-er, and it means that we are stron-ger, when we sing our songs like one. 2. Ti-ny Like the spar-rows, tweet, tweet, tweet. When the lit-tle come to-geth-er, then a rock be-comes a feath-er! When the Like the spar-rows, tweet, tweet, tweet.

1. Kad se mnogo malih složi,
   tad se snaga stoput množi,
   a to znači da smo jači,
   kad se skupimo u zbor.

2. Mala iskra požar skriva,
   kap do kapi rijeka biva,
   hajde zato svi u jato,
   kao vrapci, živ, živ, živ.

Chorus:
   Kad se male ruke slože,
   sve se može, sve se može!

1. *When the little come together,*
   then we fly like birds of feather,
   and it means that we are stronger,
   when we sing our songs like one.

2. *Tiny sparks can make wildfire,*
   drop by drop the river's higher,
   so let's sing our songs in choir,
   like the sparrows, tweet, tweet, tweet.

Chorus:
   When the little come together,
   then a rock becomes a feather!

Translation by Nikola Vranić "J.R. August" (2022)

CHILDREN'S SONGS GREECE

149
Οταν θα πάω κυρά μου στο παζάρι
When I'll Go to the Market, My Lady

["The Little Rooster" (Το κοκοράκι) is a very popular song for children in Greece, although originally composed in 1941 as "a funny song" by Joseph Corinthios (1908-1992) to lyrics by Nikos Fatseas (1914-1990). Year by year people have realized its usefulness, since it is ideal for children to learn how animals sound. With every verse, one more animal and its voice is added to the previous ones. Thus, the animal list could go on indefinitely, sometimes turning this into a game of memory and creativity. So, in this so called "accumulative song", the lyrics say that 'I will buy you a little baby rooster, the baby rooster cock-a-doodle dee". Then next time: "I will buy you a fluffy little hen, the little hen cluck-cluck, the baby rooster cock-a-doodle dee", – and so on.

By Thomas Louziotis, president, Hellenic Choirs Association

Lyrics: Nikos Fatseas (1914-90) Music: Joseph Korinthios (1908-92)

1. Όταν θα πάω κυρά μου στο παζάρι
   θα σου αγοράσω ένα κοκοράκι,
   το κοκοράκι κικιρικικί
   να σε ξυπνάει κάθε πρωί.

2. Όταν θα πάω κυρά μου στο παζάρι
   θα σου αγοράσω μία κοτούλα,
   η κοτούλα κοκοκό,
   το κοκοράκι κικιρικικί,
   να σε ξυπνάει κάθε πρωί.

3. Όταν θα πάω κυρά μου στο παζάρι
   θα σου αγοράσω μία γατούλα,
   η γατούλα νιάου νιάου,
   η κοτούλα κοκοκό,
   το κοκοράκι κικιρικικί,
   να σε ξυπνάει κάθε πρωί.

4. Όταν θα πάω κυρά μου στο παζάρι
   Θα σου αγοράσω ένα πουλάκι
   Το πουλάκι τσίου τσίου
   η γατούλα νιάου νιάου,
   η κοτούλα κοκοκό,
   το κοκοράκι κικιρικικί,
   να σε ξυπνάει κάθε πρωί.

5. Όταν θα πάω κυρά μου στο παζάρι
   Θα σου αγοράσω ένα σκυλάκι
   Το σκυλάκι γάου γάου
   Το πουλάκι τσίου τσίου
   η γατούλα νιάου νιάου,
   η κοτούλα κοκοκό,
   το κοκοράκι κικιρικικί,
   να σε ξυπνάει κάθε πρωί.

6. Όταν θα πάω κυρά μου στο παζάρι
   θα σου αγοράσω ένα κοκοράκι,
   το κοκοράκι κικιρικικί
   να σε ξυπνάει κάθε πρωί.

1. Oh, when I go my lady to the market
   I will buy you a little baby rooster,
   the baby rooster cock-a-doodle dee,
   will wake you up right next to me.

2. Oh, when I go my lady to the market
   I will buy you a fluffy little hen,
   the little hen cluck-cluck,
   the baby rooster cock-a-doodle dee,
   will wake you up right next to me.

3. Oh, when I go my lady to the market
   I will buy you a purring little kitten,
   the little kitten meow-meow,
   the little hen cluck-cluck,
   the baby rooster cock-a-doodle dee,
   will wake you up right next to me.

4. Oh, when I go my lady to the market
   I will buy you a beautiful canary,
   the canary tweet-tweet,
   the little kitten meow-meow,
   the little hen cluck-cluck,
   the baby rooster cock-a-doodle dee,
   will wake you up right next to me.

5. Oh, when I go my lady to the market
   I will buy you the cutest little puppy,
   the little puppy woof-woof,
   the canary tweet-tweet,
   the little kitten meow-meow,
   the little hen cluck-cluck,
   the baby rooster cock-a-doodle dee,
   will wake you up right next to me.

6. Oh, when I go my lady to the market
   I will buy you a little baby rooster,
   the baby rooster cock-a-doodle dee,
   will wake you up right next to me.

Translation by Monika & Stavros Xenides (2023)

CHILDREN'S SONGS   ROMANIA

150
O lume minunatã
A world so full of wonders

A dedication to childhood, a song full of life and joy sung with great pleasure by all children, a particularly charming song expressing so much optimism that it pulls anyone out of the routines of everyday life. According to its author, this hit took no longer than thirty minutes to compose in 2004, thanks to a spontaneous idea he had on his way home. Even nowadays, the tune is still trending: It is sung by many children in kindergarten, schools and by various bands in shows – and it's appreciated each and every time.

*By Dr. Grigore Cudalbu, National University of Music, Bucharest, UNMB/
Romanian National Association of Choral Music, ANCR*

Lyrics: Mihai Constantinescu (1946-2019)   Music: Mihai Constantinescu (1946-2019)

Allegro di gioia ♩ = 132

1. E o lu-me mi-nu-na-tã în ca-re veti gã-si Nu-mai co-piii
   O lu-me cu mult soa-re si mii de ju-cã-rii
   Pen-tru co-piii În lu-mea cu po-vesti si flori
   veti în-tâl-ni Nu-mai co-piii Si o lu-mea i-no-cen-tei pãs-
   tra-tio ori-cear fi Pen-tru co-piii

1. A world so full of won-ders, as hap-py as can be for you and me!
   This world that's full of sun-shine, with all these toys you see
   kids play-ing free! This world so rich in sto-ries is
   where you'll al-ways see kids play-ing free! This world of in-no-cence, keep
   it as it should be, for you and me!

Fine

Chorus:
    E-o lume minunată în care veti găsi
    Numai copii!
    O lume cu mult soare si mii de jucării
    Pentru copii!
    În lumea cu povesti si flori veti întâlni
    Numai copiii!
    Si-o lume a inocentei păstrati-o orice ar fi
    Pentru copiii!

1. Ieri am fost si noi copii
    Dar timpul ne-a schimbat
    În viată am pornit si vise am împlinit
    Asa, cum ne-am dorit.
    Gânduri bune câte-am strâns
    Si tot ce-am învătat
    Copiilor să dăm iubirea ce-o purtăm
    ce-i bun, să le arătăm.

Chorus:
    Eo lume minunată...

Bridge:
    Ce zâmbet poate fi mai sincer, mai curat
    Ce ochi stiu a vorbi atât de adevărat?

Chorus:
    ||: Eo lume minunată... :||

Chorus
    A world so full of wonders, as happy as can be
    for you and me!
    This world that's full of sunshine, with all these toys, you see
    kids playing free!
    This world so rich in stories is where you'll always see
    Kids playing free!
    This world of innocence, keep it as it should be,
    for you and me!

1. We were children yesterday,
    but time did come to grow,
    in life we got our start and wishes from the heart
    came true for me and you!
    All the good that came our way
    and that did help us so!
    To children we should give the love for which we live
    and teach them to forgive!

Chorus:
    A world so full of wonders...

Bridge:
    What smile could ever shine more honestly at you,
    whose eyes know how to speak without a word, yet true?

Chorus:
    ||: A world so full of wonders... :||

Translation by Beck Corlan & Alex Szollo (2022)

CHILDREN'S SONGS   HUNGARY

151
Kis kece lányom
White Is the Dress

"1907, Felsőireg, Tolna county" – was written on the manuscript of the famous composer and folksong collector Béla Bartók (1881-1945), when he recorded this folksong, sung in our time mostly by girls. "White is the dress my daughter is wearing/ White is the rose her sweet hand is bearing./ Lemon and spearmint, rosa canina/ I'd join the dance if I had a partner". The melody, with different lyrics became very popular among the scouts, and has remarkable number of arrangements for voice, choir, piano, etc, by eminent Hungarian composers.

By Ágnes C. Szalai, called by the National Association of Hungarian Choirs and Orchestras, KÓTA

Lyrics: folk poem   Music: folk song

1. Kis kece lányom fehérbe' vagyon,
   Fehér a rózsa, kezébe' vagyon.
   ||: Mondom-mondom, fordulj ide,
   mátkám asszony, :||

2. Citrusi menta, kajtali rózsa,
   Elmennék táncba, ha szép lány volna.
   ||: Mondom-mondom, fordulj ide,
   mátkám asszony, :||

1. White is the dress my daughter is wearing,
   white is the rose her sweet hand is bearing.
   ||: Turn and face me in the bride's dance,
   I implore you, :||

2. Lemon and spearmint, rosa canina,
   I'd join the dance if I had a partner.
   ||: Turn and face me in the bride's dance,
   I implore you, :||

Translated by Rachel Hideg (2021)

CHILDREN'S SONGS   ITALY

152
Alla fiera dell'Est
Highdown Fair

This song, released in the homonymous LP by Angelo Branduardi in 1976, has a very particular genesis. The melody 'sounds' almost archaic, like a relic from an ancient folk tradition, and with lyrics which are a sort of lullaby, much loved by children. Both melody and lyrics are, in fact, inspired by "Chad Gadya" (One Little Goat), a song of Jewish tradition (an essential and genetically fundamental component of the great Italian melting pot). What appears as an innocent lullaby is actually a metaphorical narration of history seen from a biblical perspective and embraces a period of time ranging from the myth of creation to the fall of the Roman Empire! The closing of the story returns to the beginning. Alpha and Omega. The cultural sensitivity of Branduardi, a great lover of traditional cultures and ancient music, has given the history of Italian song an evergreen pearl that combines simplicity with great depth.

By Alfonso Santimone, National Academy of Jazz, Siena

Lyrics: A. Branduardi (1950-) & Luisa Zappa (1952-)   Music: A. Branduardi (1950-)

(* * Sing 1 time in first verse, 2 times in second verse, 3 times in third verse etc.)

1. Alla fiera dell'est, per due soldi
   un topolino mio padre comprò.
   E venne il gatto
   che si mangiò il topo
   che al mercato mio padre comprò.

1. At Highdown fair for two farthings
my father bought me a little white mouse.
Along came a grey cat
and ate up the white mouse
my father bought in the market square.

2. Alla fiera dell'est, per due soldi
   un topolino mio padre comprò.
   E venne il cane
   che morse il gatto
   che si mangiò il topo
   che al mercato mio padre comprò.

3. Alla fiera dell'est, per due soldi
   un topolino mio padre comprò.
   E venne il bastone
   che picchiò il cane
   che morse il gatto
   che si mangiò il topo
   che al mercato mio padre comprò.

4. Alla fiera dell'est, per due soldi
   un topolino mio padre comprò.
   E venne il fuoco
   che bruciò il bastone
   che picchiò il cane
   che morse il gatto
   che si mangiò il topo
   che al mercato mio padre comprò.

5. Alla fiera dell'est, per due soldi
   un topolino mio padre comprò.
   E venne l'acqua
   che spense il fuoco
   che bruciò il bastone
   che picchiò il cane
   che morse il gatto
   che si mangiò il topo
   che al mercato mio padre comprò.

6. Alla fiera dell'est, per due soldi
   un topolino mio padre comprò.
   E venne il toro
   che bevve l'acqua
   che spense il fuoco
   che bruciò il bastone
   che picchiò il cane
   che morse il gatto
   che si mangiò il topo
   che al mercato mio padre comprò.

2. At Highdown fair for two farthings
   my Father bought me a little white mouse.
   Along came a black dog
   and jumped on the grey cat
   who ate up the white mouse
   my father bought in the market square.

3. At Highdown fair for two farthings
   my father bought me a little white mouse.
   Along came on old stick
   and beat off the black dog
   who jumped on the grey cat
   who ate up the white mouse
   my father bought in the market square.

4. At Highdown fair for two farthings
   my father bought me a little white mouse.
   Along came a fire
   and burned up the old stick
   which beat off the black dog
   that jumped on the grey cat
   who ate up the white mouse
   my father bought in the market square.

5. At Highdown fair for two farthings
   my father bought me a little white mouse.
   Along came sweet water
   and put out the fire
   which burned up the old stick
   which beat off the black dog
   that jumped on the grey cat
   who ate up the white mouse
   my father bought in the market square.

6. At Highdown fair for two farthings
   my father bought me a little white mouse.
   along came a great ox
   and drunk all the water
   which put out the fire
   which burned up the old stick
   which beat off the black dog
   that jumped on the grey cat
   who ate up the white mouse
   my father bought in the market square.

7. Alla fiera dell'est, per due soldi
   un topolino mio padre comprò.
   E venne il macellaio
   che uccise il toro
   che bevve l'acqua
   che spense il fuoco
   che bruciò il bastone
   che picchiò il cane
   che morse il gatto
   che si mangiò il topo
   che al mercato mio padre comprò.

8. Alla fiera dell'est, per due soldi
   un topolino mio padre comprò.
   E l'angelo della morte
   sul macellaio
   che uccise il toro
   che bevve l'acqua
   che spense il fuoco
   che bruciò il bastone
   che picchiò il cane
   che morse il gatto
   che si mangiò il topo
   che al mercato mio padre comprò.

9. Alla fiera dell'est, per due soldi
   un topolino mio padre comprò.
   E infine il Signore
   sull'angelo della morte
   sul macellaio
   che uccise il toro
   che bevve l'acqua
   che spense il fuoco
   che bruciò il bastone
   che picchiò il cane
   che morse il gatto
   che si mangiò il topo
   che al mercato mio padre comprò.

   Alla fiera dell'est, per due soldi
   un topolino mio padre comprò.

7. At Highdown fair for two farthings
   my father bought me a little white mouse.
   Along came a butcher
   and slaughtered the great ox
   which drunk all the water
   which put out the fire
   which burned up the old stick
   which beat off the black dog
   that jumped on the grey cat
   who ate up the white mouse
   my father bought in the market square.

8. At Highdown fair for two farthings
   my father bought me a little white mouse.
   And the Angel of Death
   came for the butcher
   who slaughtered the great ox
   which drunk all the water
   which put out the fire,
   which burned up the old stick
   which beat off the black dog,
   that jumped on the grey cat
   who ate up the white mouse
   my father bought in the market square.

9. At Highdown fair for two farthings
   my father bought me a little white mouse
   and last came the Lord
   who threw down the Angel
   who came for the butcher,
   who slaughtered the great ox
   which drunk all the water,
   which put out the fire
   which burned up the old stick,
   which beat off the black dog
   that jumped on the grey cat,
   who ate up the white mouse
   my father bought in the market square.

At Highdown fair for two farthings
my father bought me a little white mouse.

Translation by Peter Sinfield (1978)

CHILDREN'S SONGS LATVIA

153
Aijā žūžū lāča bērni
Hush-a-bye, My Little Bear Cubs

Songs continue to play an important role in raising and educating Latvian children. Seemingly every family for several generations has sung this lullaby in which child care is figuratively sung with affection. Mum and Dad have gone to the woods for honey and to pick berries, leaving behind either siblings or grandparents as caretakers. On the parents' return, the little child will have earned a reward for sleeping peacefully. When singing this smooth melody, the chorus imitates the rocking – Hush, Hush, Hush-a-bye (ai-jā, žū-žū) – which creates both a free and soothing mood. Since its first publication in 1921, it has attracted the attention of many composers and has been performed countless times both for choir, solo song with as well as an instrumentally.

By Rūta Kanteruka, president, Latvian Music Teachers' Association, LVIIMSA

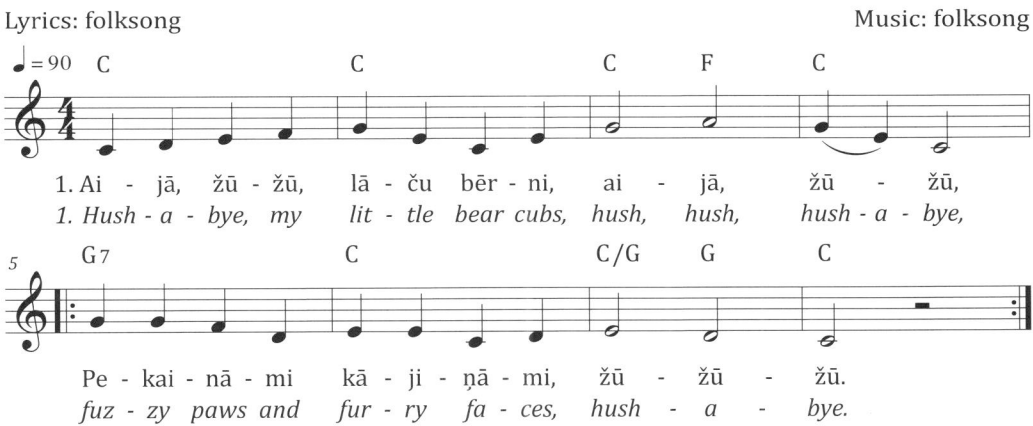

1. Aijā, žūžū, lāču bērni, aijā, žūžū,
   ||: Pekaināmi kājiņāmi, žū-žū-žū. :||

   Hush-a-bye, my little bear cubs, hush, hush, hush-a-bye,
   ||: fuzzy paws and furry faces, hush-a-bye. :||

2. Tēvs aizgāja bišu kāpti, aijā, žūžū,
   ||: Māte ogu palasīt, žū-žū-žū. :||

   Father went to hunt for honey, hush, hush, hush-a-bye,
   ||: mother to the berry bushes, hush-a-bye. :||

3. Tēvs pārnesa medus podu, aijā, žūžū,
   ||: Māte ogu vācelīti, žū-žū-žū. :||

   Here comes Father with his honey, hush, hush, hush-a-bye,
   ||: mother brings her berry basket, hush-a-bye. :||

4. Tas mazam bērniņam, aijā, žūžū,
   ||: Par mierīgu gulēšanu, žū-žū-žū. :||

   Lovely treats for little children, hush, hush, hush-a-bye,
   ||: all of you who sleep so sweetly, hush-a-bye. :||

5. Kas vilkami, kas lāčami, aijā, žūžū,
   ||: Mežā kāra šūpulīti? Žū-žū-žū. :||

   Who hangs up the forest cradles, hush, hush, hush-a-bye,
   ||: for the wolf cubs, for the bear cubs? Hush-a-bye. :||

6. Lieli vīri uzauguši, aijā, žūžū,
   ||: Nešūpoti, neloloti, žū-žū-žū. :||

   Grandmama hangs up the cradles, hush, hush, hush-a-bye,
   ||: who will thank her, who will help her? Hush-a-bye. :||

Translation by Māra Walsh Sinka (2023)

CHILDREN'S SONGS   THE NETHERLANDS

154
Dikkertje Dap
Dickory Dee

'Dikkertje Dap' is a legendary children's song from 1950, based on a poem by Netherlands' best-known children's book writer Annie M.G. Schmidt (1911-95). It tells the story of a little boy who travels to the zoo every morning at a quarter past seven to talk with the giraffe. His name, Dikkertje Dap, seems to suggest he is both chubby and brave. Or in the words of the writer Ruud Hisgen, "It's about a child whom the Dutch consider to be 'the real deal'". According to legend, composer Van Westering's song was rejected both by record companies and by radio for being "too classic and uncommercial". They were proven wrong, since it became national repertoire and was recorded multiple times by various children's choirs, singers and bands.

*By Christiane Nieuwmeijer, Leiden University of Applied Sciences
& Lieuwe Noordam, Prins Claus Conservatorium, Groningen*

Lyrics: Annie M.G. Schmidt (1911-95)   Music: Paul Christiaan van Westering (1911-91)

1. Dik - ker - tje   Dap   klom op   de trap,   's mor - gens
1. *Dic - ko - ry   Dee   got up   the tree   eve - ry*

vroeg om kwart o - ver ze - ven, om de gi - raf een klon - tje te
day at twelve af - ter se - ven, to give gi - raffe some vegg - ies from

ge - ven. Dag Gi - raf! zei Dik - ker - tje Dap, Weet je,
hea - ven. Hi Gi - raffe said Dic - ko - ry Dee   You know

wat ik heb ge - kre - gen?   Ro - de laars - jes   voor de
what my moth - er gave me?   Yel - low boots for   when it's

1. Dikkertje Dap klom op de trap,
    's morgens vroeg om kwart over zeven,
    om de giraf een klontje te geven.
    Dag Giraf! zei Dikkertje Dap,
    Weet je, wat ik heb gekregen?
    Rode laarsjes voor de regen.
    't Is toch niet waar? zei de giraf,
    Dikkertje, Dikkertje, Dikkertje,
    Dikkertje ik sta paf.

2. O Giraf, zei Dikkertje Dap,
    'k moet je nog veel meer vertellen;
    Ik kan al drie letters spellen,
    A, B, C, is dat niet knap?
    Ik kan ook al bijna rekenen,
    ik kan mooie poppetjes tekenen.
    Lieve deugd, zei de giraf,
    kerel, kerel, kerel, kerel ik sta paf.

3. Zeg giraf, zei Dikkertje Dap,
    Mag ik niet eens even bij je
    stiekem van je nek af glijen?
    Zo, maar eventjes voor de grap,
    Denk je dat de grond van Artis
    als ik neer kom, heel erg hard is?
    Stap maar op, zei de giraf,
    Stap maar op en glij maar af.

4. Dikkertje Dap klom van de trap
    met een griez'lig grote stap
    op de nek van de giraf.
    Zette Dikkertje Dap zich af...
    Roetsjj, daar gleed hij met een vaartje
    tot het eindje van het staartje.
    Boem! Au!
    Dag, giraf, zei Dikkertje Dap,
    morgen kom ik weer hier met de trap.

1. Dickory Dee got up the tree
    every day at twelve after seven
    to give giraffe some veggies from heaven.
    Hi Giraffe, said Dickory Dee,
    you know what my mother gave me?
    Yellow boots for when it's rainy.
    You're kidding me, said the giraffe,
    Dickory, Dickory, Dickory,
    Dickory, that's great stuff.

2. Oh Giraffe, said Dickory Dee
    I have got so much more to tell you.
    These are the letters I write and spell too:
    A b c, and d e f - Gee!
    I can almost count to fifty!
    Draw nice figures, very nifty!
    Oh goodness me, said the giraffe,
    you're so clever, clever, clever, that's great stuff.

3. Hey Giraffe, said Dickory Dee,
    will it be okay if I climb up
    and then glide down your neck for a fun time?
    Just for the heck of it and the glee.
    Do you think the earth around here
    when I hit it, is a real fear?
    Just step on, said the giraffe,
    Just step on and then glide off.

4. Dickory Dee got off the tree
    with a craz'ly mighty leap
    to the neck of the giraffe.
    Firmly Dickory Dee took off...
    Woosh he shot down without fail
    down to the tuft on the tail.
    Boom! Ouch!
    Bye Giraffe, said Dickory Dee.
    Soon you'll see me here again at the tree.

Translation by Arnold Mühren (2021)

Copyright © Uitgeverij De Toorts. International copyright secured. All rights reserved. Reprinted by permission

CHILDREN'S SONGS   LITHUANIA

155
Du gaideliai
Two Little Roosters

The traditional Lithuanian folk song "Du gaideliai" (Two Little Roosters) is the most popular song among Lithuanian children. It is sung in the family, in kindergartens, and at schools. The song is often staged and acted out by children because of its humorous plot and realistic characters: farmyard birds and animals.

By Dr. Arvydas Girdzijauskas, Lithuanian Choral Union, LCHS

Lyrics: folk poem   Music: folksong

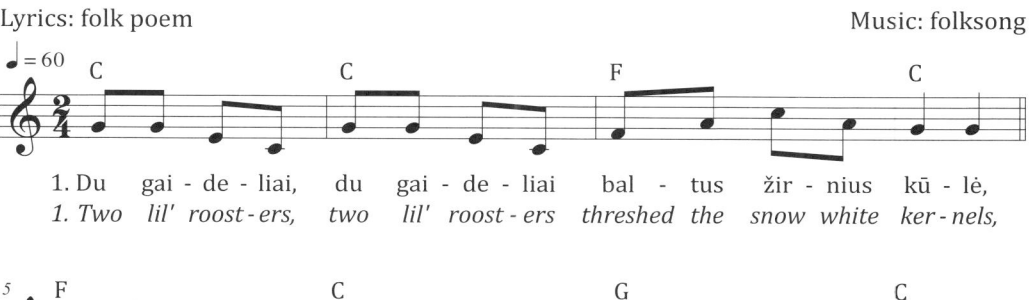

1. Du gaideliai, du gaideliai
   baltus žirnius kūlė,
   dvi vištelės, dvi vištelės
   į malūną vežė.

2. Ožys malė, ožys malė,
   ožka pikliavojo,
   o ši trečia ožkytėlė
   miltus nusijojo.

3. Musė maišė, musė maišė,
   uodas vandens nešė,
   saulė virė, saulė virė,
   mėnesėlis kepė.

1. *Two lil' roosters, two lil' roosters threshed the snow white kernels, two lil' chickens, two lil' chickens took them to the old mill.*

2. *Goat was grinding, goat was grinding mama-goat – his helper. And the kid goat, that cute fellow sifted all the flour.*

3. *Fly was mixing, fly was mixing buzzing bug brought water, sunshine cooking, sunshine cooking, moonbeams baking sweet buns.*

Translation by Gabriella Žičkienė (2022)

CHILDREN'S SONGS MALTA

156
Ninni la tibkix iżjed
Don't Cry Sweet Baby Jesus

This religious song from 1846 is synonymous with the Maltese Christmas. It was written by Indri Schembri (1805-1875), a Jesuit Priest who lived among Maltese nationals in the city of Algiers. In the refrain, the word 'Ninni', which means 'sleep', is used. This word is frequently heard when Maltese parents are putting their young children to sleep. The word stems from Italian 'ninna nanna'. The song also encompasses a religious aspect as it reflects how everyone should be in awe of how the Son of God was born a poor and simple child.

By Dr. Albert Pace, School of Performing Arts, University of Malta

Lyrics: Indri Schembri (1805-1875) Music: Indri Schembri (1805-1875)

Chorus:
Ninni, la tibkix iżjed, Ninni, Ġesu' Bambin. Ħallih għalina l-biki, Għax aħna midinbin.
Don't cry sweet baby Jesus, don't cry and go to sleep. Leave us to cry, poor sinners for we deserve to weep.

1. Ejjew, ejjew, ja Anġli, Missema, mija, mija. Hdejn Alla li ħalaqkom, Bambin ġewwa l-fisqija.
1. Come forth, come forth from Heaven, come forth in hundreds, oh angels, come witness your creator: a baby in a manger.

Kant alternattiv għall-istrofi li mhumiex ritornell /
Alternative version of non-refrain verses.

1. Ej - jew, ej - jew, ja Anġ - li, Mis - se - ma, mi - ja, mi - ja. Ħdejn
1. *Come forth, come forth, from Heav-en, come forth in hun-dreds oh an-gels. Come*

Al - la li ħa - laq - kom, Bam - bin ġew - wa l - fis - qi - ja.
wit - ness your cre - a - tor: a ba - by in a man - ger.

Chorus:
   Ninni, la tibkix iżjed,
   Ninni, Ġesu' Bambin.
   Ħallih għalina l-biki,
   Għax aħna midinbin.

1. Ejjew, ejjew, ja Anġli,
   Mis-sema, mija, mija.
   Ħdejn Alla li ħalaqkom,
   Bambin ġewwa l-fisqija.

Chorus:
   Ninni, la tibkix iżjed...

2. Ejjew, taraw b'għajnejkom
   Lil Alla Kbir tal-Ħniena,
   Bambin sabiħ u ħelu
   Ininni ġo benniena.

Chorus:
   Ninni, la tibkix iżjed....

3. Ejjew, araw, o rgħajja,
   F'kemm faqar, f'kemm tbatija,
   Is-Sid ta' kollox twieled,
   Bin Alla, il-Messija.

Chorus:
   Ninni, la tibkix iżjed...

Chorus:
   Don't cry sweet baby Jesus,
   don't cry and go to sleep.
   Leave us to cry, poor sinners,
   for we deserve to weep.

1. *Come forth, come forth from Heaven,*
   come forth in hundreds, oh angels,
   come witness your creator:
   a baby in a manger.

Chorus:
   Don't cry sweet baby Jesus...

2. *Behold this God of mercy*
   a beacon for all faithful,
   the cutest new-born baby
   asleep inside a cradle.

Chorus:
   Don't cry sweet baby Jesus...

3. *Don't be afraid, oh shepherds,*
   to leave your flocks behind,
   your sheep are taken care of
   by angels in the sky.

Chorus:
   Don't cry sweet baby Jesus...

Translation by Joe Julian Farrugia (2022)

CHILDREN'S SONGS   LUXEMBOURG

157
Léiwe Kleeschen
Dear Saint Nich'las

The poem by Willy Goergen (1867-1942) was dedicated to the patron saint of children, Saint Nicolas, the Luxembourgish version of Santa Claus. The melody was created by 12-year-old Pëppy Beicht (1907-76), a child born into a family of musicians and composers, which has thus created what may be the best known and most sung Luxembourgish song of all time.

By Robert Köller, Union Grand-Duc Adolphe, UGDA

Lyrics: Willy Goergen (1867-1942)   Music: Madeleine, «Pëppy» Beicht (1907-76)

1. Léi - we Klees - chen, gud - de Klees - chen Bréng eis Saa - chen, al - ler-
1. *Dear Saint Nich' - las, good Saint Nich' - las, bring us things that we all*

hand, Fir ze ku - cken, fir ze schmaa - chen, Aus dem schéi - nen Him - mels-
love, things to cud - dle, things to guz - zle, sent from heav - en up a -

land. Bei der Dier do stinn eis Telle - ren Bei - e - neen an en - ger
bove. At the door we've put our sauc - ers, side by side in one long

Rei 'T läit och Hee do fir Däin Ie - sel Do - fir bréng ons Spill - ge -
row, and some hay to feed your don - key, so please bring us good - ies

zei. 'T läit och Hee do fir Däin Ie - sel Do - fir bréng ons Spill - ge - zei.
now! and some hay to feed your don - key, so please bring us good - ies now!

De 'Kanner:

1. Léiwe Kleeschen, gudde Kleeschen
   Bréng eis Saachen, allerhand,
   Fir ze kucken, fir ze schmaachen,
   Aus dem schéinen Himmelsland.
   Bei der Dier do stinn eis Telleren
   Beieneen an enger Rei
   ||: 'T läit och Hee do fir Däin Iesel
   Dofir bréng ons Spillgezei. :||

De 'Mausi:

2. Léiwe Kleeschen, gudde Kleeschen,
   bréng ons Saachen allerlee,
   mir eng Pëppchen, an eng Wéichen,
   onsem Charly eng nei Lee!
   Dann nach eppes fir de Mëndchen,
   domat sinn ech extra frou,
   ||: sou e klenge Schocklasbëndchen
   gëff mir Kleeschen heemlech zou. :||

De Butzi:

3. Léiwe Kleeschen, gudde Kleeschen,
   bréng ons Saachen schéin a gutt,
   bréng e Päerd mir an eng Gäissel,
   wéi dir där am Himmel hutt!
   Mat Kamellen eng kleng Tiitchen,
   Äppel, Biren, Hieselnëss,
   ||: awer maach och, gudde Kleeschen,
   dat's de d'Mama net vergëss. :||

De 'Mamm:

4. Léiwe Kleeschen, gudde Kleeschen,
   lauschter och wat d'Mamm dir seet,
   maach mir frou meng häerzeg Kanner,
   't ass fir mech déi gréisste Freed.
   Laang nach looss se Kanner bleiwen,
   't ass déi schéinst, déi glécklechst Zäit,
   ||: well d'Erënnerung un déi Stonne
   grad wéi Gold um Liewe läit. :||

The children sing:

*1. Dear Saint Nich'las, good Saint Nich'las,
bring us things that we all love,
things to cuddle, things to guzzle,
sent from heaven up above.
At the door we've put our saucers,
side by side in one long row,
||: and some hay to feed your donkey,
so please bring us goodies now! :||*

A girl sings:

*2. Dear Saint Nich'las, good Saint Nich'las,
bring us goodies, we can't wait—
I would like a doll and cradle,
Charlie needs a new school slate!
Pop in something nice to nibble,
that would make me really glad,
||: like a secret bar of choc'late,
of a kind I've never had. :||*

A boy sings:

*3. Dear Saint Nich'las, good Saint Nich'las,
bring the goodies that we love!
Bring a pony, whip and saddle,
just like yours in heav'n above!
Add some sweeties and some toffee,
apples, pears and hazelnuts,
||: But remember, good Saint Nich'las,
Mum as well, no ifs or buts! :||*

A mother sings:

*4. Dear Saint Nich'las, kind Saint Nich'las,
listen to their mother's voice,
Bringing joy to happy children,
that will make my heart rejoice.
May they long enjoy and treasure
hours of gladness, free of strife,
||: for the memory of pleasure
shines like gold throughout our life! :||*

Translation by Edward Seymour (2021)

CHILDREN'S SONGS   BELGIUM

158
Vrolijke vrienden
Jolly and Merry Good Friends

Bob Davidse (1920-2010) was a presenter, singer, guitarist, and under the name of Nonkel Bob (which means Uncle Bob) he created and produced many children's programs on the Flemish television during the fifties and sixties. Generations of children were raised with his programs. Thanks to his editions of songbooks with guitar chords, many musicians in Flanders learned how to play the guitar. Vrolijke vrienden (Happy Good Friends) was a big hit. The music is simple, the text warm. Everyone is able to sing this song; it is an ideal song for in a classroom or local youth movement.

By Liesbeth Segers, Koor&Stem

Lyrics: Bob Davidse (1920-2010)   Music: Bob Davidse (1920-2010)

Chorus:

Vro - lij - ke, vro - lij - ke vrien - den, Vro - lij - ke vrien - den, dat zijn wij. dat zijn wij.
Jol - ly and mer - ry good friends, jol - ly good friends, o yes, that's us. yes, that's us.

1. Als wij sa - men gaan kam - pe - ren in het bos of op de hei, dan klinkt het wel dui - zend ke - ren
1. When we're go - ing for a camp - out in the woods or on the heath, then we feel like shout - ing loud:

vro - lij - ke vrien - den, dat zijn wij.
jol - ly good friends, let's come and meet.

Chorus:
    Vrolijke, vrolijke vrienden,
    Vrolijke vrienden, dat zijn wij.
    Vrolijke, vrolijke vrienden
    Vrolijke vrienden, dat zijn wij.

1. Als wij samen gaan kamperen
   in het bos of op de hei,
   dan klinkt het wel duizend keren
   vrolijke vrienden, dat zijn wij.

   Vrolijke, vrolijke vrienden...

2. 's Morgens komt de zon ons wekken
   en de vogels zingen blij.
   Dan is 't tijd dat wij gaan trekken
   door de dennen, bos of hei.

   Vrolijke, vrolijke vrienden...

3. Twee of drie die koken 't eten
   brengen lekk're dingen mee.
   Dat is iets dat wij wel weten,
   wie op kamp is eet voor twee!

   Vrolijke, vrolijke vrienden...

4. En gaat stil de avond komen,
   zingen, dansen wij bij 't vuur.
   Tot wij in ons tent gaan dromen
   in het late, late uur!

Chorus:
   Jolly and merry good friends,
   jolly good friends, o yes, that's us.
   Jolly and merry good friends,
   jolly good friends, o yes, that's us.

1. When we're going for a camp-out
   in the woods or on the heath,
   then we feel like shouting loud:
   jolly good friends, let's come and meet.

   Jolly and merry good friends...

2. When the rising sun awakes us
   and the birds are singing their song
   then it's time to get ambitious
   in the forest all day long.

   Jolly and merry good friends...

3. Cooking team preparing dinner
   bringing sweets for you and me,
   hungry stomachs, growling inner,
   we eat in the open under the tree.

   Jolly and merry good friends...

4. And when late night clock has come,
   we sing and dance around the fire.
   In our tents we dream and hum
   tomorrow's a new day in the shire.

   Translation by Stijn Meuris (2022)

CHILDREN'S SONGS   ESTONIA

159
Rongisõit
Train Ride

"Rongisõit" (Train Ride) is a well-known Estonian children's song, with music by legendary Estonian choral composer Gustav Ernesaks (1908-93). With an easy melody, it has become very popular in kindergartens. Lyrics are by the cherished children's writer and poet Ellen Niit (1928-2016), who in her lifetime published more than 40 books translated into 18 languages. In the lyrics of this song, she populated the train with animal passengers – cats, dogs, pigs and goats – and ever since one question has been repeated by many generations of Estonians: "Oi-oi-oi, ai-ai-ai, so what became of the passengers?"

By Kaie Tanner, Sec. General, Estonian Choral Association, ECA

Lyrics: Ellen Niit (1928-2016)   Music: Gustav Ernesaks (1908-93)

(Verse) 1. Rong see sõitis tsuh-tsuh-tsuh,
piilupart oli rongijuht.
Rattad tegid ra-ta-ta,
ra-ta-ta ja ta-ta-ta.
Aga seal, rongi peal,
kas sa tead, kes olid seal?

(Chorus) 2. Seal olid kiisud, seal olid miisud
seal olid väiksed kirjud kiisud.
Kiisud sõitsid Türile,
sõitsid külla Jürile.

(Chorus) 3. Seal olid suured mustad kutsud,
seal olid väiksed roosad notsud.
Kutsud sõitsid Torilasse,
notsud sõitsid Porilasse.

(Chorus) 4. Seal olid sarvilised sikud,
sarvilised sikud-sokud.
Sokud sõitsid Karjaküla,
Karjaküla-Marjaküla.

(Verse) 5. Rong see sõitis tsuh-tsuh-tsuh,
piilupart oli rongijuht.
Rattad tegid ra-ta-ta,
piilupart jäi tukkuma.
Oi-oi-oi, ai-ai-ai,
mis siis sellest rongist sai?

(Verse) 6. Rong see sõitis tsuh-tsuh-tsuh,
kuni kraavi läks karpuhh!!
Oi-oi-oi, ai-ai-ai,
mis siis reisijatest sai?
Oi-oi-oi, ai-ai-ai,
mis siis reisijatest sai?

(Chorus) 7. Kõik nad läksid uperpalli,
uperpalli-kukerpalli.
Kiisud jooksid sabad seljas,
kutsud jooksid keeled väljas.

(Chorus) 8. Kümme notsut kukkus kraavi,
kümme kutsut laskis traavi,
sarved segi sikkudel,
sikkudel ja sokkudel.

(Verse) 9. Kiisud ei saand Türile,
külla minna Jürile,
kutsud ei saand Torilasse,
notsud ei saand Porilasse,
sokud ei saand Karjaküla,
Karjaküla-Marjaküla.

(Verse) 1. Chooga-chooga, chuff-chuff-chuff,
loco driver Duckling Duff.
Train wheels singing rat-at-taa,
rat-at-taa and tat-at-taa.
But again, aboard that train,
do you know all names who came?

(Chorus) 2. There were tabbies, cream and ginger,
kitties of all hues, blues singers.
The kitties went to Tiri-Lee,
just to visit Youri-Lee.

(Chorus) 3. There were large and blacky doggies,
there were small and pinky piggies.
The doggies went to Tori-Laa,
the piggies went to Pori-Laa.

(Chorus) 4. There were big and horned billies,
some were smart and others silly.
They were off to Karya village,
Karya village, Marya village.

(Verse) 5. Chooga-chooga, chuff-chuff-chuff,
loco driver Duckling Duff.
Train wheels singing rat-at-taa,
the driver fell asleep – aha!
Oh the woe! Oh the woe!
What all happened, do you know?

(Verse) 6. Chooga-chooga, chuff-chuff-chuff,
the train went off the rails – carwhaff!
Oh the woe! Oh the woe!
Where the passengers could go?
Oh the woe! Oh the woe!
Where the passengers could go?

(Verse) 7. All they went down harum-scarum,
harum-scarum, no alarum.
The kitties ran with tails like pistols,
the doggies ran as to a whistle.

(Chorus) 8. The piggies fell into the ditch,
the doggies ran without a hitch,
the billies had their horns entangled,
horns entangled, nerves all jangled.

(Verse) 9. The kitties saw no Tiri-Lee,
no hello to Youri-Lee,
the doggies saw no Tori-Laa,
the piggies saw no Pori-Laa,
the billies saw no Karya village,
Karya village, Marya village…

Translation by Doris Kareva (2021)

Copyright © the authors. International copyright secured. All rights reserved

CHILDREN'S SONGS   SPAIN

160
Hola Don Pepito
Hello Master Biggens

Once upon a time in the 70s and 80s there was a group of clowns – Gaby, Fofó, Miliki and Fofito – who had a TV show which made all children in Spain laugh: "Los Payasos de la Tele" (the TV Clowns). Their songs were extremely catchy whereas their lyrics didn't make much sense, and the kids loved them. In this famous song, by Puerto Rican comedian Ramón Rivero "Diplo" (1909-56), Don Pepito and Don José greet each other and ask about their respective grandparents every time they meet, "Hello, Don Pepito – Hello, Don José" and start over, speeding up the tempo in each repetition to end up screaming "Goodbye, Don Pepito – Goodbye, Don José". There is nothing better than finishing a song screaming out loud!

By Julio Muñoz & Maria del Carmen García Jiménez, Escuela Superior de Canto de Madrid, ESCM

Lyrics: Ramón Rivero "Diplo" (1909-56)   Music: Ramón Rivero "Diplo" (1909-56)

1. E - ran dos ti - pos re - que - te - fi - nos.___ E - ran dos
1. They were two strange and quite spe - cial fel - lows,___ they were two

ti - pos me - dios chi - fla'os.___ E - ran dos ti - pos___ ca - si di - vi - nos.
cer - ti - fied lun - y guys.___ They were two fel - lows,___ not ver - y mel - low,

___ E - ran dos ti - pos des - ba - ra - ta'os. 2. Si se_en - con -
___ they were two fel - lows, al - most di - vine. 2. If they crossed

tra - ban en u - na_es - qui - na,___ o se_en - con - tra - ban en
paths while out on the main street,___ or they crossed paths while in

el ca - fé,___ siem - pre se_o - í - a___ con voz muy fi - na___
an - y hall.___ You al - ways heard, in___ a voice so sweet,___

1. Eran dos tipos requetefinos.
   Eran dos tipos medios chifla'os.
   Eran dos tipos casi divinos.
   Eran dos tipos desbarata'os.

2. Si se encontraban en una esquina,
   o se encontraban en el café,
   siempre se oía con voz muy fina
   el saludito de Don José:

   Chorus:
   Hola, Don Pepito.
   (Hola, Don José)
   ¿Pasó usted ya por casa?
   (Por su casa yo pasé)
   ¿Y vio usted a mi abuela?
   (A su abuela yo la vi)
   Adiós, Don Pepito.
   (Adiós, Don José)

1. They were two strange and quite special fellows,
   they were two certified luny guys.
   They were two fellows, not very mellow,
   they were two fellows, almost divine.

2. If they crossed paths while out on the main street,
   or they crossed paths in any hall.
   You always heard, in a voice so sweet,
   the super greeting of Master Small.

   Chorus:
   Hello Master Biggens.
   (Hello Master Small)
   Did you pass by my house yet?
   (By your house I did just call)
   Did you see my Grandma?
   (Yes, your Grandma I just saw)
   Goodbye Master Biggens.
   (Goodbye Master Small)

   Translation by Nan Maro Babakhanian (2022)

Copyright © 1957 Peer International Corporation. Copyright Renewed. International Copyright Secured. All Rights Reserved.
Reprinted by Permission of Hal Leonard Europe Ltd.

CHILDREN'S SONGS   SLOVAKIA

161
Kukulienka, kde si bola
Cuckoo Dear, Oh, Where Did You Stay?

One of the best known and most popular folk songs for the youngest in Slovakia. Children learn this song already in preschool due to its accessible melody, rhythm and harmony (various variants of harmonic accompaniment are possible, simple and more complex). And since songs about animals tend to be favorites, Kukulienka is attractive in its content. Together with other relevant songs, rhymes or poems, it is also suitable for dances or dramatic performances.

By Dr. Eva Čunderlíková, Slovak Music Teacher Association, AUHS / Academy of Music Bratislava, VŠMU

Lyrics: folk poem   Music: folksong

1. Kukulienka, kde si bola,
   keď tá tuhá zima bola?
   Hajaja, kukuku, sedela som na buku,
   hajaja, kukuku, sedela som na buku.

2. Sedela som na tom dube,
   kde Janíčko drevo rúbe.
   Hajaja, kukuku, sedela som na buku,
   hajaja, kukuku, sedela som na buku.

3. Sedela som na tej lávce,
   kde Janíčko krpce láce.
   Hajaja, kukuku, sedela som na buku,
   hajaja, kukuku, sedela som na buku.

1. Cuckoo dear, oh, where did you stay
   till that winter went away?
   Hie-yie-ya, kukuku, I sat on the beech tree, coo,
   hie-yie-ya, kukuku, I sat on the beech tree, coo!

2. On that oak I sat as I should;
   Johnny's there, chopping up his wood.
   Hie-yie-ya, kukuku, I sat on the beech tree, coo,
   hie-yie-ya, kukuku, I sat on the beech tree, coo!

3. On that bridge I sat and I mused;
   Johnny's there, mending both his shoes.
   Hie-yie-ya, kukuku, I sat on the beech tree, coo,
   hie-yie-ya, kukuku, I sat on the beech tree, coo!

4. Keď som včera prala šaty,
   stratila som prsteň zlatý.
   Hajaja, kukuku, sedela som na buku,
   hajaja, kukuku, sedela som na buku.

5. Vrabec kričí spoza kríčka,
   že je prsteň u Janíčka.
   Hajaja, kukuku, sedela som na buku,
   hajaja, kukuku, sedela som na buku.

6. Sova volá spod jedličky,
   že je prsteň u Aničky.
   Hajaja, kukuku, sedela som na buku,
   hajaja, kukuku, sedela som na buku.

4. *Yesterday, when I washed my clothes,
   my gold ring vanished, where? who knows?
   Hie-yie-ya, kukuku, I sat on the beech tree, coo,
   hie-yie-ya, kukuku, I sat on the beech tree, coo!*

5. *Sparrows cry: "We can tell you where:
   Johnny's house: your gold ring is there."
   Hie-yie-ya, kukuku, I sat on the beech tree, coo,
   hie-yie-ya, kukuku, I sat on the beech tree, coo!*

6. *Hear the owl: "I can tell you where.
   Annie's house: your gold ring is there."
   Hie-yie-ya, kukuku, I sat on the beech tree, coo,
   hie-yie-ya, kukuku, I sat on the beech tree, coo!*

Translation by John Minahane (2023)

CHILDREN'S SONGS   CYPRUS

162
Αγιά Μαρίνα τζιαι τζιυρά
Santa Marina, Lady Fair

This is the most famous lullaby in Cyprus. St. Marina was a martyr who lived in Antioch towards the end of the 3rd century A.D. She is believed to be the protector of children. In Western churches she is known as St. Margaret of Antioch. In Cyprus, mothers pray to Saint Marina to put their children to sleep, take care of them and bring them back bigger and stronger.

By Egli Spyridaki, Music Academy ARTE

Lyrics: Traditional   Music: Traditional

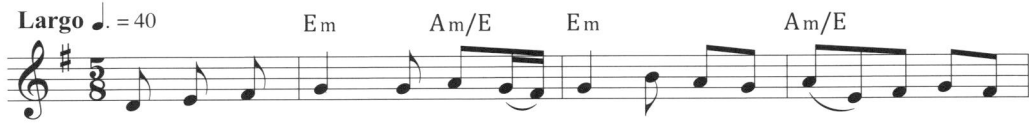

1. Αγιά Μαρίνα τζιαι τζιυρά,
   που ποτζιοιμίζεις τα μωρά,
   ποτζιοίμισ'το μωρούδιμ μου
   τζιαι παρ' το πέρα, γύρισ' το.

2. Να δει τα δέντρη πώς αθθούν
   τζιαι τα πουλιά πώς τζιελαδούν,
   πώς τζιελαδούν, πώς σιαίρουνται,
   πώς πάσιν πέρα τζι' έρκουνται.

3. Ύπνε που παίρνεις τα μωρά,
   έλα, πάρε τζιαι τούτο,
   μικρό, μικρό σου το 'δωσα,
   μεγάλο φέρε μου το.

4. Μεγάλο σαν ψηλό βουνό
   τζι' ίσιο σαν κυπαρίσσι,
   τζι' οι κλώνοι του ν' απλώνουνται
   σ' ανατολή τζιαι δύση.

1. *Santa Marina, lady fair,*
   who lulls the tiny babes to sleep,
   tenderly lull my little one,
   take it afar and bring it back.

2. *That it may see the trees in bloom*
   and hear the birds that sweetly sing;
   how sweet their song, how they rejoice,
   how they fly afar and they return.

3. *Sandman, who takes the babes away,*
   come, take my tiny one with you.
   A tender child I give to you,
   full' grown up bring it back to me.

4. *High as a mountain bring it back,*
   and straight and tall as a cypress tree,
   spreading its branches far and wide,
   upto the eastern and western glade.

Translation by Ayis Ioannides (2021)

CHILDREN'S SONGS — IRELAND

163
I'll tell me ma

The precise origins of this traditional children's song are unknown, however a variant of the words appear in a song entitled The Wind in the 1898 publication, "The Traditional Games of England, Scotland and Wales (Vol II)" by Alice B. Gomme. The author associates the song with a children's game in which: 'A ring is formed by the children joining hands, one player standing in the centre. When asked, "Please tell me who they be," the girl in the middle gives the name or initials of a boy in the ring (or vice versa). The ring then sings the rest of the words, and the boy who was named goes into the centre'. In the version collected by Gomme the city in the refrain appears as a noble or golden city. The song is well-known in Ireland with either Belfast or Dublin named as the city depending on which part of Ireland it is sung.

By Mark Armstrong, SING IRELAND

Lyrics: traditional Music: Traditional

♩ = 104

Chorus:
I'll tell me ma when I go home, the boys won't leave the girls a-lone. They pull my hair, they stole my comb, but that's al-right till I get home. She is hand-some, she is pret-ty, she's the Belle of *Bel-fast ci-ty. She is court-ing, one, two three. Please won't you tell me who is she? 1. Al-bert Moo-ney says he loves her, all the boys are

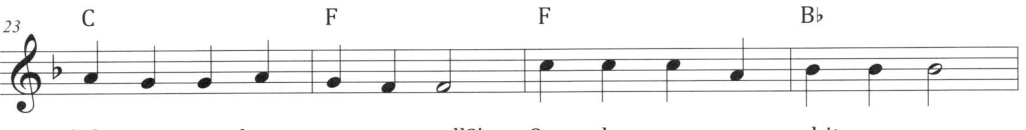
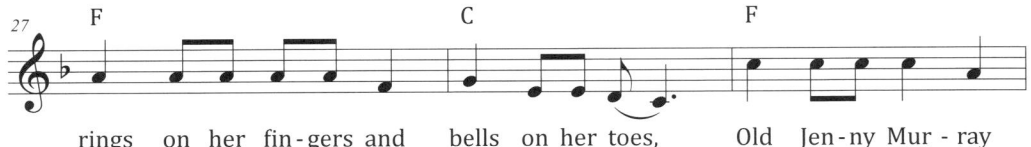

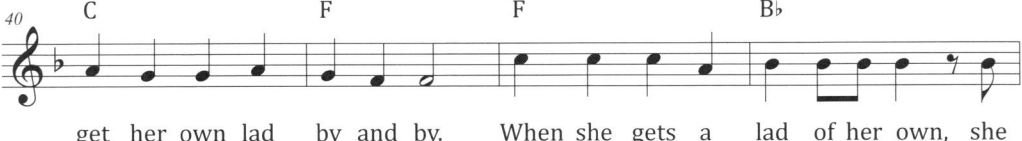

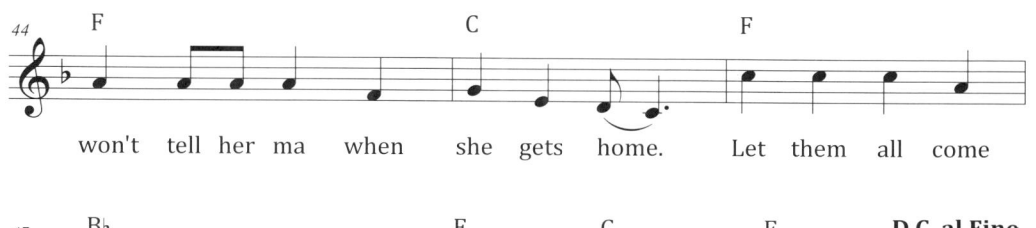
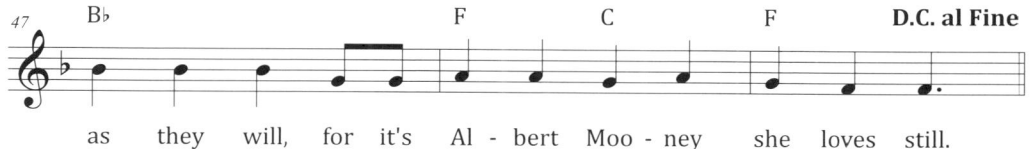

Chorus:
    I'll tell me ma, when I go home,
    the boys won't leave the girls alone.
    They pull my hair, they stole my comb,
    and that's alright till I go home.
    She is handsome, she is pretty,
    she's the belle of Belfast city,
    she is courtin', one, two, three,
    please won't you tell me who is she?

1. Albert Mooney says he loves her,
   all the boys are fighting for her.
   They rap at the door and they ring at the bell,
   saying 'Oh, my true-love are you well?'
   Out she comes as white as snow,
   rings on her fingers, bells on her toes,
   Old Jenny Murphy says she'll die,
   If she doesn't get the fellow with the roving eye.

Chorus:
    I'll tell me ma, when I go home...

2. Let the wind and the rain and the hail blow high
   And the snow come tumblin' from the sky
   She's as sweet as apple pie
   And she'll get her own lad by and by.
   When she gets a lad of her own
   She won't tell her ma when she gets home
   Let them all come as they will,
   For it's Albert Mooney she loves still.

Chorus:
    I'll tell me ma, when I go home...

CHILDREN'S SONGS PORTUGAL

164
A loja do Mestre André
Master Andrew's Music Shop

'A Loja do Mestre André', is a famous children's song that apparently seems to exist in quite a few foreign languages. In Portuguese, it enumerates in a manner of cumulative song a series of small, little musical instruments with which children can gradually form a band in order to play and sing together, laugh, and very happily muck around.

By Manuela Encarnação & Nuno Bettencourt Mendes, Portuguese Music Teacher Association, APEM & Jorge Alves, Association for Choirs in Lisbon, AMLC

Lyrics: Traditional   Music: Traditional

1. Foi na lo-ja do Mes-tre André que eu com-prei um pi- fa-ri-to, ti-ro-li-ro-li-ro um pi-fa-ri-to. Ai o-lé, ai o-lé, foi na lo-ja do Mes-tre André. Ai o-dré. 2. Foi na lo-ja do Mes-tre André que eu com-

1. 'Twas at Master Andrew's shop that I bought a litt-le fife, fee fee fee fee fee, a lit-tle fife, hip hip hop hip hip hop, 'twas at Master Andrew's shop. Hip hip shop. 2. 'Twas at Master Andrew's shop that I

1. Foi na loja do Mestre André
   que eu comprei um pifarito,
   tiro-liro-liro um pifarito.
   ||: Ai olé, ai olé,
   foi na loja do Mestre André. :||

2. Foi na loja do Mestre André
   que eu comprei um pianinho,
   plim plim plim, um pianinho,
   tiro-liro-liro um pifarinho.
   ||: Ai olé, ai olé,
   foi na loja do Mestre André. :||

3. Foi na loja do Mestre André
   que eu comprei um tamborzinho,
   tum tum tum, um tamborzinho,
   plim plim plim, um pianinho,
   tiro-liro-liro um pifarinho.
   ||: Ai olé, ai olé,
   foi na loja do Mestre André. :||

4. Foi na loja do Mestre André
   que eu comprei uma campainha,
   tlim tlim tlim, uma campainha,
   tum tum tum, um tamborzinho,
   plim plim plim, um pianinho,
   tiro-liro-liro um pifarito.
   ||: Ai olé, ai olé,
   foi na loja do Mestre André. :||

5. Foi na loja do Mestre André
   que eu comprei uma rabequinha,
   Chiribiri-biri, uma rabequinha,
   tlim tlim tlim, uma campainha,
   tum tum tum, um tamborzinho,
   plim plim plim, um pianinho,
   tiro-liro-liro um pifarito.
   ||: Ai olé, ai olé,
   foi na loja do Mestre André. :||

6. Foi na loja do Mestre André
   que eu comprei um rabecão,
   Chiribiribão, um rabecão,
   Chiribiri-biri, uma rabequinha,
   tlim tlim tlim, uma campainha,
   tum tum tum, um tamborzinho,
   plim plim plim, um pianinho,
   tiro-liro-liro um pifarito.
   ||: Ai olé, ai olé,
   foi na loja do Mestre André. :||

*1. ´Twas at Master Andrew´s shop
   that I bought a little fife,
   fee-fee-fi a little fife,
   ||: hip hip hop, hip hip hop,
   ´twas at master Andrew´s shop. :||*

*2. ´Twas at Master Andrew´s shop
   that I bought a small piano,
   plang-plang-plang, a small piano,
   fee-fee-fi, a little fife,
   ||: hip hip hop, hip hip hop,
   ´twas at master Andrew´s shop. :||*

*3. ´Twas at Master Andrew´s shop
   that I bought a little drum,
   tum-tum-tum, a little drum,
   plang-plang-plang, a small piano,
   fee-fee-fi, a little fife,
   ||: hip hip hop, hip hip hop,
   twas at master Andrew´s shop. :||*

*4. ´Twas at Master Andrew´s shop
   that I bought a little bell,
   ding-ding-ding, a little bell,
   tum-tum-tum, a little drum,
   plang-plang-plang, a small piano,
   fee-fee-fi, a little fife,
   ||: hip hip hop, hip hip hop,
   ´twas at master Andrew´s shop. :||*

*5. ´Twas at Master Andrew´s shop
   that I bought a little fiddle,
   didle-didle-dee, a little fiddle,
   ding-ding-ding, a little bell,
   tum-tum-tum, a little drum,
   plang-plang-plang, a small piano,
   fee-fee-fi, a little fife,
   ||: hip hip hop, hip hip hop,
   ´twas at master Andrew´s shop. :||*

*6. ´Twas at Master Andrew´s shop,
   that I bought a big low fiddle,
   dong-dong-dong, a big low fiddle,
   didle-didle-dee, a little fiddle,
   ding-ding-ding, a little bell,
   tum-tum-tum, a little drum,
   plang-plang-plang, a small piano,
   fee-fee-fi, a little fife,
   ||: hip hip hop, hip hip hop,
   ´twas at master Andrew´s shop. :||*

Translation by Luísa Sobral (2023)

Song categories

FREEDOM & PEACE
1. Ha én rózsa volnék
2. Le chant des partisans
3. Grândola Vila Morena
4. Die Gedanken sind frei
5. Η δική μου η πατρίδα
6. Modlitba pro Martu
7. Bella Ciao
8. Na Kráľovej holi
9. Man binder os på mund og hånd
10. Πότε θα κάνει ξαστεριά
11. Tema '79 (minn 'Ġensna')
12. Over de muur
13. Finlandia-hymni
14. The Fields of Athenry
15. Saule, Pērkons, Daugava
16. Oj Triglav, moj dom
17. Acolo este țara mea
18. De Feierwon
19. Laisvė
20. Änglamark
21. Moja domovina
22. Koit
23. Brenna tuat's guat
24. Една българска роза
25. Ik hou van u
26. Dziwny jest ten świat
27. Libre
28. Ode an die Freude

LOVE SONGS
29. Ne me quitte pas
30. Το Γιασεμίν
31. Tuulevaiksel ööl
32. Z tobą chcę oglądać świat
33. Så skimrande var aldrig havet
34. Σ' αγαπώ γιατί 'σαι ωραία
35. Aš mylėjau tave tau nežinant
36. Grace
37. Sinua, sinua rakastan
38. Lásko má, já stůňu
39. Sah Ein Knab Ein Röslein Stehen
40. Xemx
41. Amar Pelos Dois
42. Vyznanie
43. Ce bine că ești
44. Tavaszi szél
45. Si tú no estás aquí
46. Hey Du
47. Mag Ik Dan Bij Jou
48. Weit, weit Weg
49. Светът е за двама
50. Kvinde Min
51. Hymne à l'amour
52. Almeno tu nell'universo
53. Dan ljubezni
54. Cesarica
55. Viņi dejoja vienu vasaru

NATURE & SEASONS
56. Canção do Mar
57. Põhjamaa ("Laul põhjamaast")
58. Хубава си, моя горо
59. Mediterráneo
60. Η βρύση των Πεγειώτισσων
61. Le Sud
62. Kertész leszek
63. Song for Ireland
64. L-Aħħar Bidwi f'Wied il-Għasel
65. Wiosna, ach to ty
66. In die Berg bin i gern
67. Kai sirpsta vyšnios Suvalkijoj
68. Geh aus, mein Herz, und suche Freud
69. Μες στου Αιγαίου τα νερά
70. Impressioni di settembre
71. Slovenija, od kod lepote tvoje
72. D'Margréitchen
73. Au înnebunit salcâmii
74. V dolinách
75. Tik Un Tā
76. Myrskyluodon Maija
77. Vi elsker vort land (Midsommervise)
78. Dalmatino povišću pritrujena
79. Chválím Tě Země má
80. Mijn vlakke land
81. Öppna landskap
82. Het regent zonnestralen

Song categories

FOLKSONGS & TRADITIONALS

83 Uti vår hage
84 Ljubav se ne trži
85 Pūt, vējiņi!
86 Ciuleandra
87 Hej sokoły
88 Černé oči, jděte spat
89 Whiskey in the Jar
90 Kungla Rahvas
91 Bruxelles
92 Hull a szilva
93 Malhão, Malhão
94 Φραγκοσυριανή
95 À la claire fontaine
96 Излел е Делю Хайдутин
97 Asturias, patria querida
98 Τηλλυρκωτισσα
99 A ja taka dzivečka
100 Teka teka šviesi saulė
101 Der Mond ist aufgegangen (Abendlied)
102 I Danmark er jeg født
103 'O Sole Mio
104 Kein schöner Land in dieser Zeit
105 Viva Malta
106 Kättche, Kättche bréng mer nach e Pättchen
107 Kje so tiste stezice
108 Brabant
109 On suuri sun rantas autius
110 Auld lang syne

FAITH & SPIRITUALITY

111 Stille Nacht, heilige Nacht
112 Il testamento di Tito
113 Erdő mellett estvéledtem
114 Zdravo Djevo
115 T' 'Αϊ Γιωρκού
116 Ktož jsú boží bojovníci
117 I østen stiger solen op
118 Foi Deus
119 Αι γενεαί πάσαι
120 Ave Maria
121 Von guten Mächten
122 En etsi valtaa loistoa
123 Ако си дал
124 Ag Críost an Síol
125 Iddečidejt
126 Pie Dieviņa gari galdi
127 Tyliąją naktį
128 O Mamm, léif Mamm do uewen
129 Dominique
130 Midden in de winternacht
131 En vänlig grönskas rika dräkt
132 Glej zvezdice božje
133 O, ce veste minunată!
134 Daj Boh šťastia tejto zemi
135 Zegarmistrz światła purpurowy
136 Palve (Looja, hoia Maarjamaad)
137 La Saeta

CHILDREN'S SONGS

138 Au clair de la lune
139 Na Wojtusia z popielnika
140 Детство мое
141 Guten Abend, gut' Nacht (Wiegenlied)
142 Kekčeva pesem
143 Päivänsäde ja menninkäinen
144 Jeg ved en lærkerede
145 Idas sommarvisa
146 Vadí, nevadí (Není nutno)
147 Åba Heidschi bumbeidschi, schlåf långa
148 Kad se male ruke slože (Himna zadrugara)
149 Οταν θα πάω κυρά μου στο παζάρι
150 O lume minunată
151 Kis kece lányom
152 Alla fiera dell'Est
153 Aijā žūžū lāča bērni
154 Dikkertje Dap
155 Du gaideliai
156 Ninni la tibkix iżjed
157 Léiwe Kleeschen
158 Vrolijke vrienden
159 Rongisõit
160 Hola Don Pepito
161 Kukulienka, kde si bola
162 Αγιά Μαρίνα τζιαι τζιυρά
163 I'll tell me ma
164 A loja do Mestre André

Member states

AUSTRIA
23 Brenna tuat's guat
48 Weit, weit Weg
66 In die Berg bin i gern
104 Kein schöner Land in dieser Zeit
111 Stille Nacht, heilige Nacht
147 Åba Heidschi bumbeidschi, schlåf långa

BELGIUM
25 Ik hou van u
29 Ne me quitte pas
80 Mijn vlakke land
91 Bruxelles
129 Dominique
158 Vrolijke vrienden

BULGARIA
24 Една българска роза
49 Светът е за двама
58 Хубава си, моя горо
96 Излел е Делю Хайдутин
123 Ако си дал
140 Детство мое

CROATIA
21 Moja domovina
54 Cesarica
78 Dalmatino povišću pritrujena
84 Ljubav se ne trži
114 Zdravo Djevo
148 Kad se male ruke slože (Himna zadrugara)

CYPRUS
5 Η δική μου η πατρίδα
30 Το Γιασεμίν
60 Η βρύση των Πεγειώτισσων
98 Τηλλυρκωτισσα
115 Τ' 'Αϊ Γιωρκού
162 Αγιά Μαρίνα τζιαι τζιυρά

CZECHIA
6 Modlitba pro Martu
38 Lásko má, já stůňu
79 Chválím Tě Země má
88 Černé oči, jděte spat
116 Ktož jsú boží bojovníci
146 Vadí, nevadí (Není nutno)

DENMARK
9 Man binder os på mund og hånd
50 Kvinde Min
77 Vi elsker vort land (Midsommervise)
102 I Danmark er jeg født
117 I østen stiger solen op
144 Jeg ved en lærkerede

ESTONIA
22 Koit
31 Tuulevaiksel ööl
57 Põhjamaa ("Laul põhjamaast")
90 Kungla Rahvas
136 Palve (Looja, hoia Maarjamaad)
159 Rongisõit

FINLAND
13 Finlandia-hymni
37 Sinua, sinua rakastan
76 Myrskyluodon Maija
109 On suuri sun rantas autius
122 En etsi valtaa loistoa
143 Päivänsäde ja menninkäinen

FRANCE
2 Le chant des partisans
51 Hymne à l'amour
61 Le Sud
95 À la claire fontaine
120 Ave Maria
138 Au clair de la lune

Member states

GERMANY
- 4 Die Gedanken sind frei
- 39 Sah Ein Knab Ein Röslein Stehen
- 68 Geh aus, mein Herz, und suche Freud
- 101 Der Mond ist aufgegangen (Abendlied)
- 121 Von guten Mächten
- 141 Guten Abend, gut' Nacht (Wiegenlied)

GREECE
- 10 Πότε θα κάνει ξαστεριά
- 34 Σ' αγαπώ γιατί 'σαι ωραία
- 69 Μες στου Αιγαίου τα νερά
- 94 Φραγκοσυριανή
- 119 Αι γενεαί πάσαι
- 149 Οταν θα πάω κυρά μου στο παζάρι

HUNGARY
- 1 Ha én rózsa volnék
- 44 Tavaszi szél
- 62 Kertész leszek
- 92 Hull a szilva
- 113 Erdő mellett estvéledtem
- 151 Kis kece lányom

IRELAND
- 14 The Fields of Athenry
- 36 Grace
- 63 Song for Ireland
- 89 Whiskey in the Jar
- 124 Ag Críost an Síol
- 163 I'll tell me ma

ITALY
- 7 Bella Ciao
- 52 Almeno tu nell'universo
- 70 Impressioni di settembre
- 103 'O Sole Mio
- 112 Il testamento di Tito
- 152 Alla fiera dell'Est

LATVIA
- 15 Saule, Pērkons, Daugava
- 55 Viņi dejoja vienu vasaru
- 75 Tik Un Tā
- 85 Pūt, vējiņi!
- 126 Pie Dieviņa gari galdi
- 153 Aijā žūžū lāča bērni

LITHUANIA
- 19 Laisvė
- 35 Aš mylėjau tave tau nežinant
- 67 Kai sirpsta vyšnios Suvalkijoj
- 100 Teka teka šviesi saulė
- 127 Tyliąją naktį
- 155 Du gaideliai

LUXEMBOURG
- 18 De Feierwon
- 46 Hey Du
- 72 D'Margréitchen
- 106 Kättche, Kättche bréng mer nach e Pättchen
- 128 O Mamm, léif Mamm do uewen
- 157 Léiwe Kleeschen

MALTA
- 11 Tema '79 (minn 'Ġensna')
- 40 Xemx
- 64 L-Aħħar Bidwi f'Wied il-Għasel
- 105 Viva Malta
- 125 Iddeċidejt
- 156 Ninni la tibkix iżjed

NETHERLANDS
- 12 Over de muur
- 47 Mag Ik Dan Bij Jou
- 82 Het regent zonnestralen
- 108 Brabant
- 130 Midden in de winternacht
- 154 Dikkertje Dap

POLAND
26 Dziwny jest ten świat
32 Z tobą chcę oglądać świat
65 Wiosna, ach to ty
87 Hej sokoły
135 Zegarmistrz światła purpurowy
139 Na Wojtusia z popielnika

PORTUGAL
3 Grândola Vila Morena
41 Amar Pelos Dois
56 Canção do Mar
93 Malhão, Malhão
118 Foi Deus
164 A loja do Mestre André

ROMANIA
17 Acolo este țara mea
43 Ce bine că ești
73 Au înnebunit salcâmii
86 Ciuleandra
133 O, ce veste minunată!
150 O lume minunată

SLOVAKIA
8 Na Kráľovej holi
42 Vyznanie
74 V dolinách
99 A ja taka dzivečka
134 Daj Boh šťastia tejto zemi
161 Kukulienka, kde si bola

SLOVENIA
16 Oj Triglav, moj dom
53 Dan ljubezni
71 Slovenija, od kod lepote tvoje
107 Kje so tiste stezice
132 Glej zvezdice božje
142 Kekčeva pesem

SPAIN
27 Libre
45 Si tú no estás aquí
59 Mediterráneo
97 Asturias, patria querida
137 La Saeta
160 Hola Don Pepito

SWEDEN
20 Änglamark
33 Så skimrande var aldrig havet
81 Öppna landskap
83 Uti vår hage
131 En vänlig grönskas rika dräkt
145 Idas sommarvisa

Song titles – in original language

99	A ja taka dzivečka
95	À la claire fontaine
164	A loja do Mestre André
101	Abendlied (Der Mond ist aufgegangen)
17	Acolo este țara mea
124	Ag Críost an Síol
119	Αἱ γενεαί πᾶσαι
153	Aijā žūžū lāča bērni
123	Ако си дал
152	Alla fiera dell'Est
52	Almeno tu nell'universo
41	Amar Pelos Dois
35	Aš mylėjau tave tau nežinant
97	Asturias, patria querida
138	Au clair de la lune
73	Au înnebunit salcâmii
110	Auld lang syne
120	Ave Maria
162	Αγιά Μαρίνα τζιαι τζιυρά
7	Bella Ciao
108	Brabant
23	Brenna tuat's guat
91	Bruxelles
56	Canção do Mar
43	Ce bine că ești
88	Černé oči, jděte spat
54	Cesarica
79	Chválím Tě Země má
86	Ciuleandra
72	D'Margréitchen
134	Daj Boh šťastia tejto zemi
78	Dalmatino povišću pritrujena
53	Dan ljubezni
18	De Feierwon
101	Der Mond ist aufgegangen (Abendlied)
140	Детство мое
4	Die Gedanken sind frei
154	Dikkertje Dap
129	Dominique
155	Du gaideliai
26	Dziwny jest ten świat
24	Една българска роза
122	En etsi valtaa loistoa
131	En vänlig grönskas rika dräkt
113	Erdő mellett estvéledtem
13	Finlandia-hymni
118	Foi Deus
68	Geh aus, mein Herz, und suche Freud
132	Glej zvezdice božje
36	Grace
3	Grândola Vila Morena
141	Guten Abend, gut' Nacht (Wiegenlied)
1	Ha én rózsa volnék
87	Hej sokoły
82	Het regent zonnestralen
46	Hey Du
148	Himna zadrugara (Kad se male ruke slože)
160	Hola Don Pepito
58	Хубава си, моя горо
92	Hull a szilva
51	Hymne à l'amour
102	I Danmark er jeg født
5	Η δική μου η πατρίδα
60	Η βρύση των Πεγειώτισσων
117	I østen stiger solen op
163	I'll tell me ma
145	Idas sommarvisa
125	Iddeċidejt
25	Ik hou van u
112	Il testamento di Tito
70	Impressioni di settembre
66	In die Berg bin i gern
96	Излел е Дельо Хайдутин

Song titles – in original language

144 Jeg ved en lærkerede

148 Kad se male ruke slože (Himna zadrugara)
67 Kai sirpsta vyšnios Suvalkijoj
104 Kein schöner Land in dieser Zeit
142 Kekčeva pesem
62 Kertész leszek
151 Kis kece lányom
107 Kje so tiste stezice
22 Koit
116 Ktož jsú boží bojovníci
161 Kukulienka, kde si bola
90 Kungla Rahvas
50 Kvinde Min
106 Kättche, Kättche bréng mer nach e Pättchen

64 L-Aħħar Bidwi f'Wied il-Għasel
137 La Saeta
19 Laisvė
38 Lásko má, já stůňu
57 Laul põhjamaast
2 Le chant des partisans
61 Le Sud
157 Léiwe Kleeschen
27 Libre
84 Ljubav se ne trži

47 Mag Ik Dan Bij Jou
93 Malhão, Malhão
9 Man binder os på mund og hånd
59 Mediterráneo
69 Μες στου Αιγαίου τα νερά
130 Midden in de winternacht
77 Midsommervise (Vi elsker vort land)
80 Mijn vlakke land
6 Modlitba pro Martu
21 Moja domovina
76 Myrskyluodon Maija

8 Na Kráľovej holi
139 Na Wojtusia z popielnika
29 Ne me quitte pas
146 Není nutno (Vadí, nevadí)
156 Ninni la tibkix iżjed

150 O lume minunată
128 O Mamm, léif Mamm do uewen
133 O, ce veste minunată!
28 Ode an die Freude
16 Oj Triglav, moj dom
109 On suuri sun rantas autius
103 'O Sole Mio
149 Οταν θα πάω κυρά μου στο παζάρι
12 Over de muur

136 Palve (Looja, hoia Maarjamaad)
94 Φραγκοσυριανή
126 Pie Dieviņa gari galdi
57 Põhjamaa ("Laul põhjamaast")
10 Πότε θα κάνει ξαστεριά
85 Pūt, vējiņi!
143 Päivänsäde ja menninkäinen

159 Rongisõit

34 Σ' αγαπώ γιατί 'σαι ωραία
39 Sah Ein Knab Ein Röslein Stehen
15 Saule, Pērkons, Daugava
45 Si tú no estás aquí
37 Sinua, sinua rakastan
71 Slovenija, od kod lepote tvoje
63 Song for Ireland
111 Stille Nacht, heilige Nacht
49 Светът е за двама
33 Så skimrande var aldrig havet

115 Τ' 'Αϊ Γιωρκού
44 Tavaszi szél
100 Teka teka šviesi saulė
11 Tema '79 (minn 'Ġensna')
14 The Fields of Athenry
75 Tik Un Tā
98 Τηλλυρκώτισσα
30 Το Γιασεμίν
31 Tuulevaiksel ööl
127 Tyliąją naktį

83 Uti vår hage

74 V dolinách
146 Vadí, nevadí (Není nutno)

429

Song titles – in original language

77 Vi elsker vort land (Midsommervise)
55 Viņi dejoja vienu vasaru
105 Viva Malta
121 Von guten Mächten
158 Vrolijke vrienden
42 Vyznanie

48 Weit, weit Weg
89 Whiskey in the Jar
141 Wiegenlied (Guten Abend, gut' Nacht)
65 Wiosna, ach to ty

40 Xemx

32 Z tobą chcę oglądać świat
114 Zdravo Djevo
135 Zegarmistrz światła purpurowy

20 Änglamark

81 Öppna landskap

147 Åba Heidschi bumbeidschi, schläf länga

Song titles – in European English

24	A Bulgarian Rose
53	A Day of Love
62	A Gardener
141	A Good Evening, a Good Night (Lullaby)
150	A world so full of wonders
4	All My Thoughts Are Truly Free
119	All the Generations
116	All You Mighty Warriors of God
75	Anyway
97	Asturias, Beloved Homeland
120	Ave Maria
132	Behold the Little Stars of God
7	Bella Ciao
85	Blow, Wind!
108	Brabant
91	Brussels
121	By Gentle Powers
47	Can I Be With You
124	Christ's Is the Seed
86	Ciuleandra
135	Clock Master of the Purple Light
42	Confession
161	Cuckoo Dear, Oh, Where Did You Stay?
78	Dalmatina, Worn Out by Your History
22	Dawn
157	Dear Saint Nich'las
154	Dickory Dee
126	Dieviņš Keeps a Lavish Table
29	Do Not Leave Me Now
129	Dominique
156	Don't Cry Sweet Baby Jesus
95	Down by the Clearest Fountain
48	Far Away
13	Finlandia Hymn
52	Flame
139	For My Wojtuś From the Ashes
94	Francosyriani
19	Freedom
27	Freedom
122	Give Me no Gems nor Gifts of Gold
68	Go Forth, My Heart, and Seek Delight
36	Grace
3	Grândola, Swarthy Town
92	Grapes and Plums
160	Hello Master Biggens
87	Hey Falcons!
46	Hey You
152	Highdown Fair
43	How Lovely You're Here
153	Hush-a-bye, My Little Bear Cubs
51	Hymn to Love
35	I Have Loved You and Kept It a Secret
144	I Know Two Larks Are Nesting
109	I Long for the Shore So Bleak and Bare
66	I Love Mountains
34	I Love You Because You're Beautiful
79	I Praise You, Mother Earth
163	I'll tell me ma
99	I'm That Kind of a Girl, You See
125	I've Decided
145	Ida's Summer Song
1	If I Was a Rose
123	If You Have Shared
45	If You're Apart From Me
102	In Denmark I Was Born
117	In Eastern Skies the Sun Climbs Up
17	In My Beloved Land
83	In Our Meadow
69	In the Aegean Waters
74	In the Hills
118	It was God
103	It's Now or Never
82	It's Raining Sunrays
158	Jolly and Merry Good Friends

Song titles – in European English

142	Kekec's Song	111	Silent Night
		147	Sleep Well
50	Lady Oh Lady	71	Slovenia, Where Do Your Splendours Come From?
138	Lit up by the Moonlight		
73	Locust Trees Are Going Crazy	63	Song for Ireland
134	Lord, Oh Let This Earth Be Happy	2	Song of the Partisans
41	Love for the Both of Us	56	Song of the Sea
84	Love Is Not for Sale	65	Spring, Oh It's You
88	Lovely Black Eyes, Time to Sleep	26	Strange Is This World
		40	Sun
164	Master Andrew's Music Shop	15	Sun, Thunder, Daugava
76	Maya of Storm Islet	44	Swelling Breezes
59	Mediterranean		
77	Midsummer Song	137	The Chant
21	My Croatia, My Home	72	The Daisy
80	My Open Land	131	The Earth Adorned in Verdant Robe
5	My Own Fatherland	14	The Fields of Athenry
140	My Sweet Childhood	18	The Fire-Wagon
		60	The Fountain of Peyia
113	Night fell Upon the Willow Grove	30	The Jasmine
104	No Better Land	64	The Last Farmer in Honey Valley
57	Northern Land	101	The Moon Is Risen, Beaming (Evening Song)
128	O Mother, Up Above Us	54	The Queen
28	Ode to Joy	23	The Roof's on Fire
93	Oh Winnower, Winnower	33	The Sea Did Never Shine So Brightly
38	Oh, My Queen, My Heart Aches	61	The South
16	Oh, Triglav, My Home	143	The Sunbeam and the Goblin
127	On That Silent Night	112	The Testament of Tito
8	On the King's Highland	98	The Woman from Tillyria
96	Once Came Out Delyo the Hajduk	70	The World Became the World
81	Open Country	49	The World Is for Two
12	Over the Wall	11	Theme '79
		9	They Try to Tie Us, Lips and Hand
90	People of Kungla	55	They Were Dancing for One Sweet Summer
136	Prayer		
6	Prayer for Marta	159	Train Ride
		155	Two Little Roosters
100	Rising, Rising, Bright Sun Rising		
106	Rita, Rita, Bring Another Litre	114	Virgin Mary
39	Rose on the Heath	105	Viva Malta
115	Saint George's Day	32	Want to See the World With You
162	Santa Marina, Lady Fair	77	We Love Our Land (Midsummer Song)
130	See, Amid the Winter Night		
110	Should Old Acquaintance Be Forgot	67	When Cherries Ripen in Suvalkija

Song titles – in European English

149 When I'll Go to the Market, My Lady
148 When The Little Come Together
10   When Will There Be a Clear Sky
20   Where Angels Tread
107 Where Are The Footpaths
89   Whiskey in the Jar
151 White Is the Dress
31   Windless Night
133 Wondrous Tiding, Joyful Feeling
146 Worry or Not

58   You Are Beautiful, My Forest
37   You, It Is You, It Is You I Love
25   Your Love's So Sweet

Composers

Abela, Paul   11, 64
Acda, Thomas   82
Afonso, Zeca   3
Alifantis, Nicu   43
Aljaž, Jakob   16
Andersen, Kai Normann   9
André, Fabrizio De   112
Armenteros, José Luis   27
Avsenik, Slavko   71

Bach, Johann Sebastian   120
Bambost, Lars Van   25
Barthel, Pierre   128
Beethoven, Ludwig van   28
Beicht, Madeleine (Pëppy)   157
Belar, Leopold   132
Bernard, Romain   46
Brabec, Jindřich   6
Brahms, Johannes   141
Branduardi, A.   152
Brauns, Mārtiņš   15
Brel, Jacques   29, 80, 91
Bródy, János   62

Castellari, Corrado   112
Chydenius, Kaj   37
Colclough, June   63
Colclough, Phil   63
Constantinescu, Mihai   150

Davidse, Bob   158
Deckers, Jeanne Paule Marie
    (Jeannine)   129
Dedić, Arsen   148
Capua, E. Di   103
Dimitrov, Emil   123
Ditkovskis, Olegas   35
Dujmić, Rajko   21

Eiffes, Jean   106
Ernesaks, Gustav   159

Fabrizio, Maurizio   52
Ferrer, Nino   61
Fietz, Siegfried   121

Geboers, Sander   47
Gheorghe, Tudor   17, 73
Goisern, Hubert von   23, 48
Gopar, Rosana Arbelo   45
Goranov, Georgi   58
Grech, Dominic   40
Grech, Tiziana   125
Grechuta, Marek   65
Gruber, Franz Xaver   111

Hanzely, Peter   74
Harder, August   68
Helismaa, Reino   143
Hermann, Karl August   90
Herrero, Pablo   27
Hrušovar, Tadej   53

Janes, Alberto   118
John, Pete St.   14
Jouannest, Gérard   29, 91

Kalniņš, Imants   55
Kalogjera, Stjepan Stipica   54
Kazasyan, Vili   140
Kernagis, Vytautas   67
Kiriac, Dumitru Georgescu   133
Korinthios, Joseph   149

Lange-Müller, P.E.   77
Larsen, Kim   50
Lehotský, Janko   42
Lundell, Ulf   81
Lutteman, Hugo   83

Marly, Anna   2
Masytė, Eurika   19
Mazzucchi, A.   103
Menager, Laurent   72
Meuris, Stijn   25

Composers

Monnot, Marguerite   51
Moschos, Aristeides   34
Munnik, Paul De   82
Mussida, Franco   70
Mägi, Tõnis   22, 136
Mårtenson, Lasse   76

Naujalis, Juozas   127
Neikova, Maria   49
Nielsen, Carl   144
Niemen, Czesław   26

O'Meara, Frank   36
O'Meara, Sean   36
Ovsenik, Vilko   71

Portelli, Freddie   105

Riada, Sean Ó   124
Riedel, Georg   145
Rivero, Ramón (Diplo)   160
Rozenboom, Jan Willem   108

Schembri, Indri   156
Schierbeck, Poul   102
Schulz, J.A.P.   101
Serrat, Joan Manuel   59, 137
Sibelius, Jean   13, 122
Smit, Léon   12
Sobral, Luísa   41
Spalato, Tedi   78
Stabulnieks, Uldis   75
Stipišić-Delmata, Ljubo   78
Stipišić-Gibonni, Zlatan   54
Svoboda, Karel   38

Taube, Evert   20, 33
Tokas, Marios   5
Trindade, Ferrer   56
Tutić, Zrinko   21
Tätte, Jaan   31

Uhlíř, Jaroslav   79, 146

Valchev, Dimitar   24
Vamvakaris, Markos   94

Vinter, Ülo   57
Vodopivic, Marjan   142

Wagenaar, Rogier   47
Werner, Henrich   39
Westering, Paul Christiaan van   154
Weyse, C.E.F.   117
Wodecki, Zbigniew   32
Woźniak, Tadeusz   135

Zinnen, Jean Antoine   18

Åhlén, Waldemar   131

Lyricists

Acda, Thomas   82
Afonso, Zeca   3
Andersen, H.C.   102
André, Fabrizio De   112
Armenteros, José Luis   27
Attila, József   62

Belar, Leopold   132
Bergstedt, Harald   144
Bernard, Romain   46
Bonhoeffer, Dietrich   121
Branduardi, A.   152
Breij, Claudia de   47
Brel, Jacques   29, 80, 91
Brito, Frederico de   56
Britvić, Drago   148
Bródy, János   1
Burns, Robert   110

C. Sant, Alfred   64
Čaklais, Māris   55
Capurro, G.   103
Chorążuk, Bogdan   135
Cibotaru, Arhip   73
Claudius, Matthias   101
Colclough, June   63
Colclough, Phil   63
Constantinescu, Mihai   150

Davidse, Bob   158
De Munnik, Paul   82
De Wilde, Wim   25
Deckers, Jeanne Paule Marie (Jeannine)   129
Drachmann, Holger   77
Druon, Maurice   2
Dujmić, Rajko   21

Fatseas, Nikos   149
Ferrer, Nino   61
Freiligrath, Ferdinand   4

Gasolin'   50
Gerhardt, Paul   68
Goergen, Willy   106, 157
Goethe, Johann Wolfgang   39
Goisern, Hubert von   23, 48
Gopar, Rosana Arbelo   45
Grech, Dominic   40
Grech, Tiziana   125
Grechuta, Marek   65
Gudev, Bogomil   140

Helismaa, Reino   143
Henningsen, Poul   9
Herrero, Pablo   27

Ingemann, B.S.   117

Ján Gruska, Viliam   134
Janes, Alberto   118
Jekkers, Harrie   12
John, Pete St.   14
Jonynas, Antanas   35

Kangur, Villu   136
Karavelov, Lyuben   58
Kessel, Joseph   2
Kiriac, Dumitru Georgescu   133
Kofta, Jonasz   32
Koskenniemi, Veikko Antero   13, 109
Kovič, Kajetan   142
Kuhlbars, Friedrich   90

Lauzi, Bruno   52
Lentz, Michel   18, 72
Lindgren, Astrid   145
Lundell, Ulf   81
Lutteman, Hugo   83

Machado, Antonio   137
Mahoney, Ray   11
Marcinkevičius, Justinas   19
Martinaitis, Marcelijus   67
Meeuwis, Guus   108

Lyricists

Mogensen, Mogens   50
Mogol   70
Mohr, Joseph Franz   111
Müllendorff, Charles   128
Mägi, Tõnis   22

Nenițescu, Ioan   17
Niemen, Czesław   26
Niit, Ellen   159

O'Meara, Frank   36
O'Meara, Sean   36
Oksanen, Aulikki   37

Padura, Tomasz   87
Pagani, Mauro   70
Perica, Petar   114
Peteraj, Kamil   42
Piaf, Édith   51
Pliekšāns, Jānis Krišjānis (Rainis)   15
Porazińska, Janina   139
Portelli, Freddie   105
Prenen, Harry L.   130

Rada, Petr   6
Rivero (Diplo), Ramón   160

Schembri, Indri   156
Scherer, Georg   141
Schiller, Friedrich   28
Schmidt, Annie M.G.   154
Serrat, Joan Manuel   59
Sheehan, Father Michael   124
Sobral, Luísa   41
Štaidl, Jiří   38
Stănescu, Nichita   43
Stare, Marjan   71
Stipišić-Delmata, Ljubo   78
Stipišić-Gibonni, Zlatan   54
Svěrák, Zdeněk   79, 146

Taube, Evert   20, 33
Tochev, Dimitar   49
Topelius, Zachris   122
Tutić, Zrinko   21
Tätte, Jaan   31

Valchev, Nayden   24
Vamvakaris, Markos   94
Velchev, Ilya Borisov   123
Velkavrh, Dušan   53
Vetemaa, Enn   57
Virtanen, Jukka   76

Wirsén, Carl David af   131

Yaşin, Neşe   5

Zālīte, Māra   75
Zappa, Luisa   152
Zeman, Ľuboš   74
Zemljič, Matija (Slavin)   16
Zilliacus, Benedict   76
Zuccalmaglio, Anton Wilhelm Florentin   104

Special mention

A shout out to the founding board members of the EU Songbook Association, *Jens Svane Boutrup* (DK) and *Jon Egeris Karstoft* (DK), as well as engaged board members *David Drachmann Laureng* (DK), *Liesbeth Segers* (BEL), *Nuno Bettencourt Mendes* (POR), *Ruta Kanteruka* (LAT) and *Egli Spyridaki* (CY): The European Parliament's *European Citizen's Prize 2023* was given to the project for your volunteer spirit, tenacity and creativity. Also, special mention to supporters *Jens Marsling Bäckvall* (Web-app), external accountant *Jens Tage* (DK), our organisational lawyer *Bruno Månsson* (DK), publishers *Henrik Sebro* (GAD) and *Dansk Sang Publishing, Musiklærerforeningen Dansk Sang (The Association of Music Teachers in Denmark),* and *Hal Leonard Europe*, to *Rakkerpak Productions* (DK), to *Aage & Johanne Louis-Hansen Foundation*, who secured the publication, and last but not least, to *Wawa Wang*, resonant spouse of the project leader, for generously granting him the opportunity to work unpaid part-time during the completion of the project, and for spiritual support through the storms.

Thank you list. In gratitude (2015-2024):

Austria: Alicia Edelweiss, Ewa Geiger & Sarah Marchant (Blankomusik), Sabine Schebrak; **Belgium**: Iris Raspoet, Pascale Ulrix, *Conservatoire royal de Bruxelles*, Quinten Van Wichelen, *Kunstenpunt*, Danny Fish, *Clari Cantores*; **Bulgaria:** Gina Kafedjian, Ekaterina Savova, Elka Nedeva, Daniela Kaneva; **Bosnia**: Aleksandar Sasa Skoric; **Croatia**: Srđana Vrsalović (HRSK), Silvija Prozinger (*Croatian Embassy to the Kingdom of Denmark)*, Ivana Skračić; **Cyprus:** Annette Chrysostomou, **Czechia:** Jakub Kratochvíl (UČPS); Veronika Trojanova (*Royal Danish Embassy*), *Nadace Český hudební fond*; **Denmark**: Magrethe Vestager (European Commissioner), Turf Böcker Jakobsen (*Aage og Johanne Louis-Hansen Fonden*), Stine Bosse (*The European Movement, DK*), Stine Hove Marsling, Elsebeth Øberg Pedersen, Peter Marsling, Anne Hove, Rikke Øberg Pedersen, Dorte Palle Jørgensen og Mads Gordon Ladekarl (*Rakkerpak Productions*), Sune Hansen og Maria R. Rasmussen (*European Parliament Office, CPH*), Mogens Halken (SAG), Jørgen Emborg (RMC), Henrik Sveidahl (RMC), Eva Hess Thaysen (DKDM), Diana Amika & Emma Sørensen, Uffe Østergaard, Michala Petri, Pernille Weiss (MEP), Lasse Schwanenflügel Piasecki, Jens Kaad, Fhv. Indenrigsminister Morten Østergaard, Christina Holm Eiberg, Fhv. Kulturminister Bertel Haarder, *Institut français, KODA*, Suvi Andrea Helminen, Kenneth Sorento, Toke Odin, James Avery, Thorkild Jacobsen (P2), Henrik Hartmann (DR), Simon Jespersen, Marie Hove Marsling; **Estonia:** Karmen Rõivassepp, Anete Kruusmägi; **Finland**: Ahti Viluksela (*Sulasol*), Anu Ahola (FMQ), Monica Nieminen-Mahjoubi, William von der Pahlen, Elina Ohl; **France**: L'Association des Amis de Pontigny-Cerisy (AAPC), Isabelle Replumaz, Jean-Baptiste Bonaventure, Quentin Richard, Mustapha Tossa, Jessica Sestili, Teresa Terracciano, Diane Jean, Louis Guillonnet, Pierre Godin, Aurora, Corinne McOran-Campbell; **Germany**: Goethe-Institut (Zentrale, München) – (The Goethe Institute), Europäische Bewegung Deutschland e.V (The European Movement), Sabine Verheyen (MEP), Karin Schroeck-Singh, *Saxon State*

Ministry for Art; **Greece**: Margaritis Schinas (VP European Commissioner), Yiorgos Psychas, Nikolia Apostolou, Anna Strati, Eleni Dracoulacou; **Hungary**: David Zsoldos (Hungarian Music Council), Iván Fischer, Nora Wagner-Varady (*Embassy of Hungary in Denmark*), Tamás Czuczor, Orsolya Magosi; **Ireland**: www.irishprimaryteacher.ie (blog); **Italy**: Sonia Biagiotti (Coro Diapason), Maria Sara Farci, Stefania D'Ignoti; **Latvia:** Krista Čaka, Solvita Sejane (Musica Baltica); **Lithuania:** Sigita Einikiene (MICL), Ramunas Kontrimas, Dalia Satiene; **Luxembourg:** Marc Meyers (CVL); **Malta:** Mary Ann Cauchi, Fleur Cilia Buckett; **Netherlands:** Friso Wiersum, Martijn van Schieveen (*European Cultural Foundation, ECF*); **Poland:** Klaudia Kocimska, Maciej Balicki, Anna Woźnicka-Hrnčić *(Ministry of Culture)*, Sylwia Holeksa-Wilkowska (*The Stanislaw Moniuszko Academy of Music in Gdansk*), Kate Wyrzykowska, Aleksandra Białkowska; **Portugal:** Sofia Sá, Maria Angélica Roberto (*Grupo Coral Stravaganzza*), João Gil, André Alves, Sílvia Schiermacher (*Embassy of Portugal Copenhagen*) and Ms. Sara Gil, Ana Rita Gomes Do Canto, Salwa El-Shawan Castelo-Branco (*International Council for Traditional Music*); **Romania:** Dan Şumălan (Asociaţia Profesorilor din România, APR), Adina Florescu, Adrian Marin Ciora, Nicolae Gheorghiţă, Bogdan Cameniţă, Calin Cosmaciuc, Georgiana Manole; **Slovakia:** Janka Kubandova (Viva Musica! Agency), Svetlana Waradzinová & Katarina Haskova (VSMU), Klara Orgovánová (The Roma Institute, Bratislava), Silvia Woloszynová; **Slovenia**: Mihela Jagodic (JSKD), Klemen Weiss & Aleksij Valentinčič (DSS), Eva Debelec (Zbor sv. Nikolaja Litija); **Spain:** Ana Fuentes Martínez, Carlos Marlasca Morales, Jaime Velazquez, Prof. Dr. José A. Rodríguez-Quiles y García (University of Granada), Víctor Pliego de Andrés (RCSMM), Paloma O'Shea & Pilar Pertusa (*Paloma O'Shea Santander International Piano Competition*), Olga Montes & Rodrigo García, Isabel Pérez (*Universal Music Publishing*), Alfonso Gentil Álvarez-Ossorio (Ministry of Culture), Veronica Martinez Rios; **Sweden:** Lycke Berling, Robert Nilsson (Ministry of Culture), Marie Halling (KMH), Jörgen Adolfsson (*Svenskt visarkiv*), Maja Marsling; **the UK:** Julian West, Jayne Hughes, Rachel Greaves; **USA**; SurveyMonkey, Google Translate, *National Public Radio* (NPR); **Taiwan:** Leikim Peng, An-Loo Wang, Angus, Mae-Mae & Hua-Hua.

Quotes about the EU Songbook

The European Union Songbook Project organized by the European Union Songbook Association symbolically affirms the richness of European cultural diversity. It is an excellent example of intercultural dialogue so dear to Portugal and to be followed in the future.
Former Minister of culture, Graça Fonseca, Portugal

The EU-Songbook is a genius model, since it is a civilian project that EU hasn't interfered with. We are entering a new phase in EU where culture is the defining element, and in my view, EU will fall apart if cultural initiatives do not arise. EU's biggest threat is not the Euro. On the contrary, the greatest threat is if we do not build a cultural community.
Peter Duelund, head of Nordic Institute of Culture, Denmark

Such initiatives contribute immensely towards the European Integration as the follow the path of coexistence and cultural exchange which bring together our peoples and our cultures. The end result will be nothing short of exceptional and the songbook will convey the spirit and ideals of us all across Europe and the world.
Former Minister of Education, Culture, Sport and Youth, Mr. Prodromos Prodromou, Cyprus

Under the title 'Voices of Peoples in Songs', Johann Gottfried Herder published a collection of folk songs in 1807 – the title would fit well for the EU Songbook! The EU is increasingly becoming a unit, but the strength of this unit is its diversity. If the peoples of EU would contribute to the Songbook, thus somewhat better understanding this diversity, much would be gained. "Who sings together, do not shoot each other" – what more is to be won?",
Dr. Helmut Brenner, Kunst-universität Graz, In Memoriam

As Minister of Culture, I cannot stress enough what an important contribution music and singing together can make to cultural exchange. I am therefore very happy about this beautiful project, which in a musical way promotes both unity and exchange within Europe.
Former Minister for Justice, Culture and European Affairs, Anke Spoorendonk, Schleswig-Holstein, Germany

We greatly appreciate this initiative that contributes to the dissemination of cultural heritage in a European context.
Minister president of Flanders, Jan Jambon, Belgium

I welcome the EU Songbook, an initiative that reflects the cultural diversity and richness of the EU in the commemoration of the 70th anniversary of the establishment of the Union.
Hon. Dr Owen Bonnici, former Minister for the National Heritage, the Arts, and the Local Government, Malta

As a land of choral music, we in Estonia, welcome and applaud to the idea of the EU Songbook giving us the excellent possibility to get acquainted to the singing tradition and culture of different European nations, especially valuable in the times when we cannot meet in person.
Undersec. of Art, Ministry of Culture, Taaniel Raudsepp, Estonia

They are right, when avoiding financial support from the EU-Commission: It would've been a kiss of death. Such a project from the grass roots is both joyous and uplifting. I hope the songbook will be followed by a cd, since I and probably many others are curious after hearing the songs in their national versions.
Former EU-Commissioner, Ritt Bjerregaard (1941-2023, R.I.P.), Denmark

I am impressed by the interesting concept and pan-European scope of the European Union Songbook project organised by your association. Preserving cultural diversity in the context of pan-European unity is crucial for the development of the cultures of individual countries and for the establishment of exchanges and dialogues between them.
Former Minister of Culture, Boil Banov, Bulgaria

A symbol of European diversity and unity at the same time.
Former Minister of Culture, PhDr. Lubomir Zaorálek, Czechia

In particular, the 6 songs selected from Greece, represent centuries old traditions, both urban and rural, that embody the history, values and aesthetics of the Greek people. This intangible national treasure merits every effort to be preserved and promoted abroad, thus the European Union Songbook is perfectly aligned with the efforts and goals of the Greek Ministry of Culture.
Former Minister of Culture and Sport of the Hellenic Republic, Dr. Lina G. Mendoni, Greece